HAPPY AFTERLIFE

PART TWO

BY

STEPHANIE HUDSON

Happy Ever Afterlife - Part 2
The Afterlife Saga #12
Copyright © 2020 Stephanie Hudson
Published by Hudson Indie Ink
www.hudsonindieink.com

This book is licensed for your personal enjoyment only.
This book may not be re-sold or given away to other people. If you would like to share this book with another person, please purchase an additional copy for each recipient. If you're reading this book and did not purchase it, or it wasn't purchased for your use only, then please return to your favourite book retailer and purchase your own copy. Thank you for respecting the hard work of this author.
All rights reserved.
This is a work of fiction. Names, characters, places, brands, media, and incidents are either the product of the authors imagination or are used fictitiously. The author acknowledges the trademark status and trademark owners of various products referred to in this work of fiction, which have been used without permission. The publication/use of these trademarks is not authorised, associated with, or sponsored by the trademark owners.
Happy Ever Afterlife - Part 2/Stephanie Hudson – 2nd ed.
ISBN-13 - 978-1-913769-29-1

When thinking about who I was going to dedicate this book to, I didn't have to think very hard. This person was the one who planted the seed in my mind, and from that the Afterlife saga grew from ten books to twelve and to what I hope you will all think is a beautiful Happy Ever After...life.

Claire Boyle, my wonderful PA but above all my fabulous friend. I dedicate this book to you as it is only fitting for it stemmed from an idea that found its way into two more books. I would be lost without your constant support and can't thank you enough for all your hard work.
Love Stephanie. X

Being There.

A true friend is sometimes hard to find,
To have your back, when you're in a bind,
Finding patience, when my life's a mess,
To bringing round wine, and classing PJ's as being dressed.

To knowing what to say when times are the worst,
Holding my hand and being the one to call first.
Making me laugh or giving me a big hug,

When my deadlines are due and all I do is shrug.

*You accept me for who I am and my quirky ways,
Even when I drive you nuts when my mind's in a daze,
You never cast judgment or comment on my messy hair,
You are always there for me, my wonderful friend Claire.*

Author Insight

I want to start this book by explaining the reasons behind its very existence. As many of you know I don't usually do things in the 'Normal' way and although a lot of you may think that some of these chapters should have made the last book, I made the decision to do things this way to give people the option to choose. Which is why I think you, the fabulous fans of the saga, deserved this explanation.

When writing the last book in the saga I knew I wanted it to end with an epic bang, one I think it deserved after all this time. But in doing so, I had to make the heart-breaking decision to leave out all the 'fun chapters' which could have only happened after the 'Near end of the world as we know it' ending.

However, not long after starting to edit these chapters I once again became lost in the story and before I knew it, there was not just one book, but two.

So, make yourself a cuppa, grab a few snacks and sit back and enjoy this little slice of heaven for our girl Afterlife Heroine, Keira Draven.

After all, I think she deserves her very own…

Happy Ever Afterlife.

WARNING

This book contains explicit sexual content, some graphic language and a highly addictive Alpha Male.

This book has been written by a UK Author with a mad sense of humour. Which means the following story contains a mixture of Northern English slang, dialect, regional colloquialisms and other quirky spellings that have been intentionally included to make the story and dialogue more realistic for modern-day characters.

Please note that for your convenience language translations have been added to optimise the readers enjoyment throughout the story.

Also meaning…

No Googling is required ;)

Also, please remember that this part of a 12 book saga, which means you are in for a long and rocky ride. So, put the kettle on, brew a cup, grab a stash of snacks and enjoy!

Thanks for reading x

PROLOGUE

Standing at the mouth of Hell was a strange feeling but doing so without facing off an army of Titans and being there of your own free will, was taking things to a whole other level. But then again, I never believed the reasons for me ever being back here would be because Draven had been the one to drag me.

So, now what faced me was the real truth about my husband's hidden world, one that he ruled in secret and one he had tried to keep from me. A kingdom so hideous that it made my own world's worst serial killers look like a bunch of bullies at a playpark!

I didn't understand it back then, when I was naively walking along the only path that led me to him…to the man I loved. But little did I know where that path would really lead me. Because down here, well that path was a charred crumble of broken remains leading me to somewhere I was never expected to go.

Oh yes, I may have been down here a few times now, but both times were to save the man I loved and preventing any future from happening where we wouldn't be together. But a future I had never accounted for was one where I would be facing a new enemy of the likes I had never known before.

Because how could you fight against your own body?

Against your own soul.

Against your chosen, eternal love.

I had no answers to this, and not even in the face of the monsters that surrounded me now could I say why he had sent them. My new enemy, whose hand had slashed through the demonic air, sealing my fate and cutting into my heart right along with it.

The one that gave the order to have me in chains. The one that then ordered me to be brought to my knees at the feet of a King.

A King that would make me beg and prove that I not only loved the Angel that had already captured my heart, but also a Demon that would *demand it*.

No, this was no longer Draven's Hell…

It was mine.

CHAPTER ONE

BECAUSE HE LOVES YOU

'Queen of the Netherworld and seventh slave, you will come to me and...I will make you my slave in Hell.'

"Keira?" I heard my name being called in my mind in a questioning way that didn't really make sense in the light of what was happening right now...or should I say, in the darkness of what was happening now. As I was still being dragged down through the water with the demonic hand I now knew belonged to Draven's demon. He was still holding me, but with each call of my name, his grasp on me began to loosen. As if hearing my name from a voice he knew was having an effect on him.

"Keira!" I knew that voice, even though it sounded as if it was coming to me through a fog of jumbled memories. I decided I needed to look back, as though this was the last thing I needed to do before I ran out of air. So, with his hold on me slowly slipping away, I turned my body in the water so that I was now facing the surface.

Even through the cloudy black liquid I could now see a figure standing there looking into the pool as I once had done. I started to reach up, my arm floating as if that was all the fight I had in me and in doing so I heard the growl in my mind as an arm banded itself around my torso. It was as though the action was done as one last desperate attempt to keep me locked to him.

This was it, he wasn't going to let me go. He would fight, which meant I would have to also. So, with the last of my breath, I twisted in his hold and I don't know why it mattered, but I issued him a warning I was surprised he even listened to. I sent out the power of thought that even in my own mind, sounded like the desperate cry it was.

'Let me go, you're killing me!' I don't know why, but in that single second the arm disappeared as if this was never his intention. As if killing me wasn't what he wanted, but more like abducting me was and this had been his only way. Then, as I made my way closer to the surface, I stared, stunned by what I could now see. It wasn't the voice of someone I knew calling my name that belonged to the shadow above…

No, because that shadow was me.

I tried to make sense of this in my mind but came up with nothing other than still feeling the overwhelming need to breathe.

"KEIRA!" Suddenly the voice screamed this time, as I reached up trying to claw myself through the water back to the surface and back to my other body.

This was when I heard one last threat in reply, echoing around the confusion in my mind. I knew it was one I no choice but to take seriously.

As my fingertips were just about to break the surface, he

told me as a demonic growl in my ear,

"I will be waiting for you…in Hell"

I woke with a startled breath as if gasping for air, bending my body over double in order to fill my lungs and rid myself of the burn.

"Keira?! Jesus, what just happened!?" I heard a voice shouting at me, but it started off sounding muffled until finally I was able to focus.

"Sophia?" I said her name as a question as she continued to rub large circles on my back.

"Yeah, it's me, thank the Gods, because I think if my brother had found you he would have freaked, and shit soul weed roots!" I laughed at this only it came out spluttered.

"What happened?" I asked after finally feeling steady enough to stand up without swaying.

"I should be asking you that. I came down here when I saw the door was open and thought, hey this is Keira, my crazy, 'I like to do dumb shit' sister in law, she must be down here." I shot her a frown and she motioned to the room and pool we were still stood in front of, making her point.

"Okay, so yeah, you can have that one…what else?"

"What else? I came down here and saw you just stood like a Jikininki demon staring down at the pool in some weird trance," she said getting slightly more high-pitched, no doubt because she was still coming down from her moment of panic.

"A what now?"

"Think Zombie only with more teeth, none of which are rotting or blunt and also throw some self-loathing in there for good measure," she said taking me by the arm and steering me away from the pool.

"Aww, that can't be fun."

"They eat the flesh of human corpses and then steal from them to use as bribery. We are not exactly talking pillars of society here, Keira." I made a 'Eww' face and said,

"Fair enough. So, getting back to the Zombie Keira, that being the 'less flesh eating and more zoned out variety', what the hell happened?" I asked looking back over my shoulder at the shimmering dark pool.

"You tell me, I was only the one who found you like that, not the one who put you there...what did you see?" I stopped dead at her question and turned to face her stunning doll like features, beautiful even at the height of her confusion.

"How did you know I would see anything?" I asked frowning.

"A guess," she said in a tone that even she knew I wouldn't buy into what she was trying to sell me, which was basically supernatural bullshit. In the end all I had to do was pull a Draven and raise an eyebrow at her.

"Fine, jeez, my brother rubbing off on you much...you know I remember a time when you used to be more accommodating to my bullshit."

"Yeah, well what can I say, a few trips to Hell and back and you learn a few things," I said without even thinking about where I nearly just ended up...or had I? I mean it wasn't like I had just been pulled out of the water. Or was it like there had been Draven's demon down there shaking his fist at us like some defeated bad guy from Scooby Doo, shouting 'You pesky kids!?'.

"I don't even want to know what that look is all about," she commented holding her hands up in defeat.

"No, you really don't," I agreed as I continued to follow her out of Draven's private vault, just thankful that once we made it through the painting she started talking. She had just pressed it shut with both hands and then when the locks clicked into place, she leant her forehead on the painting and released a sigh.

"Is it that bad?" I asked, taking in the unusual sight of Sophia looking lost for words.

"Come on, I mean I gathered pretty quickly that it wasn't some ancient pool of tranquillity or anything," I said making her straighten her shoulders before facing me in an obvious posture that said, I can do this, but I just don't want to.

"No, but it is a pool direct from the river Lethe."

"Okay, well that doesn't sound so bad." I said obviously jumping the gun when she asked me back,

"Do you know what the Lethe is?"

"No, but it sounds nice…is it not…*nice?*" I asked when she started shaking her head at me.

"Well, that depends on your take on nice when referring to one of the five rivers in Hell," she replied wryly.

"Wow, definitely not tranquillity then…and you're right, not exactly what I would class as *nice* either," I said after a sudden expel of air.

"That would be a no," she agreed and let's face it, with her being a demon and all, and not forgetting having a father that currently resided in Hell as one of its rulers, then yeah, she would definitely be the expert here.

"Aww man! Seriously, why is it all Draven's pads have to come with weird shit? I mean rats I can live with. Hell, even a damn temple and creepy ass crypt I won't draw the line at and well, don't even get me started on dungeons, as no offense, but around you guys, my husband says he's taking me to a castle for our honeymoon and I just know there will be a dungeon or two…but finding a bathroom surprises me, go figure…"

"Keira dear, your point?"

"My point dear sister, is that why is it always the last bloody thing I expect to find is the very thing I always bloody find! I mean Jesus, Ffffing Christ on a pogo stick!" I said dramatically throwing my hands up in the air so that my massive sleeves ended bunched up near my shoulders.

"Now who has been…?"

"Don't say it!" I warned holding up a hand to stop her from throwing a Pipism in my face.

"So, these 'normal' things?" she asked, putting a hand on her hip as if what I was asking for was insulting and not having a strange demonic pool of water that tried to drag unsuspecting victims down to Hell was a completely reasonable request.

"Yeah, you know, like a home cinema or a hot tub…I mean at this point I would even shrug at a Playboy mansion style sex grotto, as it's not exactly as though I don't know what happens at your private parties. Seriously, why can't you guys just have normal shit in your house, uh?" I asked making her laugh as we left the gallery and made our way presumably back down to where the party had already started.

"Because, I don't know if you have noticed this yet, that in there is my brother's version of 'normal shit'," she told me, making me wince because I knew she was right. But even so that didn't stop me from saying.

"Yeah, well it wasn't that long ago that I fell through the floor and into a pit of rotting rapist corpses, being eaten by a guy we always thought was a woman, so you know…God, I miss Ranka!" I said first with a shrug of my shoulders and then finishing this by looking up at Heaven as if this was where I would find her. Sophia just patted the top of my head until I was looking down, after giving me a little shake of my head to remind me where she had likely founding her resting place. If Hell could ever be filed away in that 'RIP' category.

"In my brother's defence and at this point, what I like to think as a positive note, he didn't know that was there either," she reminded me referring once again to Ranka's unconventional snack bar.

"That doesn't exactly give me the warm and fuzzies here, Sophia," I said looking at her side on. She looked thoughtful a moment and then shrugged her shoulders just like I had, before agreeing,

"No, I suppose not."

"Okay, so I know it's not what you would call the norm…"

"Having a Hellish pool of water in the middle of a private vault, one that had been cut into the mountain and hidden behind a big ass painting of yourself…no, definitely far from the norm there, Sophia," I agreed sarcastically, one she smirked at.

"Why would he even have it?" I asked before she could try and convince me that it wasn't that weird again. She sighed, (something that was quickly becoming a habit around me) and then threw another shocker my way.

"Because of you." My mouth dropped open forming a little O shape before snapping shut again, looking around as if the walls held the answers and no surprises when they didn't, my mouth dropped open again. Thankfully, these fish like actions were enough to get her to put me out of my misery and stop me imitating marine life.

"The water from the Lethe is known to have many properties, and the master of the Lethe is known to have control of them all as the river flows through his home," Sophia told me as we walked through yet another long hallway, this time, instead of being adorned with my handsome husband, it was one lined with colourful tapestries of landscapes. There were even ladies lay in a garden full of fruit trees, draped seductively in the grass about to eat golden apples. Medieval Knights bearing the red templar cross across their white tunics stood proud against the back drop of a castle in the distance.

"Properties like…?" I questioned, leaving it hanging in the air and rolling my hand around to prompt her to say more.

"Well, to humans it is mostly like losing time, known as the Ameles Potamos, which means the river of un-mindfulness. Named after the Greek spirit of forgetfulness and oblivion. It is said that one sip is all it will take to lose the essence of your mind that helps hold on to reality…although, you would think being in Hell this would be enough to achieve that." I snorted at that and had to agree,

"Uh, I would say the verdict is a big fat yes on that one." She gave me a coy look in return before carrying on.

"To our own kind of course it has a different effect, one quite the opposite in fact."

"How so?" I asked in a curious tone, one overshadowing the worry I should have been expressing.

"Well, it can have the power to show you a glimpse into the future or, if on the receiving end, have the power to grant you strength to succeed in your goals. Bringing you clarity…of course it has also been known to drown those stupid enough to fall into its depths, succumbing to their own foolish power when being made to believe they are in no danger until it is too late…it's fickle that way." Yeah, I could believe it, considering it felt like it was trying to consume me whole at the time…or better still, the demon that lurked beneath it had.

"Where for humans it can conceal the truth, for one such as my brother, it can shine light on it." My eyes grew wide hearing this.

"Okay, so I get it, handy thing to have in your private secret room. But the one question I do still have is…what does that have to do with me?" Sophia gave me a small smile before telling me Draven's own truth.

"He would use it to try and seek out visions of you."

"What?!" I shouted making my slightly overly dramatic response echo in the large space.

"Is it really so hard to believe? He may have been told by the Fates that you were destined to find him, but that didn't stop him searching anyway he could. Trust me, if he had found you first, he wouldn't have sat back on his heels and just waited another decade for you to come knocking on the castle door." Yeah okay, so knowing her brother as well as I did, I could see that.

"Wow, I had no idea."

"But of course you didn't, and Dom would no doubt like to keep it that way." Her look said it all. I gave her a salute and said,

"Mum's the word." Which ended in her cocking her head at me like a parrot listening to a new sound.

"It means I won't say anything." She frowned as if trying to make sense of it, which had me smirking to myself. All this time on Earth and there were still things her and her brothers didn't know. Okay, so it wasn't exactly state secrets or the cure for the common cold but still, it was enough for me to have my small moment of being smug.

"So now the important question remains."

"And that is?" I soon wished I hadn't asked.

"What did you see in the pool?" Her folded arms told me getting out of this question wasn't going to be easy.

"Uhh…nothing much, anyway so this thing tonight, is there going to be haggis, 'cause you know, not the biggest fan of the whole heart, liver, and lungs meat thing, stuffed into an animal's stomach.?" I said and as soon as I had, I wished that my voice had remained even (as a high-pitched voice was usually dead giveaway of someone lying). I also knew I had gone too far, too soon into the whole change of subject thing. Damn it, why couldn't I ever be cool?!

"Keira! By the Gods woman, why can't you go one minute without getting into some shit!" Sophia said stopping abruptly and calling me out on my lie. As let's face it, if it wasn't something bad then why feel the need to lie about it. Bugger, I knew I should have just gone with something light-hearted like, 'Oh it showed us all drinking mulled wine around a roaring fire singing carols to a snowy Christmas this year'.

Alright, so yes that was probably an even more far-fetched vision to say, as I couldn't exactly see Ragnar singing Frosty the Snowman wearing a fluffy Santa's hat. If anything, it was more likely to be 'Santa's got a bag of *Souls*'. The demonic Afterlife version of Soul Saints Orchestra!

"Okay so yes, some weird shit has been happening lately but please just listen to why I haven't told you or anyone for that matter…well other than Lucius, but that totally didn't count as, well he kind of walked in on it…although now that I think of it, I did kinda shout his name in my head and…" I finally stopped rambling on when I heard Sophia groaning. I looked back to where she had once again stopped walking, to see her rubbing both her hands on the side of her temple as if trying to ease the headache I knew she didn't have, because I was pretty sure demons couldn't get headaches. Although, this was me we were talking about here, I mean if there was one being alive that had the ability to evoke a first headache on any of the Dravens it was inevitably going to be me.

"Gods Keira, it's not even been a month!"

"I know, I know!" I said throwing my hands up in the air before deflating back down along with my shoulders until finding myself sitting on the floor amidst all the material. I must have looked like a crumpled wilted flower.

"Hey, come on now, I am sure it can't be that…oh…ooh right it's bad isn't it?" I nodded my head to indicate a big fat unfair yes and she winced. She gracefully dropped down beside me, once again making me ask myself the unimportant question of how in God's name she could pull such a swan-like move without slumping down like a dead weight, as I had in such a dress.

"Well, look on the bright side, I am sure Pip is getting bored of being on Adam lock down and is just dying to get up to some mischief, so YEY on that one," she said saying the word 'yey' and pretending to wave a little victory flag at me, making me laugh.

"Oh yeah, Pip will love this one alright," I said on a groan and a roll of my eyes.

"Look, whatever it is we will face it and deal with it like we always do…don't worry. Besides, I am sure once my brother knows what…" she trailed off when I started shaking my head desperately, telling her that one; he didn't know and two; please don't tell him. Then she closed her eyes and let out another groan of frustration, this time one that made her look a lot like her brother, as she was holding the bridge of her nose with her thumb and forefinger.

"I swear one of these days I am going to bash both your heads together," she said before giving me her hand to help me up off the floor.

"Why?" I asked as it was clear now from the sounds of music that could be heard we were only a staircase away from joining the party.

"Because it's clear neither of you have learnt anything over the past few years," Sophia said, and on some level, I knew she was right. But then again, in this situation she had no idea what the consequences of telling Draven could be. Which was why I reached for her hand and made her look at me before telling her,

"I will make you a deal, if you just give me tonight, then tomorrow I will tell you everything and then at the end of hearing it, if you still think it's a good idea to tell your brother, then we will…but please, just give me this." I asked this last part in a pleading voice as I looked back over my shoulder indicating the party I knew was below.

She gave me a fleeting, conflicted look before finally giving in to my wishes with a shrug of her shoulders.

"Fine, but you have until tomorrow and then you will tell me everything." I nodded frantically before grabbing her to me, pulling in for a grateful embrace. She made a kind of 'Umpf' sound before relaxing and patting my back.

"How are we going to…?"

"Leave my brother to me," she said interrupting my question on how we were going to manage getting me away from Draven long enough for that unfortunate conversation to take place. After all, lately Draven hadn't been too keen to let me out of his sight for long. But looking at Sophia's cunning eyes, I knew exactly what she was planning so said with a groan of my own,

"It's going to include shopping, isn't it?" Her smile said it all.

After this we continued toward where the noise was coming from and I looked over the balcony to see the stunning ballroom below. I stumbled a step forward and had to grip onto the wooden railing in front of me just to hold me steady.

"Sophia?" I whispered her name in a hushed question as what now faced me was beyond anything I could ever have imagined. If anything, it looked just as beautiful as our wedding down there.

"My brother wanted it to be a surprise," she answered, knowing what it was I was asking. Oh yeah, it was a surprise alright. Even from up here I could see all the effort that had gone into something like this. It was incredible and felt as though I had just stepped through another Janus gate into a very different past.

The massive room beneath us looked completely different now it was full of colourful life, no longer just a bare open space. No, now the wood panelling was a back drop to the ivy covered free standing candelabras reaching up like black iron hands. Each held massive church pillar candles in rich golds and reds that cast a warm glow against the dark wood.

Great long tables framed the sides of the room, leaving a huge space in the middle for people dancing. Twirling bodies covered in lush materials of twisting silks, velvet and satin as they were spun by their smartly dressed partners. A sea of colour all moving in perfect sync to the band that played, higher up on a raised dais over in one corner.

Even the red covered tables were filled with massive platters of food and decorations the colours of Autumn, down their centres. Sparkling silver goblets being filled by servants in costumes, also playing the part in a medieval party, were dotted in and out of the crowd.

Even the walls had been decorated with long swathes of red velvet, creating curtains to frame a slightly raised seating area at one end. A beautiful table of purples and golds setting it apart from the rest, that and the thrones set behind it just ready to be filled by the guests of honour...

The King and Queen.

"He did all this...just...just because I mentioned about going to a banquet?" I asked in a stunned tone that spoke volumes as to what I was feeling. I was completely overwhelmed. I heard Sophia's sing song laugh behind me at the sight of my shock, before she approached next to me.

But it wasn't her voice that answered me.

It was his.

The King...

"No, he did this because...*he loves you.*"

CHAPTER TWO

LOVE WITNESSED BY LOVE WRITTEN

"Draven!" I shouted, giving him this as his only warning before I launched myself at him. I ran to him and threw my body into his own, one that was barely ready and in doing so it forced him back a step. Then, I wrapped my arms around him as far as they would go thanks to his wide frame and held my cheek to his chest as I breathed him in. I could feel his soft chuckle vibrate against my body as he encased me in his arms, ones that had no problems holding all of me to him.

"Miss me, little one?" he teased after reaching down to tip my head back, so I could look up at him. By the Gods, he looked handsome. His hair had been pushed back, half contained by a tightly wrapped black ribbon tied into a knot. This made his strong features all the more striking and I found I couldn't help myself from reaching up and running the pad of my thumb over his perfect lips.

I ended up tracing along the smile my actions brought him, and I felt him grip my side and pull me harder to his body.

"I can't believe you did all this for me," I told him, and he leant his head down to increase the intensity of his response, when he whispered fervently,

"I would do anything for you."

And I hated to admit this to myself, but the only thing in that moment I wanted to say was 'even if that meant you might hurt me, would you stay?' but I already knew the answer to that, which was why I was so scared.

After all, it had happened once before.

But I didn't say that. Nor did I give any clue as to where my thoughts were leading me, hand in hand with my biggest fear.

I saw Draven look up and nod to Sophia who was still behind me. I looked back at her and saw her nod silently in return before descending the stairs, leaving us to have our moment. Draven soon brought my attention back to him as I felt his finger hook under my chin again.

"By the Gods, you're beautiful." I gave him a small shy smile in return and knew I was blushing. The second I felt it bloom across my cheeks I heard him groan, knowing that he too hadn't missed it.

"Blushing in my arms only makes me want to discover just how far that flushed skin has travelled to," he told me on a lust fuelled growl and bending enough so that he could bite my cheek, holding the flesh there just before the point of pain.

"Draven." His name left me on a whispered breath, one I didn't yet know if it was said in a plea for more or less.

"What my love, what do you ask of me?" he answered in that demonic purr that was the complete opposite of the demon in him that now terrified me.

"I…I…don't know," I admitted, now feeling more breathless at the sight of him.

"I know what you need…always!" he said before crushing his lips to mine for an all-consuming kiss. I reached up to

grab him to me in a possessive way from a fear that he would leave, and his response was a rumble of approval. He held me to him, banding an arm around my waist as he picked me up, so he could walk with me without breaking our connection. His other hand was in my hair and the second I felt his fingers getting closer to the mark on my neck I pulled back panting.

"My ravished queen, my utter perfection," he told me as he continued to walk me backwards, after gathering up my skirts and tossing them to one side so that he wouldn't step on them. Then I quickly found a wall at my back and before I knew what was happening his teeth were at my throat. However, he didn't bite me and the fist that suddenly made me jump as it punched against the wall next to me, was testament to how much restraint he was battling against.

"By the Gods, what it is you do to me!" he told me looking tortured, prompting me to place a palm against his cheek. He leaned into my touch as if feeding from it and after taking a deep breath he started to calm the pounding in his heart.

"Just one look at you and my heart aches with desire to have you and make you mine again and again." I bit my lip feeling the tears welling up in sight of such love, and it nearly broke my heart knowing what I was keeping from him.

"Oh honey," I whispered, burying my head into his neck before I could become overwhelmed into telling him everything. Even the sound of me calling him this had an effect on him, as I felt his body shuddering against mine when holding me tighter.

"I want to steal you away," he admitted, making me giggle into his neck before telling him.

"You can't do that, we have a party to get to…a party you threw for me, remember?" I said making him groan in frustration this time.

"Yes, and remind me again why I did that?" he said pretending to sound exasperated making me laugh again.

"Because you love me, remember." Hearing this, he dropped his fake annoyance and instantly grinned down at me.

"Besides, we may not have now, but we a whole lot of *later…naked later,*" I teased waggling my eyebrows at him in what I knew was a comical fashion, as he burst out laughing.

"Mmm, yes indeed and then it will be your turn to show me just how much you love me in return," he teased back with a sexy bad ass grin, one that always made me turn to putty in his hands.

"Challenge totally accepted," I said with a cheeky grin and a sneaky lip bite, *his not mine this time*. Then he let me slide down the length of him until I was back steady on my feet.

"Now, I do believe you owe me a medieval date, Mr Draven," I said holding out my arm for him as if I was the gentleman. He looked down at me and, with a shake of his head and a chuckle, he took my hand and rested it inside his arm. He was just taking the first steps towards the sweeping staircase that led below when I pulled back, as now I had only just noticed what he was wearing.

"Keira?" he questioned, but I had stopped dead and was just staring at him like a piece of man candy I need to suck and lick all over. Holy heaven and Hot as Hell, Jesus he was stunning!

"Gods Draven, what are you trying to do to a girl."

"I am afraid I am not following," he said, clearly confused by my behaviour. So, what did I do, I decided that snorting at him would be just as sexy as the sight in front of me. Then I added to this a wave of my hand up and down his body and a very uncool,

"Uh huh, okay," ending with a giggle.

He decided that coming closer might help me get my wits together enough to explain, but in the end all I did was stare and concentrate on trying not to drool. He was wearing a high collared long black jacket, which was embroidered with deep purple thread. The wide design framed the centre of the jacket either side the opening, with embellished leaves folding back in on themselves and around the silver buttons on one side that ran down the full length of the jacket. The other side the same thread created a piping effect around the eyelets the buttons would fit into.

However, I was glad to see him wearing this open as it gave me a wonderful view of his large torso encased in a tight waistcoat, the same material as the centre of my dress. To this he added a black shirt, black cravat and black breeches with high leather boots.

And he was stunning.

"By the Gods, you're handsome." The whispered confession broke free before I could say anything different and his wide eyes proved he heard it no matter how quietly it had been spoken.

In fact, he looked like some fairy tale prince just stepped out of a fantasy book and into real life, finding me here staring at him. Actually, I started to notice that I was staring at him so much and in such a way that he started to look slightly uncomfortable…and oh my God, was that a blush I could see?!

"Keira I…"

"Oh my God, are you blushing?!" I shouted getting excited by the fact. He suddenly straightened his shoulders a little as if shocked and stated way too firmly for it not to be true,

"No…No I am not." I laughed once and said,

"You so are!"

"Keira…" he started to say my name in warning, but there was no way I was stopping with my teasing now, not when he enjoyed playing with me so much. No, it was time for a little pay back.

"Draven, seriously just the sight of you, I am finding it hard to breathe here," I said putting a hand to my chest and taking a large breath as if to prove my point. Of course, all of this was true, being around Draven looking almost painfully handsome was one hell of a sight to behold and it did often make it hard for me to breathe. He rolled his eyes as if he didn't believe me, which made me take this to the next level.

"Do you not know what it is you do to me, what your delicious body does to me?" I asked him after taking the few remaining steps closer, so I could run my hands up over his jacket to his shoulders. He looked down at me with shock and it was only now that I started to realise, that like with lovely pet names, I had never really told Draven very often how sexy I find him. Well yes, I often showed him just what he did to me, but tell him?

Well, from the looks of his expression I obviously didn't do it enough, as he was definitely surprised and hearing your wife telling you how sexy she finds you should never come as a surprise. I don't know why I'd never thought about this till now. Maybe it was because of how Draven was and always portrayed himself. Not being so arrogant as to already know how sexy he is, but more carrying himself with such confidence, I always just assumed he knew without words.

"Is that so, my little Queen?" he hummed now, looking very pleased. I bit my bottom lip and nodded my head whilst making a 'Uh huh mmm' sound.

"You know, if I didn't know any better, I would say you are flirting with your King," he teased, and I now decided to up the ante when I took his hand in mine and raised one of his fingers to my mouth to nibble on. This action was another that surprised him as he raised his eyebrows at me.

"I am, but tell me *my King,* is that a punishable offence?" I asked purring the words 'My King' and making him groan, although that could have also been the fact that I was now taking his whole finger in my mouth and sucking on it, re-enacting what I would rather be doing to another part of his anatomy.

At first, he looked lost for words and the powerplay that was currently tipped in my favour was near intoxicating. When he growled down at me I smiled around his finger before letting it go with a wet pop.

"You push me, little one," he said, growling down at me after yanking me hard to him and I swear this made my lower regions spasm with excitement. Then, as if I knew the exact words it would take to get his patience to snap, I raised up on my toes and whispered,

"Or you could push *into me* with *your big one.*" The second his eyes flashed into purple fire I knew I had him and instead of words, a demonic snarl was sounded in their place as my only warning before he bent, and I was suddenly over his shoulder. I let out a squeal in shock, granting me another grumble from his demon side, one I hoped still liked playing with me and was far from the demon my nightmares had recently shown me.

I pushed up against Draven's back to see him doing something that I couldn't make out until I noticed his phone by his ear.

"We will be delayed," he said in a stern and gruff voice, one thick with his obvious lust. I squirmed on his shoulder making him growl a one worded threat,

"Behave." I swear I giggled making whoever was still on the phone to laugh.

"An hour, maybe two if she continues to misbehave," Draven replied obviously to the 'how long' question that was asked. I felt his hand grip my thigh painfully for a second as if to drive his point home and I suddenly squeaked out,

"One! One hour!" This made him chuckle.

"Please tell me that was your sister on the phone?" I asked after he hung up. He didn't answer me but just squeezed my leg again and started to walk faster, with more urgency. Then, when Draven came to a divide in the hallway, he seemed at odds with himself on where to take me. It was almost as if he wanted to go one way but knew if he did, he wouldn't be getting exactly what he wanted. I don't know how I knew this, maybe it was just because I knew him that well, or maybe it was the way he growled before turning away from where I knew he really wanted to go.

"Draven?" I questioned as I still hung over his back.

"I do not have the time to take you how I want to, and if I take you back there, then we will not be leaving again until dawn." He growled this confession and I couldn't help but look down the hallway we were walking away from, now wondering where it was he really wanted to take me. Finally, we came to another staircase and instead of taking the stairs he simply vaulted over the banister to the echoing sounds of my frightened scream.

"Draven!" I shouted as I slapped his ass in reprimand for scaring me. He didn't even flinch but instead stormed through his home like a man on a mission, until a pair of double doors I knew well stood in front of us.

The Library.

He reared back a little before kicking the doors open in his rush to have me inside. Then, just as he started walking inside, he pulled me back over his shoulder gripping me around the waist and holding me there, so I was level with his face. I wrapped my hands around his neck and held on as he walked us across the room with purpose.

"What if someone comes in?" I whispered in his ear making him stop momentarily.

"What door?" he asked in a stern way that spoke of that fine thread that was close to snapping. I frowned, not understanding the question. This was until I looked behind him in time to see that, with a mere flick of his wrist, the panelled wall next to the door started to expand, pushing its way across the door until it consumed it. It didn't take me long before a quick scan of the place told me there was no other way in, or out for that matter.

"I'm sure you could have gotten away with just locking it?" I teased. He turned his head my way, so he could look at me when he said,

"Yes, I could have, but then again, any lock can be unlocked but take away the door then there is less chance of being granted entrance…"

"Or escape," I added much to his amusement as he repeated my words with a heated whisper,

"Yes, or escape."

After this he walked me backwards through the opulent and aged space and I had to wonder right then and there, how many of these books held words of love like the ones we were about to display to the written word?

The room was as you would have expected to find in a castle such as this, showcasing the wealth of Draven's history. With its beautiful crown moulded ceiling that was a series of cut out squares, each showing a floral design with oval pictures in the centres of a golden lion holding a sabre, with the sun at his back. Of course, I had seen this symbol a few times during my trip to the past, so it surprised me to see it here in his very Scottish castle.

But as I looked around the room, these weren't the only hints into the past, as the parts of the walls that weren't floor to ceiling books, were decorated with tapestries of war. Roman soldiers marching to a war against Persia with Draven's men on horseback with their arrows taut and ready to fly at the approaching enemy.

The rest of the room held other references to history, like massive model ships encased in glass. These done with such detail, you could almost hear the crashing waves of the sea against the bow and hear the cries of its Captain as he commanded his men.

Marble busts on carved wooden plinths stood as bodiless guards to the two large fireplaces in the room and plump Chinese style vases illuminated the space with the lamps fitted with modern day bulbs were dotted about the room. Rugs added deep rich reds, burnt oranges, subtle creams and even a hint of navy blue to the dark mahogany panelled walls, thanks to the ancient Persian designs.

The rest of the colour was created by its many book spines covering the heavy wooden shelves that lined the spaces in between objects of interest. Like the shining old globe that looked to be almost begging fingertips to spin its sphere. I even found myself wondering if there was a decanter of age old whisky hidden inside, but with Draven's body still backing me up into one of the bookshelves I didn't ponder the Earth for long.

I felt the hard leather spines dig into my own as Draven gripped my behind and hoisted me up and at the same time nodding to a sideboard. I yelped as I heard the smash of pottery as it hit the ground, thanks to its disappearing surface. This was because it was suddenly sliding along the floor at speed until soon the narrow serving cupboard was underneath me, so Draven could lower me to the lacquered wood.

Then he gathered my hands in both of his to raise them over my head in a painfully slow way and doing so by never taking his intense purple gaze from me. I looked up to see my wrists shackled in his large hands as he held them to the lip of the shelf above me.

"Draven?" I whispered his name in question as he started

to transfer them both into one, holding me with ease where he wanted me.

"I have wanted to fuck you in a library ever since that day," he said in a demonic purr as his hand travelled slowly down my arm, gathering back the large sleeve of my medieval style dress, making it bare for his touch. But his discovery didn't stop there. He continued on along my shoulder and down my neck where his hand came to rest at my throat as he shackled a more vulnerable part of me, one that made me shudder against him.

"Since I...?" I started to say my question, one that was quickly stopped when he asserted some pressure on the column of my throat before releasing it just as quickly, telling me,

"Since the day you teased my cock, little vixen."

"I don't remember it that way," I told him, adding a bite to my reply with the tone in which it was said.

"No? Then pray tell my sweetest one, which of us was it that nearly begged for the other to take pity?" Draven asked me with a raise of his eyebrow and I couldn't help but be transported back to that day that seemed so long ago. Another heart-breaking lifetime in fact. It was when Draven and I were no longer together, and I worked in the library. Of course, it had been as far away from working at Afterlife as you could have got and that's not just including the fact my wages had been pretty much a quarter of what Draven paid me. But it had served its purpose in both helping me get out of the house and stop moping around, as Libby called it, and getting my mind off Draven by keeping me busy.

But then, of course, came the day he infiltrated my private sanctuary and he did it in such a way, I had ended up being only a hair's breadth away from kissing him. And this, after a sworn vow never to kiss him ever again for as long as I lived. A vow that had lasted not even twenty-four hours after first seeing him. Looking back, I even remembered the way he seemed to be blushing when I first told him of my new job, and now after what he just said, could this really be a fantasy of his?

I also knew that before I became myself again after the Hexad cult, we had shared a beautiful night together in his library at Afterlife. And little did he know it at the time, but it was to be his last night with me as Katie before I was given my memories back. But for me and Draven, well then, this was a first and no doubt considering how long we had together, would hopefully be a first of many.

"Okay, so you begged me to take pity, but that was for being cute Draven, I was hardly ripping my top off, baring my naked breasts to you and saying, 'take me I'm yours' with Jane Austin at my back!" I said on a laugh, but I knew the second he looked down at my heaving bust line that I had lost him to other thoughts.

"Mmm, speaking of which..." he said granting me a grin. Then he hooked his fingers inside my cleavage and just before he could rip my dress off I tensed, strained my neck up and said,

"Wait!" I was actually surprised when he did stop and listen.

"Please don't rip my dress, I like this one." He smirked down at me, given that he was still taller than me even with the added height from the sideboard my backside was resting on.

"Alright little beauty, I have other means to free those bountiful gifts for me to feast upon." This was his only warning when he gripped the bottom of the corseted part of my dress before giving it a yank, making it slip further down my torso. Thankfully, it was tight enough that it didn't move much but it was enough for Draven to gather my breasts up so that most of them were now spilling over the top, overflowing into his hand. The second he pinched one of my nipples into a hard peak I threw my head back and let out a moan in pleasure. Then he moved to the other one and did the same, making me release an even deeper moan this time, yanking to free my hands as I did. However, he didn't release me but just held me in a firmer grip, adding to the intensity of it all.

"Oh, how I wanted to lift up your legs, wrap them around me and thrust into you, just before a word of protest could be uttered from your nervous, bitten lips," he said before swooping down to bite said lips, as if needing to add to the memory with a moment of truth.

"How I wanted to hear you moan my name as I took you to greater heights when chasing your release. To hear you beg it of me, so that I may gain back my control over you…" he said pausing to kiss along my neck, taking little bites along the way before continuing on with his confession.

"…So, that I might own you once more, as was my right. For you are mine now, and as you were even then…so say it… say it for me." Draven was quickly losing sight of his control and I knew this when his eyes grew darker with the purple ring around the iris turning to flames of red. So, I did the only thing I knew I could do, and that was try and give him what he needed and in doing so, hoping to tame the beast.

I wished my hands were free, so I may have added my touch to the words, but in the end all I could do was lean closer to him and whisper my vow over his lips.

"I am yours, now and always," I told him and the satisfaction I received when I saw his eyes seep back to purple made me want to howl in triumph. This had been something he needed to hear after this confessed hardship, one I knew was harder for him to live through seeing as he was forced to see me in the arms of another. I remember thinking, when I saw him that first time after so long, how relieved I had been to find him alone without some supernatural beauty on his arm.

"Mine… now and forever," he whispered before crushing his lips to mine, so he could taste the sexual moan he brought to

life with his kiss. I felt him reach down with his free hand as he gathered up all my skirt, lifting it so he could get to my bare skin. The second his fingertips made contact with my soaked panties we both sucked in a breath. I felt as though with that one touch he was igniting my senses and heating my core, making that tight bundle of nerves throb with need.

"You're soaked for me?" he asked, making me blush after he swiped his fingers over the lace and then brought them back to his lips to taste. I decided that, despite my shyness, I would give him the truth, so I leaned closer to him and told him,

"Around you my husband, I always am." This was enough to snap his control as he suddenly let go of my hand and gripped the back of my knees to yank my backside to the very edge of the sideboard.

A startled yelp later and he ripped off my panties and with a yank of his breeches he entered me in one beautifully brutal thrust. I threw my head back and cried out my pleasure, not caring that I hit the back of my head on years of literature.

I felt myself building the second he made contact, with that warmth that seems to spread throughout your entire body travelling all around me, as I felt myself close to coming undone. Like hands of pleasure were slowly crawling their way up from your toes at the same time making their way down your spine and the second they would finally meet, would be an explosion of sensation.

"Gods!" Draven hissed as he too seemed to be fighting with himself the second he could feel I was near. I gripped onto his shoulders and started trying to peel his jacket back so that I could feel more of him. He soon got the hint as he shrugged out of his jacket with my help and then let the expensive item drop to the floor.

Now, if I thought the sight of him in the jacket was sexy, this was something else entirely. I was near panting at seeing him with just his white shirt and tight fitted waistcoat straining against the movements of his massive muscles beneath the material. This combined with feeling breathless thanks to how he powered into me with such passion, he was like a man possessed.

I could feel myself on the edge just about to tip over when he suddenly grabbed my hands from exploring his body, once more so he could keep me imprisoned against the bookshelf. Now, with my hands once again shackled, he swooped down to my neck and plunged his fangs into my flesh and at the same time thrust into me to the hilt. I cried out my orgasm, screaming up to the ceiling as he roared out his own around my bloody flesh. I felt my own fangs lengthen because of it and I bit into my lip as my body still rode the wave of euphoria. I could still feel my insides quivering around him as he too shuddered against my inner walls, coating them with his seed.

Then, after licking my neck and sealing the wound, he pulled back and with my blood still coating his lips, he grinned down at me with that bad to the bone sexy grin and said the sexiest words anyone could ever hear in a library...

"By the Gods, how I love fucking my little librarian and making her scream for me."

CHAPTER THREE

FOOLISH ROMEO AND HIS UNFOOLISH JULIET

"Well, I think we can safely say I look adequately ravished by the King of the Castle," I joked as I took in my appearance from my reflection in the window and wondered what I was going to do about my hair.

"And ne'er has there been a sight more lovely than that of such beauty glowing after a lover's touch," he said making me glow a very unflattering shade of cherry. I looked back at him and took in the sight of his tall frame shrugging his jacket back over his shoulders and this time he fastened the buttons, giving him an even more masterful presence.

"Draven, did you just get that out of a book?" I teased nodding to one of the few books that had fallen onto the floor during our time spent abusing the shelf. I looked back at the evidence of not only the books lay across the floor like floating beige islands upon a sea of dark wood, but also the broken, splintered shelves they used to be nestled on.

I think it was during our third time and after Draven informed me he was far from done with his 'little librarian', that he had spun me round and taken me hard from behind. I vaguely remember looking to the side when I heard his fist lashing out into the spines before gripping the wooden shelf to aid him in his efforts. This, of course, didn't last long before giving out against his strength, surprising me that my own body fared better. Although, I wouldn't have been surprised to see fingerprint bruises at my hips where he had gripped me hard and boy wouldn't I be lying if I said this thought didn't excite me. To bear his mark on my body gave me a thrill like no other and before I knew what I was doing I was reaching up to a bite that had already healed.

Draven noticed the action and watched me with interest.

"Did I hurt you?" Draven asked now ignoring my tease about lines from books. I gave him a look of shock and shook my head,

"No, of course not, besides…new Vampy toughness remember?" I said showing him my muscles, which unfortunately were still none existent but at least it made him laugh.

"Then I am curious…" he started to say as he made his way to me. Once he was within reaching distance he gently took my hand in his and yanked me to him so that I landed pressed up against him, as was his plan. Yin and Yang sensations were a common thing around Draven, showing his gentle side whilst enforcing his strength and dominance over me.

"…what was that hidden look about?" he asked, finishing his query.

"It's not really hidden if you saw it, Draven." I complained on a chuckle instead of answering him. I felt him raise my face to meet his.

"Sweetheart, no look you give is ever hidden from me, for your expressive face often grants me more insight to your mind than your words do." In response to this I faked shock when my mouth dropped open and his bad boy grin told me he liked my reaction to his teasing.

"Then in that case there would never be a need for me to drop my guards and let you access my mind in the future, would there?" I told him, knowing the second I did I too would be granted the reaction I wanted. Draven didn't disappoint.

"Now I wouldn't go as far as to say that, and you know…" he paused first getting closer to my face before continuing,

"…to know your thoughts as they come to you… well now, I can imagine the benefits would be very rewarding, especially during certain *carnal acts.*" He finished these wicked words with a firmer grip to my side as he pulled me roughly to him and sealed his sentence with a kiss. I let myself enjoy it for a moment longer before pulling back, patting him on the arm twice before saying,

"Nice try Casanova, but that would be a big fat no on that one." He growled as I walked past him closer to the window, making me smirk at my own reflection.

"Now the big question is what on earth am I going to do about my hair?" I said facing the window, so I could assess the damage. It now looked as though someone had stuck a curly blonde bush on my head.

"I don't suppose you will believe me if I told you that I think you look beautifully wild."

"Yes, 'wild' being the operative word here, Draven." He laughed once before coming to stand behind me.

"And we can't have people getting the wrong impression of me, can we?" he said making me frown back at him in our reflection.

"And that would be?"

"Why, by ravishing my delectable little Queen, one held captive with my teeth and *cock.*" He whispered this last word in my ear making me shudder against him and I felt his smug grin against my neck.

"Now, let's see what I can do," he said before placing his hands on each side of my head, pausing for a second.

"Close your eyes for me," he hummed in my ear and I did as he said, unable to deny him anything when using that soft tender tone. I felt him start to move his hands down my hair, framing it all with his large hands and other than a tingling tickle, I wouldn't have even said he had really touched me.

"There... almost respectable again," he teased. I opened my eyes and saw that he was right, my hair had not a strand out of place from when Pip had first done it. Even my makeup was back to how Sophia had first applied it, complete with lipstick, that I knew Draven had kissed off long ago. Now making me ask the question why weren't his own lips covered in the shade?

"I also have to look respectable for my Queen, do I not?" Draven replied to my unspoken question.

"How did you...?"

"Like I said sweetheart, you have an expressive face and your *wide eyes tell me everything,*" he whispered down at me and I blushed and replied in a quiet tone,

"Not everything they don't." Thankfully he took this the way I had hoped and not because of the secrets I kept from him.

"Behave vixen!" he warned, granting me a flash of his purple heat in both his eyes and the slight glow of his veins. Then, before I could come back with a witty reply, he gripped the top of my dress and with a hard tug, pulled it up. This meant it was now covering my breasts and preventing them from spilling over as they had been. Of course, it wasn't enough to get them to behave completely as thanks to my curvaceous body, I was still sporting a hell of a cleavage. One that enticed him to run his fingertips gently across my soft mounds.

"Behave, Romeo." I half teased him back, also knowing that if he carried on we would never leave this room.

"Romeo is it? Well, I like to think I have more sense than that foolish fictional being," he said with a huff making me turn to look at him.

"Foolish?" I asked frowning up at him.

"Do you not think it foolish to let anything come between a love so strong, a foolishness that causes the death of two star crossed lovers by their own hands?" he asked light-heartedly giving me a tap under my chin with his curled finger, before leaving to go fix the shelf. Meanwhile, I was still stood there where he left me just replaying his words. I don't know why they affected me so much, that was until the words were spilling out before I could stop them.

"I would die for you…I…*I did die for you*…do you think that is foolish?" The second my words were out he froze and one of the books he was putting back dropped from his hand. He first lowered his head and closed his eyes as if my very words had caused him utter agony to hear and I wished in that moment I could have taken them back. He had his fists clenched at his sides and was close to shaking, which was when I could stand it no longer.

"Draven I…"

"We have both died for one another Keira, and where did it get us but steps down a foolish path we both regret taking," he said, his voice stern and on the edge.

"It isn't foolish to die for the one you love Draven, and I don't regret dying for you or dying to save all of those we love, including might I add, the whole world!" I snapped back knowing I was just making this worse, but I couldn't help it.

"Yes, but what if it had been *your* hand behind the blade and *my* heart you had plunged it into?" he snapped slashing a hand out to his side in his anger. I took a step back and my hand clutched at my heart as if that very image had been scorched upon my soul.

"Ah, I see that painted image is enough to haunt you as its reality still does me!" he growled in response to my reaction. At first, I didn't know what to say. But he was right, that image was one that had tears forming and a strange ache in my chest as though that glass blade was still there.

"Draven…why, why do this to yourself when it was always meant to be this way. When it was destined in the Fates even before we met?" I asked in what I hoped was a soothing tone for I hated to see how much this still affected him. And from his snarled words I could understand how. Because even the words spoken about committing such an act was too horrendous to even allow my mind to paint that image for long. And in the small time they had taken root, was enough to have a tear escaping down my cheek.

"Yes, well I damn the Fates and their fucking foreseen destiny! I am nobody's puppet and I would spend a thousand lifetimes cutting at their strings if they be ones that try and force my hand to harm you again!" He vowed this time with his voice giving over more to his demonic side, making me ask myself, which part of him ruled his heart more. Because like this, it was once easy to see how his demon side loved me just as his angel side did. But now, well now I wasn't as sure as I had once been. Because now I knew I had met his demon and one thing had been obvious…

He didn't like me.

But right now, I couldn't think about this. No, right now I only had one important job to do and that was being Draven's shoulders. For I needed to take his weight, a weight of pain that was holding him beneath a mountain of guilt. So, I walked up to him and placing a palm on his cheek, I raised his face up so that I could see him.

"Now I want you to listen to me Dominic, for I will only say this one last time…" I paused to take in a breath as his eyes so full of pain looked to mine, as if in this moment I held the answer to all.

So, I told him the only thing that mattered and a truth so blinding he couldn't see it for he refused to open his eyes. And by doing so, I forced him to open them and see once and for all.

"That knife was never in your hand but in that of a God. A God, Draven. A God that used you and took my life, which in the end was to be his undoing. Don't you see, the prophecy was never about *you* taking my life… it was only ever about me risking *mine to save yours*. I chose the path I walked down, and I took every step because I knew it only ever led me to one place…" I told him and then pulled his face down to mine so that I could whisper the end of my sentence with my forehead to his.

A sentence spoken to the feel of his tears landing on my cheeks, mixing with my own.

"…A place that only ever led me to you."

CHAPTER FOUR

IT STARTS WITH A KISS

After this tender moment that passed between us he simply took my hand in his and said,

"I believe I owe you a date, my Queen." Then he led us from the library after flicking his wrist and bringing back the door with a mere thought. We walked away from the bittersweet moment and now hopefully towards one that held just the sweet.

As we walked in silence back the way we came, I knew I wasn't the only one with heavy thoughts resting on their mind. For me it was thoughts consumed by once more facing an unknown future with the man at my side. But for Draven?

Well, I could only imagine it was consumed by one single moment in time. One that would no doubt stay rooted within him for many years to come. A painful reminder every time he looked to the girl by his side who was now his wife and eternally bound to him. All I could hope for was a short time trying to find the light in the darkness so that he may finally make it out to the other side…not years of doing so, or even worse…*a lifetime.*

I knew my words had only helped sooth his guilty soul for a while, but knowing Draven as I did, I knew it wouldn't last for long. And from the looks of that thoughtful expression, I knew it was a lot shorter than I had hoped for.

But then again, it was a traumatic experience after all and I knew from my own experience that those weren't exactly easy to get over. It had taken me years to get over what Morgan had done to me, and even longer to stop caring about the evidence of such a time still left on my skin, like showing my scars to the world.

Hell, I can't even remember the last time I had even been conscious of them being there. But this wasn't like a scar on his skin that would remind him each time he saw it. No, this was far worse. This was like a scar on his soul, one he would feel deep within him every time he looked at me. Every time he saw me smile, laugh or moan in rapture. Every time he saw a hint of the girl he loved, he would forever be plagued by then seeing that life fade from my eyes by his own hand. And no matter how many times I tried to rid him of that guilt, he would simply hold onto it tighter.

So, the question was…

Would he ever let go of it?

As we approached the staircase that led down into the ballroom, I knew the answer to that question was one I would be asking myself for some time to come and that thought made me squeeze his hand tighter. He looked down at me and took my bitten lip as a nervous reaction to seeing all the people below and not the real reason I was feeling this way.

"You ready?" he asked me, and I found I could only nod in return, too afraid of what my mind would let slip with words. The second we started to descend the stairs it turned out that our entrance was to be a grand one, whether we liked it or not. Or should I say...whether *I liked it or not.*

Suddenly the band stopped playing and a ballroom full of people all paused and looked up at us before they started to clap. I felt my feet nearly slip on a step and I instantly gripped onto Draven tighter as if needing more than his mental support this time. The second he felt it he decided to take matters into his own hands...*literally.*

"Draven!" I shouted his name as I found myself being swept up into his arms. The crowd loved it and went crazy cheering for us. And I could hear Pip's wolf whistle above it all, finding her easily in the crowd as a colourful beacon bouncing up and down like an excited child.

"Just in case you fall for me again," Draven told me softly, making me grin up at him after first trying to bury my head in his chest to hide myself from the shame of being on show. In the end I had no choice than to just let Draven carry me down the stairs and across the grand banquet hall until we arrived at our royal looking seats.

"You know when I mentioned about going to a medieval banquet, I didn't mean that I had to be the queen at one," I teased as Draven took the steps two at a time to the raised platform where our long table was positioned at the head of the room. He chuckled at my comment and then let me down before waiting for the room to grow silent.

"I would like to thank you all for being here tonight in helping me surprise my beautiful..." 'Say wife, say wife, say wife' I repeated over and over in my mind.

"...wife," he said looking at me as if he had heard my silent plea and I released a sigh in relief, which turned out to be premature. His tender smile soon turned into a bad boy grin when he then added,

"And my ravishing Queen! For she knows not the pleasure

she grants me just by seeing her smile. So, once again I thank you all for aiding me in making that happen...To eternal happiness!" He shouted this last part whilst raising his glass as the whole room did the same. The rest of the room shouted out the same in chorus making the words 'Eternal Happiness' thunder out and echo in the huge room.

After this he pulled out my throne-like chair for me and the second I had sat down he nodded to the room, indicating they should all do the same. Draven was the last to take his seat and he rolled a hand in the air to signal to the waiters that food could now be served.

"So, what do you think?" Sophia asked nodding to the ballroom full of colourful life, as she was now sat next to me.

"I think it's..."

"Tote bag, Amazebollocks!" Pip shouted from next to her, making me laugh, as I was pretty sure that was pip code for 'totally amazing'...well it was either that or she had a canvas shopping bag full of men's chopped off balls under the table and thought her collection was amazing.

"What she said, only with less male parts," I said making her giggle before moaning,

"Aww, but those are the best bits! You're no fun," she teased and Draven, overhearing this, grabbed my hand in his and raised it to his lips to kiss before informing her,

"I disagree...she was extremely fun moments ago." This made everyone sat at our table laugh, which turned out to be for longer when they heard me growl at him despite my red cheeks.

"That's adorable you know," he told me, giving my fingertip a little nibble.

"Yes, well it won't be adorable when I am growling whilst chopping off your balls and adding them to Pip's Tote bag of Amazing bollocks," I said making him a raise an eyebrow at my threat, but then Pip popped her head around Sophia and said,

"Uhh...my what now?" I laughed along with everyone else and Sophia, knowing my thoughts, nudged her and said,

"I will explain later."

"Okay, but you know I collect beanie babies and condoms from around the world...right, not man dangler ball bits?" At this I burst out laughing and unfortunately snorted a few times with it.

"Oh dear, you set inner piggy free again, Pip," Sophia said smirking when I shot her a glare, one she took about as seriously as a caged chihuahua wearing a tiara and pink tutu, baring its teeth.

"I must say I do hope that I can get that inner piggy to come out to play later?" Draven commented before taking a sip from his goblet looking mischievously at me over the rim. Again, I growled but quieter this time and just before I asked,

"Not unless there is something you're not telling me?"

"Like?" he enquired taking the bait and lowering his cup.

"Like how you have a farmyard fetish and I should start calling you Farmer Dom?" I teased making him pause for a minute before slamming down his goblet as he burst into raucous laughter. I jumped at the sudden reaction and the room seemed stunned for a moment before they all started to join in the laughter. Although I was pretty sure that no one but those close to us knew why.

"Now that's what I call bringing home the bacon!" Pip shouted slapping a hand to Adam's back before she cackled out her own sweet sing song laughter. He just fixed his now crooked glasses that had also slipped further down his nose and smiled at his animated wife's reaction to her own joke.

"Tell me, my dear one, for I am curious, but would this fantasy of yours include you naked and covered in mud?" Draven purred in my ear making me roll my eyes before telling him,

"I think you missed the point, Draven."

"No, I think you will find that I...*never miss the point,*" he said whispering this last part and at the same time reaching under my skirt and skimming along my inner thigh. I shivered against his touch and looked down trying to hide my blush from everyone else. I only looked back up again when I heard a plate being placed in front of me and the smell of the honey baked ham nearly had me salivating. Okay, so now all I needed was fresh bread, some mayo, crisp lettuce, maybe a slice of cheese or two and a knife to put the beauty into action. Oh, and some sliced banana with a dollop of mashed potato and the whole thing dipped in Bisto instant gravy...oh yeah, now that would be...wait a second, that would be gross!

"Now that's a thought I very much wish to know." Draven's voice brought me out of my inner food turmoil.

"You mean you don't know? My eyes and expressive face didn't tell you all you need to know?" I teased making him smirk.

"Well, if I were to venture a guess it would be that at first you were ready to devour the ham in front of you with gusto, but then it looked like someone had come along and dumped vomit all over it as you suddenly looked utterly disgusted," he said making me wrinkle my nose at the thought.

"Eww," I muttered before he carried on.

"Now, seeing as I am at a loss to know why or what caused this sudden change of heart, I am forced to surrender my weakness to the mistress of my answers and simply ask," he said making my lips twitch at his chosen words.

"I like the sound of that...hey do you think we could upgrade me from Vixen to that? 'Mistress of answers' has got a nice ring to it I think," I said humming to myself and tapping a finger on my bottom lip as if I was deep in thought.

"Now I think it is you that missed the point my dear," he retorted making me drop a hand to his trousers at the same time as I sucked in my bottom lip looking at him. Then I grabbed his semi hard erection and gave it a squeeze, instantly feeling it grow as I repeated his own words back at him.

"No, I think you will find that...*I never miss the point, Draven.*" This time I was the one smiling at his deep rumbling growl, one that told me along with what was now over filling my hand, that it was a sound emitted from being turned on.

"Oooh spit roast! Slip me some skin, Baby Boo Bot!" Pip shouted excitedly, pointing now at the plater of roasted pork and crackling that was being brought around by a waiter dressed in a blue tunic.

"Oh, and the po ta ta as!" she added making me forgot Draven's leg and swing my head to Sophia and ask,

"The what?"

"I think she means she wants potatoes, but then considering she also calls your breasts tata titties, then who the hell knows," she said wryly with a shrug of her shoulders. But Pip hearing this informed us,

"No, they are now known as baby mama milking jugs, and yes I meant the potatoes." Now I know when hearing this I should have focused on my new breast nickname. Or better still, even ask myself why she thought it necessary to have a series of nicknames for that part of my anatomy. However, this wasn't what I went with, because my stomach demanded something more for me when I blurted out,

"Potatoes!" making Draven shoot me a look along with everyone else on the table, after just shouting this at the top of my voice for some weird reason.

"Can you pass them to me please!" I said way too forcefully, making Pip give me a quizzical look before dropping the serving spoon in the bowl with a clatter and passing the bowl to Sophia without taking her eyes from me.

"Uhh…yeah, sure thing Tootie bean," she said in that 'What the Hell' tone.

"Thanks." I said nearly snatching the silver bowl from Sophia and ignoring her comment of,

"Okay there, little Miss Grabby."

"Sweetheart?"

"Um?" I answered Draven after piling the roasted potatoes on my plate making sure to only pick the big ones.

"You okay?" he asked making me just nod once before scanning the table for what else I was looking for. Okay, so I know I must have looked like a woman slightly possessed right in that moment, but I couldn't focus on caring about anything else but my new mission.

"Yeah, could you pass the butter…over there… that's it, can you pass it down please," I said waving a hand to Zagan, who was sat at Draven's side in place of his brother, which reminded me, where was he and Ari? Draven frowned as the dish was passed up to him but must have decided not to say what was on his mind and instead just watch this play out.

"What is she doing?" I heard Sophia ask her brother after a few minutes of watching me dissecting my potatoes.

"Is she building a tower like I did?" Pip asked with a long piece of crackling in her hand before she bit off the end with a loud crunch. I shot Pip a frown only to find that yes, she had indeed built a tower from potatoes and what looked like different condiments in between to act as the cement in this crazy edible construction. Okay, so I couldn't talk about other people's brand of crazy, not considering I had been the one not long ago to build a tower out of toilet rolls!

"No Pip, I am not building a tower, although I have to say, impressive," I said waving to her food art with my fork. She gave me a wink before breaking off a piece of her sweet covered dress and using the lollypop to scoop up some of her food, which I think was a creamy fish dish. Either way it didn't look like a great combination, but once again, who was I to judge.

"May I ask what they did to offend you so?" Draven asked nodding down to my plate and the fact that I had taken all the crispy skins off the roast potatoes and had scooped out the filling before mashing it up with the back of my fork.

"Oh nothing, just making mashed potato," I said after dumping an unhealthy amount of butter on top and mashing that in there too.

"Okay...sweetheart if you wanted mash..."

"Oh hey! Excuse me!" I shouted to a waiter as he was going past us and completely interrupting my poor husband in the process.

"Who me?" the server asked looking startled.

"Yes you, would you mind doing me a favour please," I said as he first shot a worried look to Draven who was no doubt an intimidating presence at my side, and one who was making his ownership known as I felt a hand on my shoulder claiming me. I rolled my eyes once, before continuing on.

"Do you think you could get me a banana?" I asked making Draven stiffen next to me and suddenly start coughing as if he had choked down a heavy swallow. I tried to ignore Sophia's giggle which was followed quickly by Pip shouting,

"Oh, my giddy God's uncle, did she just ask for a banana?!"

"Keira?" Draven's stern voice was saying my name in question but come on, what did he expect me to do with it, wave it in the air and tell the room to excuse us, as we were leaving now to go and fornicate with fruit?

"Umm...sure, I think we have some in the kitchen." The

poor server, who at this point looked like he wanted nothing more than to just run away and hide, muttered nervously.

"Thank you, oh and if you could also grab that gravy jug when you're on your way back, that would be wonderful," I said nodding down the end of the table where Adam had been pouring it and stopped mid flow as soon as I said this, only to find everyone now staring at him.

"Sure thing," the guy said before rushing off back to the kitchens.

"Alright, what is with you?!" Sophia demanded, and I just shrugged my shoulders and said,

"What? I just fancied one after this," I said nodding down to my makeshift pile of mashed potatoes now surrounded by discarded golden shells with little pools of butter in between the pale peaks.

"She can eat what she wants, Sophia," Draven said firmly, making me smile up at him before kissing his jaw in thanks.

"Whatever," she muttered in amusement, when I turned and stuck my tongue out at her. A few minutes later as I was just taking small mouthfuls of my potatoes, I saw the waiter coming back. I sighed in relief as for some reason it just wasn't hitting the right spot.

"Here you go, Miss." The young guy said handing me the bowl of fruit and placing down a new gravy boat.

"Mrs Draven!" my overbearing husband corrected making me roll my eyes and the waiter first looked fearful before I said,

"Thank you, that's very kind of you."

"Yes of course, Mrs Draven," he corrected, now looking slightly less scared as he left me to my strange bounty.

"You know if you wish me to wear a sign around my neck saying 'property of Dominic Draven' so that you will relax and be less frightening to the common mortal man, then I am willing...you know, all in the name of peace and tranquillity and all," I said looking back over my shoulder up at him making him raise an eyebrow at me.

"Mm, keep it up sweetheart and it won't be a sign of possession you wear around your neck, but a chain I have wrapped around my fist that's attached to the... *collar around your neck.*" He said this last part as a sexual purr down in my ear making him grin against my neck when he felt me shudder because of it. Wow, can anyone say wet panties, it felt like the buggers were melting off like pouring hot water on tissue paper!

Shortly after Draven's BDSM bombshell, his attention was taken away by a question of business from Zagan and Takeshi and for once I was thankful for this. Now I had chance for my overactive mind to go on sexual overdrive thinking about me chained to Draven as he took possession of my body.

"Oh, by the Gods, what is she doing now?" Sophia said to herself after raising her hands up to the side of her face in a dramatic sigh.

"What?" I asked, pausing just before I took a bite of what was now a banana in my hand that had a big heap of mashed potato and gravy on the end.

"Gods Keira, what in Heaven's name are you eating?" Draven asked now he had his attention brought back to me. I looked down at the banana that had been half eaten wondering to myself when I had even done that.

Pip suddenly burst out laughing before filling the rest of us in on what was so funny.

"Oh, watch out, it looks like the Tootie baby machine just hit the level CRAVE ME on the preggy scale!" Pip shouted after first clapping her hands and getting excited. I opened my mouth ready to deny it but looking down at what should have been the most disgusting combo in my hand, then really, was I in any position to argue? So instead I just shrugged my shoulders and said to Draven,

"What she said." Then I took a big bite of my potato covered banana and moaned as my taste buds started to sing! Draven gave me a loving look as though the sight of his wife moaning around a banana dripping with gravy and mashed potato was the most natural and sexy thing in the world.

"She can eat whatever she wishes as long as it makes her and the baby happy," Draven said softly, making me want to melt up next to him, especially as he rubbed a large hand over my belly in a tender loving way.

"Great, now he is going to make sure it's on the menu of every restaurant we own, just in case you might want to go there," Sophia commented dryly, only with one look at her and the wink she gave me, I knew it was said to tease her brother and not me. So, I decided to get her back as I leaned into her and said,

"Yeah, but it's for a good cause...*Aunty Sophia.*" After I whispered this last part to her she shot me a look of shock as if she hadn't fully realised until now what me being pregnant would mean and bring to her life...*to all our lives*. Her beautiful wide chocolate eyes went from being surprised to tearfully overwhelmed in seconds and it was when that full bottom lip of hers found her way into her mouth that I knew I had her.

She didn't say anything but instead she grabbed my hand under the table and gave it a squeeze, telling me in that one gesture that we were sisters and we were in this together.

Draven being Draven hadn't missed our exchange and he rewarded me by first giving me a warm tender look. This was swiftly followed with action when he hooked me around the neck and pulled me in for a kiss. I tried not to flinch as I felt him close to my birthmark, but I was too late.

I felt something there start to get hot. I sucked in a deep breath, holding it in as he continued to kiss me for fear that any minute now it was all going to go terribly wrong. As if I would knowingly be releasing a Draven Demon King Kong onto the world, and then later on, amongst all the rubble, there I would be,

Stood in the midst of it all saying the words…

And it all started with a kiss.

CHAPTER FIVE

THE FLOWER OF SCOTLAND WILTS

Draven's fingers flexed once, then twice on my birthmark as he continued his kiss and the heat it caused felt almost like a brand. I was just about to pull away, still in fear of what I would see once I did, but then something different happened. Instead of War of the Demon Worlds breaking out, like I thought, Draven just tapped his fingers on my neck a few times more before releasing me.

I didn't realise but I had even closed my eyes and the second I felt a shiver pass through me I was snapped out of it. It was that feeling people get when they say someone just walked over their grave. Well, it was like that only for me it felt more deeply rooted. As though someone hadn't just walked over it, but more like first dug it, pushed me in and then buried me alive before doing some boogie dance moves over it!

Thankfully, this feeling soon passed, and the rest of the meal continued on without a hiccup. Now that my belly was happy with its unconventional meal consumed I found myself sat there, content and taking in the rest of the ballroom. I had to admit that I felt quite bad that there weren't many here that I knew. Which also made me a little sad. I guess I was getting so used to seeing everyone in our supernatural inner circle that I missed the usual faces. But then I realised that now that the war was over, it was time they all got back to ruling their own kingdoms and for everyone to continue on as before. Living their lives the way they always had before I had come along and put an 'end of the world' spanner in life's works.

Jared had his freaky circus fight club and his Hellbeasts to keep him busy. Vincent and Ari had their own issues to deal with, which for some reason I knew I was being kept in the dark about.

I had been disappointed not to see them, but according to Sophia they were currently in London still trying to follow the breadcrumbs in discovering Ari's past. I knew this was something she needed, and I didn't blame her, for I could only imagine how hard it must have been waking up each day and not knowing who you truly were.

It was bad enough when I thought my name was Katie and having to learn it was all a lie. But no matter how much I knew she had to do this, a part of me also wished that she wouldn't. That she would just look at the man who obviously loved her, seeing Vincent the way I knew he wished she would see him and then just let herself be happy. But then again, what did I truly know? After all, in Draven's world, it wouldn't have been a stretch to say that I was being kept in the dark about what was really going on.

The truth was I missed Ari and wished she would just come home.

As for the rest of them, last I heard RJ would barely leave Jack's side, who unfortunately still hadn't woken up. Draven assured me that everything was being done to try and discover why, along with Seth who had left on his own mission of discovery. But then again, they were another pair that had yet to come together and stop fighting the cosmic pull that fate had thrust upon them.

And last I heard about Lucius, was that he too had returned to his own domain and was... well, doing what Lucius did best...ruling with an iron fist and no doubt a sadistic grin. I smirked to myself when thinking that he was probably finally getting some peace these last few weeks without me around getting myself into trouble. But then again, something in this told me that he no doubt still worried, considering what happened the last time I saw him.

I couldn't say that I blamed him, as I was somewhat of a liability in their world and let's face it, when a person needed more than one hand to count the amount of times they had been kidnapped, then yeah, the cards were never in my favour.

As for Sigurd, as usual I had no clue, only that he wasn't here. Not that this surprised me as he was your typical lone rogue who wasn't exactly the best team player. Sure, the war had been won with him fighting by our side. But as for being an active council member, then well, let's just say that I wasn't going to hold my breath any time soon waiting for that one.

Which left Draven's usual council on the top table, along with Pip and Adam who were looking more and more like a permanent addition to our family. I had to say this made me more than a little happy, it filled me with joy!

I felt blessed to have Pip in my life as she had become such an important person to me over the past few years that I didn't know what I would have ever done without her. And the thought of not seeing her for months on end wasn't something I ever wanted to think about. Besides, from the looks of things, I don't think Pip was all too thrilled with the idea of being separated either and when it came to Adam, well the motto 'happy wife, happy life' was more like his life's mission and mantra.

I was just starting to take in the rest of the room when I saw Mack step onto the small stage just as the last song ended. The band had been playing throughout our meal but now that most had finished, it looked as if they were about to kick it up a notch. Which begged the question, what was Mack now doing up there? Well, I was about to find out as someone handed him a microphone.

He was dressed like a rock version of a Scotsman and I had to say, looked very handsome in that rough and ready kind of way. He wore an unconventional kilt that was made of black canvas material, pleated at one side, with a large flat panel that wrapped around the front. Its waistband was a series of embossed leather straps etched with what looked like Celtic symbols and the same design was on the square leather bag that was attached to one side.

To this cool gothic take on a traditional Scottish attire, he added a simple white shirt tucked in the kilt, and was rolled up at the sleeves, showing off not only an impressive amount of muscle but also his many tattoos. He wore this shirt unbuttoned around the neck with a loose black silk tie knotted low, that was covered in black leather skulls on the shiny paisley pattern. Heavy biker boots, that were only half laced up, and thick bands of buckled leather around both wrists completed the outfit. His shaved mohawk had been braided many times and then twisted back into a leather tie that showcased his handsome features.

I frowned as I saw the few couples dancing now leaving the open space in the middle, and I wondered what was about to happen. Was there to be an act announced? Then with a nod to Draven from Mack, I looked back in time to see Draven respond in kind before the sound of bagpipes suddenly filled the room. Two men walked around the stage from both sides and started to play the proud Scottish sound, along with two more that followed playing large drums hung around their necks. They were all dressed similar to Mack but then when they stopped playing I was left stunned when I heard a beautiful male voice start singing. I shot back to the man in question and felt my mouth drop when I saw it was in fact Mack who was filling the room with such beauty with his harmonious voice…

> "O flower of Scotland
> When will we see your like again
> That fought and died for
> Your wee bit hill and glen
> And stood against him
> Proud Edward's army
> And sent him homeward
> Tae think again"

It was when Mack continued on to the second verse that Draven stood, turning to me and held his hand out for me to take. I looked up at him in question when he said,

"I believe I owe my Queen a dance." At first, I wanted to say no as I knew I would no doubt just make a fool of myself and him for that matter, but then the second I hesitated, he gave me a smirk as though he knew where my thoughts lay and said,

"Put your hand in mine Keira, for I would never let you fall." The second he said it and the moment I put my hand in his, I couldn't help but remember his demon's threat that day…

"Then we will watch as you fall and what will you do…when you have no wings to catch you?"

I shuddered at the thought, as this had been what he had said that night and this was what I now had replaying over and over again in my mind as Draven escorted me to the dance floor. Everyone rose to their feet as we made our way around, making my face hot and flushed from being the centre of attention.

After the second verse the bag pipes started up again just as we made it to the middle of the dance floor. Draven gave my body a small tug and pulled me tight to his frame so that now we could dance just as the chorus was sung by not only Mack, but also the rest of the band. It was a beautiful moment and I soon found myself getting lost in not only the words but also by Draven's warm touch. He guided me around the floor with ease and made me feel like I could actually dance.

I felt a bit like a Scottish princess in that moment as my heavy skirt flared out to the side every time Draven would spin us around. In fact, I found myself so lost in the moment that I soon forgot about the crowd of people surrounding us all clapping and cheering. I just looked up at Draven and found myself captivated by his purple eyes gazing down at me as he continued to control our movements, making us both move together as one.

Before I knew it, the song had ended just as Draven brought me closer still, lifting me with an arm around my waist so that our lips were mere inches apart. Then he kissed me quickly before the next song started to play, which had a different vibe and was one less lively.

I was at least glad to see that now others had started to join us on the dance floor. They each took to the steps with practiced ease so that now we all flowed around the room, rotating around the space like a finely tuned cog powering a machine none of us could see.

I had no idea what I was doing but just knew that if I held onto Draven then I would be okay. Then the people all started to get closer to us and we moved faster around the room, making me feel as though if I let go at any minute, I would soon get swept up in the storm around us. As I spun around I would notice people staring at us, laughing in a kind of sinister way. The men who had once played the bagpipes on the stage now stepped forward with violins and girls rose from their seats to play their flutes when their time came.

"Draven?" I said his name as my panic started to mount as the images around me started to blur the second we travelled faster. I felt him lower my body backwards, holding my waist in a tight grip and as the tempo of the luring new song started, I let my head fall back. It felt as though I was drugged and now the woman's voice that was filling the room, singing in a different language felt as though she was putting a spell on me.

It was only when I started to really focus that I noticed the room was slowly changing around me. The rich and sunny colours of autumn started to morph into the shadows giving way to the darker side of my fears. I frowned as the panelled walls started to turn from mahogany to muted colours of grey stone, framed by crimson banners with a demonic looking symbol at their centres in painted tarnished gold.

Then mighty stone pillars seemed to shoot up from nowhere and now stood tall around the room in the image of mighty giant sentinels looking down at all the people. Equally large stone weapons of death held firmly in their grasp and helmets of burnt gold sat atop lowered heads. They each looked down, holding the plinths upon their colossal shoulders which then became part of the structure of holding up the scalloped roof. One that was carved to look like dragon scales in between the series of arches.

It was as if someone had taken the room and expanded it, stretching it to three times its size. I couldn't understand what was happening as I knew I wasn't dreaming, for I could still feel Draven's hands on me. Was this part of the spell, part of the magic of the evening? Well, looking at all the people now cloaked and wearing gruesome masks, I had to say that it was unlikely.

I felt as though I had suddenly been dumped in some demonic version of that childhood classic movie, Labyrinth, but if that was the case then did that make Draven, Jareth and me Sarah and was I, at some point, to smash my way out of this illusion?

This thought finally brought me to my senses enough to pull myself back up and face the man that still held me, hoping like never before, that it was still the same man I treasured and loved.

It wasn't.

I released a muted cry of shock that left me on a breathless whisper as I now gazed upon Draven wearing a mask of death. It even looked to be made from real bone and was the shape of a decorated horned skull that fit snugly over the top part of his face, cheeks and nose before following the curve of his top lip, covering it slightly. However, the fangs I saw gleaming just under it were all his and I couldn't help but try and pull away at the sight.

This seemingly innocent trance I had been ensnarled into had quickly spiralled into my nightmare, and I needed to escape. His grip tightened on my waist as he snarled down at me. Then I looked into his eyes, ones now painted black beneath the skull to look even more intimidating. I started to struggle in his hold before demanding of him,

"Let me go, Draven!" At the time and even when I said this, I didn't think for one minute it would have an effect on him, but then suddenly he surprised me by letting me go. I let out a small yelp of shock as I expected the pain to follow, but it never came thanks to the massive frame of Draven now behind me. He caught me by the arms and with a quick, gentle push, I was back to standing upright before I felt him disappear. It happened in seconds and I stood for a moment, too stunned to move. Then, coming to my senses, the impossible world around me snapped sharply into focus, I whipped around ready to face this new version of Draven.

But he was gone.

"Draven?" I whispered his name, quietly pleading for him, the Draven I knew, to return and save me. I looked around the space where I stood, desperately trying to seek him out, but all that met me was this new demonic reality. Each of the guests who had once held demonic masks to their faces, had now changed yet again. No, now what covered their appearance were the stiff dead and tortured leftovers from the humans they had peeled the faces from. Haunted features frozen in time were all the humanity that remained in this world... their death and me still living.

I felt sick as I tried to push my way through them all, knocking into one man and making him lower his fat human face mask, one he had stuffed a golden apple into its mouth. But the second the face was lowered I soon wished for the grim face of death back, as what lay beneath it was far worse than that of staring at a bloated corpse.

Rotting red flesh hung in sags by his cheeks and three rows of yellowish brown teeth were in place of his lips. A protruding bloody bone from his chin that looked to have been forced somehow through the raw flesh that surrounded it. In fact, it looked more like a horn, that tapered down into a blunt point. One that at some point he thought must have been a good idea to get pierced, as it also had three large hoops tunnelled through the centre, hanging down overlapping each other. The centre of his eyes reminded me of lizard skin that seemed to burn brighter green in the cracks, as he looked me up and down.

I stumbled away from him and tried to squeeze past the others, this time without touching them and as I did, I felt a presence watching me as I went by. I turned in time to see who I thought was Draven, but as he turned his back on me, he became lost in the crowd and quickly disappeared.

"Draven...Draven?!" I said his name again only this time a group of people all dressed like gothic buccaneers started laughing at me. Their masks were scarred skulls held to their faces by a skeleton hand and a forearm they all held by the bone. One of them even had a small model pirate ship nestled amongst plumes of red feathers in the brim of her fur trimmed hat.

I turned away from their mocking stares and cackling laughter as I weaved my way through the crowd in search of him. What was this place? Why was I suddenly here and not there, back in my own time?

Was this what had happened, had I somehow been transported to another time, or worse, was this a glimpse into my future? I had no answers but only an endless stream of questions that were leading me down a deeper road to nowhere. No, my only hope was to find Draven and try to get him to explain what had happened, or to at least speak with him to assess what the Hell was going on!

But that in itself seemed like an impossible task, as first I had to find him and find him amongst a sea of demons no less. The music seemed to increase its tempo into a darker more sinister theme and it became more like the drums of war than that of a ball, as I fought my way around the crowded space. I kept seeing a glimpse of him every time I turned around, catching him for a second, staring at me through the crowd with an intensity that had me near cowering from him.

I passed a group that started snarling at me through moving dead lips, ones that seemed to be attached to the rest of the mask with hammered rivets so that the jaw could move. I took a step back and straight into a hard body, where hands came to hold the tops of my arms to steady me. I felt the deep growl rumbling up my back as it travelled up his chest before sounding by my ear. It was a terrifying sound and I shuddered as a chill crept up my spine. At first, I thought it was directed at me, but when I saw the once snarling group in front me start to lower their heads in submission, I knew it was at them not me.

"What a pretty little slave you will make for me," his rough raspy voice hummed in my ear just before he let me go. I spun on my heel so that this time I would catch him with an outstretched hand. But the second I turned he was gone again and my fist closed around the empty space he had once filled. I let my arm drop and I swear I could hear his amusement in the background as he witnessed my hopelessness for himself.

"...A beauty with chains against this delicate skin." I turned again the second I heard his voice in my ear, feeling his lips touching the delicate skin he spoke of.

"Draven!" I shouted this time, when once more I was faced with nothing but our hellish audience. I could hear his laughter echoing around the huge space and I looked up and around to see where it was coming from. This was when I noticed the whole ballroom was surrounded by a high balcony, one that curved around the room's massive stone warriors that this time, all seemed to be watching me. That's when I saw a shadowed figure stood there above us all, reminding me of times long past, back in Afterlife. I knew it was Draven thanks to his white bone mask that caught the flickering candlelight. He was watching me, hands gripping the banister as if he was holding himself back from just jumping down and claiming me.

Then someone bumped into me, first from behind and then to the side and I had to take a step forward to right myself. I looked up just in time to see a small cloud of stone dust float down, falling to the floor from where his hands had crushed indents in the railing. The red of his demonic eyes burning bright through the holes in his mask.

A commotion to my side made me look away and I saw the two who had bumped into me drop to their knees, clutching at their throats as if they had been poisoned. Then I felt the bile rise up as I watched in chilling disgust as their necks started to melt, as if the contents of their stomachs had been filled with acid and it was overflowing up their food pipe.

I turned away from the sight before I threw up and stumbled back a step. This time people moved out of my way pretty quickly, no doubt too afraid to receive the same fate forced upon them by their master. My gaze snapped back to where he had been on the balcony, only to find it now empty.

What was he playing at here? I felt like some small helpless mouse being played with by a demonic cat. He was toying with me, enjoying the game of chase, one that I knew was impossible to outrun. But I knew I had to try because right now, I knew that trying to find him was more dangerous than trying to get away from him. The game had changed and whereas before I thought he was my only hope, now I knew he would only lead to my destruction.

So, I looked around and spotted an arched doorway, hoping that it might help lead me home, or even better…

Break the spell.

But as I felt myself gaining distance and squeezing my way through the crowd with only a handful of people still left between me and the door, the sound of his commanding voice made me stop. Frozen against my will the second he said that foreign word.

"Keira, BATILTU!" Hearing the sound of my name, coming this time from the Draven I knew, made me turn to face him but the second I did I knew then it was a trap. Because the Draven I knew and loved didn't face me now.

No, he had just made me believe it was, as another way to control me. I looked back at him to see the room had now halved, split down the middle creating a path straight to him of parted damned souls standing either side. And right at the end of that demonic path stood the man himself looking just as powerful in his suit as if he'd been clad in battle gear ready to charge his army into the war on Hell.

I wanted to cower away from him the second he raised his hand and motioned me forward with a flick of his fingers. The only defiance I managed was to shake my head at him telling him no, not the running towards that doorway as fast as my legs could carry me that I had been hoping for.

Everyone first looked to me and then back to their master to see what he would do next. I then had to wonder how many of them were surprised to see him smirking because of my refusal or did they just know something I didn't. Thankfully, in the end, my senses must have kicked in because I decided not to stick around any longer to find out.

He must have known what I was planning because my last look back at him had him shaking his head at me, telling me no. A firm warning I ignored. So, with the last of my will as my own, I turned and ran from him to the archway not far from reach. I didn't even need to push past anyone as, like the others, they quickly parted as if I was Moses in a dress running for his life before a sea named Draven came crashing down all around me.

Then, just as I was about to reach it, I heard a thundering noise that made the floor beneath me shake and at first I thought the floor was going to split open beneath my feet. I even looked down half expecting to see a mighty crack in the mirrored floor in between my legs ready to open up into a chasm, plunging me deeper into the belly of this Hell.

But that didn't happen. No, what did happen was that the

arch opening was there one second and then the next an almighty stone axe was being hammered down over the entrance, now blocking it entirely. I followed the smooth carved rock up to find the colossal warrior now looking down at me as if I was an ant he was waiting for permission to crush with his foot.

I staggered back about five steps, still unable to lower my astonished face from the giant that had just come to life. It was only when I saw it move his head slightly to look beyond me that I turned too. And what I saw had me looking towards the cause, utter dumbfounded to find Draven there commanding the gigantic stone warrior with only a flick of his hand. If I was scared enough to run from him before, then now I was utterly terrified and had quickly hit a state of desperation. So, when he made his next command of me, I found myself shaking my head in panic.

"Come to me now!"

But if this was my only chance to run from this nightmare, well then, I was going to take it…

So, I took it and ran.

CHAPTER SIX

HELL AWAITS

"*Come to me now!*"

Needless to say, I didn't, but instead I continued to back up putting even more space between us. The whole room gasped at the sight of my defiance and Draven seemed to shake his head slightly as if disappointed. Although, it was hard to tell considering his face was still mostly hidden thanks to his mask of bone.

Then I saw him nod to behind me as if he was signalling to something and I soon found out what. I screamed when I felt the rumbling beneath me again but the second I took a step to steady myself, my back hit an unexpected wall.

I stiffened against it and the moment it started to move, pushing me forward against my will, I knew that I had been wrong. It was no wall but instead one side of a giant's axe that Draven was commanding the sentinel to push forward and in doing so, forcing me back to him.

It reminded me of the Draven in my human life, the one

who had forced his will upon me many times, using objects in the room to make my body yield to his command. Well, I think it was safe to say that this was taking things to a whole new level, as an enormous stone axe at my back beat a desk or a chair any day of the demonic week!

Thankfully, I came to my senses pretty quickly, so it didn't end up pushing me the whole way to Draven. I ran from the thing the first second I could get my bearings enough to do so. I backed away, turning to check I was putting enough distance between me and the rock, when I stepped into the demonic hard place I was in the middle of. I whirled around and found the puppet master himself now right in front of me.

"Wh...what do you want with me?" I asked stumbling back a step. Then I heard the drums and violins start to play as he stepped into me, reaching out to grab me and gripping me tightly on my side before pulling me into him.

"I believe I owe my Queen a dance," he said, mocking Draven's earlier words, making me wince. I turned my gaze from his, needing in that moment to get away from it, if only for a second.

"Now Nga Rugummum Wardum," he growled in a barely contained demonic demand, before he nodded to the side. I wondered what he was commanding now, but then when a woman's voice started to sing once more, I wasn't asking myself this for long. He clasped my hand in his at the same time his fingers flexed at my side before he started to move us into another dance. It wasn't long before her words started to seep into me, luring me deeper and further into this other world,

His world.

> *"One kiss, my bonnie sweetheart*
> *I'm after a prize tonight*

But I shall be back with the yellow gold
before the morning light
Yet, if they press me sharply, and harry me through the day
Then look for me by moonlight
Watch for me by moonlight
I'll come to thee by moonlight
though Hell should bar the way"

After this verse, a louder chorus of violins and flutes started to play, and I looked around to see the reason they had started to echo all around the room in different places. I sucked in a deep breath as Draven started to dance me around the room just as the orchestra appeared above. Startled at the sight of them now all balancing on the railing above, I flinched in his hold as one by one they opened their demonic wings and stepped off the edge. They all fell to the far end of the room, where there had once been a top table overflowing with plates of food, flowers and candles. Only now it had been lost to this demonic kingdom along with the rest of the room.

Two sweeping staircases of grey stone arched outwards up to a higher platform above reminding me of…

"Afterlife." I uttered the name in hushed surprise and on a breath that was barely audible. But of course, he heard it. I knew when I saw his eyes burn brighter as he looked down at me, controlling every movement my body made. With my hand in his, he gripped it tighter in his grasp as I looked to where the orchestra all landed on the steps in a staggered way that looked beautifully choreographed.

They started to walk down the steps and on to the stage in between the grand staircases to a raised platform, like the stage was in Afterlife.

"What is this place?" I couldn't stop myself from asking as

the more of the place I took in, the more it started to look familiar but a twisted Hellish version. He continued to dance me around the space and at first, I didn't think he would answer me.

"This is your Afterlife," he told me, and I couldn't help but jolt in his hold just with the sound of his harsh tone.

"No...no this is...*this is Hell!"* I said, pausing first to look around and seeing that it did indeed look as if Afterlife had been rebuilt in a Hellish image. Everyone here was like a tortured soul that couldn't leave, not that they would have ever wanted to.

Chandeliers hung low from different points on the ceiling that looked more like twisted charred bones of the creatures slain to create them. Long candles that looked like wax spine bones flickered, casting an eerie glow against the crimson red banners that hung like floating blood-stained ghosts. And everything being reflected from the mirrored glass floor that looked as though any minute someone would fall through the mercury liquid we stood on.

He laughed when I said this, a throaty sound that again made me shudder against him. He seemed to like this reaction to him, this fear I had because I felt his fingers flex again against my side, digging in slightly, in a possessive action. Then he continued to dance with me around the ballroom, snarling and growling at those that got too close. I don't know why but it seemed the longer he had me in his arms the more protective he seemed to become, pulling me away from any potential threat and tighter into his body.

I had to question his actions as this obviously was not *my Draven* but then again, it also seemed far from the demon Draven I had encountered by the willow tree that night in my dreams. Which begged the question...

Who was he this time?

Because to begin with he seemed to almost be playing with me as he watched me struggling my way through the crowd to find him. I had felt his eyes on me and the brushing of his body against mine, like a sudden breeze catching me off guard and leaving me feeling cold from its fleeting touch.

But now, with his hands taking command of my body, holding me in such a way as though he would never let me go, I had to ask myself why the change? But more importantly, how would I ever get away from such power?

The song came to an end and Draven slowed us down until the last of the notes were played. I looked around the room and saw that now the rest of the demons had moved right back, giving us a large space as if they were getting ready for something. My panicked eyes darted back and forth between each of them, but it was only when I heard a demonic growl that I froze, as fear replaced all other reasoning.

"You will look at me and only me!" his voice demanded and as if he had me connected to a string, my head yanked quickly back to him to find eyes burning down at me.

"Why am I here?" I asked him after shaking my head a little, trying to make sense of this once more. He turned his head to the side as he looked down at me as though he was trying to understand both my question and the little mannerism that went with it. In fact, with the way he looked at me it felt as if I was being studied, not just watched. As if he was meeting me for the first time and was somewhat fascinated by what he found.

"Because it was summoned," he said after taking the time to decide whether he should say anything or not. I frowned up at him and again, because it was habit, I shook my head as if this would help…but really, when did it ever?

"I don't understand…what does that mean?" I asked him and the second I saw his lips raise on one side into a grin that was nothing short of evil, I knew it wasn't going to mean good things. I was right as he lowered his head down closer to mine so that he could give me my answer, dripping with confidence, shadowed in intimidation and drowning me in dominance.

"It means little slave... *you're now mine!*" he said in that guttural rasp that was only ever really heard when his demon came out to play. Then he motioned with a nod of his head for another song to start playing and the moment his orchestra began I soon found myself once again in his tight grasp.

"Palladio?" I asked, the second I recognised the piece of music, only strangely I couldn't say from where or how I knew. He didn't answer me but instead spun me around at the same time as everyone else stepped back on the dance floor, as if this was their cue to join us. Then, gripping my hand in a certain way, he flicked his wrist and I found myself turning into him, so that my back was now to his front.

"Palladio...*for the tortured souls within us,*" he told me cryptically on a whisper in my ear, before releasing me back into the dance. One I now noticed was the exact same as everyone else's, as I was just held out on an extended arm like the rest of the partners were.

This was when I first looked to them and then down to the mirrored floor as he brought me back to his hold. It was as if we were in a room full of moving parts, all twisting and turning to drive something bigger. Like an open-faced clock, that was a series of cogs all ticking down the seconds until my fate was decided. A driving force, all giving power to their puppet master in the centre.

"What does that mean?" I asked him when he referred to the song and the tortured souls he spoke of.

"He was weak!" he said turning angry at my question, snarling the words and that glow in his eyes turned hotter, blood red as though he was staring straight into the image of the death he had created. I tried to pull away from him, but the second I surprised him enough to get my hand free he was at me, reaching out and snagging my hand only to twist me around again. Then he would release me, and I would try and run again, only to be faced with a wall of laughing demons, faces hidden under their death masks.

I was seconds away from pushing past them only to once again find myself captured by the hand and pulled back into his twisted dance. He was toying with me again, as if this... everything I was, everything *we were*...well, it was all just a game to him. As if our love meant nothing to him, as if all we had shared together hadn't happened...as if we had...

Never existed.

I felt my heart be crushed, yet at the same time anger started to seep into my veins and at the height of my rage I snapped. He had just let me go on a turn and I stopped myself from spinning, stomping my foot to the ground.

"NO!" I shouted with fists clenched and I didn't realise the impact it would have, but the second my foot touched the glass floor it cracked all around my shoe. Then almighty cracks branched out like broken fingers reaching all around me, as if daring anyone to come near, with threatened death. The whole room stopped, and mid-dance froze in their partners hold, to look at me. This was when I started to notice what my actions had really shown me as I looked down at the floor.

"Gods!" I hissed, losing my anger at the sight of something else and stepping back at the vision now reflected up at me. It seemed I hadn't only cracked the mirror but also smashed the illusion Draven had me under. Because what was once a room full of demons all hiding under human masks was now a sea of humans all consumed in demonic flesh.

Elongated faces, twisted in pain and without skin, screamed out silently in their agony. Blood oozed from slices, cuts, gashes, and every natural and unnatural orifice on their bodies. Rows of teeth, horns and bone torn up ripped through flesh. Wet, dripping or stretched skin and scorched matted hair all made for a gruesome sight of surrounding faces that haunted me from below.

Tortured souls.

"ENOUGH!" A booming voice brought my attention back and as my gaze found his, it was as if he had clicked his fingers as all masks dropped together in a wave of action. I screamed and turned to run away from them all, him included, as now the demons were no longer a reflection my mind could convince itself wasn't real. No, now there was nothing to prevent that sight from forming life in front of me and the threat was as real and deadly as they come.

"No!" I shouted as I ran straight into his body and pulled back the second I touched him.

"I have not finished with you yet, my *Wardum àm Kad nga Shi'*" he said as he captured me in his grasp and speaking words I didn't know the meaning of or even recognise as a language I had ever heard before.

"Let me go!" I shouted back as I struggled against him.

"Nahu…calm yourself little slave or you will feel pain," he whispered down in my ear, tightening his grip on me as if to prove his point. I decided the wisest course of action at that moment was to cease my struggles and just let him have his way. And in doing so, maybe gaining enough trust to take him off guard. After all, I needed to find a way out of this place, wherever this place was, because for all I knew I had been unknowingly sucked through a portal into Hell. Which seemed more likely by the second.

"So, my new pet can be trained after all," he mocked, making me growl at him and in doing so evoking a moment of shock before he chuckled. It was a throaty sound, one that didn't belong to the usual sexy sound of Draven when he laughed.

"I can scratch too if you would like to see it!" I snapped up at him and even though he still hid most of his face under that skull mask, I could see in his demonic eyes he was excited by my sharp tongue and witty reply.

"And how would you do that, my Rugummum Sag',as, when you and your claws are *chained to my bed?"* He finished off this rhetorical question with a gravelly tone, one that spoke of both his need to dominate me and obviously liking the image he painted. My mouth dropped open and I frowned up at him. I was in shock because wasn't this version of Draven supposed to hate me, unless this wasn't his demon I was talking to at all and it was *my Draven* trying to break through?

Because I knew, after that nightmare and back in his secret vault, that Draven's demon was trying to get rid of me, so that he could take back control. Something he thought I had taken away from him. I don't know how but somewhere along the line and after the battle we won thanks to my death, a switch had been flipped within him. Which now meant that his demon was able to take control and overpower every other essence that was Draven, *mainly his Angel side*.

And this now begged the most important question of all…

Was I the key to freeing him?

The turmoil in my mind continued as he took up the dance once again, only this time it was one that was slow and sensual, which only ended up adding to the bombardment of questions I was quickly burying myself under. Questions like why was I here and how? Was this a dream and if so would I just wake up? Or more worryingly so, was this real and if it was, then how would I ever make it back home?

So, I decided my only course of action right in this moment was to use what I had and see what would happen. And right now, the only thing I had was my feminine charms and curvy figure, so it was time to see if Draven's demon was a boob man. Release my inner Tittanian as Pip would say. It was just a shame I was minus my three Boobateers, who would no doubt help me kick some sense into Draven's demonic ass!

"I thought you didn't like me?" I asked in a soft voice, one that was trying for innocent and seductive. He jerked back slightly as if surprised by my question and in the submissive manner I had asked it. Then he growled low and yanked me hard to him and snarled,

"Does it feel as though I don't like you!" This wasn't really a question as the second he pressed me tighter to him I could feel his impressive hard length bulging against his tight breeches.

"But…but…then why?" I asked looking up at him with big beseeching eyes that spoke volumes of my confusion.

"Why?!" he repeated and yet again it was a word barked at me.

"Yes why, why am I here, why do you keep me… call me your slave… why do any of this…?" I paused to motion to the haunting and Hellish ballroom with a hand I had yanked free only to have it quickly taken back into his. As if he feared I would run again and he wasn't taking that chance.

"…Why force me to see this part of your world. Why do you… *want to make me fear you?"* I asked softly, this time pulling free my trapped hand that was pressed between our bodies so that I could reach up and bravely touch his masked face. I did so slowly, as if any minute I was expecting the wild beast I knew prowled in wait deep within him to strike me down.

His reaction wasn't what I expected. It was almost as if he had forgotten his place in all this and the second I showed a bit of affection back, something in him seemed to snap. I felt something hard grow by my side where his hand was, and I looked down to see that where there had once been a man's hand, now it was no longer.

I remembered that hand, or should I say that demonic fist. Sucking in a startled breath, I watched as darkness overtook sun-kissed skin as if he had dipped his hand into molten lava and the second he pulled it out, it started to cool and harden into an indestructible substance.

Long, black and deadly claws formed at the end of thicker fingers, that were more pronounced at the joints and knuckles. If anything, it looked like some kind of demonic armour had replaced his skin and then been soaked in the thickest black tar. Scales of horns ran up his arm in a line like the spikes you would find framing each side of a crocodile's tail. Only they weren't made of flesh or any other organic substance but looked more like black forged metal plates hammered to deadly points.

I wondered where I had seen this arm before and then it hit me. It looked almost identical to Draven's gauntlet he wore that day in the past when I was sat upon his throne with him. His sharp claws teasing dangerously against my skin just before he declared me to be his queen in front of his kingdom. Which had me asking the question, had it been made in his demon's image?

I could see the pulsating power of raw crimson energy coursing under the plates on his arm like lava glowing beneath the crust and between the cracks in his rock amour. My eyes followed the streams of Hell's fuel up his arm, noticing the change as it happened. Starting with the material of his jacket drying up as though baked under a desert sun for a thousand years. Then, as he flexed his muscles, the once luxurious material started to crumble then float away in a grey dust. Blown away as if an imaginary wind had carried it, leaving only the raw body of a demon Warrior King underneath.

My mouth dropped open and just before my hand could

drop from his mask, he covered my hand with his. It was as if time had been switched to slow motion as I even felt my movements whisper through the space, as I moved cautiously to look at my hand now consumed by his.

His body was still changing, and I watched in horror as one of the last parts of him to be taken over was the hand that now held mine to his face. Power washed over him like a wave of rolling volcanic rock scales of obsidian, overtaking the last visible parts of his human form. His black talons were the last thing to grow as they pushed from the top of his fingertips, tearing through his skin and curling around until they reach their desired length.

Once again I tried to pull away, afraid they would cut into my own flesh and only stopping when they started to pierce through the bone mask he was touching over my hand. I had to say that when I saw them stab through the mask as though it had been made from paper, I was just glad that his fingers long surpassed mine. Because let's put it this way, I don't think I would have needed to worry about ever applying nail vanish to that hand again.

Thankfully though, with his hands dwarfing mine, his claws didn't touch me, but instead embedded themselves into the skull mask, making it crack and break around each claw with a snap. Then once he had hold of it he pulled the mask away along with my hand, as it was still wedged in between them both. And it was in this petrifying moment that I realised that his transformation wasn't yet complete.

No, for now I was to come face to face with the true image of Draven's demon and this time, there would be no hiding behind the shadows. There would be no cloaked features from view or spoken words from the darkness. Because now, there was nothing left between us.

The veil was being lifted and for once I would now have to face my own demons...

The one I had married.

"Draven?" I heard myself ask on a terrified breathy whisper, but then when I saw his eyes first seep to black before a deadly ring of fire circled the iris, I knew my mistake had been one of many. The first being that I allowed myself to ever believe I had a hope of taming this beast with my body. I knew that just from the death's hold he had on my side, that with one squeeze of his hand he could have ripped out half my intestines. Then where would my body be to help me? In pieces at his feet that's where.

"Draven is no more," he answered me and the second he said this the mask was truly gone and in its place was the face of ...

A Demon King.

That same demonic summoning started to take over his face and as it had with the rest of his body, the power seemed to seep up from under his skin, leaving behind a shell of an image of the man I loved. His chest was now bare and full of too many muscles to count as he now looked completely shredded of a single ounce of fat. I mean the Draven in my world was ripped and cut into what was a dream and drool worthy body, but this...well this was something else! It looked as if he had grown at least another half his body size and with it came a strength and physique of the likes I had never seen before.

Now the transformation was complete I could see that the black plates on his arms were in fact, some kind of amour. Amour that seemed to come from within him and be called forth at will, like when he did so with his demonic swords from his wrists. It was still a part of him, as it not only covered his flesh but also pierced up through it, interweaving itself around his powerful frame. But it was chosen at this moment to only cover his arms, sides, lower stomach and legs, leaving most of his torso bare.

It was amazing to watch as much as it was frightening. Seeing the way it rippled as if alive, which I guess it was. A series of spikes reached up from his massive shoulders with the shorter ones reaching up level with his chin. The two larger ones were set further back and twisted up level with the top of his head. They looked similar to horns, but I knew they weren't because I was now looking up at his altered face and had something to compare them to. Because now came the biggest and hardest change of all.

And like he had said…

My Draven was no more.

The second I felt his own hand release his hooks on the mask, I too let it fall from my grasp. Time seemed to slow down as the mask fell to the cracked floor and the second it smashed into pieces I couldn't hold it in any longer.

I screamed.

I pushed myself from him and caught him off guard enough that I too fell backwards to the floor. I landed hard on the thick glass, hearing it crack further beneath me. I started to scramble backwards like a crab, but no matter how much distance I put between us it still seemed as if he towered above me like the master he was. He crossed his massive armoured arms across his chest as he gazed down at me in annoyance.

"Wh…what…what are you?" I stuttered out in fear as I no longer faced my husband. I wanted to scream it wasn't him, that it was someone else entirely but deep down I knew that wasn't true. Because he was still there if I was truly honest with myself and if I allowed myself to look deep enough.

But it was as though his once handsome features were being overwritten. Like his eyes that had become deeper set into his face, making his bone structure above them more pronounced.

This made the skin around his eyes darker in shadow, creating a malevolent and black hearted edge to his already flaming eyes. This and the line of bone that travelled from the peak in his harsh brow that reached up to his hairline. Also, his cheekbones that jutted out beneath the skin, along with nasolabial folds that framed his nose and tapered down either side to his chin. His lips and nose remained the same, with the only difference being the longer fangs that could be seen when he snarled down at me.

Even the lines and corded muscles in his neck seemed to stand out more than I was used to seeing. But surprisingly this wasn't the biggest change to his appearance, as that honour belonged to the huge twisted horns that were nestled further back in his hair.

They were raven black and thicker than my arm at the point closest to his head. They were also ridged all the way to the razor points that stood at least half a metre above his head, curling backwards from his face.

But the last shocking change belonged to the pigment in his skin as now instead of a body touched by the sun, it seemed to have been touched by the moon, one surrounded by the darkness. Light grey skin made for a stark and foreboding contrast to the black of his armoured arms and midnight hair that was now longer. But mainly it was the power lighting up his veins coursing through his body, making it look like he was fuelled by the core of Hell itself.

"Who am I?" He repeated my question, growling and taking a step closer towards me, making me flinch back.

"I am the Master of Hell and…" he paused before crouching low without putting a knee to the floor so that he could reach out and tip my head up with a talon curled under my chin. I daren't move too quickly, allowing his own movements to guide me, so as not to get hurt.

"...I am the Master of you." His demonic voice told me on a purr and hearing this I couldn't help my reaction any longer as I turned my face from his, danger be damned. Thankfully, he lowered his hold on me just as quickly, so I didn't even receive so much as a nick from his razor-sharp claws.

"I am no man's slave!" I snapped back at him, releasing my words on an angry hiss. At this he started laughing, a gruff throaty sound as he raised himself back up to once more tower above me.

"You may be no man's slave, my beautiful little fool, but you forget, for here I am no man...HERE I AM GOD!" He roared, bellowing the admission with arms raised outward addressing the room and making them howl, snarl, growl and cry out their submissive acceptance in sight of a being that clearly ruled over them.

"I don't belong here," I whispered after jumping at the sight of his commanding presence, one that seemed invincible. It was even barely said but he heard it, even through the noise of the thundering crowd that all lay witness to their master's crushing will thrust upon us all. He looked down at me as if to judge for himself what to say next and when he spoke, I don't know why but I didn't believe him. It was almost as though what he said and what he *wanted* to say were two different conflicting things. Which is why I shook my head in denial when he told me,

"No, but the King of your world does, and Hell has only one place for you, my Pet."

"As your fucking slave! That will never happen!" I threw at him with hatred, one that I could tell affected him enough to make him snarl in anger down at me. It was as if he wasn't used to being faced with such disrespect and disobedience.

"Your fate was decided long ago," he threw at me with a slash of his arm out to the side. Sparks of power flew out in his anger and I flinched before doing something suicidal.

"No!" I shouted back at him, hitting my fist once more to the floor. He watched me and my defiance as if blown away by my lack of fear shown. Oh, I felt it all right, but I knew that in this moment what good would it really do me? After all, if this creature, this Hellish being and master of my nightmares wanted me dead, then I knew it would have happened by now. Or if not, then nothing I said would stop the inevitable fate he spoke of. And speaking of fate,

"Yes! I know this because I was the one who fucking sealed it! Now yield to me mortal and kneel," he bellowed down at me and then pointed to his feet. I let the rush of anger seep through my veins and I felt my fangs spring forth, bursting from my gums as I sensed the threat of another.

"Never! I want to go home!" I screamed up at him banging a fist against the floor again, even harder this time creating more cracks in the black glass.

"You will be home…*soon my Wardum àm Kad nga Shi,*" he said calling me this name again, the ancient language flowing from his lips as though he spoke it every day.

"But until then, so be it…*time to run from me, little rabbit…*" he told me, and I cried out in fright when one of his swords emerged from his wrist. But this time taking a more demonic looking blade full of spikes, a serrated edge and a wicked curve in the middle before heading down to his feet. I started sliding my body backwards trying once more to put distance between us, trying to escape his wrath. But that didn't stop him from lifting his sword and telling me,

"Run…whilst you still can," before hammering his sword down and impaling the glass at his feet, creating a lightning bolt of power to travel along the crack heading straight for me. Then the glass shattered beneath me and I screamed.

"NOOOO!" I knew it was a haunting sound, even to my own ears as it echoed around me.

Just as I started to fall I reached out a hand in hopes of being saved. But nothing would save me now. I knew that when I heard his last threat issued in just one word and a name I didn't understand followed, before he sent me back to await the Hell he had planned for me…

"Soon, my Shi."

CHAPTER SEVEN

BLAMED

I screamed the second I felt as if I'd landed and I fell forward over the table in front of me to the sound of plates and goblets clattering to the floor.

"Keira?!" I heard Draven's panicked voice next to me and I jumped near out of my skin. I scrabbled backwards and almost ended up in Sophia's lap as I tried to get away from him. His eyes widened in shock at seeing me now terrified of him and the second they turned pained and devastated, I hated myself for being the one to put that look on his face. It didn't take me long to realise that I was back to the time before we danced, and I wondered for a fleeting moment if everything that had just happened to me was because he had touched my birthmark? Had it gone back to that time?

I was about to try and explain myself the second Draven reached for me, but stopped when Zagan called his name in an alarmed tone,

"Dom! Takeshi." Upon hearing this he snapped his head around to see for himself what was wrong with his council member and the second he did, he growled. Takeshi was currently slumped back in his seat with eyes of milky white crying contrasting black tears. No sound came from his lips, but they moved like he was silently speaking in a trance.

"Oh, God no!" I whispered just before my hand covered my mouth. But it was too late. It was already out and in doing so I had implicated myself just with my guilty tone alone. Because I knew, the very second I saw Takeshi in that state, that this was my fault. I didn't know how or why, I just knew that I was the cause.

And now Draven knew it too.

He looked back at me and pinned me with a knowing frown as now he had a pair of guilty eyes staring back at him to add to the hushed regret in my whispered cry.

"Ragnar, take him to his chambers, I will join you in a moment." Draven issued his order and I looked up in time to see my old friend and bodyguard emerge from behind a screen of tight latticed woodwork. It was almost as though he had been positioned there to watch the room unseen, which had me now questioning Draven's motives for doing so?

I knew what *I* was hiding from him, but the question was, what was *he* hiding from me?

I watched as Ragnar stepped up to the platform and with Zagan's help, started to move Takeshi so he could be lifted from his chair. But Draven wanted my attention and made this known when I felt my chair suddenly slide along the floor, as he yanked it closer to his.

"Draven I..." I started to say something but what, I wasn't really sure. However, I was interrupted when suddenly a hand slapped down on the back of my chair, making me jump and this time it didn't belong to Draven.

Ragnar had just walked behind us with Takeshi in his arms, and at first it had looked as if he been doing this whilst his burden was unconscious. But now I cried out in shock as I looked into a pair of haunting eyes of cloudy milk, that were solely focused on me. Then his lips started to move, and it was as if there was a time delay as foreign words followed the action seconds after spoken. Only the words that were heard might have come from his lips, but it wasn't his voice.

No, it was the voice of...

Draven's demon.

"Amaru za-e Esharra, Wardum àm Kad nga Shi" Draven's face turned to steel the moment the words were heard, and I flinched back when I saw his accusing eyes shift sharply to me.

"Take him and inform me the moment he has seen it through!" Draven demanded, his voice hard and unmoveable. I gulped back a choked breath at the tone and just as Ragnar pried Takeshi's death grip from the back of my chair, he had one more message for me.

Only this time, it was one I could understand all too well.

"That's what happens when you try and run from me, little slave..."

"Now Ragnar!" Draven snapped, ripping Takeshi's hand from my chair himself. Ragnar started moving again, now he was free to do so but the second he did, Takeshi started laughing. He threw his head back over Ragnar's arm, eyes bleeding with black tears now streaming down his forehead and to his hairline. His laughter a disturbing sound, and that of a demon taking possession of another. A laughter that only stopped to add a single threat...

"...Soon my white Rabbit."

I shivered and closed my eyes against the sound, knowing now that I couldn't get away with it. My biggest fear was about to come true as Draven knew there was something I was keeping from him. Okay, so he didn't know what it was yet, but for Draven, well he only needed to know that it was something to do with me lying to him and that was enough for the rest of my cards to come tumbling down around me.

"Sophia, take Keira back to our room, I will be there shortly." He snapped out the order and at the same time my eyes snapped open. But seeing the way he was now looking at me, then I kind of wished I hadn't. He looked so disappointed and angry. An anger I could tell he was barely keeping a lid on.

Seeing him like this and having the other extreme to compare him to and I could now see how much of his Angel side held him back. How much it ruled over his emotions so that he could continue on with life without exploding into the rage, one I knew bubbled so close to the surface. And now, because of me, that surface was even closer.

"Dom, I don't think..." Sophia started to say but was quickly shut down when he snapped,

"Now, Sophia!" I bit my lip and flinched, tearing my gaze from his and hating that all of this night had been ruined. All the effort made in gifting me the perfect medieval banquet and in the end, I had never even danced with my king. No instead, I had been lured and then forced into dancing straight into my nightmares, only to fall. And when granting one last look at Draven, it was true what his demon had said to me that night...

I had fallen and for once, Draven... well...

He hadn't caught me this time.

I could hear the argument ready to lash out from Sophia's lips, so instead I placed a hand over hers as I turned to her.

"It's alright Sophia, let's just go," I said in a deflated tone, making her first look surprised by my easy acceptance, then she looked angered by it.

"Fine! But Dom, I am warning you now, that you'd better turn up with a damn good excuse as to why you're treating her like this, or so help me, *I* will be the one who forces *you* to sleep on the couch!" she snapped making him growl. But she didn't care, no, she looked too furious for that. Instead she stood, slapping her napkin to the table before turning to Pip and demanding,

"Let's go, Squeak." Pip who had been watching this whole scene play out like she was watching some dramatic soap on telly, looked up with a lollypop still sticking out of one side of her mouth.

"Uh…oh, right, that would be me then, laters my favourite man meat provider!" she said, giving her husband a little tap on his cheek before standing.

"Come on honey, let's go bitch about the opposite sex and their clueless and insensitive overreactions," Sophia said which was also my cue to leave. And hearing this from his sister prompted only another growl from him. But I decided not to look because really, what good would come if I did? He was angry and to be honest, the only reason I could see why was because now he knew that I had been keeping something from him. What else could the reason for his cutting behaviour towards me be? No, it had to be that, it had to be because of lies. A river of lies, I felt in this moment, I was drowning in.

"Keira…" The sound of my name coming this time from a more tender place, I couldn't help but turn to look back at him. He was stood also and for a second it looked as if he wanted to reach out to me, to pull me to him for an embrace. However, he didn't do any of these things and the second his features turned serious again, I knew both he and I had lost the moment.

"Yes, Draven?" I asked in a deadpan tone at the sight of his cold manner.

"You are not to leave the room…Understood?" I closed my eyes a second as I took a deep calming breath so as not to make a scene and my answer came in the form of a nod before I opened my eyes again.

"Sophia?" He said his sister's name as a one worded

question, demanding the same answer from her. She however, unlike me, didn't answer calmly but instead snapped,

"I'm not her fucking jailer Dom, she is free to do as she pleases, you don't like it, then I suggest you fucking hurry!" Then she grabbed my hand and pulled me with her, ignoring the warning snarl coming from her angry brother.

The three of us quickly made our way around the raised dais and crossed the centre of the room towards the staircase. I was half way up it when I had the urge to look back, no longer caring who saw me or was staring our way. No doubt they had all witnessed what had happened at the table anyway, so what was one more thing to gossip about.

So, I gave into my urge and looked back at the only man I cared to see. But I was surprised that I had to look for him, as he was no longer sat were we had been. No, instead I found him stood by the screen that Ragnar had been behind. I frowned, squinting my eyes trying to see why he would now be there when he stepped to the side and I got my answer. That and the glimpse of a cloaked figure he was looking down at.

He looked angry as he scanned the room behind him, looking over his shoulder with a glare. I saw the way his hand gripped the wooden screen as it started to splinter under the pressure of his wrath and the hooded figured took a step back, clearly afraid.

"Come on, let's get out of here," Sophia said, pausing to find me staring at Draven and the second she said this, it was as if he heard her because his eyes quickly found mine. For a moment we seemed locked in a soundless gaze, as if we were both trying to read each other's thoughts.

But then the inevitable happened and as we both came up empty, all I received was a nod from him, giving me that silent order to go. I gave him one last look that screamed out what my lips wouldn't allow and that was my utter disappointment. One directed at both him and myself. Not that he would know that because the second he gave me his unspoken order, he turned his back on me and directed his attention to the small cloaked figure. His actions just made my curiosity grow tenfold as he pushed the person further behind the screen, no doubt because he now knew I was watching.

Yep, so it was now confirmed. I wasn't the only one keeping secrets, that much was obvious.

Surprisingly, we all remained silent as we walked through the halls and back to where Draven had demanded me to be. Even Pip had made it all the way back without speaking but this was most likely down to Sophia. Every time Pip looked as though she was about to ask something, Sophia would just pull something sweet off her dress and hand it to her, telling her without words not to speak, just to suck.

However, the second we made it back to the room, she calmly closed the door and with her hands still holding it behind her, she said,

"Right, now why don't you tell us what has been going on." To which I took a deep breath, faced Sophia and couldn't help but blurt out,

"I am being terrorised and stalked by Draven's Demon." To which they both replied at the same time in an echoing surround sound shriek.

"WHAT!"

"HOLY SHIT BALLS, WHAT YOU SAY!?"

"Ssshh, wanna say it any louder as I don't think the ballroom full of supernatural people and their amazing hearing abilities, quite heard you both freaking out, along with my husband who I really, really don't want to find out."

"You mean he doesn't know!?" Sophia shrieked bracing her hands at the door in her surprise.

"Holy haberdashery, Batman!" Pip said slumping down into

the winged back chesterfield in the corner, losing a few fizzy cola bottles along the way. Was it wrong that in that moment and height of my mental turmoil I wanted to pick them all up and stuff them into my mouth, hoping somehow the sugar rush would help?

"Not now, Pip," Sophia said making her pout.

"Why not, trust me if there was ever a time for an awesome Robin quote it's when he says something like that and blows up the 'oh my fucking goblin' meter!" I looked at Sophia, cocked my head to the side and shrugged my shoulder, agreeing with Pip,

"She has a point." But I don't think Sophia agreed at all, when all she did was release a growly breath of frustration. Then she held the bridge of her nose with two fingers and closed her eyes, reminding me of her brother when he too was frustrated with me. In fact, I was starting to think I made a lot of people do that around me. I think if I hadn't already had a mind full of 'Holy shits' right then I would have questioned how much of an annoyance I really was for the Supernatural world and its big players. Lucius alone had said it enough times.

"Okay, let's start from the beginning, should we?" she said after a moment of calm, although I wasn't sure how long that would last after I had finished telling them everything. I released a sigh and, like Pip had, deflated down to sitting on the bed. Sophia took one look at me and knew that right now I needed support if I was ever to get this all out. So, she pushed off the door and came to sit down next to me. Then she put an arm around me and pulled me to her side for a hug. Pip, seeing this, jumped up and said,

"Hey, don't leave me out, I want to get in on some girl on girl action." Then she raced over to us, surprising me by how nimble she could be in that dress, however she did lose more sweets along the way, gobstoppers and cherry lips this time.

"You do know that means lesbian sex, right?" I informed her making her wink at me.

"Well, if I had a dangly piece of man meat to swing that way and my love rug ever fancied a cleaning lady, then you Biaches would totally get the job!" Sophia and I looked at each other and gave the same questioning looks, trying to gauge if either of us knew what she meant.

"Oh, for the love of Rasputin, I mean that if I ever turn sexy lesbo, then I would totally do you both, but as it turns out I like meat to go with my pale gravy... Capisce?" Pip said holding the tips of her fingers to the tip of her thumb, as she waved her hand in the air like an Italian mobster when saying this last word.

"Yeah, you like men, we got it, now can we please move away from Pip's vagina and its sexual preferences and on to more pressing matters, please," Sophia said turning to look at me once more, after first aiming most of this sentence looking around me at Pip. Someone who, at this moment in time, just held up their hands in defence and said,

"Yeah, I'm game for info upload to begin."

"Okay so on that note, where to begin?" I asked myself, only getting an answer from Pip anyway,

"Well duh, at the beginning silly...*I mean jeez, she just said it.*" This last part was said to Sophia behind my back and also in a comical way by using only one side of her mouth. She also did this behind her hand in a not so secretive tone. I ignored her and so did Sophia after only rolling her eyes before coming back to me.

"Right well, I guess it started right after the battle..." I began, knowing that it was best not to leave anything out. Which meant that ten minutes later I was done, having included everything from me and Draven on the couch acting strange when he first touched my birthmark. To the most recent events that happened not even half an hour ago. By the time I had finished Sophia looked as though she had swallowed a bug and Pip looked like she was getting ready to swallow a whole swarm of them.

"Oh, come on guys, say something!" I said pretty much pleading and throwing my arms down as if this would help with trying to extract information out of them.

"Uh…I don't know what to say." Sophia replied first, and Pip snorted and said,

"I think the words you're looking for are Holy Tintinnabulation!"

"No, no, I think you'll find the word I am looking for is a lot stronger than that," Sophia corrected dryly.

"Holy fuck a duck hole?" Pip asked, this time making me snort but that was mainly at the disgusted look Sophia now gave her when moving slightly away as she said,

"Eww, no!"

"And Tintinnabulation is any better?" I asked wondering what the hell it meant.

"Well, considering it means the sound of ringing bells and not entering the realms of bestiality, then yes, I would say it's better. Right, well now we have wrapped that up, can we please get back to trying not to freak out about the fact my brother's fucking demon is trying to take over his body and in doing so, making you his fucking slave!" Sophia snapped, clearly losing it towards the end and to be honest, when put like that, then I couldn't say I really blamed her. Pip's solution to this was to simply pull a red twizzler off her dress and hand it to Sophia.

"Here, eat this, you clearly need it." Surprisingly, Sophia just took it and tore a big bite off the end, pulling at the bottom so it stretched, reminding me of an angry child that needed the sugar rush.

"It tastes like vodka!" she shouted after swallowing.

"Yeah, I know, I told you that you needed it! Besides, I soaked most of my sweets in vodka first before I put them on, see how big my gummy bears and babies go?" Yeah, now that she mentioned it, there was a strong aroma of alcohol drifting my way and she was right, those were big gummy bears.

"So, the Lucius thing, seriously Keira what were you thinking?" Sophia said, determined to get back on track. This was when I stood up and threw my hands up in the air dramatically saying,

"I don't know! I panicked okay!"

"Well yeah, I am not surprised." Sophia agreed before continuing.

"But why Lucius, why not call me or Vincent, someone that didn't include…"

"Who, the only person I knew that had the power to control Draven?" I threw back making Pip pop her lolly from her mouth, point it my way and say,

"Baby mamma's got a point." Sophia shot her a look telling her 'not now' and carried on.

"Okay, but you do realise that when Dom knows about this, then that just made it and the shit street you're now living in, about ten time worse!"

"Ha, yeah but I think you can add on a couple of million shit fits to that ten times worse bit!" Pip added, now making me frown at her and give her my own 'not now' look.

"Of course, but I am not going to tell him!" I said dropping the mega bombshell that Pip would no doubt have named something like the megalodon shark of all bombs dropped.

"WHAT?!" Again, this came from Sophia.

"What else do you expect me to do here?" I asked shaking my head a little.

"Uh, tell him the truth, I know it's a foreign concept for you both, but you could at least try it sometime, for all our sakes." I gave her a pissed off glare and snapped,

"That isn't funny!"

"No, and it wasn't supposed to be," she replied calmly.

"Look, I get it okay, so much shit has happened between me and Draven and yes, I agree, most of it because we have kept stuff from each other or worse, lied to one another, but this time it's different!"

"How…just how is this time any different, Keira?" she pressed, and I could understand why she did but right in that moment, I really didn't have it in me to explain my reasons…or so I thought.

"It just is, okay?"

"Yeah, but how?!" she asked again, this time losing her patience and in turn I lost mine.

"Because I don't want to give him another excuse to leave me again, okay! Because I don't want another one of his lackies turning up outside my door telling me he's gone or that he's dead to me! And I don't want another string of letters telling me goodbye and how he is sorry, but I should just move on with my life…that's why, Sophia." I told her and the second I did her face softened with her understanding.

"Oh, Honey."

"Oh, Tootie Cakes." They both said at the same time and my shoulders slumped as I now took the place Pip had used, falling back into the corner chair.

"Sweetheart, do you really think that will happen again, that my brother could do that, put either of you through that?" she asked, nodding to my belly after I raised my head up from the hand it had been resting on.

"All I know is that Draven will only see this as one thing, that he is a danger to not only me this time, but us both…" I said pausing to cradle my stomach and the precious life now growing inside, telling them without words the severity of it all.

"Think about it Sophia, and look back at what I have to go on here…" I said pausing to take a breath.

"Think about what happened in the past when Draven believed that he could be a danger to me, he went as far as forgoing the bloody prophecy for Christ sake, he turned his back on saving the whole world Sophia, just so that he could save my life! So yeah, hearing this, it's not a massive stretch of the imagination to believe he will just leave again." Finally, explained like this, I could see her coming around to my way of thinking, as come on, it wasn't exactly as if she could deny it. This time it was her own shoulders that slumped in defeat for we both knew she couldn't deny it anymore.

"Yeah, yeah, I know, she makes a good point," Sophia said before Pip could say it again and now I wanted to kiss them both as Pip winked at me and Sophia finally admitted that I was right.

"So, does this mean you're not going to tell him?" I asked in that hopeful tone, one that turned out to be rewarded when she said,

"No, I am not going to tell him."

"But he's your brother!" This surprisingly came from Pip, making me frown at her.

"Sorry, my bad Toots but come on, I thought that being blood and all, meant that she would want to give him the 'hell Bro, what's wrong with your demon ass' low down…but Yey, for team Keira that she doesn't… eh?" she said waving an imaginary flag at me.

"He may be my brother but that doesn't mean he is always right and I learnt not long ago that sometimes my brother's choices aren't always what's best for others, despite what he thinks. Besides, I have been more loyal to you and your choices for a while, so why break tradition now," Sophia said standing up as if it was all decided. I walked over to her and pulled her in for an embrace and hugged her to me.

"Oooh, do me, do me! I wanna get in on the action!" Pip said jumping up off the bed and coming over to us and then trying to wrap her arms around us both to give us a squeeze.

"This still doesn't mean I'm a chick muncher," she said eyeing us both one after the other. We both groaned at the same time saying a joint,

"Yeah Pip, we know."

"We know."

"Anyway, getting back to the problem at hand, you do realise that I am the least of your problems, right?" Sophia said after we had all hugged it out.

"What do you mean?" I asked, looking back up at her as I was currently sat down trying to take my shoes off, as my feet were killing me.

"Are you forgetting something, because I am pretty sure it wasn't coincidence that Takeshi had a vision the second Dom's demon tapped into your mind?" she told me, and I already knew this was true. Of course, the biggest question of all was…why?

"Yeah, it must have something to do with that doohicky on your neck, like a demonic switch or even better, like a TV remote for Hell…I wonder if you could pause or fast forward… what?" Pip said stopping mid flow when she saw our 'not impressed' faces.

"Uh, yeah right, what am I going to do next, pulled DVD's out my ass and twist my breasts to control Netflix? I don't think so some…"

"Just wait a minute, she could actually be on to something here," Sophia piped up, making me drop a shoe and give her my best, 'what the Hell' look, one I had practiced to a fine art since meeting these people. And when I say people, what I really meant was the other half of my soul and his family, which just so happened to come with a cruise boat load of Supernatural baggage!

Pip stuck her tongue out at me, giving me an 'I told you so' look and making me roll my eyes before saying the obvious,

"I think you need to explain Sophia, before my head explodes or worse, your brother comes back here and his goes off first."

"Well, think about it, what major event occurred just before this started happening?"

"Oh, I know this one! She died! It's she died, right?" Pip shouted ending it with a fake stab to the heart and a dramatic death with her falling back onto the bed.

"And she was like...Bluurrraaa brrraaains," she added now sitting up slowly with her arms out in front of her and pretending to be a zombie. I gave her a death glare making her giggle before covering her little breasts and saying,

"I take it back, please don't eat me!"

"Yeah right, you're wearing a dress made of sweets for Gods' sake, like you don't plan on getting eaten tonight.," Sophia said wryly. Pip smirked at me then gave me a wink, replying with,

"You wanna see my underwear, it's made from candy floss and edible paper." Then she waggled her eyebrows at me in a cartoon comical way.

"There are just no words, Pip," I said shaking my head on a chuckle. She bowed at the waist and said,

"Danke schön" which thanks to the 'leftover school days' folder in my brain, I knew meant 'thank you very much' in German.

"Please, for the love of Harpie blood, can we just stick to a conversation long enough before your private parts have to come into it, or is it time to see Sheila again, Squeak?"

"Nah, I dropped that bitch long ago, get this, she told me to start writing my impulses down first before following through with action," she said finishing with a snort of disbelief before continuing,

"Shushuh, yeah, like that was ever gonna happen! I told her, I said look honey, there just ain't enough paper and ink in the world to contain this level of genius in words. Then I walked out, stole a marker and an apple from stuck up bitch on reception and fucked Adam on the way home." I took a deep breath and closed my eyes a second trying to get my head around everything she just said and then did something Sophia was silently telling me not to with a shake of her head.

"I know I am going to regret this, but why the apple and marker, Squeak?"

"Oh well, I went into the bathroom and wrote on myself all the things I wanted him to do to me, with arrows and shit." She said this by using both her hands to point to her lady parts. As if we needed any help knowing precisely where Pip would draw the sexual aid and where it would point to. Hell, it wasn't like Adam would have needed a map, not when you know your way home!

"And the apple?" I asked wondering why I felt the need to know.

"Ha! For his mouth of course," she said in a way where she thought it should have been obvious because she even pointed a thumb over her shoulder at me to Sophia, like I was the biggest joker on the planet.

"But of course," I muttered dryly before moving on to more practical stuff, like my future in Draven's world and just how long I was hoping to stay in it without a Hiroshima Hell bomb exploding, namely Draven's demon.

"Ookay, so anyway back to the important stuff and firmly

off the fruit stuffed Adam," I said trying like Sophia to get back on track.

"Oh, it was firm alright, but I was the one getting stuffed!" she said with a giggle and a slap of her thigh.

"Pip!" I reprimanded.

"Alright banana girl, chill your preggy hot potato, gravy knickers."

"What does that even mean?" I asked with a shake of my head.

"I don't think it matters what it means as we have ourselves bigger problems!" Sophia said slowly looking towards the door. Me and Pip then both did the same, as if any minute we were waiting for a purple hulk sized Draven to burst through the entrance.

"Shit, that isn't good!" Sophia suddenly shouted, and I looked to her and before she said anything, I knew.

I knew because seconds later I heard it.

Seconds later we *all heard it.*

"Oh no," Sophia murmured.

"Oh, fuck a doodle!" Pip squealed.

"Oh, Bollocks!" I cried.

Then, as the mighty roar was boomed through the hallway beyond, we all collectively flinched the second we heard it and this time it was an unmistakable sound.

The sound of...

Draven's rage.

CHAPTER EIGHT

THE HELL AFTER THE STORM

The second we heard the demonic roar we all froze, and panic started to set in with me. Had I been too late to stop this from happening, had Draven's demon already broken through?

"Right, listen to me now, if you are dead set on keeping this from Dom then I suggest you do the one thing you're shit at," Sophia said suddenly coming up to me and grabbing the tops of my arms.

"Why do they say dead set anyway?" Pip muttered to herself in the background, but I tried not to focus on that and more on the importance of what Sophia was saying right now.

"You mean lie, right?" I replied making Pip snort a laugh.

"Not helpful Pip…yes, I mean lie," Sophia said after shooting Pip daggers.

"We need time to figure this out but until then, you are going have to come up with a pretty good excuse as to why you blacked out and then came to, acting terrified of my brother,"

Sophia reminded me, looking dire. And what on earth could I say to that!

"Oh, I know!" Pip shouted racing to me and hip bumping Sophia out of the way. Then she slapped her hands together and rubbed them as if she was warming herself up for something. I saw her eyes flash a brighter green and take on a more cat like look before she placed her hands over my stomach. I didn't really feel much and after a few more seconds of looking down at what she was doing I looked back up at her.

"Uh, Pip…not sure what you are trying to accomplish here, but I don't think it's working," I said making her smirk at me and then wink, which for Pip usually didn't mean good things. Naughty, despicable and rude things yes, but good…rarely.

"Well duh, honey Tootie bag, it won't happen straight away as we need Mr Angry Pants for that first," she told me instantly making me worried.

"Oh no, Pip what have you done?" But this time the worried tone came straight from Sophia but was a question right out of my brain as I was on the verge of asking the very same thing.

"Look, he will be here any second, so let's rap and snappy this 'oh dippy shit moment' up, shall we…? Tell him the reason you blacked out was you felt lightheaded and woke freaked out because hey, you blacked out, so why the hell wouldn't you be… right?" She paused nodding at us both and prompting us to do the same, which we did, like puppets.

"And Takeshi?" Sophia asked thankfully reminding me of this fact that I would have to explain.

"You have no cluedomundo what happened to Takeshi, that's what! And you're freaked out because of it… Then turn on the 'Aww it's a shame, comfort me big man…that type of gig… then if he starts to doubt you then you ramp it up, boom baby!" she said slapping a hand to her other one in front of my face making me jump.

"Ramp what up?" The question came from me this time.

"Being preggers that's what! He starts to doubt you then you guilt his ass and say, 'hey, guess what dipshit, I am pregnant, my body is changing and my hormones are doing a number on my fragile head, so give me a friggin' break' then in about fifteen minutes you are gonna throw up," she said as my jaw fell open in an unattractive way.

"Uh, say what?" Sophia said for me and Pip pushed on my chin, closing my mouth before patting my cheek.

"You're having a baby Honey, your hot rod bod is going to change and with it, lots of shit the King doesn't yet understand because let's face it, number one, he's a Supernatural overlord who has never dealt with women having babies and well number two, he's also a man," she said and as much as this all made sense, the only part I was focusing on was the question I asked,

"I am going to be sick?"

"Girls gotta have morning sickness, right? Okay, so we have about ten seconds until he bursts through this door and if I were you, make it count by looking sick," Pip said before pushing me backwards, so I landed on the bed and then she grabbed a glass of water from the side table, she dipped her fingers in it and flicked water on my face.

"Hey!"

"You know, I am in awe of you right now," Sophia said to her, giving her an adoring look. Because no matter how much Pip seemed to play the fool and not make sense during about ninety percent of the time during a crisis, it was the genius ten percent that always got us through. Her ideas on how to solve a problem was quickly gaining legendary status and seeing as now Sophia was looking at her admiringly, I would say that she knew it too.

"You can kiss me later kitten, but right now…as in one, two, three…and here we go," Pip replied and we all looked towards the door as she counted down. And she was spot on as the second she finished her last word, the door banged open and there stood an angry Draven.

"Both of you, leave… *now!"* he demanded with fists clenched to his sides.

"Draven!" I reprimanded considering I was playing a part here and knew this reaction was the best one to go with. I felt guilty going down this path and projecting that guilt back on to him as I knew the second he thought there was something wrong with me physically, that his focus would switch pretty quickly. But then, what else could I do, as it wasn't as though I was brimming over with choices here?

All I knew was that I couldn't chance his demon side beating him in this inner battle, one he didn't even know he was fighting against. But just because he couldn't fight it himself, it didn't mean that I couldn't do it for him and by the Gods I was going to do everything in my power to conquer it, even if that meant lying to him. And even if it meant taking me back to the gates of Hell again and demanding they let me in so that I could beat my husband's demon into submission. Then I would do it!

Okay, so I knew even thinking this was a massive stretch of my abilities, as it seemed highly unlikely I would, one; have to go to such drastic measures and two; even if this was the case, the chances of succeeding such a thing was anything from highly unlikely, to not a chance in Hell. Mainly at the lower end of that scale.

So, if it meant lying to him yet again and carrying yet another bucket load of guilt around with me whilst I did it, then so be it. Because honestly, I was not willing to face the consequences of failure. No, all I could hope for was that we found a solution and could figure this out, and soon. Because looking at Draven now, and I would say he was getting closer to letting his demon win without even knowing it.

"I don't know what is going on with you Dom, but whatever it is, getting a fucking lid on it before you end up hurting those you love!" Sophia snapped looking back at me and giving me a nod before walking past Pip and snagging her arm as she did. Draven watched them walk by him with a stern frown over the side of his shoulder, looking down at them.

"Come on Pip, let's go and find all the good scotch my brother has been hiding. We will see you tomorrow Kaz and like we said, it should pass soon but if not, I hope you start to feel better," she said adding to the ruse, making Draven's gaze quickly snap back to me the second he heard something might be wrong.

"Yeah, same goes here, honey buzz. Oh, and I hear ginger biscuits help," Pip added with a wink behind Draven's back before they exited through the door. Sophia made sure she slammed it shut showing Draven how pissed off she was. However, Draven didn't even flinch as the second the door was closed he came over to me and lifted my face up so that he could study it.

"What's wrong? Do you feel unwell?" he asked in a clipped tone and I could tell he was trying for patience. Now I knew if I just gave into him and told him straight away that I felt a little unwell then that would only arouse suspicion. Because if the real reason for me nearly passing out earlier was to do with being pregnant, then wouldn't I have been angry by his cruel dismissal of me? So, as horrible as it was, I knew I had to act as though I was pissed off with him and boy did I ever feel like a bitch doing it. Which was half of the reason I tore my face from his hold and stood up to put distance between us.

"Oh, so you care now do you?" I asked him after picking up

my shoes from where I had dropped them and carrying them over to the dresser just for something to do.

"Of course, I care! Why do you even ask that of me!?" he snapped, and, in that moment, he sounded completely clueless as to how to deal with a hormonal wife.

"Oh, I don't know Draven, maybe because I nearly blacked out because I was feeling lightheaded and sick, and then came to feeling disorientated only to find you looking at me as if I had done something wrong," I said sounding strained and hoping, no, more like *praying* that he would take my tone for the right reasons, not the honest ones.

"You were feeling sick?" he asked focusing on that part.

"Yeah and I still do," I told him, and this part wasn't a lie as, thanks to whatever Pip had done, I now felt as if I would shortly be getting acquainted with the toilet in a more intimate way.

"Then why didn't you tell me?!" he accused making me frown back at him.

"Well, it's not exactly like you gave me much chance before you were barking orders at me to leave! I mean, you even looked at me as if it was my fault what happened to Takeshi, which I still don't know because you didn't take the time to tell me before you were lashing your orders at me and your sister!" I snapped, finding myself shamefully playing the part of scorned lover far easier than my good conscience should have been allowing me to.

"So, you're telling me that you had nothing to do with that?" he asked me in a sceptical tone, and I gave him my best incredulous look in return.

"You're seriously asking me that!?" He had the audacity to fold his arms across his chest and silently stand by his question with merely a nod.

"No, I had no clue what happened to Takeshi and to the best of my knowledge I certainly didn't have anything to do with it!

But how dare you even ask that of me!" I shouted and standing by at least knowing the first part was true, as I still didn't know why Takeshi had reacted that way to my vision. My biggest guess was that he had been possessed for a short time. Like some kind of a sticky residue left over from Draven's demon. But like I said, this was only a guess and not something I would know fully until speaking with Sophia and Pip tomorrow. I might have found out tonight if we'd had more time talking things through and spent less time on Pip's vagina and its preferences.

At least after this he had the good sense to look slightly guilty, which only ended up making mine ten times worse and boy didn't he just pick up on it.

"Then tell me Keira, why look so guilty, for I didn't need to read your mind to know that's how you felt?"

"Oh right, and I guess you couldn't possibly have been wrong!" I threw back at him, thinking this the simplest explanation…*a man got something about a woman wrong.* It wouldn't exactly be the first time in history, that was for damn sure.

"I know what I saw, and I acted upon seeing it," he stated firmly, but even to me this sounded like a cop out. However, I knew that in this moment I was going to have to pull out the big guns as much as I hated to. Because I felt myself quickly losing this battle. So, I took a deep breath and said what I knew needed to be said.

"And in doing so you ended up ruining a perfectly good night and making me feel uncared for and untrusted. So, well done with that one, Draven."

"Now just wait a minute, that is not…" he started but I quickly interrupted him.

"Yeah, you did and now look where we are, all because it obviously didn't occur to you that a look of guilt could be mistaken for shock, fear or worry that I had just nearly passed out over the table. And then seconds later Takeshi is having a freak out and issuing what sounded like threats at me!" This time he started to really look annoyed, but I could tell it was shifting and more aimed at himself.

"And that is something I am trying to get to the bottom of, don't you understand that?" he said trying for more calm now when speaking to me.

"Oh, and you think you will find it by interrogating your pregnant wife who feels like shit and is going to hurl any second, because if you do, then you can just leave right now!" I said trying to resist the urge to stamp my foot like an unruly teenager. I was even panting and about two seconds away from growling.

"Are you quite finished?" Draven asked me, and I opened my mouth ready to tell him what for when the second I did, I felt it coming. I threw a hand over my mouth and ran as best I could in this dress into the bathroom, only just making it in time. I threw up everything I'd eaten, silently cursing Pip. But then seconds later I knew I couldn't be too annoyed, as one thing became clear… it obviously had worked.

I felt Draven kneel down beside me, take my hair in one hand to hold back from my face whilst he rubbed soothing circles on my back with the other.

"Better?" he asked in a tender tone, all traces of frustration and annoyance now long gone. I nodded my head after no longer feeling the need to heave. He handed me a tissue and I shamefully used it to blow my nose and then the next piece to wipe my mouth.

"Come here, sweetheart," he said gathering me up in his arms and standing. He swept my dress out to the side and carried me back into the room so that he could lie me on the bed.

"I am sorry for not believing you, can you forgive me?" he whispered before bending down so he could bestow a gentle kiss on my forehead. I was thankful for this as it gave me a few seconds so that he wouldn't see the wince of pain in my eyes as that ball of guilt twisted tighter in my belly.

"It's already been forgiven, now we just need to forget it and not speak of it again," I said hoping he would get the hint and change the conversation.

"What did I do to deserve such a beautiful and forgiving wife?" he said making me groan and in turn him chuckle.

"I wouldn't go that far, you might have some more grovelling to do yet," I said making him laugh this time and I was just glad that the storm had passed and for once, quickly. Yep, I may feel like shit, but it had to be said that Pip was a little genius.

"Anything my Queen desires," he hummed into my neck as he peppered kisses there.

"Well, you changed your tune pretty quickly."

"I was a fool who believed something more was going on and that you may have been keeping something from me." Hearing this nearly made me groan out loud. No, thankfully I just kept quiet and silently was smacking myself on the forehead, telling my inner conscience what a bitch it was.

"How do you feel now?" he asked, and I sighed in relief that we were thankfully off the subject.

"A little queasy, but better after throwing up." Which wasn't a lie.

"But what about Takeshi, what happened to him?" I asked both because I genuinely wanted to know and also because I knew it would look odd if I didn't. Draven ran a frustrated hand through his hair and then rested it at his forehead when he flicked all his fingers out saying silently, that he still had no clue.

"He is still asleep after his ordeal, but I hope once he wakes, then he will be able to shed light on what happened." This, as you can imagine, didn't bode well for me and my future. It sounded awful of me but all I could hope for was that Takeshi fancied taking some extended time off work and stay in dreamland for as long as possible. Well anyway, at least until me and the girls could figure this out.

"It is usual for him to still be asleep?" I asked repeating in my head, 'please say yes, please say yes'.

"Well, considering this whole thing is unheard of, then I have no clue on the matter," Draven told me, sounding once again extremely frustrated.

"What do you mean, I thought he got visions all the time?"

"He does, but this wasn't a vision," he replied, and this was when my inner panic started to lean in to brace for impact position.

"Then what was it?" I asked because I knew I had to. As really what I wanted to do was cover my ears with my hands, shake my head till dizzy and sing, 'Lalalala not listening, lalala'. But then I would be zero percent closer to finding out how to stop this, so I held my breath and waited for him to answer.

"It was a demonic possession and one done by an extremely powerful being at that." Draven's reply had me almost cringing in on myself. Oh yeah, he had been a Hell of a powerful being alright, I thought ironically.

"But how would that even be possible?" I had the foresight to ask and anything I could work with at this stage I was only too happy to go digging for, as I doubted Draven would have just accepted my answer of 'Oh just curious' when waking up in the middle of the night asking random questions when they suddenly came to me.

No, I needed to find out everything I could and now, whilst

Draven and I were still talking about it. Because now the time made sense...middle of a deep sleep, not so much.

"I have my theories, but for now I won't know for sure until he wakes up." Oh shit, Draven having theories was bad. As in way, way bad. Because usually his theories led him to places like, following us to the fountain and finding us just after stepping back through the Janus gate...*that type of bad.*

"And these theories are?" I asked in a delicate tone, one that was trying not to sound too pleading. He raised an eyebrow at me in question and I was suddenly worried that I had gone too far, too quickly.

"Well seeing as you ask, at first I believed you yourself knew the reason..." I opened my mouth ready to deny everything or confess, whichever one my panicked mind blurted out first, when thankfully he stopped me.

"But after what you told me and seeing for myself how you are obviously experiencing the natural occurrences of pregnancy, then my only theory left is that an unknown enemy is out there conspiring against us and using demonic means to do so." Wow, okay so my face said it all as I was utterly shocked.

"Why would you think that?"

"Because, ever since the day of our wedding and the war that unfortunately followed it, I have felt odd," he admitted, making me close to gasping. So, all this time and he did feel as though something was wrong.

"Odd?" I questioned.

"It's strange, as if someone is trying to control me. My anger for example is far too quick to fire and I find myself battling with my demon, as if someone is trying to bring him to the surface." Okay, so this was definitely one of those 'oh shit moments' because now knowing that he felt this too was a game changer. It meant one simple fact…time was running out and faster than I thought.

"That's…oh God, I don't know what to say…why haven't you…?"

"Told you? Because I didn't want to worry you. I know I should have been honest but until tonight, then I believed mostly it was just the dreams I have been having." I could only nod at this as what could I say, 'yeah you're right, you should have been honest with me'…I mean I was currently being forced into acting like a bitch, but that didn't mean I was going to be an even bigger bitch for the sheer hell of it. No pun intended.

"What type of dreams?" I asked cautiously.

"That's not important," he said suddenly pulling back and obviously not liking where this conversation was quickly heading.

"Draven, come on, you know you can tell me and I promise not to freak out." Which was another lie. I was already freaking out and had been for a while now.

"I…I can't explain it," he said, turning his back to me and raking a hand through his hair once more.

"Just try, I mean, why not just tell me what you see in these dreams?" I asked because I had to. I just couldn't let it go now. He took a deep breath and then let it out in a heavy weighted sigh.

"Because I see you," he said after a long painful pause and my mouth dropped open. Not because of what he had said but more in the way he had said it. As though it had been a bad thing. As though it was something that haunted him.

"And that's a bad thing because…?" I let my question linger and after spending a good minute or two staring out the window he finally answered my question without looking at me. I don't know why but I got the distinct impression it was because he was fearful of what he may find in my eyes when I finally knew the truth.

"Because in them you are not my wife…" he said like a broken man and I had to confess that on hearing this I gasped in horror. But then if I thought that was all the surprise I was in for well, then I was definitely mistaken.

"So…so if I am not your wife then…*then what am I?*" I asked, having to pause as the emotions became too much. This was when Draven finally turned back around to face me and in doing so continued to drop the biggest bombshell of all…

"You are my slave."

CHAPTER NINE

ALIENS AND DEMONS

"Are you alright?" Draven asked me, now looking concerned as I could imagine I had gone deathly pale as I felt all the colour drain from my face.

"Yeah, just...well, just thinking about everything you said and why you dream of me like that?" I said because it was both true and what Draven would have expected to hear. He came to sit down next to me and pulled me into his embrace.

"It will be fine Keira, I will figure this out, but you need to promise that you will leave this to me...yes?" Okay, so this was the point where I knew if I said the words, agreeing to that promise, then it would no doubt come back to bite me in the ass and in the form of hurting Draven. So, I did the only thing I could think to do, I suddenly put a hand to my forehead and faked feeling nauseous.

"Here, drink this, you need to replenish the fluids in your system," he said, handing me a glass of water from the side table.

"Better?" he asked rubbing my back and touching my forehead to see if it was hot or clammy.

"Yeah, although I wouldn't mind having some help getting out of this dress," I said knowing that the time had passed for gaining anymore answers tonight. Besides, I could see the strain in his eyes and what telling me something like this had done in taking its toll.

So instead, I decided light-hearted playfulness was the way to go, so I waggled my eyebrows at him, making him laugh and shake his head at me. After this he made short work of getting me out of my dress and when I saw him swallow hard at the sight of my fancy lace black underwear set, I felt bad that this was one night it wouldn't be for a good cause.

No, instead of doing what he looked like he wanted to do, he simply undressed me before fetching me something comforting to wear. It was a pair of super soft, comfy Pyjamas that were light grey check trousers and a white vest top to match, one that had a patch work of hearts in the same material all over it. Then, once dressed again, he tucked me up in bed and just before I could complain thinking that he wasn't going to join me, he started removing his jacket.

Then came the hard part and that was watching as he took off his sexy suit and gifted me with the sight of his beautifully toned and muscular body. I swallowed down my sexual lump the size of a man's testicle and decided to say something, for I feared if I didn't, I would only start drooling.

"So, I take it this isn't the usual attire worn back in those days?" I asked, genuinely curious as of course, this was me we were talking about. Little Miss one million questions. He turned to look at me over his shoulder just before ridding himself of the shirt.

"Let's just say I was happy to see the back of codpieces, puff sleeved jackets and fur trimmed capes," he told me making me laugh because honestly, I couldn't see Draven wearing any of those things...one of them especially, which is why I said,

"Codpiece?" He turned fully towards me with the amusement clear in his eyes. His lips twitched as he fought off a grin and he added,

"Yes Keira, I, along with most men at the time, wore the garment." I smirked when trying to keep my face straight as I made a 'Umm mm' sound.

"Something on your mind, sweetheart?" he enquired in a nonchalant tone as he took off his boots and breeches leaving me forgetting how to form words.

"Uh..." He chuckled at me and I knew he was secretly loving the effect he had on me, especially when naked. I knew this by the grin and the little shake of his head as if he was wondering what to do with me. Meanwhile, I was just hoping it involved something that once upon a time hid behind a codpiece. Of course, after I was sick and Draven acting as if I was now some breakable china doll, I knew this outcome would be unlikely.

"You going to give me an answer, love?" he asked as he got into bed beside me after throwing back the covers. I smirked and then lifted the covers back up over his chest and then I took a peek, looking down at his impressive man danglers as Pip called them. Granted it wasn't the sexiest name in the urban dictionary, but then again, not a lot of what Pip said when describing things sexual could ever be classed as sexy. Cute and hilariously funny, yeah totally, but sexy...not ever.

"See anything you like down there?" Draven teased as I still had the covers tented above him.

"I was just wondering if you had to get yours specially made or something, as I don't see you having much need for a codpiece, not someone of your size...or was it worn as a way to fend off all the ladies with grabby hands?" I teased making him playfully growl at me before trying to nip at my lip. I dropped the covers laughing and then, knowing how we wouldn't be doing anything 'fun' tonight, I nodded to the remote control on his side of the bed.

"So, part of your punishment is that I get to pick something to watch, so pass it over," I demanded, making him roll his hand a few times as he bent at the waist, mimicking a royal bow.

"But of course, m'lady."

"So, what about me, I gathered I was also missing some authentic parts to my outfit?" I asked without looking at him as I flicked through the online video library looking for a classic and knowing how much Draven really needed to catch up on popular culture. Or should I say, more like introduced to it for the very first time, EVER!

"Well, I didn't want to see your beautiful golden hair covered with a tight curled, powered wig or have certain desirable attributes covered by that of a stiff laced, high neck ruff," he said looking down at my breasts and running the back of his hand teasingly across them.

"Desirable attributes, eh?" I asked faking my surprise.

"Very desirable...and as I said, covering such would hinder my view of such bountiful fruit, one that looks ripe for the tasting," he said on a hum before leaning down to kiss the one closest to him. I let my head fall back and released a moan but unfortunately it didn't last as it seemed that was all I was getting.

"You looked ravishing tonight," he said, and I blushed before whispering a small,

"Thank you." Then I glanced back at the screen as I tried to hide my red face and ended up blurting out,

"Alien!" causing Draven to look at me peculiarly.

"Excuse me?"

"The movie, it's a classic, trust me we have to watch this!" I said getting excited as I hadn't it watched in years and to be honest, I was more looking forward to seeing Draven's reactions to it. Although, if his sceptical look was anything to go by, then I was no doubt in for a frowny good time.

"You like this?" he asked me when I snuggled back after plumping up my pillows and said,

"Uh yeah, what's not to like, it's a horror based in space and as far as I am concerned, the only mythical thing left for me to watch in a movie without thinking, oh well they got that wrong, or well I have met them and they don't look like that or eat brains and suck blood...I'm sure you're getting my point here." He gave me a sideways grin and said,

"Yes love, I get your point."

"Ooh, I just love the intro, it's so moody," I said making him grin before telling me,

"It's lines that spell a word sweetheart, I don't think its Oscar worthy."

"I am surprised you even know what the Oscars are," I teased him back making him tickle my sides and pull up my vest, so he could get to me.

"Actually, I think you will find this won an Academy Award," I informed him in my best know it all voice.

"Oh really, is that so?" he teased back in his best, 'Isn't someone a clever clog' voice.

"So, when do the aliens make an appearance?" he asked at the scene of the crew all eating and drinking around a table after coming around from cyber sleep.

"There is only one alien in this movie, hence the name, but in the second movie there are loads," I told him glancing back for a second finding him looking at me and hiding his smirk behind his hand. I wondered with that look if he wasn't asking me questions just to see my reaction and getting his entertainment that way instead of the movie.

"Besides, they have to get to the alien planet first before the egg things can explode on that guy's face," I said nodding to the screen and the first poor bastard that gets killed.

"Mmm, sounds very educational," he murmured making me turn back and smack him playfully on the arm. Something that prompted him to put his arm around me and nestle me closer to him. We continued to lie there, and I could tell Draven was finally getting into the movie, as he kept asking questions. This made me laugh and tease him about being 'one of those people' and when he asked what that meant exactly, I told him,

"It means you're someone who is curious and wants to ask questions all through a movie because you're not patient enough to watch it and find out," I said on a chuckle.

"Why would I do that when I would much prefer to hear it the way you tell it…now what in Hell's name is that thing!" he shouted when noticing the screen and seeing what was now lay beneath the helmet they had to crack off the guy's head.

"That is a facehugger," I told him smiling.

"Ooh, now watch this bit, it has acid for blood and when they cut into its leg in a minute they find that the blood eats through the ship." I told him, explaining stuff before he even asked.

"Now who is the impatient one?" he commented with a grin.

"Well, you know that old saying, if you can't beat them, join them," I said nudging his arm and waggling my eyebrows at him, making him groan when really, I knew all he wanted to do was smile and chuckle. In the end we missed a few bits because this teasing led onto play fighting and me hopelessly trying to pin his arms down, which I knew was never going to happen. It was only when I recognised the iconic scene coming up that I detangled myself from him saying,

"Oh, this is the bit, we have to watch this part!" I shouted getting back into position with a little excited bounce and Draven made an exaggerated moan, like my fidgeting was affecting him.

"Oh hush," I reprimanded, slapping him on the chest.

"Well, he recovered quickly," Draven commented dryly seeing them now all sat around eating and laughing as if just hours before the guy hadn't had a facehugger curled around his head.

"Just watch," I told him and seconds later the guy started coughing and choking before falling dramatically to the table.

"By the Gods, now what is that thing!" Draven exclaimed once the creature had burst from the guy's chest, splattering blood around the room as his ribcage cracked open outwards.

"Now, that is the alien and known at this stage as the famous chestbuster," I told him, feeling myself for once being the one with a world full of knowledge.

"At this stage?" he asked as now I could tell he was deep into the movie.

"Let's just say it gets bigger…much, much bigger," I said using my hands to indicate its rapid growth.

"You know, I think I am going to like this movie after all." I laughed when he said this.

"Well, that's good to know considering we are already half way through it," I commented on another giggle.

After this point we continued to watch the rest of the movie without fooling around and I must have fallen asleep at some point, because it was only when I felt Draven shout next to me that I jolted awake. This was when I realised that all the other crew members were dead, and Ripley was running for her life through steam filled hallways to try and stop the ship from exploding, only to fail.

"Does she get out…? What are you doing, just leave the damn cat!" Draven said making me cry out,

"What? No! She can't leave Jonesy." He gave me a little smirk telling me he had said it to get this very reaction and was teasing me.

"So, she did get away," Draven mused prematurely, making me hide my knowing grin, for I knew what was coming next. But although I knew to expect it, I still jumped out of my skin, letting off a little scream just like I did every time when the Alien's hand shot out right next to Ripley. I had to smile because even Draven, mighty King of the supernatural world, flinched in surprise himself, but at least he didn't let out a girly scream like I had. I laughed at myself as I had automatically buried my head into Draven's chest making him chuckle too.

"What is she doing now?"

"I think this is the clever bit," I told him not giving much away.

"Well, I don't think she is going to get far if she plans on escaping into space," he said watching her slowly stepping into a space suit. I smirked, kissed his bare chest once and whispered over his skin,

"Just watch." And we did as Ripley moved into position and then started to force the alien out of its hiding place before blasting it from the ship out of the airlock and then finishing it off with the ship's thrusters.

"Now that looks almost as hard to kill as a Horo-matangi demon," he said once it was all over and Ripley was now doing her 'This is Ripley, last survivor of the Nostromo' bit.

"What's a Horo…manty…whatever you said, demon?" I asked, getting the name completely wrong towards the end and making him chuckle because of it.

"It's a creature that lives in the Lethe, and if I had to describe it, then I would say it looks similar to a large reptile in the figure of a man." I wanted to ask at this point did it look like the Spiderman Villain, the Lizard, who started life as a scientist who turned himself that way after an experiment went wrong. Although to be fair, I think that this was the back story for most comic book characters, that was if you took away the billionaires with fancy suits, the genetic mutants and dudes from outer space.

"What's the Lethe again?" I asked remembering Sophia telling me about and now focusing less on fictional characters and more on myths that were no longer very mythy thanks to Draven. Okay, so not sure 'mythy' was an actual word, but I would better my sticker collection that Pip would start using it regardless.

"The Lethe is the river of forgetfulness, which makes for a good hunting ground for the Horo-matangi as they prey on those searching for forgiveness and are haunted with regret for their sins."

"So not exactly like talking to a priest in the confession box then?" I said making him laugh, then pull me to him so that he could kiss me on the forehead.

"No, more like asking for forgiveness and then finding yourself eaten for your sins. Of course, on occasion they find themselves in the human world as the river links to Lake Taupō in New Zealand and it's where many of the creatures break through from Hell and into an underwater cave on the reef there."

"But what do they do there?" I asked naively.

"Well, mostly lurk in wait for the poor unsuspecting canoeist paddling down the wrong creek, before they strike." I looked back at him in horror and he ran his thumb over my lips pulling the bottom one from my teeth.

"Don't worry sweetheart, I have people who reside in the area and monitor the problem, one of whom you have seen a few times at the club," he said surprising me. This meant that I spent the next hour bombarding him with questions of his 'main business' in this world, which was about as far from the stock exchange and board meetings as you could get.

In the end I fell asleep to the sound of his voice and being held as he stroked my back and arms in that totally blissful way.

I woke the next morning to find two things that surprised me and at the same time made me want to burst out laughing. The first was to find a fresh pot of tea next to my side of the bed and with it a small plate of what looked like ginger biscuits. The next thing was when I rolled over to thank Draven for being so thoughtful, I found him sat up in bed reading a huge book with the title, 'What to Expect When You're Expecting'

"Some light reading?" I asked in an amused tone.

"Did you know that our baby is about the size of an apple seed right now?" Draven told me staring intensely at the book and therefore missing the tender warm look I gave him.

"Really? That's cool, what else does it say?"

"That during this time you will start to develop different symptoms, like morning sickness, light headedness, frequent urination, fatigue, food cravings and aversions to other foods like red meat, abdominal cramps..." he told me, making my face drop after hearing the depressing list.

"Right, well I think that's a bit too much information for so early in the morning," I muttered rolling over and pouring my tea, whilst stuffing a biscuit in my mouth just for something good to focus on.

"Have you had any vaginal bleeding or increased vaginal discharge?" he asked, making me nearly choke on the mouthful I had been in the process of swallowing.

"Jesus, Draven! No, I haven't and no offence, but you would be the last person I would tell if I had," I told him after I had finished coughing. He looked totally affronted by my answer.

"But why?!" he asked frowning at me

"Because it's embarrassing that's why," I argued making him now lose the frown and replace it with a soft smile.

"Sweetheart, it's not embarrassing, it's the most natural and beautiful thing in the world." At this I snorted.

"Yeah, well tell that to Libby when she would pee herself every time she laughed too hard, coughed or sneezed... I think she ended up washing the sofa cushions about six times during her pregnancy."

"That really happens?" he asked now looking shocked.

"Uh, yeah! And considering you have a thing for collecting antique furniture, then I think it's safe to say it wouldn't be worth much after its got a big pee stain in the centre of the 16th century cushions." Hearing this he waved a dismissive hand at me and said,

"I don't care about that, all I care about is you and your wellbeing. I don't want you to be in pain or feel discomfort." This time I gave him a soft smile in return. Then I leaned over to him, cupped his cheek and said,

"That's sweet Honey, but I think all of the above is inevitable. Besides, you keep bringing me tea and biscuits in the morning and I would say you're in for a winner," I said making him give me a sideways grin.

"So, have you had any vaginal bleeding?" he asked after a moment of silence. I groaned out loud and shouted,

"Draven!" He gave me a look that silently asked what my problem was with asking this, but seriously, even for someone as far removed from the human world as Draven was, he still should have known the obvious answer to that one.

"Okay, so I think that is enough reading for one day," I said taking the book off him, this time making him moan.

"I mean, is there anything positive in this book, other than having the baby at the end?" He smirked and said,

"Not unless you consider constipation or mood swings one of them," he replied with a smirk, one that quickly turned into a grin when I growled at him.

"I feel one coming on now," I said dryly.

"Then I suggest you use the bathroom, or that will really embarrass you."

"Draven! I meant a mood swing not needing the toilet!" I shouted making him throw his head back before roaring with laughter.

"I know sweetheart, I was teasing you," he told me after finally controlling his laughter enough to do so.

"Maybe not the safest thing to do around a hormonal pregnant Vampire, you do remember I have fangs now…right?" I said trying for my best, 'don't mess with me Mister' face, one that even without the aid of a mirror, I knew was useless.

"Yes, but mine are bigger," he said in a cocky tone and added to it by leaning into me and showing me a closer look as his fangs started to grow. I didn't know whether it was because I was now a Vampire or because I just loved it when he bit me during sex. But I had to say the sight of him with his fangs out, which for Draven was a rare sight, was getting me all hot and bothered and wet and horny.

"Yeah, is that so?" I teased back shifting closer to him and pressing my breasts into his chest.

"Mmm." At this point he could only manage a murmured agreement and a nod as he looked down at my cleavage, one he seemed captivated with.

"Then maybe you should put them to good use, baby," I said in what I was hoping sounded like a sexual purr. The moment I saw his eyes flash purple I knew it had worked as he had me under him in seconds. His hands ran up my arms as he pushed

them up above my head and he looked down at me as if any second, he was going to ravish me until breathless and screaming.

Well, a girl could hope.

Then, as he started to lean down to kiss me, his fangs started to retract.

"Stop!" I shouted louder than I had intended. His hold on me relaxed as he questioned my reasons for shouting this. So, I strained my neck up, so that my lips were that bit closer to him when I whispered,

"Don't take them back...*I like them, it's hot.*" His eyes flashed a darker shade of purple, showing me his surprise before they narrowed down at me in that carnal way.

One I knew meant I was definitely in for good things...good and wonderful naughty things.

Draven didn't disappoint but then again...

When did he ever?

CHAPTER TEN

LOOKING FOR NESSIE

"Seriously Pip, you thought this was a good place to have our crisis meeting?" Sophia complained as we all swayed back and forth on the deck of the boat we were now all stood on.

"What did you expect, you did say she could pick the place?" I told her and in doing so pretty much telling her silently 'I told you so'.

After waking that morning to Draven's baby brain and ginger biscuits, one that deliciously turned into us making love, I was quickly informed that the girls were stealing me away for the day. At first Draven had been reluctant to let me go but with one scowl from his sister and a snapped,

"I think it's the least you could do!" had him relenting pretty quickly. Then he picked up the baby book from where I had kicked it to the floor during sex and he came to kiss me briefly on the lips, telling me,

"Have fun sweetheart, I will see you later. Be safe." Then he walked out of the room after first stopping to give Pip's shoulder a squeeze, and Sophia a kiss on the forehead, as way of a silent apology.

"Well, it was her turn," Sophia said in response to my argument.

"Damn straight it was and think yourselves lucky as it was this or fetish night at the Torture Gardens," Pip said as she, for some unknown reason, concentrated on looking over the edge of the boat.

"What the hell is the Torture Gardens!?" I screeched making Pip look back over her shoulder at me, as she was bent over and showing me her pert little ass, that was covered in a lycra catsuit. The wink she gave me was as naughty as they came, and had it not come from someone that look so darn cute, then I would have shivered.

She was currently wearing an all in one body suit that, the second I saw her, she informed me was actually called a 'snuggle suit' and she did this when hugging herself. It was mainly in shades of blue and covered in flying unicorn ponies and clouds of lightning bolts and strangely, eyeballs with wings.

To this she had added a bright pink leather jacket that had the sleeves cut off and was biker style. Its collar was covered in spiked studs and the rest of it was covered in every type of patch and pin badge you could think of. From bands she liked, her favourite swearwords, movies quotes, to fluffy little clouds and unicorns pooing out rainbow curly turds. Oh, and then the biggest patch of all saying, 'My Bad, fuckers, I'm a Boobateer!' which was on her back, displayed proudly in a cartoon speech bubble. To this she'd added a pair of steel toe capped cowboy boots covered with pink flames, complete with pink spurs.

But getting back to my question about the Torture Gardens, which only one word out of that name did I like, and it certainly wasn't the first one!

"You don't want to know," Sophia replied instead of Pip,

who just started laughing. After this it didn't take a genius to link fetish with the pain in the title, when the place was called the Torture Gardens. Which meant my best guess was that it was the name of a BDSM club. So, in that case then yes, I did consider myself lucky to be on a boat on Loch Ness, instead of watching Pip swinging a whip in poor Adam's direction.

But speaking of our usual male entourage, they had of course escorted us here, but that was about as far as they were willing to go, seeing as Adam didn't like boats, as in one little bit. But even more surprising was to hear how Zagan wasn't fond of the water either and in fact, in all his years, he had never even learned how to swim. So that only left Ragnar, our resident Viking, who obviously didn't have a problem with boats, water or swimming in it, as he had it ingrained in his DNA. But one hand to his chest from Sophia was all it took to prevent him from stepping on the boat back at the dock. She only needed to say one thing to explain her actions,

"Girl time." This had been enough to get him to relent from bodyguard duties and give in to Sophia's demands.

"Well, I think Dom would have given birth to Harpies if he had known you were taking his pregnant wife to a sex club, as that's not exactly the girly day out he had in mind," Sophia said on a laugh.

"Yeah right! Like I was ever scuba'cidal enough to take her there!" Pip said chuckling.

"Scuba'cidal?" I asked because I knew if I didn't it would plague me for the rest of the day.

"Suicidal," Sophia answered quickly, before then asking her own question, one slightly more important than mine.

"So, this was the plan all along?"

"But of course, they don't have what I need in a sex club... which if you ask me is a crying shame," she said shaking her head like this was indeed a travesty. Meanwhile, me and Sophia were a lot less stuck on the 'sex club crying shame' and more on the 'what the hell is she up to now?' bit.

"Besides, it gives me a chance to see Nessie," Pip said as she continued to dangle a sandwich bag full of lucky charms over the side of the boat, as if this would help in luring the mythical creature to her.

I was about to say something along the lines of 'surely Nessie isn't real' or 'I don't think that's gonna work, Pip', when I felt a hand on my shoulder. I looked to Sophia to see her giving me a little shake of her head, so I took her advice and let it go.

"So, you do have a plan…right?" Sophia asked instead of my Nessie comment. Meanwhile, I zipped up my navy waterproof jacket, trying to fight off the cold chill the movement of the boat created.

"Yeah, 'cause we kinda need to be informed if you do, seeing as I kind of have an important part to play in it! So, no offense Pip, but what the hell is this plan?" I asked as I took a seat on the slatted wooden bench that was positioned in the middle for the tourists to enjoy the view…or the kids to Nessie watch, like Pip.

"Hell being the right word there, Captain Tootie no beard," Pip said with a grin and a pop of her blue bubblegum. Sophia sat down next to me after first inspecting the bench making sure it was clean. I smirked to myself knowing of her strange aversion to dirt or germs.

She then flicked out her expensive designer jacket that was a light grey shade and was in a poncho style with bat sleeves and a black leather belt. Skinny jeans and knee high grey boots completed the look.

As for me, I was the only one that looked dressed for the trip, being the practical one without even knowing it. Light blue jeans that were frayed a little around the bottom from being that little bit too long for me. Underneath my jacket I had on a thin red cotton sweater that had a black Aztec design on the sleeves. To this I'd added a blue and red tartan scarf, one Draven had bought me when we went to spend the day in Edinburgh. And now I was currently tapping one of my converse skull shoes against the leg of the bench as I waited for the conversation to kick start into a faster gear. That being the gear that would shed light onto what I was hoping would be known as 'Operation kick Draven's demon's butt and save my pregnant ass from becoming a slave in Hell'...then one named 'how to achieve this in ten easy steps'!

Yeah that would have been nice, something easy for once.

Okay, so granted 'Operation kick Draven's demon's butt and save my pregnant ass from becoming a slave in Hell' was a long-winded code name for a mission, but I could work on it later...what I couldn't do later on however, was talk about this with the girls and form a plan in front of, well, *anyone.* Which was why I was getting impatient and which was hence why the shoe tapping began.

But in the end, after the 'Tootie no beard' comment, all she said was,

"Patience my twisted knicker sisters, all shall be revealed in good time." This didn't bode well for good things ahead, I knew this but other than just sit there and wait, what else could I do? She said she had a plan and I had to trust that she knew what she was doing. As scary as that was with someone like Pip, sometimes, she really knew how to deliver the outcome you were hoping for.

"I take it that last night ended more smoothly than it began?" Sophia asked making me smile, one she also took as my answer.

"And this is definitely something you think is going to get worse?"

"How could it not, I mean, this is me we are talking about," I replied, and Pip shook her cereal bag at me and said,

"She makes a fishy good point." Sophia rolled her eyes before coming back to the 'fishy good point' at hand.

"So, the only clue you have to all of this is your birthmark?"

"Yeah, I mean Draven seems to think that someone else is behind it all, which reminds me, he had someone hiding behind a screen during the banquet, they were wearing a cloak, so I couldn't see who it was, and he didn't tell me who...did either of you guys know?" I asked hoping they would, but with a shrug of Sophia's shoulders and a confused Pip biting at her lip ring, I would say that was a big fat no from them also.

"Well, someone must know...oh wait, what about Ragnar? He was the one who seemed to be guarding whoever it was," I said looking back to where we had boarded the small boat as if we would see them all still standing there.

"Ha, you really think he would break that easily after my brother had issued his orders?" Sophia asked looking from me to Pip and back again. Pip just grinned and I followed suit when in the end all three of us nodded and said in unison,

"Yeah".

"We can totally break him, especially Tootie 'miss favourite Viking' pants over there, besides, she is with child now, you know how they won't be able to resist doing something she asks...hey, can you cry on demand?" Pip asked, still refusing to give up her search for Nessie, as she still shook her bag over the side.

"No, and I don't know anyone that can do that."

"Uh, yeah you do," she replied before slapping her ass and saying,

"You're looking at her skilful little ass right now....what? I only do it when Adam won't give me what I want, it's no biggy...Jeez, and this look coming from a fecking demon bad ass... like you never did it with Mr hot and pale commander of Hell's Legions, Miss Prissy Pants." Once Pip was finished she tried folding both her arms across her chest but realised the flaw in this was then having to give up her fishing for a sea monster. So instead, she decided to go for the usual, hand on cocked out hip look.

"I never cry in front of Zagan!" Sophia screeched out in annoyance.

"Oh no, well what about when Dom was being a dicky Dom and forbade you to see our Kazzy Toot brain, Uh?" Pip said reminding her and my head shot round to Sophia's to see her trying to drill a hole through Pip's forehead with none existent laser eyes.

"You cried?!" I asked making her turn her scowl from Pip's satisfied, cocky know it all expression.

"Of course I cried, it was like losing a sister," she finally admitted, and I threw my arms around her for a hug.

"I felt the same way," I told her softly making her body relax into my hold on her.

"No fair, I wanna get in on the mushy crap!" Pip complained making me laugh and Sophia groan.

"Yeah well, taggly tale tellers don't get to do the mushy crap...did I say that right?" Sophia said first to Pip and then to me.

"Close enough," I replied with a smirk.

"The hell they don't! Move over bitches, this 'I'm so cute I could die' snuggle suit is coming over, Nessie hunt be damned!" Pip said putting down her lucky charms on the side and running over to us to 'get in on the action' as after all, she was a sucker for a girl hug.

"So cute I could die snuggle suit?" I had to ask.

"It's the name of my body suit, isn't it fabulous? Ugh, just look at those scarily cute little pegacorns prancing all over the place. They just KILL me. Not to mention all the stormy clouds disgusting. It's so cute, I think I'm going to DIE!" she replied making me and Sophia frown at each other in question, as even for Pip standards it didn't make much sense.

"What, it's what it says on the Black Milk description on their website, that and it's lined with fleece, see, so snuggly," Pip said unzipping it down the front and pulling it to one side, exposing one of her little naked breasts as she did so. I turned my head away and said,

"Whoa there, Pip, we believe you, now put the Tatas away."

"Jeez, woman don't you ever wear a bra?" Sophia asked, tucking back a stray curl from her twisted bun in a less awkward way than me openly averting my eyes.

"Oh, come on, it's only a boobie, and besides I am wearing a bra, see…" she said pointing to her nipples.

"That's not a bra Squeak, that's just a couple of kid's band aids," Sophia replied sounding as though she was dealing with a three-year-old that wanted to go to the supermarket dressed as a superhero.

"Yeah, but it totally counts as I have my nipples covered." I shot her boob a brief look to see that yes, she did have her nipples covered with superhero plasters that crossed over making an X shape.

"This one is DC, but the other one and my favourite nipple, is Marvel," she told us proudly.

"You have a favourite nipple?" I couldn't help but ask.

"Yeah, doesn't everyone?"

"Nope."

"No, not really." Me and Sophia both answered making Pip shrug her shoulders and make a 'Huh' noise.

"I have one other Pip induced question," I said as she finally zipped up her all in one suit.

"Fire at Will…Poor Will, he's always getting shot at and

pistols at Dawn, what did she ever do?" I ignored this and pressed forward to fire at Will.

"Okay, so leaving poor Will and Dawn out of this, what is a pegacorn?" I asked as my brain was still stuck on what she had said earlier about her 'snuggle suit'.

"Well, I think it's when Pegasus and a Unicorn have a love child...that or it's just a pregnant Unicorn, I haven't decided yet."

"Oookay right, well now that's all settled, and the important stuff is clearly out of the way, can we move on to the problem at hand?" Sophia said sarcastically. Pip just stuck her tongue out at her showing us her candy stripe balls attached to either side of the bar.

"Sure thing, boss a'wooney, so when do you want me to start trying to find my wizardry pokery?" she asked making me quickly wonder if I had missed something vital here, as I know I was prone to day dreaming and getting lost in my own thoughts. But I was sure I would have noticed a conversation with the words 'And that will solve all your problems'.

"So, you definitely have a plan?" Sophia beat me to this question, and in doing so unknowingly answered one unspoken, as it was clear she didn't know either.

"Yeah, of course I have a plan, what do you think we are doing on this damn boat?" Pip told us on a chuckle.

"Uh...looking for the Loch Ness monster?" I said, now well and truly confused. However, the second I said it I knew I had made a mistake at some point along the way. Because now Sophia had covered her face and groaned into her hand before I saw Pip's green eyes flash in anger. Then, just before she started to blow, I noticed the deep sway of the boat before the bag of lucky charms slipped off the side and into the water.

"She is not a monster!" she declared, crying out and stomping her foot.

"She is just misunderstood and no wonder she doesn't like humans…" she carried on with her rant.

"Uh Pip…" I murmured trying to interrupt her the second I saw that there was a commotion in the water next to the side of the boat, but she wasn't listening.

"I mean, she was here first! Yes, woopydo one thousand four hundred years ago and the first human spots her because she had a cold and can't disguise herself during a sneeze and…"

"Okay seriously Pip, I think you need to see this," I tried again but Pip was still too deep in her own rant to notice that now the boat had started to tip slightly as if something was pulling it down on one side. I even held on to the bench but seeing as Pip was already leaning casually against the cross bar that held up the canopy above us, she obviously couldn't feel the boat tipping.

"And then they go on to say that she isn't even real and it's impossible for her to hide so long, but excuse me Mr Nelly Nessie misbelievers…"

"Yeah, not hiding anymore here, Pip," Sophia said as things on the boat suddenly start to slide and we could hear the captain behind the wheel cursing like a…well like a sailor.

"As if you will find her…the lock is around seven hundred and fifty feet deep and holds more water than in all of the lakes and rivers of England and Wales combined…but oh no, nowhere for her to hide…"

"PIP!"

"SQEAK!" Sophia, and I both screamed at the same time as the second massive splash of water came over the side, just as she said,

"What…oh?" This 'oh' ended up finishing as water hit her and us, making us all scream this time as we got soaked.

"I don't ken what's wrong, we mist be caught oan something, haud oan!" The Captain shouted from the front of the ship, one it was sounding as if was getting harder and harder to control.

"I think we are going to have to take over this. Pip, you try to control your…pet thingy and I will knock out our human witness," Sophia said after throwing her now wet hair back from her face and taking charge. I can't say I was thrilled at the idea of her knocking out anyone, let alone the poor guy that was only trying to make a living by bringing tourists out on his boat for a relaxing hour on the Loch. Well, I bet he will regret the day he let us unsuspecting delinquents on board, that's for damn sure!

"Oh dear, I think she's… having a… sugar rush…usually I only… give her a few at… at a time!" Pip shouted having to keep pausing every time the boat rocked violently. Meanwhile, I was holding on to the rail for dear life, telling myself that from now on Pip was NEVER allowed to pick our days out!

"That's the captain sort…Holy Mother of Gods!" Sophia started to say before screaming the end of her sentence in shock. I turned just in time to see what looked like a giant sea monster rising up over the side of the boat. It had a huge rounded head with a strange flat, wide mouth, with long whiskers. It's body, from what I could see of it, was shaped like a whale only its fins were much longer and thinner, like tentacles of a giant octopus.

A row of spiked scales ran down the centre of its back in a zigzag formation with higher, sharper spikes at the centre points that were tinged blue. But everything else was a shimmering light grey that made its thick skin seem almost translucent…oh and it looked to be the size of a bus!

I was just about to scream, when Pip turned her head and stuck a finger over her mouth,

"Ssshh, you will scare her." My mouth was still open from

the scream I still had at the ready and I turned to Sophia and whispered,

"How can we scare that!?" Then I heard a mooing sound and turned around to find Pip was now communicating with the large beast by sounding like a farmyard animal. To be honest, the more you looked at it, the less intimidating it looked, 'cos if it wasn't for the sheer size of the thing, you would actually have said it was quite cute.

"It looks like a gigantic sea cow," I muttered in disbelief.

"Yeah it is, or at least what they would have looked like in the Jurassic age," Sophia told me trying to also keep her voice down.

"But how? Why?"

"Think demonic interference as opposed to natural occurrence and you will have your why and how," she answered, speaking side on and like me, not taking her eyes off the creature.

"Gottcha," I replied as I watched Pip reaching out her hand to try and tame the startled beast.

"Hey babydoll, mummy missed you, yes I did, come here Moomoo and give mummy a kiss," Pip cooed as the creature lowered its head obviously taken with her.

"Uhh, is that wise Pip?" I asked a little louder this time making it snort out a load of what looked like snot, as it bristled its whiskers, that now had been decorated with strings of slimy mucus. Okay, so the thing might have been cute before that happened and the same went for Pip who was now covered in the stuff too.

"It was until you said that!" she snapped wiping the sticky clear liquid, that really resembled dog drool, from her face.

"What did I do?" I whispered this time just to be on the safe side.

"Uhuh, beats me," Sophia replied reverting back to a

whisper and obviously like me standing on the cautious side of things.

"Look, she is skittish okay, and she doesn't trust new people…it's okay, see, they are friends, just ignore the blonde that doubted you, I mean she doesn't even have a dog," Pip said throwing an arm back my way and waving at me.

"Hey…I like dogs," I argued making Pip scowl at me once more telling me to,

"Ssshh," before giving her attention back to the pale beast who started to shudder making its shimmering skin ripple like skipping stones along the still water.

"So, is this what you had in mind when letting Pip pick our girly day?" I asked leaning closer into Sophia so as not to spook the creature. She gave a me a sideways glance that said it all…*regret and never again.*

"I would just be thankful the boat is no longer rocking," she told me and yes, there was that silver lining I thought wryly. Or at least there had been a silver lining, one that was soon blown out the sky the second Sophia's phone started to ring. Pip hung her head in what was another 'Oh shit' moment and Sophia started trying to fumble in her jacket to reach her phone to stop it ringing.

But it was too late, the creature started thrashing violently in the water in distress making the boat thrash right alongside it. I grabbed onto the pole just as I was thrown sideways and then swiftly back, only just stopping myself in time from landing on my backside.

"Oh…uh, yeah…Hi Dom," Sophia said shrugging her shoulders when I shot her a look of disbelief. She mouthed the words 'I didn't mean to answer it!'. Then she gave me a pained look and said,

"Oh that, no, no it's just…um, just a…" she paused and looked at me rolling her hand around telling me to think of something quickly. I gave her my own panicked look when Pip once again came to the rescue, although technically the problems she solved were usually ones created by herself.

"We are watching Jaws!" she shouted suddenly, just as there was another massive splash making us all hold on as the wave rocked the ship even further to the side and back again.

"Yes, yes, Jaws, we are watching Jaws...well, it's the surround sound that's why...anyway will ring you back when I can...no she is fine, no, you can't talk to her she is in the..." Sophia had to pause as the creature cried out, sounding like a cow giving birth surrounded by microphones and then pumped through a stack of concert speakers.

"IN THE TOILET!" Sophia shouted this last part after Pip crouched low and squatted, obviously giving Sophia her answer and this being the obvious reply to the question, 'Where is my wife?'.

Finally, the creature started to go back under the water after Pip's cooing was obviously not working enough against the sound of a Beyoncé's Halo which, surprisingly, was Sophia's ring tone.

"What was that noise...?" Sophia repeated looking to us both separately as it became obvious she had no idea what the movie Jaws was even about and thus became the flaw in Pip's plan. So, knowing there was little else we could do, we found ourselves both forced to play the strangest game of charades in history. And talk about it being played at an advanced stage, this was more like 'Hard core, extreme, life and death level'.

Pip started it off by pretending that her arms out in front of her was a shark's mouth, but I got this straight away because I knew what Jaws was, being that I lived in the world and all.

However, what Sophia got from this was the totally opposite.

"Just Hitler on screen...no you're right, that doesn't exactly fit the name," Sophia agreed, saying this last part through gritted teeth at the same time Pip slapped a hand to her forehead and shook it. Meanwhile, I just started shaking my head at her before doing my own impression. I formed my hand as if I was about to karate chop someone then placed it on top of my head hoping it looked like the fin of a shark. Then I wiggled around like I was lurking in some imaginary water.

"Well, I don't know there are other things involved, like there is a chicken..." she said, and my mouth and arms dropped.

'Chicken?' I mouthed at her in disbelief making her mouth back,

'I panicked'. I then groaned and prompted her to carry on and try and salvage the damage.

"No, no, not a chicken... I mean a Monster, yeah one with sharp teeth..." she improvised after Pip decided on a new method when making teeth with her fingers, this done by using both hands cupped together by her mouth. Of course, after she said monster, then Pip just threw up her hands dramatically and muttered,

"That's it, I quit."

"Uh yeah, that is probably why it's called Jaws although you're right, not sure why there are Nazis in it," Sophia said faking interest and now getting the fact that she wasn't very good at this game.

"Anyway, we'd better...No, Dom, she is pregnant, and pees a lot. Okay, yep, will do...yep I will get her to..." she started to end the call and unbelievably we might have been scot free, but it was in this moment when we realised we hadn't heard the last of 'Moomoo', aka Nessie, the Loch Ness monster. The creature must have knocked hard against the side of the boat as it fled which in turn meant the mobile phone was tossed from Sophia's hand and was currently sliding towards the edge. I could even hear Draven shouting her name as it passed me, but instead of being able to grab it in time, I missed it by an inch before it fell into the water.

"Oh shit!" I said as I looked back at the other two who were still hanging on to the boat like I was.

"Seriously, you need to watch a fucking movie, dude!" Pip said ignoring the fact that we were on a boat, one that felt as if it was going to sink any second and we had just lost the phone. A phone, I might add, that now had my extremely panicked husband on the other end, asking himself what the hell just happened.

"And you need to stop changing my ring tone to anything with a fucking Angel, Heaven or Halo in it!" Sophia snapped back, and my mouth dropped open at the fact that we were in our current situation and yet these two were focusing on movies and ringtones.

"Seriously guys, can we like do this later…? I don't know, maybe when the boat isn't…!" In the end I never got to finish this sentence as Nessie hadn't yet finished with us, as this time the boat tipped so far, there was nowhere else for us to go but into the water.

And into the water we went with one song playing through my head and it wasn't Beyoncé's Halo.

It was…

The Jaws theme song.

CHAPTER ELEVEN

THE BAD WOW

"Okay, so not the fun, girly day trip I had in mind, guys," I said after spluttering and coughing up what felt like a bucket of lake water. Oh, and not to mention I was now freezing my ass off and it felt like my nipples had become hard enough to become weapons and cut through my bra!

We had all been thrown from the boat just before it started to sink and as each of us reached the surface, the first thing I shouted to the others was about the Captain.

"I am on it!" Pip shouted, giving me a salute before nose diving under again to find what was thankfully the only other person on board. I was sure glad Pip had paid the guy for a full load and turned the other mortals away, as I think this boat trip would have ended quite differently. Think Titanic, only on a micro scale.

"Come on, let's get you out of the water, the ruins aren't far!" Sophia shouted pointing to what looked like a small stone covered beach area that held the castle's ruins up on a hill behind it. I just started swimming when I heard a break in the water behind me and I turned, whilst treading water and kicking my leggings, to see Pip was now playing life saver.

"Is he okay?!" I shouted to her as she now had her hand under his chin and was swimming whilst keeping his body afloat.

"He's breathing if that's what you mean?!" Pip said nearly catching up with me. Man, she was fast for someone so little!

"Yeah, that's what I mean, Pip," I replied on a laugh before I carried on swimming, which brought us back to now and the reason I was flat on my back trying to remind my lungs how to work.

"I had fun!" Pip said replying to my comment about fun girly trips now we were all trying to catch our breath on the stones beneath us. I knew I had to move as I lay flat on my back, because every time I took a breath I could feel the rocks digging in through my jacket.

"Yeah well, I bet that guy can't say the same thing! Are you sure he is okay?" I asked nodding to the poor unconscious Captain, who Pip had propped up like a mannequin against a bolder. But hey, at least he was still breathing. Although, that might change when he wakes up and finds his way of living is now sitting at the bottom of the Loch.

"Yeah, we should be fine and when he wakes, I will buy him a shiny new boat, so it's all good and dandy...but on another notepad binder, wasn't my Moomoo looking awesome!?" Pip said, as though what just happened was all just part of the fun.

"Well yeah, that was until she sank the fucking ship!" Sophia snapped making Pip roll her eyes at me, eyes that were currently raccooned by black makeup and lines dripping down her face. Even one of her fake eyelashes was half hanging off which made it look like a spider was crawling on her face. In the end she pulled it off and flicked it off her fingers before answering Sophia.

"Yes, well technically it was your phone that put a Nelly up Nessie's butt, so maybe next time we are on a mission, may I suggest Vibrate...which isn't something used just when you wanna get your kicks in your knicks," she said winking at me before Sophia started growling at her and then shouting,

"I don't do that!"

"Alright ladies, it happened, and we can't do anything about it, other than pray that Draven isn't at this moment freaking out enough to send out for the Coastguard or planning a rescue mission with the Scottish government." Pip and Sophia shot me a look that said it all, making me groan.

"Well either way, we can't just sit here for the rest of the day and wait for the pissed off cavalry to come rescue us," I said getting up and then ringing out the edge of my clothes the best I could. I had to say I was just glad to see I hadn't lost my scarf or then it would have really pissed me off.

"What is this place anyway?" I asked bending slightly to one side and squeezing the water out of my hair.

"This is Urquhart castle, or at least it was until a storm back in 1715 finished it off," Sophia told me looking up at the steps leading to the top.

"How much time do you reckon we were on the pleasure cruise?" Pip asked us both. I gave her a shrug, a telling sign I had no clue, whereas Sophia was definitely more helpful.

"No more than thirty minutes, why?"

"Because I just wanted to know how much time we had until the big man freak out." Pip was, of course, speaking of her own husband and the off the scale man paddy that would occur once his wife didn't come back within the one-hour boat tour time frame. Knowing Adam, he was probably still looking at his watch and counting down the minutes. Draven on the other hand was probably trying to hire a helicopter to come pick us up.

"Good, then that means we have time," Pip said clapping the wet grass from her hands before doing the same to her snuggle suit.

"Time for what?" I asked as I gave Sophia a hand with her jacket, patting off the grass from the back of that too.

"Why, the reason we came here silly!"

"What do you mean, the reason we came here…Pip, did you plan all of this?" Sophia asked in a cautious tone. Pip whipped around to us both and faked an 'utterly offended, mortally wounded, how could you ever think such a thing' look.

"Who me?"

"Pip, spit it out!" We both said at the same time.

"Okay, okay, so yeah, there might have been a tinsy tiny reason for us coming here, but I didn't plan on Moomoo sinking the Orca!"

"Orca?" Sophia asked so I told her,

"It's the ship's name in the movie Jaws."

"Yeah and one you would know if you ever watched a friggin' movie! You know, this snapping motion being a shark and all and about as far away from Hitler as you can get!" Pip said doing the same gesture she had on the boat, only doing it now with sarcasm.

"Well, excuse me for having more important things to do, like keeping the world from falling into the hands of rogue demons and angels, so basically chaos!" she argued back, making me start rubbing my forehead wondering if it would ever end.

"Ha! Yeah and how much of that job includes online designer shopping, uh?" Pip argued back.

"Okay guys let's just move on and…" I started to say but was quickly interrupted by Sophia.

"That's my down time!" she said folding her arms and huffing.

"And what do you think watching movies are for...torture for prisoners of war?"

"Pip, that's enough, she gets it, now can we please focus... *okay guess not.*" I added interrupting myself this time when Sophia snapped,

"Well, according to you they are the source of all world knowledge!"

"Uh yeah!" Pip agreed in a tone that stretched out the words like it was obvious, which only managed to make Sophia's face redder.

"Yes, well I like to read."

"Yeah, like what, a catalogue!?" Pip shouted back and this time I found my limit, hating seeing these two really arguing for the first time.

"RIGHT, ENOUGH!" I shouted before either of them could speak again.

"This is neither the time or the place! What happened back there was no-one's fault and if you start blaming each other again then I will just remind you why we are all here in the first place...because of ME, yet again! So, if you want to point fingers then do so at me. I don't care! Because I would rather be blamed any day of the week, than watch my two best friends fighting like this!" I said panting through my anger and looking at them both now. Thankfully, my dramatic speech seemed to have worked.

"So, if you are quite finished then can we get back to the reason we are here, and solve this quickly before all our men turn up and put a stop to us before we have even started?" I asked, this time in a calmer voice. Sophia nodded and then Pip followed.

"Good, now hug it out and let's get this shit over with," I

said pushing them both together and finally making them giggle. They then hugged, said their apologies and thankfully for my sanity's sake, moved on.

"Right now, that's done, can we get back to the reason we are here, Pip?"

"Well, you did say you wanted to know what the Hell's rocket was going on...*right?*" Pip said dragging out this last word.

"If I say yes, is she going to get me even wetter?" I asked Sophia making Pip giggle before saying,

"Ha! You wish chickee Tootary!" I groaned and said,

"I didn't mean it like that, I just meant that if I say yes, is this going to get me in even deeper water...and yes, pun definitely intended!"

"Well, it will get you deeper alright, but not *under* water," she replied cryptically, and I was just about to complain when she slapped her hands to her butt and said,

"Come on ass, like smart Tootie cookie said, time's a wasting." Then she started to march off towards the ruins and walked up the many steps that led to the ruined castle. It had obviously all been well set up for tourists.

"What about him?" I asked Sophia as we both walked past the Captain.

"He should be fine, I made sure he wouldn't wake until we can get him back."

"And his boat, won't that be a little odd when he wakes up to find his livelihood missing?" I asked knowing that I certainly would.

"We will no doubt think of something and besides, the cost of the new boat is coming out of Pip's pocket... come on, we'd better make sure she stays away from the tourists, that's if there are any." I continued up the stairs cut into the land until I could see an arch in the wall ahead of us. I saw Pip disappear through it before we followed, now doing so with pace in case she was the one to encounter anyone alone, not knowing what she would say.

But I needn't have worried as the second we walked through, I looked around to find the same thing Sophia did, and that was a large green area void of any people. It was definitely strange, as I knew it wouldn't have been closed on a fairly sunny day in May on a week day. But nevertheless, I looked from left to right, and up the different stone pathways leading off in different directions, only to find more stone steps and Pip walking up some of them.

We quickly caught up to Pip to find her whistling the A Team's theme song and what I can assume was smoking an imaginary cigar, mimicking the team's leader, Hannibal.

"So, where are all the people?" I asked looking around and seeing no-one but us, and also noticing that we were walking in the opposite direction, away from the large tower.

"Ah, that, well I thought I would use the good side of my brain today, as I didn't think it was going to be very practical having an audience," she said tapping on her head after first switching her imaginary cigar over to her other hand.

"What did you do, Winnie?" Sophia asked in a telling tone.

"Hey, little Miss Kettle Black, I do remember you burning down a whole college hall just to keep little Miss Trouble here out of…well, *trouble*. So, don't you ya start giving me the 'Tone'," she said motioning up and down Sophia's body as she spoke.

"Pip, just tell us what you did," I asked this time and my tone was all exasperation as the last thing I wanted was another Sophia/Pip showdown.

"Okay, okay, jeez Spanish inquisition much…look all I did was put out a weather warning on their website saying it was going to be closed for the day and then I emailed all the staff telling them to take the day off...see, no biggy." I looked to Sophia and shrugged before admitting,

"That doesn't sound that bad." Sophia on the other hand just folded her arms across her soggy wet jacket and said,

"And?" My eyes shot back to Pip in hopes she would be defensive and say, 'and nothing, that was it'. But this was Pip we were talking about and therefore,

No such luck.

"Welllll, as I was already hacking into their system I might have accidently, on purpose also hacked into their payroll and gave each of them a bonus, then erased that I ever did on file."

"Aww, that was sweet of you," I said making Sophia shoot me a look before telling me,

"Don't encourage her!"

"Why not, after all she is right, you did burn down a whole building just so I wouldn't be going to college for a few weeks," I told her in return and Pip looked as delighted as a child that was faced with two parents fighting each other over parental decisions.

"Okay, so it seems like our new team moto is going to be upgraded from 'My bad' to 'She has a point'," Sophia commented dryly, making Pip jump up and down on the spot and say,

"Great! First thing when we get back I am contacting my T-shirt guy!"

"You have a T-shirt guy?" I asked feeling stupid about three seconds after it because, let's face it, this was Pip I was talking to...of course she had a T-shirt guy!

"Well duh, I mean, doesn't everyone?"

"Nope."

"Not really no," I said after Sophia had answered too.

"Huh, I just assumed everyone did, oh well it's no biggy, you can use mine, *he's fabulous!*" she said throwing her arm up and around dramatically and speaking like some posh rich person boasting about an expensive designer. And definitely not someone who just printed designs onto T-shirts for a modest living.

I had to stifle a giggle when I saw Sophia's wrinkled nose as if Pip had just waved rotten cheese under her face, because as much as I loved her, Sophia was spoiled, and she knew it. If it didn't come with a designer label, then she just wasn't interested. Which meant I doubt very much that Pip giving us both the name for her 'T-shirt' guy was going to increase his work load by much. Not unless I was in the mood to buy some funny novelty gifts this Christmas and not unless Sophia had lost her ever loving designer mind.

We continued to follow Pip on her unknown mission and I leaned in to Sophia and muttered,

"So, do we have any idea on why we are here and what she is planning…and just so you know, when I say 'we' I actually mean 'you', supernatural connoisseur that you are?" She gave me a sideways look that I could have taken as her answer but in the end, she gave it to me verbally.

"I don't know whether to be flattered or insulted that you think I would know what she is up to, for who in all the world's realms does know?"

"Well, I think the closest answer to that question is no doubt sat on a dock looking at his watch with no fingernails left and about fifteen minutes away from going turbo," I replied, and Sophia gave me a dire head nod, knowing herself the bad cocktail mix a 'mischievous Imp named Pip', a whole lot of 'worry' and one 'Adam', made. Actually, think less cocktail and more bottle of coke shaken for a whole hour before taking the top off.

We continued on in silence after this, following the jumping Pip in front of us who, amazingly, had removed her pink cut off jacket and was pulling at the back of it, doing something I couldn't really see. The next thing I knew the biggest patch came flying off as she threw it in the air, as she said in an Arnold Schwarzenegger tone,

"Hastalavista baby! You have been upgraded!" I looked down just as I was about to step on the words, 'My Bad, fuckers, I'm a Boobateer!'. So instead, I picked it up and stuffed into my still wet jacket pocket. I did this for two reasons, but I only told Sophia one of them when she looked at me in question,

"I don't want a kid picking it up or anything." She shrugged her shoulders and took that as my answer. The other reason was because it reminded me of Pip and I thought that one day it would come in handy for something to look back on. Of course, that's presuming that I didn't just end up a slave in Hell at some point. And that something to look back on was me having a memento to go with the question, 'where did it all go wrong?'. Yep, I was definitely holding out for the less daunting scrapbooking version of the two.

"Right, now where is it...Ha over there!?" Pip started to ask herself before answering it directly after. Then she marched us further up the path until we had reached all the way to a large round stone wall. It looked as though it had once been the foundations for something. Definitely a singular room of some kind, as it had a break in the wall where a door would have been and even some old slabs on the floor, that would have probably been a path leading in. If I were to guess I would have said a store room of some kind. But like always, around so many people that were thousands of years older than me, I was about to be proven wrong yet again.

"Ah, here we go!" Pip said bouncing over to its centre, whilst I turned around to take advantage of our new position being higher up. I couldn't help but gasp as I took in the most amazing panoramic view of the Loch in all its magnificent glory. I tried to imagine what it must have been like living here and waking up to that majestic view every day.

I always loved seeing places that would offer us the exact same view as if we were there hundreds of years ago. That even though life may have altered, giving way to the modern world, there were still many places like this left in the world. Places where you could be surrounded by untouched beauty and pretend, if only for a fleeting moment, that they were being lived in, in the past. That you could forget your own world, and therefore fully immerse yourself in fantasy and escapism.

Okay, so this was how I used to view places like this but now, looking back at Pip and no doubt the next mind-blowing thing I was about to be shown…well, then fantasy was pretty much the norm for me and escapism was something like going to the dry cleaners or a check -up at the dentist. Which I was also hoping this was something I wouldn't need to do anymore because I am pretty sure one look at my fangs and a heart attack and a guilty conscious were all I would achieve that day.

"Tell me this isn't what I think it is?" Sophia asked in a tone of utter awe which I had to admit, coming from these two, didn't give me the warm and snugglies.

"That depends, whatya think it is?" Pip asked rocking back on her heels like a child playing a game with her elders. Sophia tilted her head slightly and said in what sounded like Latin,

"A Testis Circulo?" Pip's face said it all, but she nodded like a mad woman anyway, with a big grin on her face.

"It just might be," she replied like a teasing child would.

"That's…wow…just wow." I looked from Sophia and then back to Pip, trying to figure out if this was a good wow or a bad wow. And then I asked myself if there was even such a thing as a 'Bad wow', but then looking back to the girls, then yeah, I knew there definitely was. Because I wasn't living in the real world per se. I was living in their world and in their world, then even words like 'wow' were used when shit hit the fan, or all Hell was about to break loose.

Which was why my next question was, what I considered, an important one,

"And this wow, is it a good thing or a bad thing?"

Of course, I should have known not to ask. I should have known that we weren't here for some simple reason and that maybe, just maybe, it was going to be the easy way. Because when was it ever the easy way with me and Draven?

And I knew now was no different, not when Pip replied,

"Only if sending you back to the future is a bad thing?"

I had only one answer to that...

"Hell yes, it is!"

CHAPTER TWELVE

MIRROR, MIRROR

"Okay, come again?" I asked after shaking my head a few times and asking myself if I had heard her correctly.

"It's not as bad as it sounds," Sophia told me in that dismissive way that people do when they want you to move past something and quickly. I knew this when she ignored my inner freak out and started speaking again, only this time it wasn't to me, it was to Pip.

"But I thought they were all destroyed back in the 1600's?" Sophia asked, clearly surprised. Whereas I was still about 400 years stuck in the past asking myself what was going on?

"You mean after the great booming fire in London, which was to cover up the demon outbreak of 1666," she said making Sophia groan.

"Yeah don't remind me, your husband was certainly a pain in the ass for us back then," she replied making my mouth drop and Pip frown.

"Well, what do you expect, he was angry, being locked up for all those centuries and…"

"Oh, don't you give me that, we all know it was when he first met you, so you can just go ahead and take the little Miss Innocent act off the table and tell her to piss off!" Sophia argued back, but it was at this point that I held up my hands in surrender and said,

"Okay, someone is going to have to explain this one to me." Pip just folded her arms and gave us a pout.

"I take it she knows how you first met lover beast boy?" Sophia first asked Pip who shrugged her shoulders like a pissed off teenager.

"Yeah, she told me when we were in Germany together," I answered for her.

"So, you know she got sent down because of the outbreak of the Black…"

"Don't say it!" Pip shouted, hating it when people mentioned it.

"…Death?" Sophia finished, making Pip wince as if she had been shot.

"So, after being on the run, and having to hunt her ass…"

"Yeah, thanks for that by the way!" Pip interjected, sarcastically.

"Wait a minute, you hunted her and sent her to Hell?!" I shouted back at Sophia who was now not only frowning at Pip, but now at me.

"Of course I did, she managed to kill 40,000 people!"

"38, 472! And don't forget one of those had a bad heart anyway so he doesn't count," Pip said in her defence and I remembered back to that day hearing her saying the same thing to me, now giving me the strangest form of déjà vu.

"Oh yeah, 'cause that makes it better. Anyway, we found

her hunting some guy, who we now know coerced her into doing something stupid like bringing infested rats from China into the country," Sophia said in a kinder tone this time.

"My bad," Pip added, proving that this was still a much loved motto after all.

"So, what does this have to do with a Demon outbreak?" I asked wondering where these two tales would interlock.

"1666 was when Pip was sent down and as punishment was given to Abaddon."

"Oh, yeah she told me that," I said but still not really understanding, so quickly following this up with a question.

"But how did Pip meeting Abaddon cause an Outbreak topside?"

"Oh, would listen to our little Tooterina, all grown up and talking like one of us, calling it topside and all…"

"Stop trying to change the subject, Squeak," Sophia said making Pip sulk.

"The reason her meeting him caused an outbreak was to save herself from being eaten, as what she no doubt failed to mention, was after she first entertained him by dancing around and laughing, she then quickly found another, shall we say, very inventive way of doing it further," Sophia told me, and I was about to ask as my brain was obviously not up to the task at seeing the obvious, but Pip beat me to it.

"How was I supposed to know the big guy was a freakin' virgin and it was his first time and also that an orgasm was literally going to break the confines of Hell and open up a fucking window…it's not like I was playing ballgames inside the house!" she argued, meanwhile my brain was still stuck on them having sex!

"No, you were just firing them at the glass with a fucking bazooka!"

"You had sex with Abaddon the first time and broke Hell?" I asked utterly gobsmacked. She gave me a cheeky grin and then looked at her nails to blow on them before telling me,

"What can I say Toots, it was earth shattering," she said with a wink.

"Anyway, that might have technically been my fault, but the next biggy was on you guys!" she argued this time making Sophia groan.

"The next Biggy?" I asked trying to keep up with these two.

"Oh, you know when I told you about when they tried to take me off him the year later which ended up killing 80,000 people in the Shamakhi earthquake! You know that number which is double the amount of deaths my shit caused!" Pip said in a know it all tone making Sophia throw her hands up in the air as though she was dealing with a naughty child that wouldn't listen.

"Here we go again." I muttered shaking my head wondering whether I should just let these two wrestle it out and have done with it.

"Oh, I see you told her that part right but leaving out the demon horde… nice." This was when I snapped again.

"Okay, okay, enough!" I shouted getting in between them and holding a palm out to them both.

"Please tell me that these issues were dealt with years ago and we are not choosing *now*, a time where there is zero to spare, going over something that happened four hundred years ago?!" I said in that exasperated tone. They both looked at each other and said at the same time,

"She has a point."

"She's got a point."

"Yeah, totally our new motto, and Dancing Danny is so gonna get a lot of work coming his way!" Pip added, now strangely looking excited.

"Dancing Danny?"

"My T shirt guy," she told me before going back to searching the ground for something...but what, I had no clue.

"Oh, is he a dancer as well?" I randomly chose this question to ask.

"No, why?" she replied frowning. I looked to Sophia, silently asking her if what I asked was beyond the realms of comprehension, when she just shrugged her shoulders, so I thought it best at this point to just let it go.

"Never mind, so what is this thing anyway?"

"You mean a Testis Circulo?" Pip repeated, now on her hands and knees poking at the ground as if testing it for something.

"It was known as a Testis Circulo, which is Latin for 'Witness Circle' but then after the..." she paused a second and looked at Pip whose lips were pouting as she waited for what she would say next. Sophia released a sigh and decided a safer way to go was to call it something else.

"...*The incident*, the Witness circles were used as portals to gain access into this world, so therefore my brother gave the order to have them all destroyed."

"So, they were all knocked down like this one?" I asked.

"No, no, this one probably just fell into disrepair not long after King James VII and William II were driven into exile. Which then prompted the Jacobite Risings and a string of armed attempts to restore the Catholic Stuart line..." Sophia said in a way that she thought was common knowledge and I really didn't want to tell her at this point that I had no clue what she was talking about. Even as a history buff, I wasn't that hot on all the dates and names of the Royals. Which is why my confusion doubled when Pip added a scoffed,

"Yeah and they tried for about fifty years, daft buggers."

"Anyway, I can see that I am losing here, so I will get to my point, what was destroyed in the Witness Circles was what powered them, not the buildings themselves."

"So, they were used as portals?" I asked again, making sure I had this right.

"Yes, their power and purpose were reversed, so to speak, and they were used for walking into their future, not seeing into their past as was intended." This was when I finally got it.

"So that's why we are here, for me to look into my past?" Sophia first looked to Pip to see her nod, before turning to me to do the same, now that she had Pip's master plan confirmed.

"Okay, so I feel like I have to ask here…why would that help me?"

"Because, my question asking loving friend, you said if only you could go back and find out how this all began, well, this is what we are doing here." Okay so she was right, I had said that this morning and now her earlier comment was starting to make sense. She wasn't planning on sending me back to the past literally, she was just making it so that I could play it back somehow…or at least I hoped this was what she meant.

Pip still looked busy, now strangely on her knees down in front of four cut out squares that were in the higher part of what remained of the small wall. There was also a tourist plaque in front of them, obviously explaining what the room was used for, but I was too far away to see. So, I took a step forward about to walk through the gap in the wall, when Sophia held me back.

"Not yet." I frowned in question, but this was as far as I got in actual asking. Instead I watched as Pip seemed to be trying to locate something and then when she stuck her hand in the third hole she shouted,

"Boo yeah! That's the sucker!"

"No way! Is it still in there?" Sophia asked seemingly excited herself.

"Too right it is, I knew that slimly little toad Belphegor had done a shit job," she said standing up and patting the dirt off her knees.

"Wait, where have I heard that name before?" I asked recognising it being said but it had been years ago.

"You know it because that asshole Sammael and he had been partners once," Sophia answered with a sneer. And this was when the memory hit me. It was shortly after my dream of Sammael in the bathroom and shortly after me and Draven first became an item. I had just finished drawing him and had showed the picture to Draven, which was when I first learned about Sammael's past. One that included the demon Belphegor being one of his partners in crime.

"Okay so this Belphegor, I get it, obviously a bad dude…" I stopped when Pip snorted a laugh.

"Yeah, he wishes."

"What do you mean?"

"Belphegor is a drunk and a demon lackey for hire and that's it. He's about as scary and as dangerous as a bumblebee on a daisy!" Sophia answered before Pip added,

"Yeah, unless you consider his farts as a weapon, although he did manage to clear out the pub that one time he shit himself and I don't care what he said, that was not follow through but just his lazy ass that couldn't be bothered to get up and use the drunken little demon room!" Pip finished by holding her nose like she could still smell it.

"Eww."

"Yep, eww is right. Well, anyway whichever dipshit put him in charge of anything other than wiping his own ass is beyond me, but I knew the second I saw him drag his baggy ass up here, that he would be useless!" Pip said with a face of disgust.

"Wait a minute, you did something, didn't you?" Sophia

asked and this time she didn't look angry about it but instead impressed.

"I might have," Pip replied looking sheepish.

"Oh come, spill... you filled a void, didn't you?" Sophia pressed, making me wonder what filling the void meant? Thankfully, I didn't have to wait long, making this one less question I wouldn't have been able to stop myself from asking.

"Okay, so yes, I made him believe he had done it, so his slobbering mouth could go back and say, 'Mission completed' and no one would be the wiser...hence my very own personal Witness Circle," Pip told us, holding out her hands as if presenting it proudly and my only reaction to all this was,

"I have to say, neither of you paint a pretty picture of this guy."

"Let's put it this way, think Quasimodo's older, uglier and definitely smellier cousin and you're about half way there to imagining how revolting this guy is." Well, after that I would say that Pip was painting a pretty good image in my head and she knew this when I wrinkled my nose as if I was now the one smelling rotting cheese.

"Right, now let's get this Kazzy Toot show in the Dovecot!" Pip said clapping her hands and jumping up onto the wall before leaping off it like a cheesy 80's Rockstar with an air guitar and landing next to me.

"Okay, but you're definitely sure about this...right?" I asked adding this last word, aiming it at Sophia as Pip started to lead me past her. I had to say her shrugged shoulders didn't give me the confidence booster I had been looking for.

"Yeah sure, why not...? Right, so I want you to kneel down and put your hand inside the third hole," Pip said, pointing down at it. So, I did as I was told, trusting that neither of them would let me do something stupid, like say, go back a couple of thousand years in the past after first leaping through a portal that usually killed people. A thought that naturally prompted me to ask,

"Uhh...are we sure about this?"

"Totally!"

"Not really" Both answered me and neither answer had me feeling good about this, not when the only positive answer had come from Pip, our crazy but equally loveable naughty Imp.

"Okay then," I stated in a strained tone, and just as I was about to reach inside, I ended up taking one look at the sign now in front of me. This ended in me shouting,

"You're kiddin me, this is where the birds were kept!"

"Well yeah, it's a Dovecot, what did you expect would be kept in there, spare dolphins?" I gave Pip a look that said it all before squatting further down with a groan.

"Okay, now reach inside until you feel a jagged piece of rock...do you feel it?" Pip asked after watching me for a few seconds.

"Yeah, I feel it, and there is a dipped smooth bit beneath it, is that it?"

"Bingoni!" she shouted, sounding like this was a new Italian version of the game.

"Right, so that smooth bit below is like a little cup that will drain down to drip onto what is called a Hell's Opal. When that happens, you need to be stood in the centre on the mark I drew in the dirt." I looked behind me to find a symbol I had never seen before drawn there, telling me that was what she had been up to earlier.

"What's a Hell's Opal?" I couldn't help but ask, making Sophia chuckle when Pip groaned,

"I swear I am going to swap Toots for Curious Cathy if she carries on asking questions."

"What do you expect, she is still a demon baby," Sophia told her with a shrug of her shoulders.

"Hey!" I complained, one they both ignored.

"It's a precious stone that was once mined in Hell and is formed from underground caverns that connects to the river of blood that surrounds Lucifer's Palace," Sophia told me and had me utterly fascinated, which meant I was just about to ask a ton more questions when Pip ordered,

"Now stick your hand in there and let's boogie." I gave her a wry look, but knew my mind was still stuck on river of blood and palace in Hell where Lucifer lived. Things like what did it look like and did he have a cleaning lady that came once a week? But then one look from Pip and I did as I was told, sticking my hand in there. Then I waited for a few seconds. It was only after nothing happened that I had no choice but to ask,

"Okay, so what do I do now?"

"Say three Hail Marys." Pip said.

"Really?"

"No, of course not! Now just think of a time you want to be shown and then cut your hand in the jagged piece of rock, so you can feed the stone your blood," Pip told me on a giggle, but the second she said the words, 'cut' and 'blood' she had lost me.

"You want me to do what?!"

"It's only a little prick, don't be a baby!" Sophia said on a laugh.

"Ha, that's not what she said when she was trying for that baby!" Pip joked making me growl but then burst out laughing as I had to give it to her, the joke was funny.

"Okay, I can do this!" I said psyching myself up and rolling my shoulders as if I was about to go ten rounds with someone.

"Yeah and while you're at it, can you *do it* a bit quicker, as time's a wasting Tootie not yet bleeding."

"Okay this is it, wish me luck!" I said giving them both one last glance to find Pip holding both her thumbs up at me, whilst Sophia mouthed a 'You will be fine' at me. I gave them both a nervous laugh in return and then closed my eyes, before dragging my palm across the stone and crying out as I felt it tear into my skin.

"Oww!" I said holding it there after Pip told me to and when she started pumping her fingers in and out to get the blood flowing, I did the same. Then when we all heard a grinding noise she shouted,

"NOW!"

I quickly got off my knees and went to stand where she had said, as I waited for whatever was supposed to happen. Then I heard the grinding of stone against stone getting louder and louder, making me look around to see if I could spot where it was coming from.

"What's happening?!" I shouted as now I had to yell over the sound as it was getting so loud. I expected to hear a response, but when I looked to the girls I noticed that now their figures had started to merge and blur with the rest of the world. As if they were now being viewed through a cloudy veil or some warped version of reality. Pretty soon you couldn't even make them out as being two people stood next to each other. As though someone had painted them and then whilst the paint was still wet, the artist had run an angry hand through the portrait.

But this was soon to be the least of my problems, as the second my nerves got the better of me I tried to move, quickly finding myself unable to do so. It was as if the earth beneath my feet had rooted itself to me. As if, now that the offer of blood had been made, I had unknowingly signed an unbreakable pact. One that wouldn't release me of my invisible chains until the deal was done and that first meant caging me in.

"What the Hell?" I asked myself when suddenly the stone wall around me started to grow, moving around in a corkscrew as if it was rebuilding itself. Its walls grew higher and higher as though it was taking back time.

It started to reach up storeys above me until it formed a dome at the top and only then, when each stone level had nowhere else to go, did it forge together. I now knew, after seeing the diagram on the tourist plaque, that I was looking at how it was back in the day when it was first built. That was minus the hole at the top, which had closed in forming a closed roof. But each of the walls were covered with rows and rows of square holes and the only thing missing were the birds to go in them and a doorway to get out.

But the second the grinding sound stopped then another quickly followed it and this time, it was one even more scary to face. Well, that was considering now I was faced with being stuck in an enclosed space, one that didn't look the best for ventilation…or should I say more importantly…*drainage.*

Because what I now heard was the sound of gushing water as if it was travelling up the walls behind a hidden cavity.

"Oh no…no, no, this is bad, this is very…" I was quickly cut off at the sight of water suddenly bursting out and start gushing from the holes all at once. And my reaction, well it was instinctive. I crouched low and covered my head, waiting for it to land all around me, hammering into my body as it did…

But it never came.

I don't know how long I waited, wincing and bracing for impact, one I thought would no doubt kill me by drowning. But like I said, there was nothing. I knew by now I should have felt something but not even a single drop of water had dripped on me, which in the end, forced my decision to look. So, with caution, I opened one eye a tiny crack and then found myself soon staring wide-eyed and in awe of what was above me.

"Impossible," I whispered in amazement. It was incredible and like looking into a pool of water in reverse. I was now

staring up at my reflection looking down at me through the water that was magically suspended above me. It was such a mind bender that when I stood up I wobbled, nearly falling over from feeling dizzy. Almost as though I was trying to walk after first standing and being twisted around on my head for an hour.

"I don't understand?" I told myself as my head started to tilt to one side and it was like looking into a mirror on the ceiling and finding someone in control of your other self. It felt so familiar that I tried to take a step back, but found like before I couldn't move from the symbol on the ground. I shook my head as if this would help rid me of the strange feeling, but nothing worked. It was stuck to me, hanging there like the sticky remains of a memory I couldn't shake off.

Which was when it hit me where it was coming from. Which memory it was that had me now too scared to move.

It was me and Katie.

All those tortured looks calling out to me in desperation. A life being shared by two souls sharing the same body. One was sacrificed and the other got to live, but which of us was the one trapped in the water now? Which one of us had this part to play, because right at this second as I stared back at myself, it didn't feel like me.

And just like that time, I had no power over what my reflection did as she started to beckon me closer. But something in her eyes told me this wasn't right. That I wasn't to trust in my own image and the blood I had shared was creating this new fear for me now. Which was why I wanted to pull away and recoil from her, but something had me trapped, as if I just couldn't stop myself. Half of me wanted to escape the spell and the other half that was a part of me just couldn't let go.

That was also the part of me that was reaching up.

'Closer'

I could see myself mouthing the luring word down back at

myself and the second I started to pull my hand away, the water would ripple as if something beneath it was being disturbed. As if I was trying to break the connection and that wasn't right. I tried to remember why I was here in the first place and what I was on a mission to find. I knew this was my only chance at this and what if what I saw ended up being the key to all of this. What if this offer of my blood was my only shot at saving the man I loved from being ripped in two?

So, with that in mind I decided to do something stupid, hoping that eventually it would lead me to somewhere knowledge was the key. A knowledge that would lead the way for yet another journey I must take.

So, I reached back up as if ready to touch it when the image above me started to become clear again, after the ripples had calmed. And the second it did I screamed.

"AHHH!" I cried out in horror, because there I was, my face now so close to the surface it was haunting. It looked like me, but I had changed…I was now also the *face of death*. One floating in the water, as if caught there demanding to be let out of its eternal cage and mimicking me as she too was silently screaming back at me. And in that silent scream I saw myself suddenly back to that day. A day when a bloody shard of broken mirror showed me another reflection…

One of death.

This was enough to jolt me into action. I was just about to yank my hand away when suddenly her own hand burst through the water and grabbed me. I cried out and tried to fight it, but I knew the second my feet came off the ground that it was useless.

I was being dragged up into the water and the second I was pulled through, my very last thought had been a chilling one,

Why were my arms slashed and bloody just like they had been that day…The day I felt like I died for the first time?

Which was when it hit me. Pip had told me to think of a past I wanted it to show me.

And a past I did think about, *just the wrong one.*
One that was ruled by the name…

Morgan.

CHAPTER THIRTEEN

FOLLOW THE WHITE RABBIT

The second I was pulled through the water I fell forward, gasping for breath. But my reaction was caused from being dragged through the water, because the second I made it through there was none. No, instead it was simply a black void surrounding me, with only a single light shining down at me from above, one I couldn't see the cause of.

"Hello?" I called out on a breathy whisper. A tone of voice that sounded almost too afraid to find out whether it worked or not. Which was why I jumped slightly when hearing it echoing around me. The sound travelled on and on as if I was now in an endless hallway and my voice was running through the space trying to escape.

But then another sound started to fill the void and the second it did both my echo and my heart instantly froze. It was the tinkling sound of a music box playing, a song that would have me waking from my nightmares screaming, with that haunting sound still plaguing my mind. A sound that should have been so innocent as it played for the small dancing ballerina, one frozen in time. I remembered reaching out and touching her little torn skirt, thinking at the time she looked as broken as I did.

Which was when I saw it.

The light had now shifted from me, casting me back to the shadows as I was forced to watch what was to be the last of my old life as it faded away. Before watching as the blood drained from my body and, unbeknown at the time, eventually breathing new life into my veins.

It was the first day I died. But it was also the day,

I was reborn.

So, I was left with no other option as I watched my biggest nightmare play out in front of me. I dropped to my knees as my anguish hit me like being punched in the gut.

"Time to go...time to end this." I saw my old image whisper down at the box I now had cradled in my hands, knowing my time was near. It was to be my saviour one way or another. I knew this as she did. I remembered everything, even after years of trying to forget. I remembered the damp smell of the walls, and the feel of the hard concrete beneath my bruised knees. I even remembered the way my broken nail caught in my matted hair as I pushed the dirty strands behind my ear. He said that he would let me wash it one day, but he never did. He only ever lied...*he always lied.*

I watched as my other self hung her head in acceptance, knowing the time was ticking down fast and all hope was resting on my ability to go through with this. To potentially end a life that I so desperately wanted to live. I had spent the whole day and all the days after finding the box, asking myself if there was another way. But every way led to this.

At first, I thought about attacking him, hiding in the shadows and pouncing on him the second I got chance. Maybe waiting behind the stairs and reaching through the gaps to slit his ankles so he couldn't walk. So that he couldn't chase me down when I ran. Or there was even the idea that I pretended to be asleep and, when he reached over me, plunging the deadly shard into his carotid artery, making him bleed out from the neck.

But out of the million gruesome scenarios I had come up with in my mind in the hours leading up to this depressing scene of me on the floor, one question plagued me, and it was always,

'What if I missed?' This question was spoken through almost silent lips from the girl of my past. She had turned her head to look at me to whisper this over her shoulder. This was said as if the real vision of the past had been put on pause, so a version of reality could be lived for a short time. Just long enough to grant me this message.

Then it snapped back into place as she raised the box to her lips and kissed the doll, like I had that day. For she was my saviour as she represented a hope that could swing either way.

Then the second her lips left the tiny plastic figure, she stood up with it still in her hands and then threw it violently to the floor on a broken desperate sob. The box lid broke on one side thanks to a snapped hinge and my eyes flew to the wide array of broken glass splintered and scattered on the floor like crystals. Now only hoping there was one that was big enough left to do the job.

Then I spotted it and my knees collapsed, folding beneath me and I fell to the floor in slow motion. Then, with shaky hands, the other me reached out to the box lid and pulled the largest piece from the wooden frame. I remembered the waiting that followed and the way my heart hammered in my chest as it seemed like only moments before I heard him opening the front door. I flinched the second I heard his footsteps above us, noticing my other self doing the same thing.

"He's coming, do it! Do it now!" I hissed at myself, fearing, like I always did, that I would fail. That I would wake up and realise it had all been a dream. That the life I had lived on from this point was all a lie, one fabricated just to survive the days with this man. I would wake and look down at my hands shaking to see the fresh bruises marred around my wrists. The new marks, scars and signs of age and time that I was still locked in this Hell on Earth he had built for me.

So, I would scream in panic! I would cry out in my dreams for her to do it and do it quickly. Forget about granting your love to those that thought you dead. Just cut yourself,

"JUST DIE!" I screamed and finally it was in that moment that she cut through her wrists, over and over again. The largest slash being when she did it too deep, nicking an artery. Blood seemed to spray out and seconds later I slumped further over myself as blood pooled around my body, framing what would soon be known as my crimson triumph.

For I had won.

And I did it all to the haunting sound of the Nutcracker's Sugarplum Fairy, with my eyes only focusing on one thing to get me through.

A blood stained little ballerina, dancing her way through my demise. Next came the bit that always terrified me, that shadow standing at the top of the stairs filling the space, a silhouette I always saw as the Devil himself. Well, now I knew better, for in the end he was just a man. A sick and twisted dark soul that had lost its way from the light long ago. Back when he stood there and watched as his sister and her lover burned to their ashes. Back when he had been the first flame behind the inferno. And in the end, his body's resting place had become that of a rotting corpse at the bottom of a ravine, now reduced to nothing but bone long ago.

I knew all this. I knew his future and the pain he suffered at the hands of my dark knight's version of revenge. But none of this was enough. Not in this moment and the vision that played out in front of me, like a horror movie permanently on repeat. Because there he was, making his way down the stairs to me and doing so with haste, as though he cared. His version of love always made me feel sick. That panicked look as if he was about to lose someone he cared about, it made me want to spit at his feet and curse him for all eternity.

And then it came.

That accusing shout of pain,

"NO! Catherine, what have you done!?" He grabbed me and held me to him, holding his hands over the damage as if he could stop the blood from pumping out of me. I shuddered in his hold, a revulsion he mistook for being cold. Oh, I had been cold alright, my heart frozen and my soul on the edge of leaving me. I wouldn't have blamed it if it had. Just look at what I had done to us.

I tore my face away from the sight, utterly disgusted to be forced to lay witness to it all again. But then I noticed something over in the corner. It was something white and glowing, but I couldn't quite make out what it was. I squinted my eyes, ignoring the sound of my weak voice telling Morgan 'the demon made me do it'. No, instead I focused on the vision of white coming closer towards me, past what was my hovel of a living space. Dirty sheets thrown over a blow-up bed, one closer to the concrete than not. Then I could see what it was, and I gasped in shock as I saw a white rabbit hop closer, knocking over a plastic bowl and spoon as it did.

I couldn't understand what a cute, fluffy white rabbit could be doing down here, but the sight of something so innocent and pure looking made for an alarming contrast to the horrific sight in front of me. I watched as it continued to hop over towards the victim and her tormentor, being so close now it stepped in the blood, seemingly oblivious. Then it looked straight to me and I couldn't believe it when I saw a pair of startling green eyes, ones I felt I knew, staring back at me. I could even see tears in them, as if what they also had been forced to witness was just as painful to them as it was for me.

Then the rabbit shook its head making its floppy ears flick around its head before its nose twitched and it turned around to hop away. I frowned, taking a step forward, but then stopping the second I saw Morgan was still there with the other version of me and my fear wouldn't let me get any closer.

But this was when my hesitation must have triggered something, because my other self let her head roll back over Morgan's arm, one he had around her, so now she was looking back at me. Then her mouth started moving as if she was chanting something, that only seconds after she started, did it reach my ears like a haunting echo,

"Follow…follow, follow…the, the… the, the…white…white, white… rabbit, rabbit…rabbit, rabbit…" Then her head snapped back as if she had been forced to continue to play out her part and with everything in me I wished I could have helped her, where no other person had. How many hours wasted had I spent wishing that someone would come? That just one person heard my cries for help, the screams that continued until my throat was raw and no voice followed my mind's order to carry on. I hadn't wanted to give up hope, but as much as they say time's a healer, it can also feed the root of doubt giving it time to grow. Until soon you find yourself surrounded by its darkness, blotting out the sun, so that you can never see a way out.

But the rabbit, it was showing me the way. It had found me

in the wrong place and was trying to pull me out, as if it was trying to help me. I could feel it deep down, like a warmth my body needed to kick start me into action. For me to face my fears and say goodbye to this horrible place once and for all. To finally close the door on my past forever.

So, as it hopped its way up the stairs, I took a deep breath and did what everything in my body was telling me to do.

I followed the white rabbit.

It disappeared through the door and for one horrifying moment I reached for the handle and expected it not to turn, just like the hundreds of times I had tried before, all in the hope that he had forgotten to lock it properly just once. But the second I turned the knob I pushed my way through in almost a panicked way, as though he was right behind me, chasing me. I stepped through and as I did my foot seemed not to land as it should, taking far too long to do so. It was almost as if I had been stepping into this new space horizontal, only to have the world tipping around me until becoming upright again.

So, as soon as my foot had travelled the 180-degree angle, I felt the world beneath my feet once more and the second I did, a door behind me slammed shut. It took me a moment to realise where I was and the second I did, I wanted to scream in frustration. So yeah, I had skipped forward but I was nowhere near where I wanted to be in time.

I mean, I barely even remembered the shift I worked at the club as nothing really happened. It was during that point when Draven had told me he was engaged to that traitorous bitch Celina. Who, neither of us hadn't known at the time, had been stalking me and my visions of demons for years, ever since I was a child.

Of course, this had all been part of the master plan, that took years of planning and one that also included her sister Aurora. But not even Draven had known until the very last moment.

This being an unusual realisation in his world, as normally he was top of the list when it came to otherworldly knowledge.

But this vision right now would tell me nothing, I knew that. Not unless there was some hidden secret and deeper meaning to the way I was restocking the bottle fridges behind the bar. Because right now that's what I was doing. I was knelt down with the doors open and reaching for bottles out of the crate next to me to place behind the ones already chilled.

From what I could remember it had been a night like any other. Quite busy, hence the need to stock up early before my shift ended. Of course, I would still look up to the VIP every now and again, thinking back on the time I was somewhat special to have been allowed up there in the first place. A time before I had been relegated back down here, all because of my unspoken and unrequited love for a man I believed at the time to be indifferent.

But how wrong I was and as I looked at myself now, I almost wanted to reach out to her. To place my hand on her shoulder, tell her it would be alright and then whisper encouraging words about what her future would hold. One that wouldn't be long in coming. In fact, before I knew what I was doing, I was reaching out towards her but the second before I made contact, I saw something in the reflection of the glass behind the shelves above.

"The white rabbit," I whispered then turned and at the same time the other me did, only her direction, like many times before it, went straight to the VIP. I saw what she was seeing. A shadow of a man standing by the balcony's edge looking down at us. Now I knew it was Draven, but back then, it was almost as though I would convince myself that it wasn't. Because the question I always asked myself was…

Why would it be?

I turned away from my former self and decided to follow

the white rabbit again, as it obviously had something to show me. I even wondered why here but then again, my only thought when walking through that basement door had been, 'take me somewhere safe'. When really, I needed to start thinking about the right time I wanted it to show me. Or I was going to be here a long time, if it just kept showing me random parts of my life every time I walked through a door.

I walked from around the bar and across the now half empty dance floor. The band was wrapping it up for the night and the rabbit was making short work of the space between me and the grand double staircase. I remembered how imposing the place was back then, when I first entered Afterlife. It wasn't just the grand way it looked or the Gothic architecture. But it was the feel of the place. As if there had been something in the air that drugged you into never wanting to leave. Now I knew it was no doubt the fact there had been a room full of Demons and Angels upstairs feeding off the emotions of everyone below. As that must have given off some funky vibes and auras throughout the place.

But for me, it had only been one reason and speaking of reasons, I watched as the rabbit started hopping up the stairs, making me weave in and out of the few groups, just to catch up. Pretty soon I made it to the top and then faltered a step as the man himself came into view.

A Draven of the past who didn't yet belong to me, and more importantly, who in this time was…

My boss.

CHAPTER FOURTEEN

HOGTIED PATIENCE

There he was, now stood looking down at the club, like a master keeping watch upon all that he owned. And the very sight of him took my breath away. He was magnificent. It was funny seeing him like this, looking so hard and unyielding, making me realise just how different he was now. How the years had changed him, making him looked less forbidding and more, well more human.

I paused as his sister approached and I looked down the second I felt something nudge at my leg. The rabbit, that was quite small for one with such big ears, was looking up at me with those piercing green eyes.

"I want to watch," I told it, not knowing if it understood, but feeling the need to explain why I was no longer following it. It wrinkled its nose once before looking back at the scene, as if resigned to my decision and therefore was going to watch it with me.

"I really don't know why you continue to torture yourself like this and her for that matter?" Sophia said nodding down to me as I had gone back to my duty, no doubt getting lost in my thoughts as usual.

"You know why," Draven's stern voice replied, saying more than his words did and that was his displeasure at no doubt having to explain himself again.

"No, I don't. The girl all but declared her love for you and I will never understand why, instead of embracing it like you want to, you chose to break it," Sophia asked which I had to say, she made a bloody good point. Draven closed his eyes for a moment and I wondered if it was done in aid of trying to find patience when dealing with his sister or because he was remembering the pain he'd inflicted upon me.

"It was better her feelings be hurt than her body, and I refuse to allow something like that to ever happen again!" Draven snapped, gripping onto the railing and becoming close to breaking it.

"You can't wrap her in a box or put her in a pretty cage Dom, she has been living with the dangers of the world for twenty three years and has made it this far."

"Yes, and look what the world offered her, and you think ours can do better!" he snapped on a growl before taking a deep calming breath before continuing on,

"Look at what nearly happened to her Sophia, at the hands of one of our own. Do not think me fool enough to think that because she survived her own world as long as she has, that she would fare better in ours," he replied letting anger coat his words. At this I couldn't help but laugh considering all I *had* survived in his world. Hell, I hadn't just survived it, I had conquered it! I had battled against everything put in his way and mine and I had beaten it back one way or another.

I had won.

But he didn't yet know this.

Okay, so I am not saying I hadn't made mistakes along the

way, as I was far from perfect, just like most people. I was still, in essence, human and that saying was created for a reason. Being the Chosen One didn't mean everything I did worked, or the decisions I made were always the right ones. I was judged and as guilty as the next person for doing stupid shit but the one thing that remained. The one thing I could say was etched in stone and was at the root of my soul. I could always say with utter honesty, that every decision I made, it was made for love.

It was a line I walked doing so believing, at the time, that it was the right one. For that was all any of us could do. It may not always have worked out like you intended it to, but even now, like Draven's decision to hurt me and put distance between us, he did so out of fear of losing me. He did so out of love.

Was it the right thing to do? No, it wasn't. But at the time he did so with nothing but good intent. Just like he did that day when he walked away from me for what he thought was for good. He believed it was the only way to save my life and in essence I was now doing the same again. I was keeping all of this from him and it was done with the belief that if he knew, then he would just end up doing the same thing again.

Because deep down, trying to find perfection in the choices you made, were only ever going to depend on the outcome you wanted. If everything we did turned out right then, yes maybe then to some degree we could be called perfect, but the chances of that happening were slim at best. But I knew, without a single doubt to cloud my mind or my heart, that I could honestly say our reasons for doing the things we did were, well…

They were perfect.

Because what better reasons were there than love. To sacrifice what you want most in the world so that the one you loved could remain in it.

That was what Draven was doing right now and by me being here, without Draven knowing, was what I was also doing. Was it the right thing to do? Well, only time would be able to answer that question.

I could only hope that the outcome…well, that it was one of the rare perfect ones. The ones we all hoped for.

"I think you underestimate her. Yes, she experienced a traumatic ordeal at the hands of what was clearly an unsound mind." She paused when Draven growled,

"Yes, and soon to be a dead one!"

"That maybe so Brother, as is your right, but my point is that she survived," she said, making Draven look from her back down to me and he did so also placing a hand to his forearm as if knowing already about my scars and imagining them there for himself.

"We don't yet know all the details of how, but the important thing is that she *did survive* and now here she is, after all this time you have waited for her…look at her Dom, tell me honestly, why do you not just take her?" Sophia asked in a pleading tone, as if she had been asking this very same thing the entire time I had been in Evergreen Falls but had yet to receive her answer. Or one good enough anyway.

Draven released a heavy sigh, leaning against the railing and continuing to stare down at me.

"Because I love her," he said after a moment's pause and doing so after releasing another deep breath.

"But…" Sophia started to argue but he raised his fingers from the rail, to tell her silently that he hadn't finished.

"She is…she is perfect…a perfection I never knew could exist for me," he said watching me as I stood up now my job was complete, and he did so having to take a breath after only starting the sentence. I was turning around to smile at Mike for some reason I couldn't remember, but Draven seemed captivated.

"I never imagined this was what it would be like and I haven't even really spoken to her yet, not as anyone but who she sees as her boss."

"Yes, and whose fault is that?" Sophia snapped back making him frown side on at her.

"You think I don't know that this has all been my doing? That I haven't been the one to push her away?"

"Oh, I know but still I am yet to fully understand it."

"Because of who I am, Sophia!" he said unleashing his anger with his demonic voice coming through. I was so shocked my hands flew to my mouth to cover the gasp that escaped.

"What happened the first time I got even a glimpse of hope at being with her, where I could be myself for the first time. Then she saw me for who I really am, and she ran Sophia, she ran because I terrified her!" Draven said, angry this time at himself as he tore himself away from the sight of me, as if he was ashamed.

"I wouldn't be too sure about that," Sophia said after laughing. Draven shot a harsh frown her way making her explain.

"Gods Brother, you can be so blind for one so old and knowledgeable."

"Not helping me here, Sophia," Draven warned making her chuckle and me also as I knew being called old was a sore spot for him, even before I came along.

"What I mean is, she, didn't just run from you, she ran from the situation, Dom. Think about it, she woke feeling vulnerable and scared, all alone after being stabbed by that bitch, who might have shown Keira her true self. We just don't know," Sophia said, and Draven crossed his arms looking thoughtful and now listening to her words, ones that made sense.

"But what we do know is that minutes later she saw you with a pair of wings and Hell's power running through your veins and ran from what she didn't yet know." Hearing this you could see that it had clearly affected him as he turned his face away. Sophia shook her head a little as if close to giving up, but then a thought must have come to her for the next moment she chuckled and said,

"Besides, she could not have been that scared of you." At this his face shot back to hers in question, but then, as if first needing to deny any possibility of it being other than what he thought it was, he warned,

"You didn't see her face, Sophia."

"No, I didn't, but I did see it the day you crushed her heart, one I will remind you was declared the day after seeing you this way and her doing so believing everything that had happened that night to be real...so tell me, just how scared did she look when she was calling you out and demanding you tell her the truth, a demon no less, for one she thought was real...?" Sophia paused to take a step closer to him, so she could look him in the eyes when she carried on with her questioning.

"...Was she repelled, disgusted, or was she there to know the truth and in doing so hoped the kiss you gave her was real too? That the feelings she felt you bestow that night, were not ones of fantasy this time, but founded on truth and thus could be ones returned?" On hearing this he turned away from her but this time I knew, as well as she did, that it was done because she had just hit a nerve.

"I do not know what goes through her mind Sophia, which is half my problem," he said in his defence making her laugh.

"Oh, you mean for once you would have to work on your charm and woo her just like any other man who has lost his heart to a girl?" Sophia said chuckling again and in doing so annoying her brother further. Which, by all accounts, was one of her favourite pastimes. But I knew that wasn't why she did it this time. No, because if there was one thing Sophia has always strived to do and that was to see both her brothers find happiness, as she had found.

"I am glad you find this so amusing!" he snapped making her laugh again, only this time it wasn't a mocking sound.

"Believe it or not Dom, I am trying to help you."

"I think you have interfered enough, Sophia," Draven said, running a frustrated hand through his hair.

"I disagree, for if it wasn't for me then you would still be watching her from afar and she would be collecting her pension by the time you declared it safe enough." Draven let out a groan telling her she was being ridiculous now.

"I think you give far too much credit to my patience and one where there is little left," he responded, making me smile.

"Then what are you waiting for? Dom, come on, she is right there in front of you, all you would need to do is speak to her and she would be yours," Sophia argued, and I blushed knowing that they knew it would have been that easy. I watched as Draven's fists clenched by his sides as if he was holding himself back from doing just that. He followed my movements as my shift had come to an end and his moments to do as Sophia suggested were dwindling down by the second.

"He's not going to do it," I said in a sad tone before looking down at my new friend, who I found looking back up at me. It cocked its head to the side and as if it just understood me it started to comfort me by nuzzling against my leg.

"And what would I say, Sophia?"

"Oh, I don't know, maybe do something normal for once and ask her out on a date, maybe to join you for a drink. Hell's harpies, Dom, it's not like I am suggesting you propose marriage to the girl. Just for you to give her the chance to see you as someone other than her boss, one she is clearly intimidated by," Sophia argued trying to push him into action. For a second, he looked as if he was even thinking about it but just like Draven, he chose what he believed was my safety above what he wanted.

"No, not until the time is right," he said, watching as I slipped on my jacket and hooked my bag across my torso, so it hung at my side. Then I bit my lip as I took in his purple gaze burning bright as he saw me say goodbye to the others, before turning to steel as I stole one last gaze to the VIP. Just before my eyes could focus, he took a step back hiding himself from view, making Sophia release a heavy sigh, shaking her head in disappointment.

"Still think she isn't longing to be here?" Sophia said driving her point home at the sight of my actions.

"She isn't ready…and neither am I!" he snapped the second I was out of the main doors of Afterlife. Then he stormed past her and the vision of me that was witnessing all of this, until he disappeared out of the balcony, no doubt so that he could see me safely to my truck.

"I take it by your pout and his scowl that you found no joy in your meddling yet again?" I spun around the second I heard Vincent's velvety voice. There he was in all his handsome glory, looking casual but smart in an open white shirt, with a faded grey motorcycle t-shirt underneath. I could only just make out the design being the outline of a white sports bike with the name Ducati across it. His shirt sleeves were rolled up his forearms displaying strong corded, pale muscles and a leather band strapped around one wrist. To this delicious top half, he added faded stonewash jeans, a dark brown belt and biker boots peeking out from under the frayed length of denim by his feet. He looked as though he belonged on the front cover of a magazine, gracing the world with his beautiful handsome image.

"I just don't understand him," she complained making Vincent sigh before resting a hand on her shoulder in comfort.

"Sophia." He said her name as if she was missing something major.

"What?" she said turning her back now from the balcony door Draven had gone through.

"Isn't it obvious?"

"Obviously not," she snapped, making him laugh and shake his head at her.

"You may not understand him, but you must remember that he also doesn't understand himself."

"Get to the point Brother, before your halo needs changing it's so old," she said cocking a hip out. He smirked and flicked her nose before telling her.

"He has never felt this way. He is having emotions that are out of his control and he is faced with a woman he wants almost as much as he wants to keep her from harm. He is not like us." She frowned as she thought about it for a moment, focusing on what he had said last.

"You mean his Angel and Demon sides?"

"Yes, for can you not see it?" he replied, making her look back over her shoulder as if she could see Draven through the glass.

"In all the time we have been on this earth, when have you ever seen him battle against his nature like this? When have you ever seen his Angel side at war with his Demon?" Vincent said shocking me to the core. Was it possible that this was what I needed to witness or just a stepping stone to a greater understanding?

"You think his Demon wants him to take her, but his Angel is fighting against it?" she asked.

"For fear of her getting hurt like not long ago, yes, I believe this is why he has retreated further from her. You know what

Dom is like, he is the epitome of control and having Keira in his life, now strips him of that, for you can never control what you love…it doesn't work that way."

"And our dear brother is learning this the hard way," Vincent added when he saw his brother storm through the doors in what looked like a foul mood, without giving them both so much as a glance.

"How did you get so smart, eh?" she teased elbowing him in the ribs before turning around to face him again. He shrugged his shoulders and grinned.

"Well, my dear sister and little package of demonic mischief, I like to think I excel in an area neither of my siblings do."

"Oh yeah and what's that, how to hogtie a female in under ten seconds, because I wouldn't really consider that a skill when wooing a girl?" He gave her a cheeky grin in response before saying,

"You would be surprised but no, I was speaking of patience."

"Oh, I think he is exercising that in bucket loads, that's kind of the problem here, Vince," she replied sarcastically.

"I mean patience when dealing with the human girl and when speaking with her, not choosing when to strike in taking her against her will, something I know for a fact won't be long in coming." Sophia's eyes lit up and she couldn't help but ask,

"Oh, you know that for a fact do you?" Vincent smirked down at her and then leant in to whisper,

"Yes, for I know what just arrived and awaits him on his desk."

"And that would be?" she enquired in that, 'tell me now or I will use my nails and teeth' type of tone. Even I held my breath as he first looked around to see if anyone was in earshot and when he deemed it safe enough, he leaned further into her and said the words that sent chills through my core and left me unable to breathe…

"Keira's case file." So once again I found myself collapsing to my knees as a hopelessness washed over me. The rabbit jumped back in surprise, but the second it saw me lower my head in defeat it hopped back over to me and forced itself under my hands held in my lap so I was now holding it. The second it did this I started to feel better, but nothing was strong enough to get the bitter taste of bile out of my mouth.

This I knew was, at the time, a huge sore spot for me. I remembered the first time and how it felt hearing that Draven had read the file, as it was one of the most devastating things to have happened. I hated that he ever saw me that way or seeing pictures of the crime scene, knowing where he had kept me. Even seeing that room Morgan had upstairs dedicated to me and my image. It was utterly sickening.

"Now that does change things…indeed," Sophia said sounding almost gleeful.

"So, there you have it, the single thread of patience for you to snap easily and the one you were waiting for," Vincent told her what she already knew.

"And for Dom…" she started to muse, but Vincent finished it off for her.

"The excuse he was also looking for. Taking the girl and making her his forever, as now he will easily believe the girl's safety is one best served by his side," Vincent said with a smirk as he too looked happy about this. But then again, I couldn't imagine it had been an easy time for either of them to watch as their brother went through such a hard time.

"And it is," she agreed meaning that Vincent did also, when he said,

"Undoubtedly."

"Right, now go… go and convince him of such, for you

know me, if I do it, I will only end up pissing him off further, but you he will at least listen to," Sophia said pushing him in that direction, making him laugh. He did as she said and started to walk towards the imposing entrance to their home when he called back over his shoulder,

"Oh, and Sophia…"

"Yes, my dear brother of mine?" she replied sweetly now she was happy and he had been the cause. He granted her a bad boy smirk, then said,

"They never complain." Then he laughed at her revolted expression at his reference to the comment made about hog tying girls. This made me blush as though my cheeks were on fire and could have cooked eggs, even though no one could see me there. Sophia first pulled a face of disgust and then smiled as she thought of a comeback.

"No, that's because you punish them if they do, that or they usually have a gag in their mouth… so that doesn't count!" Sophia shouted back on a laugh, making Vincent chuckle as he walked away, now in search of his pissed off brother.

That just left Sophia standing there shaking her head in amusement for a second at Vincent. But then you could see the cogs start to turn as to what this new information could mean. Then me and my new furry friend both watched as she walked over to the railings where her brother had not long ago vacated. She then looked out to the club and said,

"Soon my dear sister…*soon.*" This was said just as the lights below switched off one by one, before she turned around and left the VIP the way Vincent had. Thus, now leaving me with tears streaming down my cheeks and utterly astounded at the level of love that girl had for me, even back then. How much I owed to her from the very beginning just blew me away.

I looked down at my green-eyed friend who was wrinkling its little button nose as if it too had been affected by the touching scene. Then it took a sigh before hopping off my lap and making its way towards the balcony. I wondered where it was going now so decided to get up and follow it, hoping it would lead me to another insight like this one. I couldn't describe what it felt like just seeing what Draven had gone through in that tender fragile beginning.

I think, because I only ever knew of the heartache and obsessing I had gone through myself, it was difficult to imagine Draven going through the same. So, now having the gift of seeing it for myself…well, then it felt as if I had just found some secret treasure, one that without the witness circle would have been guarded for the rest of eternity.

I couldn't help but glance once more at the door Draven had walked through. Now wondering what would happen if I followed through with what I wanted to do and walked through that door instead. Would I find him there, hunched over his desk with my nightmare past spread out in front of him? To find him looking shocked at all the details and now having a face to loath and direct all your hatred on.

Well, in the end this was definitely one thought that had me following the rabbit instead of giving into my curiosity.

So, I held my breath and the second the doors whooshed open, I stepped through wondering where, on this strange journey of discovery, it would take me next.

Problem was, I soon found out where…

And it was Hell.

CHAPTER FIFTEEN

HOLDING ONTO HELL

The second I saw what greeted me I automatically turned around and tried bolting my terrified ass back through the door. But the second I turned, taking my first step, I was faced with a vast burnt wasteland of a Hellish desert. My foot hitting nothing but the dry crust that covered the land with an audible crunch. I tried to think back to what this memory was, as it was there but almost as if tainted by something.

I couldn't understand it. I wanted to, knowing it was important but I just couldn't seem to access it properly. As if someone was blocking it or had erased part of it from my memory and what they had left behind was the crumbs of a time stolen from me. I knew this was it, as unfortunately it was a feeling I was all too familiar with, since my time at the colony.

I ended up asking myself was it because I died and came back as a demonic god thanks to the blood in the glass dagger? I knew what happened that night, even though it felt less like me that was living it and more like someone who had just been along for the wild, demon ass kicking ride. But my point was that no matter how much of an out of body experience it had been, I had still been left with the memories. Which was why, when I looked around, I knew this place had been where the last of the Hellish war had been won.

This was the aftermath left from what I had done. I knew that, the second I looked down at the colossal sized crater caused from when I had the power to see Mount Tartarus crumble into an oblivion. A place even lower than what was once thought as the lowest level of Hell. And I did so dragging the Titans down with it, thus putting an end to Cronus and his apocalypse.

Then I had met Lucifer, yes this I remembered. So, I turned around and it all started to play out in front of me as if some unknown action had started to play the past. I heard an echoing crash behind me and looked as the cracked ground crumbled further into dust and rose up forming images from my memory. So, where there had once been a wasteland of death, now the space was flooded with sand demons playing out the last moments of the battle. And they did this just as the mountain was falling into an abyss in the background, taking the emerging Titans with it.

"NOOO! WHAT HAVE YOU DONE!" Cronus roared at the sight of his defeat and watched as his fallen brothers destroyed the last of his hope for victory.

"I did what you refused to do. I gave them peace and a taste of humanity…oh and I finally buried that bitch Aurora in there with them!" The vision of my warrior self said in response to his grief. We were currently the only part of the vision that looked as it had that day, not needing Hell's crusted earth to aid in re-enacting ourselves. As it was only the battle around us that looked like sand ghosts had been forced to relive through both their end and their victory.

So, then came the time directly after the war had just been won. I looked down to see where my rabbit was in all this only to gasp at the sight. Because now, instead of the cute furry little creature I had been used to, now all I was left with was a Hellish version instead.

Its fur was now missing and in places patches of his skin. One full side of its skull was bone on show and its teeth took up half its face, interlocking like on a crocodile.

Those once sweet green eyes were now blood red and bulging against the skeletal sockets that barely kept them in place. I jumped back in fright and the second I did, I don't know how I knew, but it began to look hurt. So, I decided it hadn't hurt me so why should I be afraid now. After all, I had seen far worse than a bunny that looked more like a zombie version of its former self. Okay so yes, it had those teeth, that by any wild beast's standard, certainly looked more than capable of biting my hand off. But why would it want to at this point?

So, instead of recoiling again, I simply crouched low and held my hand out to it, knowing the second I did I had made the right decision as it rubbed its bare and rough-skinned head under my hand (the side that had skin that was).

Now, once it seemed happy again, he motioned with a look back towards my other self and Cronus. So, I looked up to see for myself as Lucifer approach just as he did that day. I smiled to myself as the handsome pirate strode forward, that impossibly tall frame eating up the space between him and my other self. I nodded my head in his presence knowing instantly who he was without needing to be told.

I continued to watch as the scene unfolded. This had been when Cronus first had his neck snapped before being brought back only so that the Devil could have fun with him again later. I shuddered at the sight of when he had his minions drag

Cronus' body away. I swallowed down the bile I could taste again, at the thought of the King and ruler of Hell's idea of fun, one I didn't think was going to be a night in with Netflix, a bowl of popcorn and nice girl to enjoy both with.

But then, this was when things started to get tricky as one second, he was running a finger down my chin after enquiring,

"So, you're the one my son gifted my blood to?"

Then the vision changed from what I remembered and instead of it playing out the way it had been in my memories, the scene started to freeze. I frowned, stepping a little closer, maybe now only about three metres away from my other self.

"Why has it…" I never got to finish that sentence as one look at my face and his fingertip that was still lingering on the end of my chin was when everything changed. Suddenly a black decay started to spread on my skin from around his touch as if he had done so with the power of Hell being forced into my body, infecting it.

I didn't know what was happening but whatever it was, it started to spread out, travelling not only along my body but now also his. It was like a fire was being ignited beneath our flesh, burning us from the inside out, and turning our skin to ash. It started to turn us both to darker shades of greys and blacks, like flaky charcoal. Then suddenly, just as it got darker still, his image burst as if it had been made from dust held together to form of a man with nothing but a glass shell. It exploded outwards the second a figure of a man emerged, walking straight through it.

It had detonated into a black mist of particles that seemed suspended in the air, moving so slow, it was as if our bodies were stuck in another time frame. Then the moving figure, still shadowed by the black cloud, did the same with my other self's body as it had with Lucifer's. A smaller ash bomb burst this time as the man destroyed the last of the memory before I could even really make sense of it.

Then as the figure stepped from the floating dust I only needed to wait a second longer before I could see who it was, making me gasp at the sight.

"Lucifer." I uttered in disbelief as it couldn't be possible. He started shaking a finger at me, making a deep tutting noise as he did as if I had been caught doing something utterly forbidden. I tried to take a step back but suddenly found myself on the edge of the canyon where I hadn't been before. Therefore, I had nowhere to go and nowhere to run. I didn't understand what was happening as this was only ever supposed to be a memory…wasn't it?

Well, now facing the Being that was said to be the most powerful in this realm than any other, I had to say that doubt had quickly turned into a certainty that what faced me now was as real as they came. And one thing was clear, he was not happy.

He stormed towards me only stopping when his massive bare chest was only an inch from mine. This time he was dressed in a long black jacket, torn jeans, with a spiked belt and biker boots, looking more this time like a Gothic rocker. His face, however, was all serial killer. A face of hard lines and features set in stone. Red fire in his eyes that you could feel the burn created when he looked at you, as though he was leaving a brand on your skin just from glancing your way.

This was when I felt the pain scorching my skin on the back of my neck, like my birthmark was burning through my flesh. Almost as if something beneath it was trying to get out and reach the surface. I felt as if it was somehow responding to being down here and now, in front of Hell's master, it wanted to show itself and its hidden power. I don't know where this thought had come from, but it lingered there in my mind like black oil on clear water.

"Oww," I moaned putting a hand to the back of my neck and his steely gaze took in the sight of my pain, now looking pleased.

"Clever little youngling," he said, confusing me as to why. So, I frowned telling him silently that I didn't understand, and this seemed to make him even more pleased.

"Ah now I see, for you are merely searching around in the dark," he said seemingly musing to himself before raising his head up, meaning that all I saw now was his chin he was that tall. Then his skin started to change on his neck, becoming rougher, like the texture of scorched sand covered scales.

"Then allow me to shed light, where there is none," he said still looking up and now cracking his neck to the side as the power of the change rippled through him, now covering his neck and chin. I squinted my eyes trying to make out what the shadows were that were now growing above his head. But then I felt the rabbit down by my feet trying to get my attention.

I looked down only for a second to see it frantically trying to tell me something. It's panicked little jumps, and stomps on the dead crust of Hell's floor were almost frantic. But then I felt a clawed finger under my chin before it was being pushed up forcefully. Meaning now the second my head was back far enough, Lucifer then looked down, now showing me the real meaning of the name…

The Devil.

And with it, *his true form*.

"AAAAHHH!" I screamed as this horned God looked down at me now as if I were nothing but an ant that needed to be crushed and one done so for his pleasure. His skin was now that of a beast, like red worn leather stretched over an abnormal amount of muscle on his torso. His head however, was a different matter. Either side of his face was cracked skin. One glowing with molten fire beneath and lighting up his veins. This followed the line under his high cheekbones down to both sides of his chin, as if parts of his face were cut into sections. Smaller spiked horns ran along his jawbone curling back towards his neck with a roll of hard skin framing each one at the point it emerged from his face.

This was the same for the two horns that also came from his shoulders but instead of being framed by hard skin these were surrounded by rows and rows of smaller spikes. However, the biggest difference had to be the shadows created behind his head for the two biggest horns I had ever seen on a demon. They started at the base of his neck and flattened to the back of his skull before splitting and curling around to the front of the sides of his head. Then they twisted up, so the deadly points were raised above him.

Like this, he now looked every inch the Devil.

I tried to step back, quickly realising my mistake as my foot felt nothing but air. I was about to fall, that much was certain, and I could only hope that it would be enough to jolt me out of this world of the past before I hit the ground. My only hope also being that it wasn't like that urban legend that when you landed from a fall in your dreams it actually meant you died in the real world.

Thankfully, I never got to find out. I might have done, that was if Lucifer hadn't caught me. He banded a massive arm around my waist and then snarled down at me as if this action and what it could have led too, annoyed him.

"This memory doesn't belong to you!" he snarled making me flinch away, bending my back as much as I could over his arm in a desperate attempt at putting space between us. Then, if I thought his demonic voice was powerful enough to make me pee myself, his roar was the stuff of nightmares!

"IT IS MINE, NOW LEAVE!" he bellowed making rocks and mountains around us break and crumble, causing landslides in the distance. I cringed, shivering in fear in his hold as I closed my eyes and waited for the pain to come, but when it did, it did it in the strangest place.

The second he said this I felt a sharp stab in my palm and when I looked down, I could now see the demon rabbit hanging off my hand where it had jumped up to bite me.

I had barely a chance to open my mouth before the world around me suddenly disappeared and I felt myself being yanked sideways. It felt as though I was falling forever and finally when I landed I did so in a world…

I finally needed to see.

CHAPTER SIXTEEN

SEXY CUTE

I ended up landing into a small body and it took me a few seconds to realise that I was back, and the visions of the past was now over. The body I was leaning into turned out to be Pip as she helped keep me steady after what was quite an ordeal. I don't know how long it took me to get back, but I know that I had to try really hard not to faint or vomit for that matter. It felt almost like coming off a rollercoaster that had turned your stomach with too many twists, turns and barrel curled loops.

"It's okay, you're back…just take deep breaths," Sophia cooed behind me rubbing large circles on my back.

"Yeah, wow Toots, you certainly know how to show a girl a wild time!" Pip said making me frown the second her words started to form a real sentence in my head.

"Wh…what do you mean?" I asked after first having to clear my throat as now it felt hoarse from screaming. I pulled back to see her grinning at me before she stuck her top teeth further out and pretended to gnaw at something.

"Oh my god! You're the rabbit!?" I shouted the second she also pretended she had ears.

"You see, now that is how you play charades!" Pip said to Sophia, making her just roll her eyes and mutter,

"Whatever." But I didn't really hear any of this, or at least barely took it in because all I knew was the overwhelming need to cry. So, I grabbed them both to me and started sobbing.

"Whoa!"

"Oh okay." Both of them said at the same time. Then the second they realised I was crying like a baby, Sophia pulled back and said,

"Hey now, what's this all about, was it that bad?"

"Nnnoo…well yeah, I mean there was that bit with me when I was back in the basement with…"

"Captain Killer FruitLoops," Pip finished off for me making me laugh and as always bringing light to a usually dark situation.

"Yeah him. And then I got threatened by the Devil, but that's not why I am crying."

"Wow, if she ain't wailing because of that then whatever she is crying about must be uber, uber bad, and I ain't talking no taxi cabs!" Pip said to Sophia making me laugh again, this time one that ended in a little snort.

"No, I am crying because I love you guys so much!" I said on another sob, making them both first look shocked and then relieved. I turned first to Sophia and pulled her in for a separate hug, telling her,

"I saw you that night, the one where you tried to convince Draven to come down to speak with me and ask me on a date. I heard everything you said and how much you tried to get him to understand that I was strong enough for your world. I heard…I heard you call me sister for the first time!" Again, I finished this sentence on another sob and I didn't know what was wrong with me. It almost felt as though something inside me had snapped or broken free and I couldn't get it contained again.

"Oh honey, you have always been my sister, since the day I first met you!"

"Yeah and lucky she only met you now, because no offence, but you were a raving, crazy ancient lady with a mean, killer resting bitch face back in the day before toothpaste and toilet roll!" Pip said referring of course to the Sophia in the past and one who tried to poison me.

"Well, I wouldn't have tried to kill her if I had known who she was now, would I?" Sophia snapped letting me go and making me giggle before I launched myself at Pip before she could respond.

"Hey Ho, Toots...aww shucks don't cry again...oh man," she said as I started sniffing.

"You were there for me every step of the way, you led me out of my worst nightmares and freed me when no other came...I love you so much, Pip!" I said grabbing her to me again and hugging her tight.

"Of course, I was, I will always be there for you, after all, you're my sister too...you both are," Pip said adding this last part looking at Sophia and making her crumble. She joined us in our hug fest, showing me that no matter how much these two could bicker sometimes, that they loved each other no matter what.

"Keira!" The sound of my name being called had me freezing in their hold before they broke away leaving me to see Draven speeding towards us. I quickly found myself doing the same towards him, not knowing what had come over me, but suddenly feeling a desperation to be in his arms again. He looked surprised for a second before I flung myself into his body and burst into yet even more tears the second he wrapped me in his arms and held me tight.

"What the hell happened!?" he snapped and at first, I thought this had been at me, but then when I pulled back to look up at him I saw he was looking straight over my head at the girls.

"Okay, so we had a little…um…mishap," Sophia said only to be barked at by her brother again.

"A fucking mishap, she is in floods of tears!"

"Ah well that, I think you will find it's what they call baby hormones," Pip interjected after raising her hand up like she was in class and about to address a really mean teacher.

"Hormones!?" Draven repeated, snapping in disbelief. It was now that I decided to intervene as I reached up and caressed his face, before telling him,

"It's okay, I am fine, I just got myself a little worked up and over emotional when talking to the girls and thanking them for always being there for me. And then I saw you and I missed you, so I just ran and then…well, then I don't know why but I started crying again because I love you so much!" I said as I tried not to sniffle but couldn't help it as, for the reason Pip had said, it was like the flood gates had been opened and I couldn't get myself together.

"Okay, okay, Ssshh my love…hey come on now, it's alright sweetheart, I missed you too," he said after his cooing just started to set off the waterworks more.

"Pp…please don't…don't be angry!" I stuttered through the tears.

"I am not angry, sweetheart," he said, and I wasn't convinced as he said this as if trying too hard at appearing calm. I knew now it was probably because he hated seeing me cry that had done it. So, I told him after sniffling,

"You look angry." He took a deep breath, no doubt to aid in calming him further, again for my benefit, before saying,

"I was worried and angry that something could have

happened to you, but now I am relieved to see you unharmed. My only concern is now for your tears my love, for I don't relish seeing you so upset," he said making me throw my arms up around his neck (with his help of course) and then I kissed him all over whilst still continuing to hiccup on the few tears here and there.

Needless to say, this wasn't a pretty sight.

"If it helps My Lord, now I would say that they are at least tears of joy, as she has kinda talked about you none stop... hasn't she Sophia?" Pip said nudging her partner in crime and making her give her brother a quick nod.

"Yeah, don't get me wrong, I love you brother but even I was getting a little fed up of constantly being told how great you are," Sophia said adding the cherry on top and before I could give her a hidden look to tell her I think she had gone too far, I felt Draven squeeze me tighter to him.

"Give us a moment," Draven asked, this time in a far calmer tone, obviously now the immediate panic and worry he spoke of had passed. Sophia and Pip left us alone like he asked and went to sit at the low wall that had not long ago been my mental cage. Then Draven turned me to face him and he did this by taking my face in both his hands, so he could also tilt my face up.

"Are you alright, sweetheart?" he asked as he wiped the tears from under my eyes with his thumbs. I smiled up at him and then nodded for fear that my emotions would only get the better of me again if I spoke. Then he leant his forehead to mine and said,

"I was so worried." I closed my eyes and told him softly,

"I am sorry, honey." He took a deep breath as if letting my words flow over him and calm him further.

"I swear that tower is looking ever closer to playing an

integral part of your future, darling," he said making me chuckle before reaching up and telling him,

"Only if you're there with me and we both throw away the key." Then I kissed him, placing my hands on his face before throwing my arms around him. He wrapped both arms around me and lifted me so that our lips were level and then he *really kissed me*. I swear at one point I felt my toes curl like the witch in Wizard of Oz… minus the house falling on top of me, of course.

"By the gods Keira, only you can manage to go on an innocent day trip on Lock Ness and end up sinking the fucking boat," he growled, which was a sound that spoke more of his growing arousal than of his frustration the sentence would suggest.

"Technically, Nessie sank the ship, that and a sugar rush from too many Lucky charms," I informed him making him first look at me as if I was going to follow up that statement with a little more info so that he would understand better. But then when he didn't get it, he just ended up shaking his head at me.

"I knew there wasn't a movie with Nazis, chickens and monsters in it," he said looking far too sure of himself, which made me realise something funny.

"Oh my God, you googled it, didn't you?!" I shouted on a laugh when he put me back down. I watched as his lips twitched before one side tipped up, making him smirk.

"I might have," he replied this time trying to hide his grin.

"So, you know it's about a giant…" I let my sentence linger before he grinned this time and said,

"Yes love, I know it's about a shark." This made me squeal with joy for some reason, as I could just imagine Draven stood there pacing the room on his phone, asking his google assistant if the movie Jaws had chickens, monsters and Nazis in it! I swear I would have paid good money to have seen his face when google answered him. Of course, now all I could think about was the first chance I got, I was asking my phone the very same question, just to see what it would have told him.

"Right, then it's decided…!" I shouted looking over my shoulder so that the girls could hear me as well, after first getting their attention.

"And what's that, my little trouble maker?" Draven asked in that pretend stern voice adding to it his folded arms. I was momentarily stunned when looking at him and how much that look would, at one time, have intimidated the shit out of me!

This thought had me revisiting my second vision for a moment and wondering what my reaction to such a sight would have been had he come down the stairs that night. Had he just walked straight up to me before pulling me to one side so that he could speak with me. Then, as I tried to make sense of what he was saying, asking me out on a date, he would silence my concerns with a gentle kiss on the cheek. This may have seemed like a small gesture now but back then something like that would have been huge!

To find out that the man you were still obsessing over and had shortly before this point pushed you away, now wanted you. Having him tell you something like he was sorry and ask if I would give him the opportunity to explain before then sealing his words with a stolen kiss. Oh yeah, now that would have been a memory worth watching, another one treasured like the thousand after it he had given me.

But now, being that he was my Draven, I just poked fun at him in the form of my fingers trying to pinch his belly before declaring,

"Movie night tonight, and first on the list is Jaws!" I heard Pip's squeal of delight at the same time I heard Sophia's groan of disappointment.

"Do you not think we have seen enough water, boats and them sinking for one day?" she asked, making me and Pip chuckle. Draven however agreed with his sister,

"Enough indeed."

"Oh, come on, it will be fun, plus Pip is up for it," I said looking from Draven to the girls.

"Pip would be up for an enema if you told her it would be fun," Sophia commented drily making Pip stick out her tongue at her.

"Well, from the looks of it I won't be doing anything fun, because my hubba bubba will have me locked up for the rest of the night…look how twisted his panties look," she said on seeing Adam running over the hill towards her, looking even more panicked than Draven had. I looked back to the man of my dreams, who then told us,

"I called him." This made Pip groan before she too went off running, shouting behind her,

"Wish me a lucky screw!" Then we watched and as she was just about to jump on she said,

"Honey, we owe someone a new boat!" Then she landed in Adam's arms before knocking him onto his back and attacking his face with kisses.

"Damn it!" Sophia moaned.

"What is it?" I asked as she watched her own husband come dashing up the hill.

"Now he will definitely let her watch Jaws," she said making me laugh before she, like us all, went running off to join her husband, only with more hugging and less attacking involved.

"How did you know about the boat?" I asked Draven, realising now that we hadn't said anything.

"I rang Adam and he told me what adventures you ladies had decided on for the day."

"And?" I asked knowing there was more.

"And let's just say I put two and two together and it equalled to three girls in trouble on a boat, that sounded as if it was sinking when I rang." Yeah okay, so I could see how he would come to that conclusion.

"So, you came running?" I asked figuratively speaking.

"No, I flew." I gave him a look of surprise and got up on tiptoes trying to see if I could spot the helicopter anywhere.

"Where did you land?"

"Right over there, but you were too busy hugging females to notice," he said with a grin making me roll my eyes.

"Well, I don't see anything, where did you park?" I asked wondering if he'd had to put some coins in the parking machine to get out a ticket. I giggled to myself at the thought of a helicopter sat in the car park with a sticker on its windshield.

But then he popped this bubble when he chuckled.

"Sweetheart, I have wings remember?" he whispered, leaning down into me and pulling me closer to him.

"Oh, that type of flying." I mused playing now with the neck of the black t-shirt he wore beneath his khaki military style jacket, one that had a high neck and what looked to be double layered with a warmer black lining.

"Why did you do that?" I then asked wondering why I even thought of Draven having to hire a helicopter in the first place. I think sometimes I forgot that he flew, as it had been quite some time since I had been in his arms when he was doing so. Not that this was something I wanted to change anytime soon, not considering I was terrified of heights and was now pregnant to add to it. I didn't think that flying and morning sickness really made for a good combo…not for Draven or the poor souls below that thought they felt rain that day…eww.

He moved closer to me, giving me that 'I am a dominant male' look, that had me nearly backing up a step whilst also wanting to rub myself up and down his hard-intimidating body like a damn cat…boy, talk about mixed emotions!

"Because, wife of mine, for all I knew you were treading water in the middle of a fucking lake, freezing to death or worse, sinking with the fucking ship! So, I wasn't about to calmly get in my car and drive over an hour to get here to see if either of those two scenarios had come to fruition…that is why." Once he had finished he was all but growling down at me as if both of these horrible thoughts had come back to the centre of his attention and now he was pissed off again.

"Well, lucky for you I completed all my swimming courses as a kid, have all my patches to prove it and can easily retrieve a heavy weight from the bottom of a pool wearing my pyjamas, whilst holding my breath…so I think we are good," I said patting him on the chest in a way that I hoped was taken as more cute than patronising.

At first, I couldn't tell if this was the case as he seemed to be at a loss for a moment as to what I had said could mean. Well, it was that or he was still processing it all. I knew it was the latter when he asked,

"Why did they make you do that wearing pyjamas and then give you a patch for it?" I started giggling before telling him,

"Never mind babe, I will explain on the way home…let's just say for now that I am a good swimmer and move on."

"I agree…so kiss me," he said seriously.

"Not that I usually need a reason, but I have to ask, why?" To this he suddenly picked me up making me squeal in shock before he yanked me to him. I felt the heat of his dominant hold seep through my damp clothes and I wished that I could have felt his fingertips pressing into my bare skin. I gripped onto him, silently telling him never to let me go, for this was where I wanted to be…

Right here, forever in his hold.

Then he growled a sexy whisper down at me, being the perfect reason why, just before he crushed his lips to mine in a mind-blowing kiss. Thus, letting me know I had achieved what I set out to with my swimming comment…

"Because you're so fucking cute!"

CHAPTER SEVENTEEN

SHOCKED BY THE JAWS OF LIFE

A little time later and after all the dominant men had enforced their warnings of careful times ahead for the future (and no more boats), we found ourselves all sat in the drawing room which had been transformed into a cinema for the evening. After the men, of course, lugged heavy furniture around at the pregnant lady's request. As nice as it was in this room, its couches were more on the antique side of comfort, meaning no comfort at all and old as dirt but definitely prettier.

So, now instead we were all cosy around the massive telly, watching the classic Jaws with only me and Pip adhering to the Pj's rule. However, at the very least Sophia had changed for a more comfortable look, being designer lounge pants in a dove grey and a loose off the shoulder cashmere sweater in a light pink colour.

Pip, of course being Pip, was wearing green monster feet slippers that looked to have been sewn onto thigh high leg warmers. She was also wearing a space invader Pyjama set, that had a flying saucer over each boob with the words 'Breast invaders' underneath. To this was a pair of shorts that she had also attached garter straps on to hold up her rainbow striped leg warmers.

I was wearing a set my mum had got me for Christmas that was a white vest top which had a big heart at the centre that said 'I' above it and 'My Bed' below. The trousers were red and covered in little beds with hearts at the centre. When I first walked out of the bathroom after showering and getting 'scent de lake' out of my hair, the sight of me wearing this made Draven's lips twitch. He had currently been lounging back on the bed at the time reading a book while waiting for me to finish. I was still plaiting my hair to one side, tilting my head as I did, when I noticed him staring at the heart on my chest.

"My mum bought them for me last Christmas...although, when she did, I doubt she would have felt the same way about them if she knew I loved my bed with a demon in it," I said finishing this off with a wink. At this he threw his head back and started laughing, tossing the book to the side before making demands of me.

"Come here and kiss your demon."

"You know that's the second time you have demanded a kiss from me today...I hope I am not sensing a pattern of you becoming greedy," I said making him grin.

"Around you, looking like that, how could I be anything else but *greedy?*" he said purring the last word after dripping it with sexual intent.

"Now, come here and give me what I crave," he added making me smirk.

"Well alright, but remember, you asked for it."

"Asked for wh..." I never gave him chance to finish before I was suddenly running towards the bed, getting ready to launch myself at him. I saw him brace as if to catch me when I skidded to a stop by the edge, leaving him looking shocked.

"HA! Gotya!" I shouted pointing at him and laughing. Then the second I saw him take a breath and start to relax, about to say something else, this was when I did jump on him playfully. Of course, in this sexy kitten act I had been going for, I hadn't accounted for my knee totally missing the bed, slipping straight off the side and therefore ending with me face planting into his chest with a groan from both of us. I lay there for a minute unable to look at him from embarrassment and shame. No doubt one he could feel seeping through his t-shirt in the form of the immense heat coming off my cheeks. I only moved to look up at him when I felt his rumbling chest as the silent laughter continued.

"Hello," he said softly, mocking me in a cute way that turned sexy when he actually started to bite his bottom lip, as if he was trying to stop himself from laughing out loud at me.

"Is there any way this is going to go, where you are going to pretend that I never did that?" I asked him, making him fight his grin even harder and making his jaw twitch this time. He didn't answer me with words, as I think he would only have ended up failing in an attempt at holding back his obvious amusement. No, instead he shook his head, telling me that I didn't have a chance. So, I growled down at him playfully and this time prompted something more from him than a pair of beautiful dark eyes currently dancing with mirth.

"Nope, still cute *baby,*" he said whispering this sweet pet name over my lips after first flipping me to my back so that he could cover me with his body. After this I soon found out that he found cute could also be sexy…in a number of ways but more importantly,

A number of times.

"Well, she's dead," Sophia commented dryly, sounding

unimpressed about five seconds into the movie as the drunken girl started running along the beach taking her clothes off before diving into the sea.

"Hey!" she complained after getting attacked by sugar coated snacks.

"Then don't ruin the build-up…it's the best bit," Pip said after throwing popcorn at her, making Zagan pick up the pieces before eating them with a grin. All the men were sat back in their seats looking casual, Zagan wearing what looked like training pants that hung low on his hips along with a black vest and a hooded zip up with some gym name on the logo. He was sat back with his arm resting on the back of the couch, playing with a loose curl absentmindedly as if needing to have that contact with his wife without even thinking about it.

Adam was also lounging back but obviously needing more than a simple touch, as he had his wife stretched out with the whole of her upper body lay over his lap, with the bowl of popcorn resting between his knees. His version of casual was swapping his shirt, tie and sweater look for a pale blue polo shirt and pale slacks.

But it was Draven who I was more interested in and thought he looked hot in his plain black t-shirt and faded jeans. Even the sight of him with his feet up in just his white socks made me smile, seeing him looking so relaxed. But what I loved even more was the way he had lifted my legs over his lap and had a hand stretched over to rest on my belly, where he rubbed little circles there.

"See, told you!" Sophia said the second the girl started to get pulled under and then tossed all over the place. All the while the guy she had been with was nearly passing out drunk on the beach.

"Well, he was a lot of help." Zagan laughed when Sophia said this, and he started kissing her neck as he chuckled against her skin. His pale hand running through her black curls to hold them out of the way was like pieces on a chess board merging. It was so heart-warming to see both my girls being adored by the men in their life, as I knew how special it was to have someone like that be the centre of your world. Someone who loved you unconditionally. It was a gift that you never took for granted...*ever.*

"Oh no, not the kids!" Pip cried making me shoot a quizzical look her way,

"I thought you had seen this?"

"Well yeah, but I still get nervous." I laughed at Pip's answer. We continued to watch until the next attack, when just as the camera got closer to the kid's legs, just about to strike, Pip threw Popcorn at me which scared me enough to scream, making everyone laugh. Draven chuckled making me frown at him, then declare

"That's it, we are never taking our kid to the beach!" Draven laughed harder at this, then pulled me closer to say,

"Don't worry sweetheart, I will be the only thing scary in the water that day." Then he finished this with a wink that had me trying not to blush and instead act cocky when I told him,

"Sure of that, are you?"

"Definitely," was his breathy reply against my neck. Ten minutes later and then came the next observation.

"Well, I can see this ending badly." This time it was Zagan's turn to comment as he saw the two guys on the dock who thought a piece of meat attached to a car tyre on a length of chain tied to the dock, was going to be a tall task against a twenty five-foot shark. Not surprisingly then, the second the tire was pulled tight, half the rickety dock fell into the water, men and all.

"And there goes another one," Sophia added making Pip wink at me because as I did, she knew they both made it out alive…that was after a very tense moment in the water. She soon found this out and again couldn't stop from commenting.

"Okay, so I didn't see that coming," Sophia admitted, making me laugh because she was just like her brother, talking all the way through the movie. Which reminded me, Draven was unusually quiet during this one.

"You're very quiet."

"I thought that was customary behaviour during a movie, and if I recall, the last time you called me 'one of those people'," he answered, surprising me.

"So?"

"So…I am trying not to be 'one of those people'," he responded with a knowing grin. I rolled my eyes before telling him,

"Yeah, but this is a shark movie, you're allowed to talk through those," I said making his smile grow.

"Oh, is that so?"

"Yeah, that and slasher horrors and disaster movies," I told him with a smirk.

"Just not movies about stalking killer Aliens?" he asked with amusement lacing his tone and a nudge to my ribs.

"Precisely…see, now you're getting it," I said laughing when he raised an eyebrow at me.

"Now that just looks like an all you can eat buffet!" Pip said making Adam laugh. It was the part where everyone thinks they can catch a shark with a fishing rod and a tiny boat.

"Such a shame," she added with a shake of her head.

"You mean they all get eaten?" Sophia asked making me nudge Draven and whisper,

"Must be a Draven family trait."

"Behave, little wife," he teased back.

"No, the opposite happens, they all survive and kill the wrong shark," Adam told her pushing up his glasses.

"You've already watched this?" Zagan asked him as Pip stuffed her face full of more popcorn, now making my mouth water.

"Only about the hundred times my wife has made me," he replied, getting an elbow in the gut from said wife in return.

"Poor bastard," Zagan muttered making Pip turn her head at him and say,

"I wouldn't feel too sorry for him as I usually let him pick the position that night, which he usually picks rodeo with chains." I choked on a cough when I heard this, sitting forward whilst Draven patted my back to help.

"Too much nympho on the info?" Pip asked and when I could finally speak again all I managed was a croaky...

"Uh, yeah."

After this, the night continued, and I found myself in a very happy place when Pip finally relinquished control on the popcorn bowl. I also managed to wrestle a few sweets off her, which I was currently opening after picking through the colours and finding a red one, which other than the purple ones were, in my opinion, the best two flavours of most sweets.

"Not sure what a 'Star Burst' has to do with this candy, but it's a damn sight better than bloody Opal Fruits that's for sure... I mean Opal Fruits? Who the hell came up with that name for them...or stuff like 'Goobers', yeah 'cause they sound nice... not! Then there's Whoppers which aren't even that big, they are just like Maltesers' shittier tasting brother and no one wants to eat him! And ever remember 'Squirrel Nut Zippers'? I mean whoever came up with that name must have met some weird ass squirrels that's for sure, and wearing little pants in the woods no less, for if you ask me how else would they have zippers?"

"Deep breath now, my Winnie," Adam cautioned as Pip was getting way to animated about this and all because I asked for some sweets.

"Okay, okay, but I bet you can't say Bananarama three times fast," she got in there, making Adam groan. But what was even more surprising was to hear Zagan pipe up and say really fast,

"Bananarama, Bananarama, Bananarama." Sophia giggled rolling her eyes back at him and no doubt at the cocky pale grin he displayed as he stretched out as if had just mastered the impossible.

"Uh, well will you look at that, maybe it's not that hard..." Then Pip was just about to open her mouth to try it herself when Adam's hand clamped over her lips to stop her. I giggled and was just about to try it too when Draven leaned into me and said,

"Go ahead and you will find yourself in the same predicament, only I won't be using my hand to silence you," he said as a sexual purr. My mouth dropped open and I screeched,

"Draven, we are with people, you can't threaten to do that... here.!" Draven looked highly amused at this, raised his eyebrows in a questioning way, and said,

"Oh, do we not kiss in public now?"

"Oh." This is when it dawned on me what he had meant, and my face went scarlet in seconds, totally giving away where my naughty thoughts had been. Of course, Draven, picking up on this straight away, threw his head back and howled with laughter, thus making me growl.

Thankfully though we moved past this pretty quickly when there was another tense moment on screen.

"Hang on a minute, the *shark expert* just said that nothing is going to happen to him whilst going to check out a boat where something clearly happened to it and the man that was driving it and whilst they are out there at night looking for a big man-eating shark...oh yeah, good plan that one," Sophia complained sarcastically, making me smirk because I knew what was coming. So, I leaned into Draven, shifting my legs off his lap, and snuggling into his side first before whispering,

"I take it with being a kick ass demon, that Sophia doesn't scare easily?"

"That would be a no," he whispered back after he once again fought his urge to laugh at me.

"Then I bet you ten pounds and the next week of remote privileges that she screams in a minute."

"You're on," he said grinning, then he paused and seemed to think a minute before asking,

"Remote privileges?"

"It means I will get to choose what we watch for the next week," I informed him, no longer needing to whisper but also keeping my voice down for this next bit.

"And that is any different than any other day, how?" he commented with a raised eyebrow, but I just nudged him and demanded,

"Ssshh," knowing that okay so he was kinda right with that one.

"Yes, Madame," he commented back like a child and making me elbow him in the belly, an action that if done any harder would have no doubt only ended up hurting my arm more than his rock-hard abs.

I looked towards Pip to see her nearly bouncing up and down on Adam, who still had his arms around her trying in vain to keep her calm, because she too knew what was coming. I couldn't help but smile at Sophia as she looked on the edge of her seat watching this. Whereas, when she first started watching you would have thought we had forced her into the room by a threat of cutting off her clothes allowance.

Richard Dreyfuss was now in the water and poking around

the hole in the boat, just prying out a shark's tooth from the wood when, after a quick turnaround, he looked back at the severed head that popped out seconds later, meaning me and Pip both shouted,

"AHHH!"

"BOOO YEAH!" And this, more than anything, was what made Sophia scream, that and Zagan getting in on the action making him jolt her from behind the second we had all made a noise. We all burst out laughing when a pouting Sophia folded her arms and said,

"That was not funny." But our reactions disagreed, especially Pip who was still chuckling ten minutes later and receiving a death glare from Draven's sister. Meanwhile, I held a hand out to Draven and said,

"Pay up, big man." He let out a throaty chuckle and took my hand in his, holding it between his teeth for a minute, making me complain verbally, but physically I was squirming in my seat. Then he told me,

"This big man will pay up later, have no worries about that, sweetheart." I soon realised after he said this that he wasn't talking about money, especially when he soothed his bite with his tongue before bestowing a gentle kiss there.

After this I don't know what happened, but I must have put myself into a sweet induced coma as the next thing I knew I was being carried out of the room to the famous sound of Roy Scheider shouting the line 'Smile you son of a Bitch!' which was pretty much the end of the movie.

The next thing I remembered was being tucked up in bed and soon feeling a warm body join me before I fell into a peaceful sleep.

. . .

I woke what could have been hours or minutes later, I wasn't sure, but I figured it was at least long enough to send Draven into a deep sleep for he didn't stir behind me when I did. The second I opened my eyes I tried not to scream when finding something staring me in the face. In the end it was the sight of it being a fluffy white bunny that was the only thing that had me stopping myself from reacting in time. Anything else though, and I would have been waking Draven up with a full on girly screaming fit.

I frowned, before rubbing the sleep out of my eyes, as if this would help at all in making sense why my Pip bunny was back. Unless of course I was still dreaming, which knowing me was quite possible. So, this time not taking any chances, I grabbed the sensitive skin under my arm and pinched myself hard. Then had to hold back the moan as the pain told me that this time I definitely wasn't dreaming. The funny part was the rabbit was watching me do this with a tilted head and a 'questioning my sanity' kind of look, if such a thing were possible to be seen on a bunny. I rolled my eyes as I didn't exactly appreciate being woken up, only to be quickly judged by something so cute, it looked like she belonged on a cartoon cereal box of a brand name 'bunny fluff bites' or something.

I then mouthed the question, 'what are you doing here?' making it shake its head at me and then thump its foot down on the bed, which was when I noticed the paper under its paw. I picked it up and got a big clue when it read,

Draven,
If you wake and I am gone, don't panic.
I couldn't sleep so decided to go to the library and read for
a bit.
Won't be long.
Love Keira

Once I had finished, I folded it back up and placed it on my pillow for him to find, as I guess it looked as though I was going to the library. Pip saw this and then jumped soundlessly off the bed with her big ears flopping all over the place. Then she waited to see if I would get the hint and follow. I had no idea how she had turned herself into who she was in my trip down not so hot memory lane... although thinking about it, Hell had been about as far from cool as you could get.

I grabbed a warm woollen wrap from the chair before slipping bare footed out of the room, hoping Draven wouldn't stir. The second I had the door closed again, something I spent a stupid amount of time trying to accomplish without making a noise, I turned back around expecting to see my white furry friend...

But she was gone.

Well, the note said I was going to the library, so my only clue was to do just that, hoping that this whole thing wasn't a mistake. So, knowing where to go and giving the bedroom door once last look behind me, I carried on. I mean, history should have taught me to stay in bed at this point and ignore this unusual calling, but the second I saw Pip's rabbit self, then I knew I had to follow my gut and follow her. I also promised myself that the first sign of trouble, aka, Draven's demon, then I was so outta there!

I continued to tell myself this all the way to the library, where I hesitated for a minute before I opened the door. The massive sigh of relief washed over me in a wave as the second I stepped inside, I saw both Sophia and Pip sat there on the chairs that were positioned around a massive fireplace, one that Pip was currently poking.

"See, I told you Alice would follow the white rabbit," Pip said without looking and I rolled my eyes at Sophia when she gave me an exasperated look over the back of the chair she now had her elbow resting on.

"Welcome to the party and when I say party, I actually mean just us two," she told me as I walked over to the empty chair.

"That's a party enough for me," I said thinking of our last one and how much it sucked for me after demonic shit got in the way.

"But of course it is, only think more the type of party that swaps games for question time and party food for none," Pip told me with a wink.

"Yeah, I guess we didn't get much time to talk after the Kazzy freak out sob show," I said making Sophia chuckle but strangely it was Pip that wanted to be serious for a minute. Which was a scary thing because if that ever happened it usually meant that the shit didn't just hit the fan, it dived bombed it!

"Forget about that shit, what we need to be focusing on is why your memory took you to Hell and straight to the big boss man himself!" Pip said shocking Sophia.

"What!? Please tell me you're joking, and this is just one of those times when you say something, but actually mean something else, and I just don't get it because I haven't watched some fucking movie!" Sophia said having a small melt down and holding the bridge of her nose with thumb and forefinger whilst she did this.

"You didn't tell her?!" was my only answer and this was directed at Pip.

"Uh, nooodamundo...exactly when was I supposed to do that, when I was being sexed up by my paranoid android hubby, who was trying to make absolutely sure my lady muffin wasn't flooded with lake water or later on when we were all watching a shark kill people... 'cause if you wanted me to just pause the movie and start chatting about you nipping to Hell for the afternoon, then I could've," Pip answered giving me no other option than to agree and say,

"Okay, so you have a good point."

"Alright, now that's out of the way can we move on to what you did see...? You know, now that we are free to talk about it...well, that is if my brother doesn't wake up, find you gone and freak out first, letter or no letter."

"Sure thing, but first... Pip, that means no fanny talk," I warned after Sophia's other good point made.

"Yeah, like it's my favourite subject...come on give me some credit, it doesn't do chicks but likes dicks, what's wrong with that?" We both rolled our eyes and Sophia groaned, but we both decided to flat out ignore the comment and get to the important stuff right away.

I spent as little time as possible getting Sophia up to date and by the end of it she didn't just looked gobsmacked, she ended up saying half to herself,

"Just how do you keep getting yourself into these things?"

"That's a damn good question, but unless you see an Oracle lying around here anywhere, then I think you're asking the wrong person," I replied sarcastically, which ended up being the joke on me because at that very moment we all got the shock of our lives as a body suddenly emerged from behind one of the bookcases.

"Did someone say they needed an Oracle?" A voice sang out and we all screamed at once, before I finally could breathe enough to utter a single name in question...

"Pythia?"

CHAPTER EIGHTEEN

POWERFUL DEFENCES

"Pythia!?" I shouted again as if just to make sure.

"Hey, that would be me," she replied giving us all a nervous little wave. It was still weird getting used to her looking this way, as I had been used to a cute little black girl with wild curly hair and colourful clothes. But like this, in what I now knew was her true form, she looked like an Egyptian goddess.

Long dark hair that shone like silk against her white casual summer dress, one that was edge in a thick border of gold and red leaves. Under this she had on a pair of dark blue skin-tight jeans and dark tan coloured boots that had straps and loose folds of leather. The whole look had that cool ethnic vibe to it, along with the headband in the same design as the border on her short dress, holding back her beautiful hair.

The white cotton against her skin brought out the glow of her sun kissed tan, and also the exotic olive green in her eyes that were jewelled with honey flecks bursting from around the irises. She was utterly breathtaking, but in an innocent way as if she didn't yet know this about herself.

Now, I know that because of this girl, in the past I had endured more heartache than I could ever have imagined…hell, we both had, Draven and I, but that didn't mean that I was going to hold it against her. Because as she said to me not that long ago, we really weren't that different her and I…minus the Egyptian Goddess part.

I had never asked to be the Electus, just as she had never asked to become an Oracle. Yet we were both used as puppets by the Fates and neither of us had any choice in the matter. For me, it was solely done for the man I loved and all the people around his life and mine, who I cared for.

But for Pythia, well she just had *no choice*. It was this, or death. So, she played her part and in doing so, somewhere along the line, she had become the bad guy in people's eyes. However, in the end everything had worked out and also, everything she had said had happened, just not the way we ever thought it would.

Which was why I got up, walked over to her and hugged her to me, replacing that look of insecurity and unsureness from her face, filling it instead with relief. So much so that tears started to well in her eyes as if this was the first bit of kindness she had been shown in longer than she could remember.

When I thought about the trouble I had caused her just by being me and by being born as Draven's Electus, she had been cursed out, hunted, and blamed for everything that had happened. But she had just been doing what was demanded of her, so yes, of course I hugged her. She was one of us and that would never change, no matter what derogatory thoughts people wanted to cling onto…like Lucius for example.

"Welcome back, honey," I told her, rubbing away one of her tears and giving her a smile that told her all she needed to know.

She gave me a nod of understanding and I took her hand to lead her over to our little 'meeting'. I was glad to see that Pip gave her a little wave and Sophia acknowledged her by getting her another chair to sit in, one next to mine.

"Well, at least we know who Dom had hidden behind that screen," Sophia said.

"Yeah, like some dirty little secret...huh? Oh...I mean, no, nothing like that...the opposite in fact," Pip said backtracking the second me and Sophia started shaking our heads at her, ending with Sophia rubbing her fingers along her eyebrows as if trying to ask the Gods for strength.

"It's okay guys, I know things are going to be a little strange," Pythia said giving us a small smile and trying to help ease the tension.

"Well yeah, sure it will be, for starters you used to be a cute little black chickadee with hair I wanted to hide things in...also, awesome dress sense back then," Pip said making her smile and me stretching the back of my neck wondering what the chances of getting through to the end of this little group meeting without Pip insulting her at some point.

"Thanks...I think," Pythia said smiling, which I took as a good sign.

"So, getting back to the reason you're here, I take it Draven had you brought here?" I asked turning to face her and ignoring the way Pip folded her legs as if she was about to start meditating.

"He thought I may be able to detect something or someone trying to control elements of his demon side," she told us, and this was something I already suspected.

"And did you?" The question came from Sophia this time.

"Yes, I did." This surprised me but then again, her next answer surprised me even more, oh, and also made me start to panic.

"You detected someone trying to pull Dom's demon through?" Sophia asked again as if needing to be sure. This time Pythia just nodded making Pip ask,

"So…who was it, crumpet?" I smirked at Pip's new nickname for her, before Pythia's answer quickly wiped it off my face.

"It was Keira."

"Uh…come again?" I was glad Sophia had something to say 'cause I was still stuck on the mouth gaping open stage, that which was quickly giving way to panic.

"Keira is the one who is pulling his Demon out?"

"Oh no…no, no, please tell me you didn't tell my husband this?" I said in a tone that was close to begging, as if that would help with an outcome that couldn't be changed either way.

"Gods, no, of course not," she said granting me about ten wishes in one and making the three of us all take a collective sigh of relief.

"Well, thank the lord's knickers for that," Pip said flopping back in her seat as though she had just run a marathon…or more like completed a sexathon, as that was more Pip's style.

"No, I knew that wouldn't have been the right thing to do and besides, as much as Dominic asked me here to help him, I am actually here to see if I could help you, Keira." I gave her a grateful look in return before asking the question I had to, not the one I wanted to.

"I hate to ask, as it's not like I am not unbelievably grateful here, but I have to ask why?"

"Because for the first time in my life I have been granted free will. I am now my own person and can do as I wish. I can be good, be bad, be anything I want as I am no longer a tool to be used by the hand of men or the will of the Gods. I am no longer held captive by the Fates and their invisible chains." With the way she said this, I couldn't help but feel proud of her and I was glad to see that she felt the same. The way she held her head high and was basically saying to the world, 'Hello, look at me, I am a survivor, I am a Being gifted with free will and I am now one of you'.

"Which means I can choose who I wish to help and more than anyone else, I wish to help you and in any way I can," she added looking to me.

"Why our Tootiseroll?" Pip asked making me give her a half smile.

"Because throughout all of this, she has been the only constant I have had in my life. Long before you came into this world Keira, I knew of you and what you would become," she said first addressing Pip and then looking back to me as if this was something she had wanted to get off her chest for a while.

"But then when I met you, I could not have ever imagined the kindness that you bestowed on me. Someone who cared for my wellbeing despite facing your own traitorous journey," she spoke again and by this time the tears had arrived, and I couldn't blame it on hormones. Pythia turned to Pip who had asked the question and asked her in return,

"So, I ask of you, can you imagine another Being in this world more worthy than her? Someone who has put people above her own wants and needs all this time? Someone who was ready to sacrifice her very life so that those she loved could live instead. To love so powerfully that she broke every barrier put in her way, experienced pain, suffering, heartache and betrayal, just with hope in her heart that the world would get the chance to go on without her... That is why I am here," Pythia said, and by the time she finished we all had tears in our eyes, but mine were the only ones streaming down the face. Okay, so maybe I wasn't the only person crying so freely, as now Pip was wailing out a sob before she launched herself at Pythia and ended up in her lap hugging her head to her bosom, telling her,

"That was fucking beautiful…seriously you are so awesome and so, so, so in our band, it's not even funny!"

"Your band?" Pythia asked whilst patting Pip's back as she was still clinging to her like a child.

"Don't worry, there's no band, just a group of three girls who always seem to have some shit we have to get Keira out of," Sophia explained.

"Yeah, usually there are four of us, but Ari is off on her own adventure with handsome Vinny boy…but you're here now, YAY! You're gonna love it!" Pip added to this, so I decided to do the same,

"Welcome to the club, honey." She gave us both a smile and then after a few more seconds that were well past awkward, I decided to give her a lifeline, which would be one of many now Pip was in her life.

"Pip, do you wanna let her go now?"

"Oh yeah, good plan…wow, she smells sooo good," Pip said behind her hand at us as she went back to her seat.

"Thank you, Pythia, I don't know what to say other than how touched I am you feel this way," I told her after smiling at Pip's 'smells' comment.

"And she doesn't mean touched as in she is going to touch herself…I remember when I had to learn that the hard way… boy wasn't that an embarrassing day for Adam," Pip said leaning closer to her making Sophia nearly choke and me slap my forehead, but thankfully Pythia just burst out laughing, seeing the funny side of Pip like we all did.

"So, getting back to why we are all here and doing so before Kazzy can shed anymore pregnant tears," Sophia said, and Pythia's grin got even bigger as she turned to me and said,

"Congratulations, I am very happy for you both."

"Yeah, but now we kinda have a big problem, as in she doesn't exactly want to play the single mom in this picture, which Big Bad Demon Dom going King Kong and losing his shit might cause." Of course, this explanation came from Pip.

"You're afraid he will leave?" Pythia asked looking shocked.

"It's not like it didn't happen before. Last time he thought he was a danger to me, he moved to a different country, closed Afterlife and pretended he was dead and forbade any one of his kind to ever see me again."

"Man, can anyone say overkill much?" Pip commented with a shake of her head.

"Okay, so I see your point," Pythia admitted making Pip add,

"Yeah, we have all been seeing the point a lot more lately." I laughed at this.

"So, you see my problem here and why I need to figure this out before Draven finds out." I told her, knowing that I wouldn't have long, because even though Takeshi was still unconscious (something I found out on our way back to the castle) he could also wake up at any minute. Now I knew there was no guarantee that he would remember anything or know what was going on. But considering one of his special gifts was seeing things and picking up on visions, then I didn't think this likely or in my favour.

"I do, but without knowing who did this to you then we…"

"Wait a minute!" Sophia said making Pip jump in there with,

"Hold on now sister Mary, come again?"

"I thought you knew about the birthmark?" Pythia said and yes, we did, but any further than that and we were still left with more questions than answers and not once did any of those question include a 'Who?'.

"You mean someone did this to me?" I asked unable to help the squeal in my tone.

"I need you to show me the mark, that way I may recognise its origins." I shrugged my shoulders and turned to face Sophia, before lifting up my hair off my neck to show her.

"Uh…am I missing something here?" Pip asked making me frown before looking back over my shoulder at them to find them both frowning at my neck.

"Okay, now I have to see this for myself," Sophia said getting up and joining them both behind me.

"Well, that won't take long," Pip commented dryly confusing me.

"I don't understand…where is it?" Sophia asked meaning I was now panicking slightly, asking myself just what was going on.

"I don't get it…did it like fall off somewhere, could it be in the shower or maybe back on the boat, I mean that wave of water hit us pretty hard," Pip said making me react by getting up out of my seat and spinning round to face them.

"Are you telling me it's gone…? Is that what you're telling me?!" I shouted, now really freaking out.

"I am not sure it is," Pythia said surprising us all.

"What do you mean? Neither of us can see it…can you?" Sophia asked with hope.

"No, but I can feel that it's still there. I think it's being hidden somehow."

"How would someone even do that?" I asked shaking my head in disbelief.

"Well, to begin with they would have to be extremely powerful and I am not just talking your average demon with some extra skills. I am talking something ancient," Pythia said in a dire tone, making me throw my arms up and growl.

"Oh, but of course it would be! Seriously, when exactly do I get a break here, because I am sick of this shit! Like I need any more enemies to add to the list, at this rate there will be enough to throw a party of the fuckers and have yearly reunions!" I said getting more pissed off by the second and Pip snorted a laugh, making Sophia shoot her a look.

"What, it was funny." Sophia just shook her head before coming over to me, taking my hands in hers and telling me,

"Look, we will figure this out, even if we have to go to Hell and back, we will, and we will be doing it together this time. You are not alone in this, honey." Then she pulled me to her and hugged me as I cried out all my frustrations. Yep, totally a hormonal meltdown.

So, what was I left with but a chasm of doubt and very little hope that I was ever going to get to a point where my tomorrow was going to lead me closer to my forever happiness. Not the ten steps back it felt like I kept taking. It was like running on some demonic treadmill, always moving but never reaching my destination.

"I am just trying to go over it in my head, I mean the witness circle took me to three points in my life but why, as none of them were connected?" I asked the girls after slumping back down in my chair.

"The witness circle is not about what *it can show you*, but more what *you can show you*," Pythia said gently as if I was close to breaking again.

"She's right. You go in there and can ask it to show a certain point in your life but sometimes..."

"Fear gets in the way?" I said finishing off for Sophia making her nod.

"You got frightened, that then led you to another frightening time in your life, if not the most traumatic. Then at the height of that fear you needed to find a safe place, which led you to Dominic," Pythia said making perfect sense.

"Okay, so I get all that but what about the next door I walked through, I ended up in Hell...*I ended up with...*

Cronus," I said uttering this last part as it all started to make sense.

"What are you saying?" Sophia was the one to ask.

"Think about this, so what did you say, one… they have to be old and very powerful…"

"Checkarino," Pip said counting off her fingers for me.

"Okay so yeah, he wins that title, considering it took an army of us to take him down," Sophia said.

"But only one God," Pythia added, nodding to me like I was still one of something. Yeah, well wouldn't that have come in handy right about now, I thought sarcastically.

"So here we have our ancient power, and two, he has more than enough motive."

"Doublely check," Pip added again making me smile at her.

"Yeah but surely, he knew it was the end for him, so why bother?" Again, this question came from Sophia.

"Well, that's just the thing, what if he didn't know, what if he just thought that he would be imprisoned back in Hell and this was like some kind of backup plan or something…? I mean, he didn't know that he was going to become the Devil's plaything, just like none of us did," I said and then couldn't help but notice the way Pythia shivered and recoiled in on herself at the sound of Lucifer being mentioned. She was almost in a protective ball.

"So, you think that he put some kind of hex on you, one that would force you and Dom back to Hell and in doing so maybe aiding in his escape?" I shrugged my shoulders as after all, this was only speculation.

"I don't know Sophia, but at the minute it's the best we have got. He might have had the means to do something like this when I took him back to Hell with me."

"But wouldn't she remember something like that?" Sophia

asked Pythia this time, who seemed to be the one who knew more about this than anyone.

"If she was as she is now then yes, she would most certainly have felt that amount of power being branded to her…but as she was then…" Pythia let her musing trail off and I decided to point out,

"I wasn't exactly myself."

"No, she was a freakin' kick ass God and I missed it…I missed all the fun that day," Pip said folding her arms across her chest and slumping back in her chair as if it was the end of the world…again.

"Uh hello, we only travelled back through time, had the most amazing wedding and then you and your husband got to be the protectors of the human world should all Hell break loose…I would hardly call that an average boring day, Pip," Sophia told her, and Pip started to grin again adding,

"Yeah and it was great cake too…not every day you get to eat great cake, I mean you may try but just because it's cake, doesn't mean it's really cake, cake…you know what I mean?" Pip said to Pythia who sighed and said,

"I do, Armi, my past keeper, she used to make the best cakes."

"Okay, so moving on from cakes…which yes, granted Pip, my wedding cake was awesome…but getting back to answers here, so you're saying it might have been possible during that time for him to…?"

"Put a Hex on you, yes I believe so. Like I said, as you are now, you would feel it, but back then, one with extreme power wouldn't feel it. As think of it like this, it would be the same as if you were stung a thousand times and having one more bee sting wouldn't make you feel just that one," Pythia said making Pip praise her.

"Oooooh, good analogy…and also that's a shitter of a day in anyone's books." Pythia blushed and said,

"Thanks, it's all I could come up with, but I think it works."

"Oh, I can do one…okay, okay, so it would be like if she was covered in baked beans and then I added on one more bean…"

"Yeah, yeah, I get it, I wouldn't feel the extra bean," I said interrupting her, making her frown at me.

"No, I was going to say it wouldn't be the one extra bean to make you sick or bust your gut when you licked them all off, 'cause that would probably happen way before you reached that bean."

"Eww, Pip, why would I even do that?"

"Uh duh, 'cause you're covered in beans and unless you're into sploshing, then you need to get that shit off," Pip said shrugging her shoulders to the others and pointing at me as if I was the nuts one. I looked to Sophia and said,

"Do I wanna know what sploshing is?"

"Not unless you're into adding messy food to your sex life, then no." I made an eww face along with Pythia, who also looked as though she was learning all this new stuff as well, making me worried we were corrupting her new innocence to human life or something.

"Besides Pip, I would just wash off the beans, but I can't believe I even needed to say that!" I said this last part more to myself than them.

"Right, let's move on from cakes, beans, sploshing and any other food source, shall we…?" I said making Pip hold up her hands to me, replying,

"Hey sister, they're your beans, you can do what you want with them." I then closed my eyes and counted to ten before carrying on, now I had the strength.

"So, what you're saying in a nut shell…"

"NUTS…she said nuts, she broke the no food rule!" Pip shouted pointing accusingly at me and looking at the other two, making me sigh.

"Sorry, what I meant to say is, in conclusion to this new information, the reason I didn't feel anything was because I had so much power that I wouldn't have known he was putting the Hex on me and since then it's kind of been hiding?" I asked facing Pythia again.

"Yes, and it would make sense, because any other time and you would have felt it, but we have a bigger problem."

"Oh great, like we need any more of those," Sophia said sarcastically, throwing her hands up and turning her back on us for a minute as if needing some time to think. I can't say that I blamed her at this point as I was close to doing the same myself.

I just couldn't understand why this kept happening to me. How I managed to find myself in these situations. All I wanted was to find a peaceful time in my life where the biggest meltdowns included things like running out of nappies whilst changing one. Or being woken up at all hours of the night for various feeds…hell, I would even take a case of mastitis at this point, where my breasts swell up and look like two globes of the earth!

"The Hex is obviously one that continues to build up its power," Pythia said, making my mouth drop and quickly shifted my mind from nappies, milk feeds and blotchy breasts.

"Come again?" I asked.

"Think about it Keira, over these weeks since the war, it started gradually and then over time has developed, growing in power and in doing so bringing out Dominic's demon more frequently."

"Oh shit!" Pip said at the same time Sophia said,

"This isn't good." Both of which became a back-drop sound to me hanging a heavy head to my hand and muttered,

"What the hell are we going to do?"

"But why can't we see it?" Sophia asked continuing with the question as I had a mini internal meltdown...*again.*

"It must be part of this kind of Hex, like a protective measure, some kind of defence," Pythia replied, and I had to say, this wasn't good news.

"So, you mean we don't know the mark, which means if we don't know what it looks like, then we don't know who it belongs to?" Sophia surmised but I was still in the dark on this one, not exactly being big on my hexes and curses.

"What do you mean?" I asked in a freaked-out tone.

"Usually a Hex can only be removed by the one who branded it," Pythia told me, and this was when my freak out started going nuclear.

"But Cronus is dead! So how do we get a dead man to break a Hex!?" This was when Pip, Sophia and Pythia all gave each other a look as if they knew something I didn't. Something that I knew wasn't good.

"What...what is it this time?" I asked looking from one to the other and back again.

"The dead can't hold a Hex," Pythia said making me frown.

"What do you mean?"

"What she means is that if the person who branded a Hex dies, then so does the Hex," Sophia said softly, for we all knew what this could mean and the horror in facing it. However, no one else would say what we were all thinking.

No one else but me.

"Then that means..." I paused taking a deep breath before saying the words I never thought I would ever have to say...

"Cronus is still alive."

CHAPTER NINETEEN

A TOWER OF CONESSIONS

The second this was said, Sophia hissed in panic, only it was nothing to do with the bombshell just dropped.

"Shit, my brother is awake, everyone out!" Everyone stood up, including me making Sophia turn to me as Pip and Pythia started running for the exit.

"Not you, you're supposed to be here remember, now pick a book and start reading," Sophia ordered before giving me a quick kiss on the cheek and following the others out the door. Then, not knowing how much time I had, I ran to the nearest shelf, grabbed any book and then sat back down to pretend to read it.

The flaw in this plan however, was *what* I had picked up to read and now having no time to change it as Draven was stalking through the door wearing nothing but a pair of checked flannel lounge pants. His massive chest and huge shoulders were on show making me lick my dry lips at the sight of all that raw untamed muscle.

"I have to say sweetheart, not a fan of waking up to find my wife missing from our bed," he said once he was close enough that he was now stood at the back of my chair and was reaching over to take hold of my chin to tilt my head, so he could have my eyes.

"I left you a note," I said gently making him raise an eyebrow down at me. Then he leaned closer to me, bending at the waist so he could whisper seductively in my ear,

"But I can't make love to a note." I shuddered after he said this as his hand slipped down to my neck and collared it with his large hand making my insides turn to mush. Then he kissed the top of my head and I could feel him smiling his victory at getting the reaction he wanted.

"What's that your reading?" he then asked, taking me off guard. In my panicked moment I tried to hide the book and said,

"Oh, it's nothing, anyway we should get back to bed." Then I tried to stuff the book down the side of me, doing so the wrong way so that he could still see the spine. Damn it! I wanted to smack my forehead when he reached down, grabbed it before I could stop him and then read out the title much to my horror,

"Male Reproductive System: Clinical Anatomy and Physiology." My only response was to groan out loud making him chuckle,

"Some light reading, sweetheart?" he teased. I grabbed the book back off him and threw it down on the coffee table in front of us.

"Ha, ha, no I was just…well, I wanted to…to check something," I said hoping this was enough to stop him questioning me on it. But then again, this was Draven we were talking about, so of course he would say something.

"I think we know that it all works, sweetheart," he said pulling me from my chair and tugging me back against him so that he could frame my belly with his hands, as now his arms were around me from behind.

"Yes, and congratulations for that, you must be so proud," I teased back making him laugh.

"I am indeed, but just to make sure to further your education on the matter, I think it best to give you a refresher course in the male anatomy, giving special attention to the important parts first, just to be sure." At this I laughed giving him a nudge with my elbow and saying,

"Smooth."

"If you want smooth sweetheart, you might have to go digging to find it," he said turning me round to face him before looking down at the evidence that proved there was indeed something smooth down there, but it also came in the form of something very, very hard. Oh, and definitely something that needed exploring in further detail.

He picked up my discarded throw, one I had forgotten about as we had been sat next to the fire. Then he swung it out around my shoulders, catching the other side before pulling it closer around me.

"Come with me," he said in that velvet voice of his that would have me doing anything he asked. He took my hand in his and led me from the room making me look back at the space and silently saying goodbye to the turbulent night.

At first, I thought Draven was just going to take us back to our room, but when he he took a different door, one away from the stairs leading to our room, I knew he obviously had other thoughts.

"Uh, shouldn't we be…whoa!" I ended my sentence on a squeal as suddenly Draven lifted me up into his arms and continued on without answering me. We passed long hallways filled with yet even more scenes of battles and wars both painted and depicted on tapestries hung high, closer to the moulded ceilings. I wanted to make a comment but one look at Draven and I could tell his thoughts were solely on two things, his destination and how quickly he could get me there. Which prompted me to ask,

"Where are you taking me?" I questioned as he started to walk through a section of the castle I knew was leading us to one of the four towers and a place I hadn't been yet. However, yet again he remained silent through this whole time with only a squeeze of my leg every now and again. This for Draven was a tell-tale sign that he was on sexual edge and to be honest by the time he made it up the last of the spiral stairs and came to a door, then I was on that edge too.

He released my legs, letting them swing down before lowering the rest of me down the front of his hard body. But the second my face became level with his, he crushed his lips to mine in a passionate kiss. His hand cupped my cheek before embedding his fingers in my hair as if he was desperate to keep me locked to him. His lips moulded to mine as his tongue searched out my taste like a man starved of food. Then, when my need to breathe became too much, he lowered me the rest of the way to the floor, his kiss following until my body was steady and now standing.

This was when I realised we were outside a door I hadn't seen before but reminded me of the solid wooden door he had once caged me up against on his rooftop. And cage me in was exactly what he did now as he pressed me against the wooden panels that were all framed by a raised piece of wood and studded all the way round with iron rivets.

His hands flattened above me either side, showcasing his greater height and making me feel even smaller because of it. He lowered his head making some of his hair come forward and I slowly reached out to push some of the soft strands back, making his eyes flash purple, glowing at my tender touch.

"What's behind this door, Draven?" I whispered the question making one side of his lips raise up and making me swallow hard at his bad boy grin that spoke of only carnal things to come.

I knew this for a certainty when he answered me.

"A place I promised would be in your future should you not behave." Then I watched as his left hand fell down the wood, skimming it with his fingertips slowly, before what I first thought was reaching for the handle that was next to my waist. But his hand lowered further until he reached inside his pocket and pulled out a key that had the elaborate end entwined in a purple ribbon.

I didn't know why, but if I were to venture a guess, I would say it looked to have been done on purpose as a reminder to himself that one day he would be using it. A day that, when he did, he would have me right here, up against the door like he did now, in this very moment.

He raised the key to the lock and the loud click as it slid into place echoed in my heart, making it thud in anticipation.

Then he simply opened the door and I stepped further into him so I didn't fall, seeing as I was still leaning all my weight against it. This was when he straightened up and turned me round with his hands on my shoulders, with the key still in hand. Then he walked me forward into the room. The second I took one look inside I gasped walking further in, this time by myself before turning around to face him.

"This...this is..." I didn't know what to say at first as it seemed impossible...could it have been true, all this time?

"You didn't lie...all this time and you weren't lying," I said finally getting my words out and seeing for myself the near insane level in which Draven, through his love for me, was willing to go to keep me safe. He didn't say anything to this, but he just stood in the doorway with his arms folded as he watched it all dawn on me.

"This is your tower, isn't it? The one you always threatened me with…all this time and I thought you were only joking," I said in freaked out awe as I looked around the room, one that had obviously been decorated with only me in mind. I knew this because, as insane as it sounded, it looked so similar to my room back at Libby's.

The colours used on the bedsheets were shades of purples with large black velvet flowers covering a middle section of it. Even the bed wasn't the usual masculine wooden four poster I was used to seeing. But instead a black wrought iron one with four spindles and a feminine pattern of swirls in between.

The circular room had stone walls and the bed dominated the centre of the room, whilst other sections of the space had been separated by partitioning walls to create what I knew was probably a bathroom, and a small walk in closest, as the whole tower room was certainly large enough. I was even amazed to find a desk and easel sat near a window looking out to the amazing view of the mountains, and a perfect place for a painter to lose herself in her art.

He had thought of everything, including books he knew I liked, a picture of my family in a frame and candles that were dotted around the room, as if this was a must for any girl's room.

"How long have you had this room like this, Draven?" I asked in a thoughtful tone as the seriousness of this had started to seep in. He took a few deep breaths, still with his arms folded across his chest as if he didn't want to answer me but, in the end had no choice.

"Since I first met you," he said making me swallow hard at the implications of that sentence and what it meant.

"But this room…it's…"

"I carried you back that day," he said interrupting me and obviously now knowing he needed to get this out before he thought better of it. I frowned in question and shook my head slightly before telling him,

"I don't understand."

"When I met you in the woods I knew nothing about you, other than you were the most beautiful creature I had ever beheld… but that wasn't enough," he told me shocking me, but it didn't stop there.

"I needed to know you. Needed to see who you were when I wasn't around, so I watched you." He continued speaking now as he lowered his arms, so he could close the door behind him.

"I remembered that day, laying you down on the sofa in case you woke sooner than expected. Even then your mind wasn't easy to control. I would try and get a read on your thoughts, being arrogant enough to think I was entitled to them." I frowned at him, about to disagree when he did it for me, in a sense.

"You were mine you see, the very second I saw you that was it, your fate was sealed along with mine…the only difference was that you just didn't know it yet."

"And this room?" I asked jumping slightly when he slammed it shut before pausing against it, looking down at the lock with his bare back still facing me. I could see the way his shoulders bunched as he tensed at my question.

"I wanted to make it comfortable for you, so I went in search of where you spent your time and had it memorised. Of course, I added to it the more your personality came through during your first months at Evergreen Falls, like the art supplies, clothes, books, that type of thing," he said still unable to look at me, so I asked again.

"Draven, what was this room going to be used for?" My voice this time was getting harder to keep steady as I started to worry that I already knew the answer to that question. He confirmed this when I heard the click of the key turning, locking us in.

"It was to be your home," he said, finally turning to look at me, as if he could no longer stand it, he had to see the effect his words had on me and what he saw was utter shock.

"No…no you…you can't be serious," I said denying it for him and shaking my head as if it would rid me from the thought.

"Back then I only had one thought, make it safe, then make you mine," he said, this time sounding far less ashamed than he should have.

"And if I didn't want to do as I was told?" I snapped but he merely shrugged his shoulders and motioned to the room.

"Like I said, your new home."

"You mean prison!" I corrected, this time making him wince.

"I didn't care if I had to spend the next hundred years making you fall in love with me Keira, so long as I did this knowing you were safe and none of my enemies could get to you," he told me making me bite my lip as I digested his words.

"Think back to when you travelled through time, Keira… what happened?" I frowned not understanding where he was going with this. So, I shook my head and started to tell him,

"I don't see what that has to…"

"Please, just try and answer the question…what happened when we met in the past?" he questioned more clearly this time. So, I did as he asked and thought about it before telling him,

"I met you in the great hall, I caused a bit of a scene, you saw it and then came over to me," I told him starting at the beginning still not seeing where he was going with this.

"Then what happened?"

"You got mad, held a blade to my throat and asked me

questions," I replied with a frown, wanting to point out that back in the past, he didn't exactly try to woo me.

"Did I hurt you, even though you struck a royal Satrap, something punishable by death or at the very least a severed hand?" I swallowed hard looking down at both my hands very much intact and uttered a small,

"No."

"Then what did I do?" he asked again, more calmly this time.

"You asked my name and..." I paused thinking back and remembering the way he had been so careful with his blade. How it had been more for show than anything else. Then, when I couldn't answer his questions to his liking, he was about to have the guards take me to his chamber when Ranka intervened. Okay, so I was now starting to see where he was going with this.

"And?" he pressed.

"And you ordered to have me taken away, but in the end..."

"In the end you found yourself in my Harem," he finished off for me, then going on to ask one more thing,

"Now for my next question, whilst you were in my care at any point did I let you go free?" I bit my lip, took a breath through the small gap I allowed between my lips, before shaking my head telling him no.

"No, I did not. Which, therefore, as much as both you and I hate to admit it, you were in fact my prisoner and one I kept close watch over."

"You weren't there, Draven," I told him softly making him laugh once only without humour.

"I may not have been there Sweetheart, but I know myself very well. You may add two thousand years between the two points and with that add a very a different society at the end of one... one I find myself living in today, but that doesn't mean anything if it gets in the way of what I want, and I wanted you," he said with purpose and a tone that I was left to do nothing but believe him. He took a deep breath and told me,

"Look at this any way you want Keira, but I know myself and I know even without being there, how I first enforced my rule over you, long before I tried to make you fall in love with me." So basically, he was saying that no matter how much time could have passed between us, his decisions would have still been the same.

But in the end, they hadn't been. Which now brought on the all-important question,

Why?

"Then why didn't you, Draven? Why didn't I just end up here right after we met?" I asked needing this and needing to know what would have happened had he followed through with his plan. Could I really have fallen in love with my captor, after experiencing it so horrendously with another? I couldn't say either way for sure as I had already been in love with Draven when going to the past. But what would have happened had I not been?

I had no answers because the fact remained I was now faced with the man I loved so deeply it felt like he was ingrained in my soul, branded to it no matter what happened. It had always been that way. But what if Draven had showed me a different side of him to start, would it have ended differently?

"Why didn't you just take me, Draven?" I asked again and in those few seconds of silence between us as I waited, it seemed like a lifetime until he replied with a firm truth,

"Because I fell in love with you first." Hearing this made me swallow hard and this ended up being my only reaction because I couldn't find the words. But thankfully I didn't need to as he wasn't finished.

"I fell in love with what I saw every day. The way you

reacted to those around you, the way you would laugh with your friends or the kindness you showed my sister. The serene look on your face when you would listen to your music whilst taking a walk and the way you always slept peacefully after reading a book...by the Gods even the way you drove your car so cautiously, checking nothing was coming the other way about five times before taking the chance to pull out," he said on a laugh and then paused, as if he was seeing it all there again. Seeing all those times, right in front of him, like he too had just spent time in the witness circle, asking of it, all he wished to see were memories of me.

"Even those shy looks you would grant me when you thought I didn't know that you were looking. The way you would fiddle with your hair nervously or that damn lip of yours would drive me to distraction! You just had no clue as to what you did to me. I would find myself willing you to trip, letting your clumsiness get the better of you, just so that you would fall into my arms and I would finally have the excuse I needed to touch you," he told me rubbing the back of his neck as if he remembered the frustration as if it was yesterday.

"But yet no matter how much I wanted to take it, to have it all and make it mine, I knew I couldn't do that to you, or in the end, *to me*."

"What do you mean?" I asked in a quiet, soft tone, telling him without words my anger was all gone.

"What I mean is that all of these day to day things made me fall even more and more in love with you each time and in the end, I couldn't take that from you, just as much as I couldn't take it from myself...I couldn't risk dousing water on the flames of your soul, one that would light me up within at just the sight of you."

"Oh, Draven." This was all I managed to utter as the tears came and heavy droplets fell down my face. But then I watched

as he let the key drop, falling until the ribbon untangled so that it was dangling down from his hand.

"But now, well now I finally get to live out one of my fantasies and thanks to what you said to me today, you unknowingly gave me the green light I needed," he told me, making me replace my loving look of adoration to one of confusion and wariness. Now my mind had gone into overload trying to recall all that I had said to him, but it kept coming up blank. What had I said to make him want to show me this now…? What could I possibly…? and that's when it hit me, and he knew it too when I saw him grin.

His words today had been the start, when he told me, *'I swear that tower is looking ever closer to playing an integral part of your future darling'*. And me thinking this an open threat as always, said in return,

'Only if you're there with me and we both throw away the key.'

And that key was now one that he lifted up, opening the pieces of ribbon so that he could place it around his neck, leaving it to hang there as a symbol of his ownership. A sign that he was master in this room and I was his captive.

I knew this

"I am not throwing away the key, Keira…" he told me as he started to take long strides towards me until he was towering above me, so now he could place a single finger to my chin, to tilt my head up to look at him.

"But I am keeping it right here…" he said pointing to his heart where its length reached, as if in some symbolic meaning, making me too the keeper of his heart.

Then he issued a promise, growling down at me one last rule,

"Firmly locked…until I am done with you."

CHAPTER TWENTY

A PRETTY PRISON OF SILK ROPE

"*Firmly locked...until I am done with you,*" he said as my only warning before he picked me up, tossing me up over his shoulder with one arm and making me cry out a little at the shock of both his strength and show of dominance.

"Draven I..." I started to say something but never finished when he delivered a swift smack to my bottom, making me yelp as the bite of the sting set in, something that instantly made me soak my underwear.

"Quiet!" he snapped sternly also adding to my arousal. Then he reached the edge of the bed and with a grab of my hips, he gave me another little toss. Which meant I soon found myself thrown down on the bed, bouncing once before my body settled. I was about to pull my legs up and sit up when he shook his head at me telling me no.

"Stretch out," he instructed firmly. I swallowed hard, again wondering what I had got myself into and was this wise playing this game when he was so close to his demon? Was it something I should stop or just trust him? I had to say that right now he looked the epitome of control, so in the end this and my soaked panties was enough to convince me to play this game of his.

So, if a bit hesitant for a submissive, I finally did as I was told, being granted a nod of approval for my efforts. Draven looked down at me from the bottom of the bed where he still stood, looking the master of my body I knew he was.

I don't know what he waited for but the second he saw me start to feel self-conscious by squirming under his intense gaze, he grinned before making his move.

"Draven?" I couldn't help but say his name in question, making him raise his finger to his lips.

"Ssshh." This was all the warning I got before he slowly started to crawl up the bed over me, looking like a predator coming to claim his kill before he devoured it. He finally got all the way up the bed until he was looking down at my face before he straddled my waist, holding himself above me on his knees.

"Do you trust me?" he asked me, his voice hoarse and thick with lust. I knew he didn't want me to speak, so instead I just nodded my head making him smile before leaning down to cup my jaw in his hand before kissing me. Once he was finished and pulled back, he knew that I still wanted more because I raised myself up with his lips. He nipped at them, telling me to behave so that I would relax back to the bed.

"Good girl," he praised when I did as I was told, then he glanced to the window for a second and by the time I did too, I saw the tasselled curtain tie drop to the floor before sliding towards his outstretched hand. If I thought it was hard swallowing before, now I was nearly gulping for breath.

"Ww...what are you planning on doing with that?" I couldn't help but whisper as my curiosity won over his previous order.

"Well, that depends," he told me running the silken length of rope through his strong hands.

"On?"

"You and your willingness to follow the rules," he told me, clearly enjoying this game, making me wonder just how long he had been craving to play it with me like this.

"And they are?" I asked, just glad he was letting me speak now…or so I thought.

"Speaking without permission for one," he said sternly making me bite my lip. His eyes homed in on the action and the purple in his eyes ignited once more.

"Now that will definitely get you punished," he said nodding to my lip and growling the first part of this sentence. But I couldn't help myself from asking once more,

"Punished?" He smirked this time, obviously expecting me to play right into his hands.

"Punished!" he said at the same time snapping the cord between his fists making me jump. I opened my mouth to speak again but he got there first by saying,

"Speak again and you will find out what, Sweetheart." He grinned in satisfaction when my mouth snapped shut in a heartbeat.

"Good, you're learning. Now, reach out with your arms above your head and hold them there. Do. Not. Move," he ordered, making me do as he asked. Then he took the length of rope and it didn't take a genius to know what he was going to do next, when he leant down over me, taking a wrist in his hand.

First, he lifted it to his mouth to kiss the inside of my wrist before then wrapping the silk cord around it a few times before securing it to one of the swirls of iron above me. Then he did the exact same thing to the other wrist, kissing it also after he had summoned the other curtain tie to his hand.

Once he was finished, he sat back over me to admire his handy work, then he shifted back, gripped my hips and then yanked my body hard down the bed. I gasped when the ties around my wrists tightened so that now I had nowhere to move to, meaning now he was satisfied. I knew this when he grinned at my reaction.

I kind of wished that right now I was wearing something sexy, like some lacy underwear but unfortunately, I was still in my pyjamas that had I been wearing when we were watching Jaws. But, as if reading my mind and my not so secret wishes, he put my mind at ease by granting me a moment of insight to his thoughts.

"Just look at you, looking so fucking innocent and so pure, all tied up and at my mercy..." he paused as he lowered himself down over me and he did this so he could whisper the last of his sentence over my mouth, one that opened in shock when he said,

"...My perfect little slave." Then his tongue swept inside, tasting my gasp for himself as every sensation in my body seemed to light up just through that one kiss. He tilted his head and he rolled to the side, so he didn't crush me. Which meant he could now use his hands on my face, tilting me further so that he could take the kiss deeper.

Once I was the way he wanted me and the best to devour me, one hand embedded itself into my hair, so he could keep possession of me for as long as he wanted, whilst his other hand slipped down from my cheek. It ran the length of my neck and down so slowly I felt myself arching up into his touch the deeper it went. I wanted it all over me, I wanted his touch everywhere. I wanted to be naked and feel his fingertips ignite my skin as he explored my body.

"You're wearing too many clothes," he told me as if reading my mind again.

"Yes," I agreed forgetting the rules and in doing so feeling him pinch my nipple hard before twisting it through my vest.

"Aaaahh," I moaned with both the bite of pain and injection of pure lust that action flooded my core with. Even half my body twisted as I squirmed around under his punishment.

"Legs down, be still!" he ordered but when I didn't do it in time, he had another idea. He leant down over me, taking the nipple closest to him in his mouth. Then over the material of my vest, he took hold of the hard little bud in between his teeth. He applied a small amount of pressure at first and I didn't realise but he was doing it to see if I would comply with his order. Then when I reacted too late he bit down harder making my legs drop to the bed and remain still.

I felt him smile around my nipple before he soothed the pain he inflicted, letting it go with a wet sound.

"There's my good girl," he whispered over my cheek before kissing it. Then he moved back to take the time to rid me of my clothes, ones he removed by opening the seams so that he could fix them later, knowing that they had been a gift from my mother. I don't know why, but this tender gesture coming from such a dominant side of him, made my arousal for him increase tenfold, soaking my core and readying myself for him further.

He pulled the material from my body as if it had been an insult being there in the first place. Now leaning back, he took the time to admire my naked body from further back starting with my breasts, running a flat hand down from my neck like before, only now continuing further down, as finally, he had nothing in his way. He cupped them, as if testing their weight and the whole time looking down as though they were forbidden fruits from the Gods. Then he continued further, teasing me and building me up to a near frenzy, one that would be soon begging him to take me, punishment be damned.

"Please." The sexual moan escaped before I could take it back and this time my punishment wasn't delivered to my

nipple but to my clit. He suddenly pinched it and continued to apply pressure to it slowly, making me scream.

"Are you sorry?" he asked in that controlled stern voice of his. I swallowed down my chosen swear word knowing that wouldn't help me right now and went for a frantic head nod instead. His grin was all that of a sexual tyrant, and holy hell if that didn't just end up turning me on even more! After this he released the pressure and ran his knuckle over the swollen bud of nerves making my body jolt at the sensation.

Again, my reaction pleased him, but then his gaze shifted and so did his focus. His hands started to run up my sides before resting against my belly, framing it with his big hands. I froze wondering what he was going to say next. At this early stage I wasn't showing yet but then this had me asking myself what would Draven be like when I did? I wasn't sure if he would like it or not, as it wasn't exactly something that men usually found sexy...or was it?

I just didn't know. But I also couldn't tell what he saw in my eyes in that moment. Maybe it was all my emotions flickering by one by one, which at this stage were more questions than anything else. All of which could only be answered by him. So, I continued to hold my breath until he finally spoke his thoughts aloud.

"I cannot wait to see this sexy little body start to swell with my baby as it grows inside you. To see your breasts ready themselves for becoming a mother, filling with milk...fuck, Keira do you know how much I look forward to the sight. My hot little body, this perfection I own, seeing it changing thanks to my seed that has taken root inside you," he said almost on a growl as if he could see for himself and the idea was turning him on. I was shocked and hated that the shadow of doubt asked myself if this would be true to life when I did actually start to grow bigger? Something must have shown in my expression as he added to this.

"I know you have no idea the amount of pleasure I find in this body as it is now, I can see it in your eyes. Just as I can see the doubt in them, for fear my thoughts might change, but I can assure you, my beautiful wife, they most certainly will not. I think you are most likely to find my insatiable need to have you will no doubt increase as your body changes, and in turn my need to explore it...*in great detail,"* he told me softly before coving my body in kisses, licks and little bites making me moan and tug impatiently at the ropes, my need to touch him mounting by the second. And with his sweet tender words still playing in my mind, I wanted to run my hands through his hair. To grip the strands and hold him to me so that he would never leave. I wanted every inch of my body to be used and adored by him. And I wanted the picture he painted so vividly of the future to come true.

"Please..." I pleaded pulling on my restraints, again telling him what I wanted. But this only ended up with him tutting above the line under my belly, just before he could reach my feminine mound. As this now made him want to punish me again and I knew this when he looked up at me, eyes seeping into darker purple when he said,

"I warned you sweetheart, *now it's time I really play."* This he said before diving lower and I found my legs spread, making way for his wide body in between. He held them apart by the inside of my thighs, his fingers biting into my tender flesh as his lips took possession of another tender part of me. The second his tongue swiped up the seam, I shuddered nearly coming undone just from his first taste of me. My back bowed off the bed in an arch of my spine before his hand shot out and pressed my body back into the bed forcefully.

Then he dipped lower, licking up my desire for him like a

man starved and doing so at the core of me. I felt him start growling against my damp folds, before unable to help himself from swearing,

"Fuck, you taste like heaven!" he told me before going back for more, seconds later giving me what I wanted and finally letting me come. Something I did the minute he latched onto my clit and started sucking it into his mouth, stimulating it with his tongue.

"DRAVEN!" I screamed his name, fighting against him and my ropes as my body bowed up off the bed again. I don't remember ever coming so hard in all my life and I knew this as I was still panting when suddenly he thrust into me, obviously unable to wait. I knew this when he said seconds before,

"I cannot wait any longer, I want what is mine…say it!" but I couldn't say it because I was too busy crying out in utter bliss as he entered me, making me whole again. The connection was an instant rush of euphoric sensations as my body released another orgasm too quickly after the first, confusing me as to whether it was still one or one of many.

Then I felt him sit up, pulling my body from under my buttocks as he thrust into me, yanking on my restraints and driving my wild need even wilder.

"Draven please…please…" I started begging and he lowered me down, this time taking leisurely long strokes inside me and managing only to drive me to near insanity.

"Then say it, say you're mine…*say it!*" he demanded and somewhere in the back of my fogged mind I knew if I wanted something, then I was going to have to do as he wished. So, I leant up as far as my restraints would allow and told him,

"I am forever yours!" and the second I did my ropes snapped and I was free…free to have him. I launched myself at his body, taking him off guard so that now I was on him, moving myself

astride him and sitting back to ride his length like a woman possessed. He gripped my hips, holding me steady as I rolled my movements so that he was stroking every nerve, lighting them up with every stroke. I didn't have to do this long before I felt it rising in me again and from the sounds of it, Draven was feeling the same.

"I...Gods, Keira...I...fuck!" he shouted suddenly bolting upright as he came with a roar and I followed him quickly after, screaming his name as my core rippled around his steely length. Then, as if having a thirst I couldn't contain, I sank my fangs into his neck drinking him down and in doing so making him growl before bellowing out another release. Something I also followed him with again, when he pulled me back, so he could take a turn. Only this time it wasn't my neck he took. No, it was my breast. The scrape of his fangs against my nipple had me crying out in bliss against his skin, as I left bloody kisses wherever my lips touched.

Finally, we came down from our sexual high together and collapsed back on the bed.

"By the Gods Keira, that was..." he couldn't seem to find the words, which was unusual for Draven. But just before I could ask, he snagged me with a hand to the back of my head pulling me to him and saying,

"You were perfection..." I let his words seep deep within me having only a few seconds to relish them before I realised what was happening. I looked up at him and his eyes suddenly started to change, which was my only warning when I saw fire in them, before it was too late. Because now his hand was on my neck and whatever was hidden beneath his fingers was now bringing out the demon in him. A demon that now only had one more thing to say to me,

"My perfect, Wardum àm Kad nga Shi..." My mouth opened, about to plead for him to release Draven back to me, when the next words out of his demon were my first insight as to what the ancient words meant,

The ones he had been telling me all this time…

"Wardum àm Kad nga Shi…"

"…Slave that ties my soul."

CHAPTER TWENTY-ONE

BITCH KEIRA

"Come on, sweetheart…time to wake." I heard Draven's voice entering my subconscious and I frowned, wondering what had happened? The last thing I remembered was Draven pulling me in for a kiss, telling me I was perfect one minute and then the next speaking an ancient language to me. I remembered eyes of fire. I remembered his voice, a deep and throaty growl lacing his words, but then one softer when telling me what those words had finally meant.

'Slave, that ties my soul.' That was what he had said to me. Now what had he meant by that? And now what was happening to him…was he back? I was almost too afraid to open my eyes and find out.

"Hey, come on now and open those pretty eyes for me," he said, and I felt his warm touch against my cheek, so this time I placed my trust in his voice. I opened my eyes and saw that it was now light outside, asking myself once again what had just happened.

"There she is, there's my girl...good morning, sweetheart," he said before kissing me gently on the lips.

"What happened?" I asked him whilst rubbing the sleep out of my eyes and trying to make sense of the last few hours. I knew it hadn't all been a dream because I could still feel the wonderful evidence of last night's tenderness between my legs. I could also see that we were still in my 'prison room' in the tower and sunlight was beaming through the tall windows.

"I think it's called passing out after incredible sex," Draven said on a chuckle, with a cocky smirk. Well, at least that look told me that Draven didn't remember all that happened after we'd had one of the most incredible nights together. I know that he had touched my birthmark, the one no one could see. But the one Pythia assured me was still there. And I think that after last night, that was easy to confirm. But this just begged the question, that if Draven's demon had come out to play at the end, then what did he play *with* exactly...as I remembered none of it?

After this strange morning of at least ten whole minutes of asking myself why, Draven soon took my mind off it as we spent time being lazy in bed together. We talked about everything and nothing as couples usually do. But it was times in the past I was interested in, as I couldn't get the image of Draven in the VIP out of my head. I wish I could have just asked him about it, but then again, I shouldn't have known about any of it in the first place, as I hadn't been there. So, I asked him a different way.

"Can I ask you a question?" I mused, half lounged over his bare chest, as I was currently running circles around his flat nipples with my fingertip and doing so with my breasts smushed up against him. I looked up to find him staring at the impressive cleavage my position created and at first, I thought he hadn't heard me. Obviously being elsewhere...lost and maybe somewhere the hills were giant breasts with rivers of breast milk running in between and he was currently riding on a magic carpet nipple across Boob land. But then he answered me and smashed the boob illusion

"I think with this bountiful view I am currently enjoying, you will find me susceptible to answering any of your questions," he teased making me pinch his nipple in return and making me laugh when he complained,

"Oww!" Although, I knew it didn't hurt, as I had seen the impossible happen to him and never once had I heard him saying 'Oww'. Which was why I called him,

"Baby." Then once my teasing him was through and after I kissed the fake hurt away, I leant back and asked him,

"Did you ever want to just do things the normal way and ask me out?" He looked taken back by my question for a moment and then totally shocked me by saying,

"Keira, don't you realise, I didn't just wish I could simply ask you out like any normal man would, I also wished for the first time in my life that I could *be that normal man."*

"You did?!" I asked nearly reaching high pitch levels.

"But of course, do you not see how much that would have been simpler, if I had just met you in my club that first night, and instead of feeling frustrated with myself that I couldn't just have you, I would have just asked you to join me for a drink like any normal man would...like I wanted to," he told me, sending my mind on a trip down memory lane. I remembered how he had first stopped at the table, staring at me as if battling with himself on what to do with the sight of me. At the time, of course, to me it had just been another intimidating time where Draven just looked unimpressed and annoyed at my presence. But then his actions usually always contradicted these times.

"But in the end what I had been left with was to stalk you in the shadows or the through the eyes of others. The only times I felt like I could breathe easy in the day was when you would start work under my roof and therefore I knew I had you under my protection." Hearing this sweet confession, I placed a hand to his cheek before reaching up to kiss him. It wasn't a mad passionate kiss that would lead to us being naked, because well, we were still naked. But instead, one that spoke only of the love I had for him, not for the passion he knew burned as always.

It wasn't long after this moment that Draven suddenly went tense in my arms and I pulled back to see him concentrating.

"Sophia needs to see me," he told me after a few seconds. After this he told me that behind one of the partitioned walls I should find some clothes in my size, which made my lips twitch this time, as I had been right…he had thought of everything. I already knew there was a bathroom behind the other as I had needed to use this not long after waking up.

So, after no time at all, I was just kicking my feet into some brand-new navy converse shoes that I was already claiming from this room as ones I wouldn't be bringing back. In fact, when looking through the racks and drawers of clothes when looking for something to wear, I had already decided that I had fallen in love with most of them. After all, it was a waste to just leave them here, right? As they were all brand new and all in my size and style. I knew Sophia had definitely been involved in this one.

"Are you ready?" Draven asked me after using the bathroom himself as he now looked as if he'd had a quick shower. His hair looked as though he'd just rubbed a towel over it for a few seconds as it was mainly still wet at the ends. He was also wearing a lot more than he walked in here with, which made me wonder if he too had his own secret stash of clothes in here. You know, for all those nights he intended to spend 'making me fall in love with him'. A task I think he would have accomplished in less than twenty-four hours, that was for sure.

So, with him now looking sexy in his long sleeved light grey t shirt and his charcoal jeans and black boots, I could then take about twenty hours off that first statement. I was wearing a navy blue long sleeved top, with light blue jeans and a chunky knit, white cardigan that was hooded and tied around the waist with a belt.

I then watched as he picked up the key he had taken off at some point during the night, as when he had woken me it had been gone. He walked over with it now in his hand and unlocked the door, after first staring at it in his palm for a while. I don't know why he did this as he seemed to be fixated with something, but then just before I could ask him, he looked back at me and asked if I was ready to leave. I decided to let it go for now.

"Yeah, but can I ask what this is about?" I asked but swiftly after this question I wished I hadn't, as his answer had me nearly falling back to the bed...

"It was about Takeshi."

We were making our way through the halls of his castle, both in silence. Me, because I was on edge, thinking the worst and wondering what would happen the second Draven knew what had been going on. And his silence was probably because he was wondering what was wrong with me.

"You look deep in thought, pet," he said giving my hand a squeeze.

"Oh, do I?" I said in what must have been an unconvincing tone as he gave me a look that said it all. But even if he hadn't, his next question did,

"Alright come on Keira, out with it."

"It's nothing, just wondering about Takeshi, that's all," I said because this wasn't exactly a lie.

"He will be fine, and I am hoping now to find him awake, but as I told you, this is nothing I want you worrying over, as I will handle whatever it is…yes?" he said, stopping me when I didn't reply straight away and with a small tug on my hand, I was being pulled into his arms.

"Keira, I need to hear the words," he told me, bringing my face up to his so that he could look at me when I lied.

"Yes Draven, I will let it go," I said knowing that right now I had to use the words carefully so that he didn't know exactly what I was going to let go of. I know it was tricky but what else could I do? I couldn't exactly say to him, 'ah that maybe very well my dear, but I think you will find in this instance it's me you have to leave it up to, as if you knew what I did, you would probably do something stupid like leave me again just to make it safe.' Nope, not a chance.

"Good girl," he said kissing my forehead and making me growl as it sounded far too patronising. However, this just made him laugh. Then, to change the subject, I took note of all the battle scenes on the walls again and said,

"I am sensing a theme here, Draven."

"You mean worrying about things that you should leave to me?" he said making me poke at him and say, shouting the first bit and then struggling to find the right word at the end,

"NO! I mean all the war… stuff!" He laughed at this and repeated,

"Stuff…you mean paintings, tapestries, that type of *stuff?*" he mocked and for some reason this made me really mad.

"Oh, just forget it!" I snapped, storming off and shocking him with my girl bitch paddy. Yep, I think Pip was right, I had some serious pregnant hormones kicking in.

"Hey, Keira wait up!" he shouted, laughing at the sight of

me stomping down the hallway and then catching up to pull me back gently.

"I am sorry, I didn't mean to tease you," he said gently, but his smile also told me he was finding my reaction funny too.

"You don't look very sorry!" I told him, pulling my arm from his hand and folding them across my chest. Again, he looked as if he wanted to burst out laughing as a smirk played at the corner of his lips. Which again, made him look as if he was trying not to laugh, which in turn just made me huff out loud, spin on a heel and march back down the hallway again. I think, after this, he decided the safest road to walk down during this 'preggy freak out' was to give me space and follow me from a safe distance behind.

We found Sophia in one of the sitting rooms, as eventually I had to wait for Draven to show me the way, doing so like a gentleman as he would hold his arm out in the direction I should go. Which ended up just pissing me off more as he would always smile down at me like he adored me and found this whole thing adorably cute...*and funny.*

"Hey, I wondered where you two...whoa, okay what's wrong this time?" she said the second she saw my scowling face.

"Nothing, ask him!" I snapped not understanding why I was so annoyed anymore, but I just was. Wow, being pregnant was weird. It was like I knew I was being a bitch, but I just couldn't help it. Sophia looked to her brother questioningly and without looking at him, I heard the amusement in his voice without needing to see the smile I knew was there.

"She got angry because I repeated her words in a mocking tone, thus teasing her," he answered, not sounding at all affected by this.

"Oookay, I have to say that doesn't sound like the worst thing you've ever done," she commented dryly, but then one look at me and she quickly changed her tune, addressing her brother again and saying,

"I meant, Dom, you bastard, how could you!?" Then she turned back to me and asked,

"Was that better?" At this Draven burst out laughing, making me growl at them both this time.

"Right, well I can see that I am not needed in this conversation, so I will just go," I snapped walking away.

"Holy shit, she really is pissed off," Sophia commented as if it was the first time she had seen me in a mood. I even stormed past Pip with only a head nod in greeting.

"Ooowee what's up her Nelly, as I know it's not his elephant if she is looking that pissappointed?" Pip asked Sophia creating what sounded like a new word for pissed off and disappointed rolled into one, making Draven groan in what now sounded like frustration.

"She's pissed at my brother," Sophia told her as I could still hear them all talking about me.

"For what, killing kittens and making a game out of it?" Pip said.

"For teasing her," Draven replied sternly.

"Oh…ahhh, oh okay, so I know what this is," Pip said as if now hit by a 'eureka' moment. Sophia didn't ask, but must have done some gesture at her for the next sentence was,

"It's the hormones. Apparently, it's not uncommon for someone expecting to also be expected to get pissy and often. The slightest thing can usually set them off, so if I were you I would hurry up, my Lord," Pip said.

"And do what? I think it's obvious that I am the one pissing her off," Draven replied, and I was getting too far across the room now to hear anything other than Pip's reply.

"My advice…*Go grovel, King.*"

The next thing I felt was Draven's arms wrapping around

me from behind and his face came to my neck to whisper into the sweet spot he knew he would find there.

"Hey now, come on sweetheart, I am truly sorry if you found my teasing insensitive...please don't go." The second he said this I felt like the biggest bitch ever and turned in his hold and hugged him, declaring,

"I am so sorry, I am being a hormonal bitch and I took it out on you...please don't hate me!" I said as he held the back of my head to his chest and rubbed my back in a soothing way. I could see side on that Pip was giving him the thumbs up.

"It's okay, hush now, it wasn't your fault, you're just going to be a little more sensitive than usual." I tensed in his hold and then repeated,

"A little more sensitive than usual?"

"Oh no." I heard Pip say as I watched when her thumbs up dance stopped and she smacked her forehead instead.

"More sensitive than usual?" I repeated again when Draven looked as though he didn't know where to put himself. Then he looked back to the girls as if needing their guidance.

"Back pedal!" Pip shouted, meanwhile I growled up at him and started walking away again.

"What the hell does that mean?!" Draven shouted back.

"Retreat! Abandon ship...TRY SOMETHING ELSE!" Pip shouted louder this time, after he obviously didn't understand Pipisms yet.

"Fuck this!" Draven growled, and the next minute I was spun back around and before I had time to argue, he framed my face with both his hands and leant down to kiss me. And when I say kiss me, I mean really kiss me, to the point that angry pregnant hormones were being overtaken by horny ones, as I was close to climbing him like a stripper's pole!

I think at one stage even Pip was wolf whistling and Sophia was applauding us. He let me down after I was panting because at some point he must have picked me up to be able to deepen the kiss.

"Okay, so for future reference, that right there, is how you handle a hormonal pregnant sensitive lady," I told him on a deep sigh, making him chuckle before agreeing,

"That, my beautiful wife, I promise I can do."

CHAPTER TWENTY-TWO

KEY TO MY HEART

Shortly after this and my bitchy meltdown, we found out that my worst fears hadn't come true after all and that Takeshi wasn't yet awake and ready to spill the demon beans. Which deep down had been what my freak out had really been about. But hey, I guess when you're pregnant, then sometimes your real feelings decided to come out in irrational ways. Who knew?

No, instead it had been advised by Mack that it might be best for Takeshi's recovery for him to be back in Afterlife, as being close to the Temple and that 'weird dead tree thingy' they had down there could help. But of course, they hadn't call it the 'weird dead tree thingy' as that would have just been weirder. No, instead it had been called the 'Etz Chaim' which at the time I had no clue as to what they had been talking about. No, it had only been when back in our bedroom packing, that Draven had told me it meant 'Tree of Life' in Hebrew.

He also went on to explain that almost every major religion

had its own version and when I asked what it really was, his answer was simple.

"It is the only living thing on Earth that links our three worlds together. Its roots draw power from Hell, its branches draw power from Heaven and its body remains locked to Earth, which traps both of these energies within its trunk," he told me which had me utterly fascinated.

"But why, I mean what is its purpose?" I asked, stuffing t shirts into my bag, which would have probably made any frequent traveller weep at the thought of so many creases to come.

"*We* are its purpose," he replied and then went on to explain that the tree is a source of energy for his kind, which was why by Alex (The bastard) gifting it my blood that day, it had ended up literally waking the dead. It was that powerful. Which was why its reason for being there was also to protect the temple, as it too was considered a place where harnessed power from the tree helps Draven do his job.

That night so long ago, when I saw him swapping one being's soul for another, to then be transferred into a younger vessel, was both done to administer punishment in one and grant favour in the other. That was the part of the power of the tree of life…hence its name I guess.

Having this conversation with Draven just made me realise how much there was in his world that I still didn't know. But the one thing that gave me comfort was that I now had an eternal lifetime to find out…well, that was if Cronus' plan didn't work and we could figure out a way to stop things before it was too late.

A few hours later and the honeymoon was over as we made our way back home. I can't say I was sorry about this, as I was looking forward to getting back to Afterlife. Wondering now if it wasn't that strange tree that had been pulling me to it all this time. Either way, I had missed the place, but I was also sad to say goodbye to our castle. *Our castle*, which I found had a lovely sound to it, I thought with a hidden smile. Oh, course it was also Mack, who I really would miss as well, and therefore made him promise to come out to Afterlife to stay for Christmas. He seemed extremely touched by the invitation and after an approving nod from his 'Laird' behind me, he agreed whole heartedly.

"Don't worry Keira, we will visit it again soon." Draven had told me when he saw me looking back at the place as we drove further and further away. I nodded and turned back round to face the road ahead of us, wondering just when that time would be and the next time we faced this journey, if we would be doing so with an extra addition to the family…

Our baby.

Before I knew it, we had all reached the airport in convoy, boarded a private jet, and was touching down in Portland in no time at all. Well, this was because I admit, I did sleep most of the way, as again being pregnant I was finding more and more ways that it was affecting my body.

I was just glad when Afterlife finally came into view. And as always, I smiled and released a big sigh of what sounded like relief, at least it must have to Draven who asked me about it.

"So now are you willing to tell me why you do that?" he asked nodding to my face and I guess the smile he had caught. He was sat next to me with his arm resting at the back of my seat and I was kind of nervous about it for most of the ride. At one point going as far as to take his hand and holding it, hoping he wouldn't notice any strange reason for it. But this didn't last as long as I had hoped, as he passed me a bottle of water. A thoughtful gesture after first hearing me complaining that I was thirsty, (another preggy thing) meaning I had to let go of his hand. A hand that went right back to behind my neck, resting there and making me flinch every time he touched it. Thankfully, he had believed my reason being that I was ticklish and hadn't felt the need to comment any more.

"Why I...?"

"Why you smile every time you see Afterlife," he asked and again I was struck with déjà vu, one I knew was from a real memory. It had been after our first meal in a restaurant and unfortunately one that happened under tense circumstances thanks to Alex standing me up. It didn't exactly go smoothly and wasn't really something I would class as being a top ten date.

One that ended just as badly as it started...

"Why do you always do that?" Draven's question startled me.

"Do what?"

"Smile in sight of my home...you always did that, and I always wanted to know." I gave him a small grin and hoped my response would mean he would drop the subject without me having to answer him.

"It's not like you to wait so long till finding out something you wish to know."

"Consider it me choosing the priorities of importance to me." I gave him a little shake of my head and a raised eyebrow, silently asking him to explain the cryptic statement.

"My enjoyment at seeing your happiness outweighed my curiosity," he said making me turn my head away, so he couldn't see how much his words affected me.

"So, are you going to tell me?"

"Not today," I replied softly to the night at my window.

"Why not?" he asked pushing the subject like I knew he

would. So, I turned my body to face him and nodded to his arms before arguing my point.

"Are you gonna tell me about them and why you're obviously hiding them from me?" For the first moment he looked taken aback and even shifted his body further back in his seat as if he was afraid I was going to reach out and touch them.

"That's what I thought," I said when I got no reply but a frown.

"Some things are meant to be left in the past."

"Including us?" I asked quickly making him wince at the power of my question.

"I...Keira, you must understand...this..."

"Oh, I understand, Draven, you want all the answers but with no questions asked. Well, I am afraid it doesn't work like that, it might have done at one time but let's just say I learnt my lesson. You can't go through life without ever explaining yourself, not to the people you're supposed to care about...well, maybe that's your lesson to learn for next time." I added this part looking back out to the night in a whisper I knew he would still hear.

"Next time?" he asked as I reached for the handle of the door now the car had just come to a stop. I didn't turn to face him, I couldn't with what I was about to say...

"Yeah, the next time..." I took a deep shuddering breath, released it and pushed open the door...

"...you fall in love."

The memory finished, and it had suddenly been as though I had been back there to that awful heart-breaking time. It may have been a different car, a different Draven and definitely a different me, but its memory lingered on as though I was seeing it back through the witness circle. Then I turned to face him and told him what I should have done that day.

"I smile because it always felt like I was coming home," I said after turning to him and watching as his handsome features turned more boyish with the type of smile he gave me now.

"You know not the pleasure hearing that brings me," he told me making me smile and it was one that mixed with a blush I didn't mind this time. Well, that was until he added,

"I will never forget the mortal wound you delivered me that day." Of course, after just having that unwelcome trip down memory lane I looked back to the window knowing what he was going to say.

"If it helps it wasn't exactly easy to say," I replied without looking at him.

"No, I can imagine it wasn't, as imagining someone you love with another never is…but then seeing it, is quite another thing entirely," he told me making me release a sigh, this time one that didn't come from a happy place. But before I could respond he beat me to it.

"I don't blame you, Gods I never could, as it was all my doing… I know this, but believe it or not, you did me a favour that night," he said, surprising me enough to look back at him.

"What do you mean?" I asked as the car came to a stop.

"Come on, I have something to show you," he told me cryptically and I was just about to ask, what on earth could he show me that would answer that question. But, as if knowing it, he placed a finger to my lips before I could speak and said the only words I needed to get me to go with him without question,

"Trust me."

So, I let him help me from the car and into what I had considered home for a lot longer than it had been officially. I wasn't surprised when we came to our bedchamber as whatever Draven wanted to show me it was the most logical guess that it would be in here. What I could never have guessed though, was *what I would find inside.*

"Welcome home, Keira," he said as he opened the door and I gasped and I mean *really gasped.* I covered my mouth with my hands and looked back to Draven with wide eyes of surprise. He smiled at my reaction and nodded to the room and told me,

"Go ahead." I turned back around and stepped inside what had now been transformed into what could officially be called 'Our room'. Because what used to be filled with every inch of Draven, now held a perfect mixture of the both of us.

Old tapestries had been replaced with some of my paintings and framed pictures of friends and family, including a beautiful one at the centre of me and my girls...my bridesmaids. There were even things in here from my room at Libby's that I had yet to move in...never thinking for one minute that Draven would want them in this room. Even some of the old furnishings had been taken out and replaced by a few comfy looking chairs, the type you just wanted to curl up in with a good book and stay a while. And the type that Draven knew I loved. One thing I did notice though was the couch Draven had first laid me down on was still there, small blood stain and all.

"I couldn't get rid of that of course, for obvious reasons," he said, clocking where my eyes had focused on. I gave him another shocked smile in return as some of my pillows from my room were even on the bed. Which was another part of the room that had taken on a slightly less masculine look and one more gender neutral. But then again, I couldn't exactly see Draven sleeping amongst pink flowers, surrounded by hearts and quotes of love in swirls of calligraphy every night. And nor would I want him to, as I liked this so much more and it was my idea of heaven. It was still purple and black, but definitely had more of a comfort vibe going on, with its sometimes cold silk and satin now giving way to soft and lush Egyptian cotton sheets.

"You're killing me here, sweetheart," he said after I had obviously been silent for too long.

"You did all this for me?" I asked him in utter awe.

"No, I did this for us," he told me, making his answer as sweet as the gesture itself.

"Do you like it?" he asked after I spun around again taking in even more of the room.

"Do I like it…Draven it's…it's perfect!" I said running back to him to launch myself at him. He caught me at the perfect height so that I could put my arms around his neck to lock him to my kiss.

"It's only perfect now it has you in it," he told me holding me close with our foreheads touching in a wonderful embrace.

"Us…now it has us in it," I said before kissing him again.

A short time later he put me down so that I could continue to explore and the second I walked a little closer to the bed, I shouted in surprised.

"Oh my God! It's my painting!" I shouted jumping up and down after seeing it now hanging over the bed in place of another that used to be there.

"But of course, I know how much you love it, so I had it shipped back here from Italy," he told me grinning and obviously happy at seeing me so excited. It was the one he had bought for me, bidding on it and then hanging it in my hotel room for me to find, one with the most touching note.

Which was why I couldn't help uttering,

"Seventy-seven reasons…"

"…To say I love you," he finished off for me and I knew it wasn't how the note finished but it was definitely one I preferred.

"I have a gift for you," he told me and I swear I released a sound only dogs could hear as it wasn't quite a squeal but was definitely on its way to becoming one if Draven continued to surprise me like this.

"What is it?" I asked after I watched him pull back the sheets on the bed to see what looked like another painting wrapped up. It was covered in thick black velvet paper and tied with a huge purple bow.

"Open it and find out," he replied in a pleased tone. So, I did as he asked and pulled at the ribbon for tearing back the paper. And the second I saw it this time I squealed, and it was loud. I also started bouncing a little in excitement at seeing our first wedding photo of the night. It had been when we were having a moment alone to ourselves, sat on the edge of the fountain, me sat in his arms. We didn't know the picture was being taken at the time, so we were still looking at each other, the love between us was simply breath-taking, but more than that, it was also...*magical.*

The picture was beautiful and one I would treasure forever. But I think he knew this would be my favourite as that's why he'd had it printed onto a canvas for me.

"Wow, it's...it's..." I tried to find the right words when he said one of them for me.

"Perfect."

"Us," I added making him smile. And it was. It was perfectly us as the way we were both so captivated with each other, with our eyes smiling and catching the soft glow of lights from the fountain.

"I left this one for you to choose where you want it to hang," he told me and this gesture I found the sweetest one yet. So, I kissed him on the cheek and whispered,

"Thank you, Dominic." I watched as that name sank in and he closed his eyes as though he treasured the sound and it had all been worth it just for that.

A short time later and after looking around the room trying to decide where it could go, I realised that Draven didn't look finished with the day's surprises. So, I decided to ask him about what started all this and our conversation back in the car.

"So, are you going to tell me now?" The way he looked at me, I knew this was going to be something serious.

"Your words had been 'my lesson to learn, for the next time I fall in love.' Well..." he paused taking a breath before confessing,

"...*You were my next time*... and consider this last gift a lesson learnt, sweetheart," he said pulling a small black box from his pocket wrapped in a purple ribbon, as was quickly becoming our tradition. I took the box off him and looked up at him with a question in my eyes.

"Open it," he told me softly, nodding down to it. So, I did as he asked, pulling on the end and watching the bow unravel. I don't know why but my hand shook a little as if what was in this box was something even more monumental than this new room.

Then I lifted the lid and it quickly fell from my fingers and landed on the floor by my feet, at the same time a silent gasp whispered from my lips. The first thing I saw was the keyring that we had bought together during that wonderful day we spent in Milan. The day we tried on silly wigs, ate ice cream and nearly kissed at the top of what felt like the entire world. The day I told him my fears, finally admitting it, not only to him but to my own heart...

'I'm falling for you again.'

And his answer to this had been as simple as it had been beautiful...

'Then let me catch you.'

So, you see, it may have been just a silly keyring to most people, one with Milan written in colourful writing across it.

But for me it was the perfect symbol of love. The day my heart gave itself again to another…

The day I fell in love with Draven for the second time.

And now the perfect symbol to go with what was attached to an even bigger symbol of perfection. Draven lifted it out of its box, one he let fall to the floor so he could take my hand in his.

Then he placed it in my palm, closed my fingers around it and lifted it to his lips to kiss my hand, as he told me that monumental thing I spoke of. The one thing I had dreamed of owning since I first met him and first saw this place.

And, as if I needed to hear it confirmed for myself, he whispered over my hand, looking directly into my eyes, as he said,

"Your keys to your new home…" I sucked in a sharp breath as a single tear started to fall, landing only when he finished with the most perfect reality to years of dreaming.

My dream of one day owning not only the key to his heart but also the keys to…

"The keys to Afterlife."

CHAPTER TWENTY-THREE

KISSING MY CRAZY AWAY

The next week came and went surprisingly without much of a hiccup and I had stupidly started to allow myself the belief that maybe our problems had gone away on their own. I would find myself wondering if the Devil had kept Cronus as a play thing for long enough and now he'd had his fun out of him, maybe he'd finally killed him once and for all. It would certainly explain why I'd had no dreams for the last week or Draven's demon hadn't made another appearance…That, or it had something to do with us being back home at Afterlife.

For obvious reasons, I was hoping for the first.

Alright, so he hadn't touched my neck and every time he got close to it, I would tell him I'd become really ticklish there and feeling guilty when the easy lie found itself coming from my lips one day…

"Must be another pregnancy thing."

After that he had stayed well away from the area, no doubt fearing the hormonal wrath of his wife. I was ashamed to say it, but after the one at the castle, I'd had another two meltdowns since. The first and second being on the same day. One when we were getting ready to go to my sister's house for dinner and Draven had bought an obscene amount of sweets for my niece. I then thought it best to address the subject in the worst way, *by snapping at him*. I swear it was almost like an outer body experience when I did it and it usually ended in me sobbing, telling him how sorry I was.

Which is precisely what I did in this instance. The second time however, started at my sister's house after they had all been joking about the crazy stuff hormones had done to Libby when she was pregnant with Ella. It was strange because I even remembered what she had been like, joking with Frank at the time myself. The only difference was that we did this when Libby wasn't around, but right now, there I was, sat there feeling worse by the second as Draven would laugh at everything Frank said.

I think it had only been my sister who had realised when they had taken things too far, nudging Frank and telling him quietly that was enough.

"Oh, but just this one more, like the time you got...what?" Frank asked when Libby started shooting him daggers from her eyes. She nodded to me and, no doubt by this point, I looked utterly depressed. Of course, there was an underlying reason today had been the day I let things get to me and like a slow burn, at some point I was going to explode.

So, it wasn't surprising that not long after this we were thanking them for having us and making our excuses for leaving, saying I was tired. Of course, Libby knew better, being there before and knowing the signs.

One night in particular came to mind as I remembered them coming back from one of Frank's work's parties and Libby came storming in the house in tears. This swiftly followed with

Frank slamming the door behind them storming in after. She had been heavily pregnant back then and this was a time just before I found out Draven 'died', so I wasn't so much in a 'zombie Keira like state'.

"You called me fat!" She accused dramatically making Frank release a frustrated sigh.

"No, I said you put on a good amount of baby weight... totally different thing that, Libs!" he argued back.

"Yeah fat! It's fine, you think I'm fat, then admit it...yeah, just go ahead and man up and tell me!" she pushed, making him throw his hands up in the air before saying,

"Fine, you wanna hear that, then yeah, you got fat, but newsflash here Libs, it's because you're pregnant! Jesus, woman you have a baby growing inside you, what did you think would happen, you would be the first skinny pregnant woman in history?!" The second he said this she screamed in outrage, picked up a lamp and threw it at him...one he caught with what looked like ease.

"Oh, you would catch it wouldn't you, you're so bloody perfect? You get to keep your hot body, but one day you will get fat, and then I will be the one everyone says, 'look how big he is' and newsflash to you honey, they won't mean this in a GOOD WAY!" Libby threatened, shouting this last part making even me wince before having to bite my lip to try not to laugh. So far, I had been forced to witness the whole thing as I had been sat on the couch during this time. And for some reason, they decided to have this argument in the hall between the kitchen and the living room.

"Yeah well first, I played college ball honey, so I can catch a damn lamp, something tomorrow you will be happy about because your mom bought it us and second, if I ever get fat, then you can be damn sure it won't be from your cooking, woman!" he threw back, making her mouth drop before she burst into tears and ran up the stairs sobbing the whole way. Frank gripped the back of his hair with both hands, bent his knees and shouted,

"FUCK!" Then it was like someone finally remembered I was in the room as he looked to me as though I held all the answers. Whereas, knowing my sister as I did, I only held one,

"Well, what are you waiting for…go grovel." I told him making him nod once before running up the stairs to catch up with her, taking three steps at a time. That night I heard lots of crying and when it did finally end, it was only for a short time before I then heard crying of a different kind. This was the point that I put on a 'shoot 'em up' action movie and I did so watching it on loud.

So yes, I knew after witnessing how crazy pregnancy could make you, what I was doing now was no different. But for a woman it strangely becomes a very vulnerable time in your life.

"Hey, are you alright?" Draven asked as I stormed down their porch steps and to the car.

"I am fine," I snapped, which was code in any scenario for 'no, I am most definitely not'. He caught up with me and just as I was opening the door, he tried taking it from my hands so that he could do what he always did, and that was open the door for me like a gentleman.

"Its fine, I got it."

"Keira, look at me," he asked making me just shake my head and get in the car, trying to keep a lid on my anger. Then I tried to ignore the deep breath I saw him take next to the passenger window before coming around to the driver's side. Then, after he folded his large frame inside, he just started the car and pulled onto the road to take us home without a word. We remained silent all the way home, with me looking out my window like a stubborn child. Then he pulled into the garage at Afterlife and killed the engine before turning to me and saying,

"Alright sweetheart, you are going to have to give me a clue on this one." His clue in the end had been a frustrated little scream before I got out the car, slamming about a hundred thousand worth before stomping out the garage. I heard Draven closing his door behind me and muttered to himself,

"Alright then." Then he followed me as I continued to navigate the vast hallways that would lead to our room.

"Okay, so I get you are pissed off here." I heard him say behind me a minute later.

"Oh, you think!?" I snapped turning around a second to throw this at him and the second I did nearly walking into a sideboard. Thankfully, he put a hand to my hip and steered me to the side of it, so I missed it. But this didn't help as it just made him even more perfect, which right in this moment just annoyed me further.

"But again, I am going to have to risk your wrath by asking why?" he said making me throw my hands up and start walking again, this time doing so with a weird hop as I bent to one side trying to hook my high heels off as I did.

"If you don't know, then that is even worse!" I told him.

"Or is it only worse in your eyes because you're…"

"Don't say it!" I snapped threatening him with a heel in my hand, but he must have said 'wrath be damned' in his mind, because he finished it off anyway,

"Pregnant?"

"AHHH!" I said throwing my shoe at him, and like Frank had that night, he caught it without even looking. He looked so calm as he lowered it from nearly impaling his face and the sight made me feel guilty, which only managed to make me more upset, which meant I had more to blame him for.

"Feel better?" he asked again with his voice so calm. I didn't answer him, well if you don't count a growl and my other shoe thrown down on the ground at the height of my tantrum, as an answer anyway. I just continued down the hallway to our room getting frustrated when I didn't recognise where I was.

"It's that way," he said directly behind me, making me jump from him and snap,

"I knew that!" Then I carried on, only now deciding that I wanted to talk.

"I can't believe it."

"What can't you believe?" he asked like I knew he would.

"Oh, never mind, you obviously don't think there is anything wrong with what you said, so why bother?" I argued, as if doing so more to myself.

"Well, maybe if you actually tell me *what* I said, then I could consider it for myself and answer that particular question." At this I turned around again and pointed a finger at him.

"Oh no you don't."

"Oh no I don't what?"

"Go and start speaking like that, with all your fancy words and old world English ways, trying to confuse me or turn me on…no, not turn me on, but you know what I mean!" I said getting frustrated with myself for not saying it right and saying way too much at that. I knew this when he raised an eyebrow down at me.

"I had no idea my, how did you put it, 'old English ways' was such a turn on, and now I know I can't imagine why I would want to stop, that being the case," he said making me now want to kiss him as much as slap him. So, I went for the latter, only on the arm not the face, like I had been tempted.

"AHH, you are so frustrating!" I shouted walking away in the direction he had told me and finally he snapped back,

"Yeah, likewise darling."

"Okay big man, you want to know why I am so pissed?" I said, again turning back to him.

"I think evidence would suggest that is what I have been aiming for this last twenty minutes," he said sarcastically, again only making me want to yell at him some more.

"Fine! So, Frank made that joke about Libby's bladder and about their couch getting a monthly spraying," I said recalling the night in detail. Draven looked like he too remembered... because yeah, of course he did, he was a freakin Jedi at everything!

"Yeah, so?" he replied frowning.

"And you said, and this is an I quote here... 'so what are you saying Frank, you recommend I invest in some plastic sheets then?' do you deny it?" I snapped folding my arms across my chest, cursing this tight dress that Sophia had picked out as being a perfect choice.

"Why would I need to deny it, it's what I said?" he said now folding his arms and mimicking my stance.

"Oh my God, you are so fucking clueless!" I screamed at him this time pushing past him and finally getting closer to our door and the second I opened it, he reached around me to pull it closed again.

"I am not taking this stupid argument in that room, so say what the Gods it is you mean, woman and end this madness!" he snapped back making me scowl at him.

"Madness...is that what you think this is?" I asked in that dangerous tone. Then he leaned closer to me, getting inches from my face so he could say more firmly,

"Pregnant madness." And in doing so, cracking what was left of my dignity. So, I screamed at the top of my lungs,

"I PEED ON OUR COUCH THIS MORNING!" And just as I did Sophia, Zagan, Pip, Adam and Ragnar all walked around the corner, hearing every bellowed word.

Then I did the only thing that was left for me and my fragile state...

I cried.

I burst into tears and threw myself into Draven's arms.

After this embarrassing announcement to the world, Draven simply took a deep breath and lifted me up into his arms. Then, without a word to the others, he opened the door with his mind and slammed it shut behind us using the same method. Then he sat down with me in his lap on the bed and silently unzipped my dress, pulling it to the side so that he could kiss my bare shoulder. Doing this, whilst lovingly holding me to him, letting me get it all out before I could cry no more.

Then he stood me up and without another word, pulled my dress down, slowly framing each side of my body as he did, until it fell from my hips to the floor. After it was now a black pool around my feet, he stood, picked me up again and after pulling the covers back, he laid me down gently.

He followed me quickly after, so that we were both lying on our sides facing each other. He covered us both up, despite the fact that he still had on his suit and shoes. But seeing as I was only wearing a black lace underwear set, then I think he cared more about getting me warm, than getting his dirty feet in the bed. Which, in that moment, I realised was him making a statement. He didn't give a damn about the sheets and I had no doubt that he also didn't give a damn about the couch.

All he cared about was me.

So, coming to this conclusion by myself, I placed my hand on his cheek and mouthed the word,

'Sorry'.

He gave me a small smile but again remained quiet as if this was what I needed, but then he ran a fingertip down my cheek, catching the tears there.

"I was just so upset and embarrassed, and I didn't want you to look at me any differently, you know." His frown told me that he didn't, so I carried on,

"It's not exactly the sexiest thing, sneezing and quickly finding yourself with no bladder control." After this he gave me a warm, gentle smile as if the whole day's moodiness had just been explained.

"I'm sorry for being a crazy pregnant lady *again."* I told him this time voicing it aloud. Again, he didn't say anything but just shifted closer to me, pushing a few strands of my hair back from my face and tucking them behind my ear. Then he leaned into me, so that I lay back with his face above me.

"What are you doing?" I asked meaning that finally this time he did speak and what he said was just what I needed to hear…

"Keeping my promise."

And keep it he did, and he did this…

By kissing my crazy away.

CHAPTER TWENTY-FOUR

PRISON FOR MY SOUL

After this day, everything started out perfect as now Draven knew how to deal with my meltdowns and he did this without a plastic sheet in sight. But like most things in life, when the getting is going good, the 'getting' decided to get a lot of messed up as it usually did when you least expected it, like today. And this cosmic version of 'messed up' started one day after lunch when my whole, perfect world felt like it had been dunked in a bucket of ice cold water.

And it did this with only three words,

"Takeshi is awake!" Zagan had said, rushing into the room where we were all sat down to eat. Sophia and Pip both looked at me. Along with Pythia, who Draven had had no choice but to finally announce was among us. Something I thought best to just act as if I accepted her visit with no explanation needed. I think, to be honest, he had been a little shocked by this, considering it was easy to 'set me off' these days. I had been paranoid for a moment when he looked at me strange, wondering if I had been too obvious. But then it turned out that a pregnant woman could pretty much get away with any strange behaviour, as it was a regular occurrence.

But now all three girls looked at me with the same barely hidden panic, I wasn't sure I was doing a good enough job at hiding. Thankfully though, Draven seemed far too occupied in getting up and going to him as quickly as possible, to notice the change in his wife's behaviour.

"Where is he now?" Draven asked pushing his chair back and standing.

"He is still in the Temple…Adam is with him," Zagan said, looking to Ragnar to see him nod. Draven didn't notice the action and I thought it a strange one, but in the end just shrugged it off.

"Good…I will be back shortly, stay here and wait for me," Draven told me, barely waiting for my acknowledgement, before he was leaving with Zagan and Ragnar, with both of them looking back at me as if to check that I was staying put and doing as I was told.

I frowned, wondering what was going on as something didn't feel right. So, I waited for them to leave the room and then pushed my chair back the same as Draven.

"What the hell are we going to…hey, what are you doing?" Sophia asked now noticing my actions.

"Something isn't right. I am going to follow them," I told them and when they all made a move to come with me, I stopped them.

"No, you stay here, it's best if I go alone as there is less chance of getting caught," I told them, now making all three of them frown at me in question.

"But why?" Pip complained, and Sophia argued.

"Yeah, we need to stick together and…" but then she was interrupted and this time it wasn't by me or Pip.

"No, she's right, something isn't right about this but if we all go then I think it will end up being a mistake. She has to go alone," Pythia said as if just now being hit with the same uneasy feeling.

"You see something?" Sophia asked.

"Only that I know she must hurry." I nodded to her and instead of saying anything else, I dashed from the room. I know they hadn't been gone long before me but with how tall the three of them were, then I knew they had no doubt made it some distance ahead of me already. This probably wasn't a bad thing, as I needed to be far enough away that they wouldn't spot me, smell me, or sense me following them...damn their Supernatural gifts.

I was just thankful that I had forgone the heels for the remainder of my pregnancy and was now wearing my comfy new converse. The ones I had kept from my pretty prison room in Draven's tower. One now known as the Tower of Lust after that amazing night we had there.

I continued on through what I once considered as the maze that is Afterlife, now after all these years, finally knowing where I was going. And also, after all this time, not getting phased by the turning of gargoyle heads, side tracked by the sight of the room of sacred treasures or even freaked out by the crypt with the tree of life at its centre. Hell, I barely even flinched when sticking my hand through the collection of dead vines, knowing that with a stab of my hand, it would be my blood that would give enough power to the tree to grant me access.

It felt strange being down here again after so long and after such turbulent events, but right now I couldn't allow myself the time to think about it. Something didn't make sense and I wanted to know what it was. Because, if I knew one thing by the way Ragnar and Zagan had looked at me, and that was whatever *it was*, they didn't want me anywhere near it. That I could bet my life on and with Takeshi now awake, then there was no telling how long that life would have left with Draven in it.

So, the second the branches slithered away like stone snakes, once more breathing life, the door was revealed, and it was one I quickly walked through. The bright light nearly blinded me as it always did. And it felt like fumbling around in the dark as you did so with no choice but to close your eyes. Finally, one more step was all it took for me to realise I was out of that strange portal and back into the world. A world that I knew held nothing but the worst of Draven's kind that were all down here awaiting sentence. I remembered how I felt the first time I had seen Draven's prison and terrified hadn't been a strong enough word to describe it.

But now?

Well, now there was only one thing I was terrified of and it wasn't the monsters held captive behind steel doors and iron bars. It was only what was left of my fate that Takeshi unknowingly held in his hands. But mainly, *if I could get there in time to stop it.*

That, or *something else.*

I had no clue what that something else could be, but I didn't have long to wait as I heard voices and followed the sounds around the corner. I swallowed hard when I saw all five of them now stood around an open cell, one that was made of the strangest and most demonic looking bars. Ones that looked to be made more out of volcanic rock with veins of molten silver running through them, than your standard, run of the mill jail cell.

Actually, they reminded me more like bones or long fingers that were meant to keep whatever was inside tightly within their clutches. And at each point where a knuckle would have been, there was a flatter piece of metal with etched symbols carved there. I knew these must have been spells of some kind, but for what I had no clue.

And now the door was open, and the cell was empty. At first, I thought that someone must have escaped and that was the urgency. I started to relax the tension in my muscles as it would make sense, this being the reason why Zagan and Ragnar had been acting strange. They no doubt knew what could now be running around free and be concerned about me being put in danger or worrying about it. Now the second this thought started to take hold I tensed again, wondering what type of danger I had then put myself in now by risking coming down here. Because, taking one look at the bad ass cage, one that looked fit for the wildest of beasts, I knew it must have been something scary and powerful for it to work at containing it.

"What is the meaning of this?" Draven demanded, looking first to Takeshi and then behind his shoulder to Zagan, Adam and Ragnar who were all getting closer to him. I frowned seeing their actions as strange and now wondering what I had missed before I had arrived.

"I am sorry my Lord, but we have no choice." Takeshi was the one to say before giving the others a nod and suddenly the blood in my veins filled with ice. I watched in horror as all three of them pounced on Draven at once, taking him off guard. The all wrestled with trying to take hold of him as Draven suddenly roared out. Then his body erupted into its demon form, knocking them all back in one explosive action with his arms being flung back.

Adam was flung back the furthest and landed hard against a wall before slumping to the floor. Draven then grabbed Zagan and spun with him before tossing him aside next to Takeshi. Ragnar looked torn about whether to charge or not and this wasn't because was scared to, but more because it had once been his master he now faced.

But a word spoken from Takeshi and a nod of his head was all it took for him to ready himself to charge at Draven, who looked as if he could barely believe what had happened to his men. He took his stance, readying himself for the fight, but shook his head once as if trying to rid himself of the biggest question of all…

Why?

Why had he survived all through the war and the horrors of death that it brought, only to be facing off his own people now? So, with what looked like a heavy heart and one last warning, he stood there ready to take on someone he had trusted enough to protect his wife.

"Ragnar, don't do this, old friend," Draven said as if fearing what lengths he would have to go to in order to stop him. And I knew what these were, when he let one of his swords free, as it grew from his hand until it reached the floor.

A clear and definitive warning.

But there was only one flaw in this plan as now there was one Being among them that none of them could ever hope to defeat.

Including Draven.

And his name was one found in the depths of Hell after being made by the Devil himself…

Abaddon.

And as if Adam knew that it was the only way to win this fight, he allowed part of his other-self free from his mental cage, doing so enough just to transform one of his arms. It was like watching Doctor Jekyll fighting against his monstrous Mr Hyde. First his suit jacket ripped open along with his shirt underneath, before disgustingly his skin followed. It looked like human flesh peeling back to reveal a layer of overstretched, worn grey leather beneath. A monster's skin being melted over hundreds of skulls as it grew to an impossible size of pure demonic muscle, reaching the floor. I couldn't help but gag as I watched this transformation taking place and doing so without Draven's knowledge, as he continued to fight, facing the other three.

I didn't realise it until I felt the wet drops land on my chest that tears were streaming down my face at the horror of it all. He was their King and now they were betraying him, every single one of them. How could they do this to him? I just couldn't understand it and my grip on the wall I was hiding up against became painful in my frustration at being unable to help him. If only I had my power back…then maybe I could…

"RAAAHHAA" The sound of all Hell breaking loose was what silenced my thoughts as the terrifying sound of Adam's beast coming out to play had me silently screaming into my hands.

He was utterly terrifying!

And just as Draven's other sword started to emerge from his hand, a half man, half beast stood up from where Draven had thrown him. And he did so now being a whole foot taller than Ragnar. He kept shaking his head as his neck was bulging, trying to complete the transformation all the way. The strain on Adam's face looked pure raw pain as he started screaming the second he picked Draven up by his neck from behind and quickly threw him into the cell before then falling to his knees. I watched as Takeshi slammed the door shut and quickly turned the ancient, demonic looking key before Draven could get back to his feet.

But the second I had seen Draven in the hands of Hell's most terrifying beast, something in my head snapped and I pushed off the wall running toward him screaming,

"NOOOO!" but this was to be in vain as the second I was seen Ragnar had me in his arms, holding me back. I screamed and clawed and hit and tried everything to get to Draven. And it was then when Adam raised his head up and saw me, roaring at the sight of me as he fought Abaddon for control. I don't know how he won against it as for one minute it looked like was going to lose it, making Draven shout out at Ragnar,

"GET HER OUT OF HERE!" begging him to get me to safety, no matter that he had just betrayed him.

"NO!" I screamed back trying harder this time, when finally, the sight of me must have snapped something within Adam as he finally started to revert back to himself. His body shuddered and shook as if trapped in a silent storm, one only raging around his body until finally still enough to speak.

"I...I...Keira, I am...sorry..." Adam stuttered out as if his biggest fear had been to hurt me, when really, he hadn't even been close to me. But the rest of them didn't look like this had been a victory, which had me questioning their motives yet again.

"Go Adam, go and find your wife, old friend, we will take it from here," Zagan told him, nodding his head to the exit. Adam didn't need telling twice as he staggered from the room, falling into the wall next to me and Ragnar. The look he gave me was one of regret and pain, making me look away in anger.

It was only when he had gone that everyone but me looked relieved the danger was over, one that no one must have anticipated. But I just looked disgusted with all of them. That was until my eyes found Draven slumped back against the wall, holding his head in his hands as if the relief knowing I was safe, was near overwhelming him. A reaction that was taking precedence over his current situation.

"Take her away and we will finish this," he then spoke before looking up at his men, eyes now filled with hate and disdain.

"NO! I am not going anywhere!" I screamed making his

shoulder slump as if hating this side of me and now having to battle against it and do so, now locked in a cage.

"Ragnar, if you please," Draven said again, only this time I'd had enough.

"LET ME GO!" I screamed as Ragnar nodded to his fallen King.

"As you wish, my Lord," he repeated making me start fighting even harder against him, until finally that anger and power I had wished would come back...*did*.

"I SAID NO!" I roared, meaning that when that anger did return it did so with a bang. As one-minute Ragnar's arms were around me and then, they were simply,

Gone.

Gone, along with the rest of his body. And all that was left of me was an angry girl with my fists clenched by my sides as I panted through my rage looking down and seeing sparks of power hissing around my skin like a layer of lightening. I don't know how it had come back, but I was certainly happy right then that it had. Now, I just had to keep hold of it long enough to get Draven free from that cell and fight my way to do it if need be, for I was not leaving this place without him.

I heard a commotion behind me and looked to my side to see Ragnar was removing himself from the wall I had forced his body into. Now when he approached, he did so keeping a wide berth between me and him. In fact, looking at the three of them, they all did as they eyed my hands warily as if I would explode again any minute if they moved too quickly.

"Now give me that key!" I demanded in a voice that was barely my own and holding out a hand to Takeshi so that he could hand it to me.

"Keira, please don't..." Zagan started to say but I cut him off with a slow precise move of my neck and a barely control response,

"I am your QUEEN!" I bellowed making them all flinch as I could feel both my fangs slip free and my eyes change, turning more to a demonic darkness as it started to take hold, at the sight of the man I loved being held in a cage.

"Now. Give. Me. That. Key." I demanded once more and this time not one shred sounded like the old me. No, it all belonged to the demon in me.

"Please, my Lord, listen to me quickly, you must calm her down or she will get hurt, I promise you this," Takeshi said appealing now to Draven and making me hiss at him. Draven also didn't like the sound of this threat and he snarled a threat of his own,

"You touch her, and you die!"

"Not by me! By you, Dominic! *You* are the one we are protecting her from!" he shouted at him making me snap and before anyone could stop me, I had him up against the prison wall by his neck. I don't know what was wrong with me, but whatever it was, I wasn't in control of it any longer. All I knew was that this man, right here in my hands, was trying to take it all away from me. *Was about to take everything.*

"Fucking Gods, Dom, what he says is true! Now get her to let him go before she fucking kills him!" Zagan said looking to Draven and pleading with him. Meanwhile, Draven looked as though the information had slammed into his soul and was trying to make sense of the intrusion there.

"DOM!" Zagan roared at him looking as though he didn't know what to do next.

"Keira, let him go, sweetheart." Finally, that voice seemed to penetrate my subconscious, one that was currently being overrun by a demonic wrath of the likes I hadn't known since facing Cronus. But his voice. It was enough to get me to drop Takeshi and shake myself free of the hold my own demon side had on me. I fell to my knees as I let it start to evaporate from me, falling forward so that my hands were flat to the floor over my head. It left me feeling weak, as if I had just been saved from drowning after treading water for hours.

"KEIRA! Let me out, she needs me, damn it!" Draven roared hitting out against the bars and making them spark with the clash of powers fighting against each other. His being the power to escape and the symbols' power to keep him locked in.

"We...*can't,*" Takeshi said now slumped against the wall with a knee up and his arm leaning against it. He looked exhausted as his other hand cradled his throat from where I had almost snapped it.

"Why not!?" Draven demanded snarling at him. This was when Takeshi took a deep breath, as if he hated being the bearer of devastating news and I couldn't help it when I lifted my head enough to warn him,

"Please, don't do it." Hearing this Draven shot an accusing look down at me before demanding this time,

"Tell me!"

"No don't!" I shouted again, but it was too late, he had already started,

"Because you will hurt her if you touch her," he said making me now hang my head as the irreversible damage hit home.

"I would never hurt her, by the Gods have you gone mad, for she's my pregnant wife for Gods' sake, I could never...!"

"Fuck Dom, will you just listen to him!" Zagan snapped that famous cool of his. But it was so out of character that it was enough for Draven to take it seriously and he nodded for Takeshi to continue the horrific truth.

"It isn't you that wants to hurt her but your...*Your Demon,*" he said as if it caused him pain to do so, but his pain was nowhere near as much as mine...or from the looks of things, now Draven's as well. I looked up to see as Draven took a step back, as if he'd been struck, before he started shaking his head in denial.

"No, it...it can't be possible."

"I am afraid it is, and your wife knows it," Takeshi said looking to me with sorrow in his eyes when he saw my tears fall on the ground.

"No...no it can't...it..." he started speaking to himself before casting his focus back to me, after what Takeshi had just told him began to sink in.

"Keira...is this true?" he asked now meaning I had no other option than to come clean. I swallowed hard after sitting up and then knowing that I couldn't speak yet, I simply sealed my fate and nodded. The looked of utter devastation on his face crushed me, ripping a small sob from me.

"But why...why by the Gods didn't you tell me!?" he threw at me angrily and I flinched, bunching my shoulders as if I felt his verbal attack physically. They all looked down at me with pity, but only one was accusing me. The rest just looked as though they wanted to help me but were helpless to do so. For maybe they all knew too, deep down what Draven would do if he'd known. Maybe this was taking it all out of my hands and these bars weren't just meant for him, but for me also...to keep him here.

"I didn't know how to," I told him in a small voice, one that nearly broke. He snarled at this reasoning, which even to me sounded pretty lame, but what else could I say. In the end I hadn't needed to as Takeshi said it all for me.

"Tell me...what did you see Takeshi?" Draven snapped, and I flinched again having to look away from his hard, disappointed gaze, one he wouldn't take away from me. No doubt doing this, so as to gauge my every reaction I had to whatever was said from this point on.

"The night of the banquet your demon was summoned to

her, taking hold of her mind and in doing so, my mind too got caught in the crossfire," he told him, now giving me insight as to what had happened.

"I saw it all, my Lord and all the times before," he said making Draven snap his head at him, shock and anger directed his way.

"What do you mean, all the times before?!"

"She has known of this since it first happened shortly after the war was won, my Lord." I released a shuddering sigh as Takeshi started sealing my fate, for there was no coming back from this.

"WHAT?!" he roared, and I sucked in a sob, trying not to cry, knowing that if I started now I would never stop.

"You knew…you knew all these weeks, Keira, and you didn't tell me?!" he accused making me silently nod my head, telling him he was right, because what else could I say right now. I didn't want my reasons why to have an audience.

"This control on her dreams, of her mind…tell me this is all I have done," he asked sternly, his voice a barely contained anger. But I couldn't help it, as I gave him his answer without details, when my eyes shot to Takeshi, ones now silently pleading with him not to go that far. Because none of this had been the worst part, no that had included Lucius and the lengths I had gone to in keeping my lies from him. It was a sticky web of lies that I had continued to weave until soon I had found it so big, I was trapped there surrounded by it all. And with that one look at Takeshi, well now he knew it too.

"I am sorry, my Queen," Takeshi said before tearing his regretful eyes from me and turning once more to his king.

"Tell me!" Draven demanded, folding his arms across his chest, one that was growing with every deep breath he took.

"Please…oh God, please don't do this anymore," I pleaded, no longer caring that I was begging him. Takeshi closed his eyes against it before lowering his head and telling Draven the worst part,

"Your demon took control over you and yes…I believe you hurt her just before you were stopped." Draven heard this and this time staggered back, having to brace himself against the wall as the true horror hit him.

"I…I harmed her, I hurt my…" He couldn't even finish that sentence and the tears that threatened now were overflowing with the same pain he felt. I stood up and tried my best to deny it.

"No, Draven listen to me, you didn't hurt me, not really…it was just…" Draven looked down at the floor with a disgusted look that broke my heart.

"Stop. Just stop it, Keira," he said in a voice that sounded so broken it was barely from the man I knew.

"But I…" I tried again but this was when he found his limit.

"I said NO!" He roared making me flinch back as his demon side demanded this of me, not just the man I knew could control it. But right now, he just didn't want to.

"I want to see it for myself," Draven suddenly demanded after silence had descended on the room like a dead weight looming over us. And speaking of that dead weight, I also felt one drop in my stomach when I heard what this next demand was.

"No, that is too far, Takeshi don't!" I warned as he started to take a step closer to his Lord. But thankfully my words made him stop and look to me for my reasons why.

"If you do this, then what is to stop his demon from coming out and this time, I may not be able to bring him back," I said, no longer caring what Draven knew. It was too late to save myself that fate now, so I ignored the look my husband gave me, which was one of pure betrayal and pain.

Takeshi seemed to think about my words for a minute and he looked to Zagan who answered his silent question, replying,

"She may be right, we don't know what would trigger it at this stage."

"But he can no longer be a danger to her if he is behind the bars," Ragnar added, making me frown at him, a look he ignored.

"Then what if his demon takes hold of Takeshi again and this time uses him, you also can't risk that…"

"What else are you hiding from me?" Draven's icy voice asked of me, cutting through my sentence with eerie calm, for he knew why I fought against this. I swallowed hard and was about to speak when he gave me another warning…

"And do not lie to me again!"

"I only do this to protect you," I told him, letting him know I was refusing him this.

"Protect me! *Protect me!* You are the mother of my child, Keira, the only being alive you should be protecting is the one growing inside your belly!" he roared making me close my eyes as more tears fell and I took a step back, ripping my watery gaze from his and I threw myself against the wall to start sobbing. I felt him take a deep breath in order to calm himself and obviously hating the sight of seeing what his words had done. But he couldn't go back now and besides, from his point of view, he had been right. Just being around him, and he was now considering each time had been a threat, so obviously he felt this way.

"Now fucking show me!" Draven snapped at Takeshi, who now was reconsidering giving his master what he wanted. I saw it in his eyes. My doubts had taken root and now he didn't know what to do with them. He found himself at war between his King and his Queen. A King at war with his demon and a

Queen at war with her heart. And it was clear he didn't know which one to choose, but in the end, it was taken from him.

As his attention was elsewhere, along with everyone else's, it that meant no one had seen what Draven had planned…or his actions. Draven had quietly been pulling forth his powers behind his back and I saw this as a snake of controlled purple flames coiled behind him like a long rope by his feet. No one else had noticed this and just as I called out,

"Takeshi, watch out!" it was too late. Draven, with a single snap of his wrist, had taken hold of Takeshi's body and was yanking him hard to the bars so that he could reach through and cover his head with one of his large hands. I ran forward but soon found myself being restrained and this time by Zagan, who hissed,

"Don't be foolish!"

And I guess, looking at Draven right now, who was closer to his Demon that anything else, it would have definitely been foolish. Takeshi's head snapped back as Draven applied his will over him, demanding his visions from him. I knew this as Takeshi's eyes looked up and started to turn milky white.

"No, no, no, please! Oh God, Draven don't! Please, don't do this." I begged and, in the end, Zagan was half holding me upright as if trying to stop my body from crumpling to the floor. As I knew, unlike the others, that the worst was yet to come. But Draven wouldn't listen. No, he was too far gone as the purple fire in his eyes flicked darker before glowing again, as everything up until the point of the banquet was playing out in front of him.

But I knew when the worst part came to him was when his wings erupted from behind him and now in his unspeakable rage they too started to fight against his demon. They started flickering and morphing back and forth into the dark wings of his angel and then into featherless skin between massive talon tipped limbs. I screamed at the sight and this sound was enough for Draven to rip himself free from Takeshi.

Takeshi would have fallen to the floor if it hadn't been for Zagan's quick actions as he spun me to Ragnar, before reaching out and catching his friend. A friend that was now once again unconscious. But Draven didn't seem concerned by what he had done, because now he was only focused on one thing. I could see that the second he had stepped back and only death had taken hold of his eyes.

Death and one name snarled between bloodthirsty fangs…

"Lucius!"

CHAPTER TWENTY-FIVE

TIME TO FIGHT THE WAR

"Draven, I can explain." I said quickly, trying to defuse the situation. But it didn't even come close to helping as I knew when he lost it.

"Get out!" he shouted making me gasp at the order.

"Draven, please listen to me, just hear me out and…"

"I SAID GET OUT!" he roared at me this time, leaning his upper body towards me, as his arms went behind him, making me fall back a few steps in fear. And when I finally steadied myself, I turned and was starting to run from the room when I stopped myself. I took a deep breath and asked myself, what was I doing? Had I really come this far, to what, give up now? Just because he told me to. Just because he thought to scare me into doing as I was told. Was that what love was? Something you gave up on when things got hard or you let fear start ruling over your heart? Had I really come all this way just to turn my back on him now? Had I fought through years of struggle, all to keep the love I felt for him alive, just to see it now be thrown away at the last hurdle.

So, I stopped running and refused to do it ever again.

"No!" I said firmly, after swallowing the lump I had lodged in my throat, one made of pain.

"Keira." he said my name in warning as if this would push me, but I just shook my head telling him,

"I said no, Draven." I said this after turning around and walking back towards him. I saw him shake his head as if he couldn't deal with this anymore. Then he motioned with his head for Zagan and Ragnar to take control before issuing his next demand.

"Take her away." Those words sounded as if ripped from him and I winced more at the pain I saw it caused him, than what his words had caused me. Zagan and Ragnar both looked at each other before back at me, no longer feeling as if that was an easy command to obey.

"Now!" Draven snapped and because of it, they took a step closer to me and I held up a hand to stop them.

"I wouldn't do that if I were you," I warned, looking to each of them.

"Please Keira, don't make this any harder than it has to be," Zagan said trying to reason with me and pulling back his hood so that I could see the pleading in his pale eyes. But he wasn't the only one with big guns.

"And what if it was Sophia in there?" I asked him, making him flinch and I knew I had hit my mark.

"And you Ragnar, what if it had been one you cared for, your wife or…or your daughter?" I said, knowing I was going too far bringing up a family he no longer had. But I had a point to prove and I knew it was one made when he paused to look back at the cell. It was now as if he was seeing it for himself and Draven knew it too when he let his arms fall to his sides from having them crossed against his chest. It was the first sight of admitting his defeat.

"I am your King," Draven said, trying one more time to get them to do as he demanded. But I turned back to him and said,

"Yes, but I am your wife and your heart." He heard this and took a shuddering breath this time as I knew my words affected him.

"You know this as do they. So, I refuse to leave and if you think that I don't have the strength in me to fight for what I know is right, to fight for what I love, then you don't fucking know me!" I snapped, swiping angrily at the tears that fell. Hearing this Draven clenched his fists and lowered his head as if he had already lost.

"Now, I know I have done things. I know I am far from fucking perfect here and you are angry with me...furious even. I get that, and you have every right to be. So, shout at me, scream at me and curse every single lie I told you, but do all those things with me stood right here...right here! Stood in the only place I belong. Because I am telling you, Dominic Draven, I am not fucking running this time, do you hear me?" I told him, finally making him look up at me as if my words were burning themselves to his very soul. And when he didn't get angry against any of it, I turned toward Ragnar and Zagan and told them both,

"So, you can go, but there is no way in Hell you are taking me with you, not without finding my blood on your hands, for *I will fight you,*" I warned, allowing my voice to take on a scary calm that was coming mainly from my own demon side, from the Vampire in me.

"And she will have us fighting right alongside her."

"Sophia!" Zagan shouted in surprise and I turned to see all three of my girls there, Sophia with her arms folded, Pip popping some bubble gum stood with her hand on her hip and Pythia looking slightly uncomfortable, but still having my back all the same.

I heard Draven snarl at them and snap,

"I might have fucking known my own sister would be involved in this!" To which she growled back at him, quickly transforming into her Demon, one far scarier to look at than her brother's. Her smoky wings floated around her body, as if helping with the transformation, shifting up and around her front before revealing a face of harsh, grey desert skin, sadistic lips and cold white eyes with black tears running down her face, ones there not through sorrow but through anger.

"And I might have known your actions would be ones against your wife, rather than who is really at fault here!" she snapped back.

"You think I did this?" he shouted gesturing to himself and as his biceps bulged his t-shirt actually tore at the sleeves.

"Of course not, but I know Keira obviously didn't, considering she has done nothing but try and solve this fucking problem before you could act this way!" I took a deep breath knowing that at this rate, I wouldn't need to tell Draven why I had done what I had, as Sophia was going to do it for me.

"Act this way?! You think I wanted it to come to this?!" he argued.

"And you think she did…? Ask yourself, Dom, why exactly do you think she kept any of this from you…uh? Taking our current situation into consideration here, that being me looking at you from where I am standing of course…*in a fucking cage!*" Sophia said trying to get her point across and I knew it did when he looked taken aback as if, until now, he hadn't even considered why. No, he had only focused on the betrayal.

"Her lies run too deep this time and so do yours, *sister!*" he snapped after a moment and a shake of his head, meaning he couldn't get past it. Sophia shook her head, only hers was done in obvious disappointment.

"Have you ever asked yourself why that is? Why my shift in

loyalty over the years?" Sophia asked, now sounding calm despite her brother's rumble of anger.

"Understanding all you do, Sophia, is a fucking eternal job I have had no choice but to endure!" Draven snapped making me gasp. His eyes cut to me but softened slightly when he saw how shocked I was to hear him say such a thing. But Sophia merely laughed and mocked back,

"As my eternal job has been nothing but helping you search for your happiness and now, you blame me for aiding not *you* but *her* in keeping it!? As for you…well, it seems that her heart is forever stronger than yours, for she seems to be the only one left who is willing to fight for it…where are you fighting, Draven…? In a fucking cage that's where!" Sophia said delivering the final blow and I knew this when he took a step back, shock clear to see for all of us.

"That's enough, Sophia." Sophia turned to Zagan and hissed at him, making her wings flick out to the sides in her anger.

"I think you made your point, sweetheart," he added no doubt trying to calm her down.

"One can only hope…but if not, then consider this before I go…" she paused storming passed us all and coming within inches of the bars to tell him.

"Love is a war, Brother…one she is fighting alone…*fighting, because of you.*" Then she turned her back on him, leaving him standing there looking hard, cold and indifferent, but I knew inside he was burning.

"If you need us, you know where we are," she whispered to me after placing a hand to my shoulder.

"Thank you, my sister," I told her back, making her nod to me. Then she decided to do what she did best in her world and that was rule, now in place of her brother.

"Help pick him up, Pip," Sophia said nodding to her when no one was looking, making me wonder what she was up to.

Whatever it was Pip obviously knew because she gave her a salute before helping Zagan where he didn't need it. She helped lift the unconscious Takeshi up enough for Zagan to swing him onto his shoulders. Then she backed up to me and pulled me into her for a hug.

"I am sorry about Adam," I told her, and she shrugged her shoulders and said,

"Ah don't worry honey, he's sleeping like a baby." Then she held me tighter and whispered in my ear,

"Got your back, my sister britches." Then she pulled back and winked after I felt her dropping something in my back pocket. I mouthed the word 'thank you' this time and she nodded before leaving with the rest of them. Ragnar looked torn as he lingered, and I knew it wasn't because of Draven's order, it was solely for my safety. I gave him a nod, telling him without words that I would be alright.

Then after a nod in return, he left, and I finally found myself alone with Draven.

And he looked as broken as I felt.

"Nothing I say right now will get you to leave, will it?" he finally asked, and it was the first time I heard him say anything since being down here, without it having a hard edge to it. He also let his muscles relax enough to sit down on the stone bench that he brought sliding to the centre of the room with a mere thought.

"You know the answer to that," I told him and unlike his, my voice didn't sound even and steady, but instead, small and fragile.

"Then I guess we had better talk," he said, and I heard the same sound of stone grinding against stone before I looked behind me to see where it was coming from, only to find a similar bench coming from the wall towards me.

"Sit," he said nodding to the bench that now mirrored his,

with only the bars between us. So, I did and feeling better for it as all the energy seemed to zap out of me at once.

"How did we ever come to this point, Draven?" I asked sounding as deflated as I felt. At first it looked as though he didn't know how to answer me, but then motioned with his hands that he didn't know before saying,

"Because lies always get in the way."

"That's not fair, Draven," I told him, sounding as pained as I was.

"No, what's not fair, Keira, is you putting the two Beings I love most in this world in danger and not giving me a single say about it!" he snapped back, and I knew he was right, but that didn't mean I had to agree with him on everything.

"And what would you have done, uh? Would you have simply taken me to one side and said, 'don't worry about it honey, we will figure this out together'…I don't think so?"

"I think you will find *I did* say something along those lines, sweetheart," he retorted, but there was no tenderness in my nickname now.

"Oh yeah, when you barely knew what was going on, you said that. But now… you think you can say the same to me after all you know…no I didn't think so." I added once he looked away and I had made my point.

"At least I would have been given the opportunity to choose, but you took that away from me, just as you did when you risked your life and went back in time." I swallowed hard as once again he was right.

"And what was the alternative to that Draven, because correct me if I am wrong, but your idea to winning against the impending apocalypse was to fight and hope for the best?" I snapped.

"Now who is being the unfair one?" he replied making me feel guilty, but not enough to stop yet.

"And what of my choices, you haven't exactly been forthcoming with me in the past here, Draven?"

"Everything I have done was to keep you safe, despite the challenges you put in front of me to prevent that from ever happening!" he growled looking at me in anger.

"Yeah, well you weren't the only making decisions based on what was best for another. You think it was easy for me? To know that I was possibly walking into my death by going back in time, you think it was fun for me, to get beaten up only to find your blade at my neck? To get kidnapped yet a-fucking-gain! Fight a demonic God for you and to end up in Rome about to be forced to marry a Vampire because he was confused and thought I was his Chosen One!" I said it all, no longer caring about his mounting rage with every word I said but needing to get it all out. No more lies between us, this was it.

The point of no return.

"Stop Keira, I fucking beg of you, stop now before you go too far!"

"No, Draven, you wanted this! You wanted everything, no more lies! You want to know what I have gone through and all for you! You want to know the pain endured and the lies of it I kept in order to save your own pain from knowing. Then so be it." At this point I stood up and told him,

"Lucius wanted to marry me because he was confused that I was his Chosen One and that only ended one way. I had to watch as you both fought to the death and one that nearly ended with my own. All that way travelled back in time, trying to save the fucking world, only to have you two fighting against me!" I said throwing my hands up like I had hit my mental limit on all that had happened to me. This wasn't just like opening the flood gates, this was blowing the bastards up!

"And all of this, only to find that bitch Layla pop up again like a demonic bad penny, trying to kill me …yet a-fucking-gain! And all for what? So that I could get back to you and live out what I was led to believe were my last days on Earth, just so that you may continue to live in a world with a piece of me in it... a piece of me in our child! So, don't you dare speak to me about making decisions based on what is best for others...what is best for the man I love and..." I started to stutter as the tears came again, until finally I finished my speech through a watery vision of Draven in front of me.

"...doing everything in my power to keep him by my side."

Once I was finished it looked as though he didn't know what to do with half of it, let alone the entirety of what I had been through and all for him.

"Gods, Keira..." he muttered as if he could barely believe it.

"So, you can't tell me Draven, that my love and protection is any different to yours, because all I can see is that yours means me being forced far from it, whereas mine means fighting for it."

"Yes, and that idea of fighting is always to do so by yourself, not by my side!" he snapped.

"Oh, I would be fighting by your side Draven, if I had a side to fight next to, before it decides what's best is to put distance between us," I said making him growl.

"And here it is! My life's colossal fuck up being thrown in my face yet again, I did wonder when you would bring it up," Draven replied sarcastically now making me angry.

"Well, this is coming from the man who just ordered his men to physically remove me because I refused to leave on my own accord, so excuse me for bringing up what would have been yet another of your colossal fuck ups, I just decided to prevent it from happening this time!" After this he knew I had made my point and silence descended between us again. He ran both his hands through his hair as he bent over holding his head there with his elbows rested at his knees as he studied the floor.

"How did this start?" he asked me, breaking the silence first.

"I am not sure, that's what we were trying to figure out," I told him, deciding it was best to get it all out in one hit. So, I took a deep breath and said,

"But it looks as if it might have something to do with Cronus," I said and this was when his head snapped up to look at me.

"What?!" he shouted as I knew he would.

"Explain!" he said one word and my shoulders slumped and I knew that everything I was about to tell him wasn't going to be easy, but it was the right thing to do. For it wasn't like our situation could get any worse and with him being locked in a cell, then it wasn't like he was going anywhere. So that at least took my biggest fear out of it.

Taking a deep breath, I told him everything, including the parts he most likely knew, and the parts that I knew he definitely didn't. And every single second of it was painful and made me feel like the worst person in the world.

"Oh Keira, by Gods woman why would you ever keep all this from me?" he said, sounding so disappointed it was making his voice thick and hoarse.

"Have you not been listening, you know why?" I said rubbing the few tears off my cheeks with the side of my hand. I watched him take a deep breath and say the words we had both been avoiding.

"Because you thought I would leave you again." I sniffed a few times holding the sob back and nodded without speaking.

"Why?" he asked, making me frown and shake my head like I wasn't sure I had heard him right.

"Why?"

"Yes, why did you think I would leave you?" he asked more clearly, and I coughed back my surprise and said without thinking,

"Because it's what you do." And the second I said it I wished I hadn't for it looked as though I had slapped him.

"Did.," he said and when he saw my face he elaborated,

"It was what I *did* Keira, not what I ever intended on doing again." And the second he said this I couldn't hold back the flood any longer. I burst into tears and started body shaking sobs that echoed in this dark cold place.

"Sweetheart, you're killing me here," he told me softly and I held up a hand asking him silently to give me a minute.

"Ssshh, please, just calm yourself, for seeing you this way and knowing I can't touch you, that I can't comfort you is like fucking torture," he told me, making me bite my lip as I finally looked up at him, with bloodshot eyes still filled with tears. He winced as if the sight caused him physical pain. But then again, seeing the one you loved the most in the world suffering this much, was never something that was going to be easy to witness. And Draven loved me. I knew that with every heartbeat and every stupid decision we equally made together or apart.

"Did you really mean that?" I asked after finally being able to get a hold on my crying.

"I made you a promise," he said, so I got up and walked closer to his cell bars. He flinched back, and I didn't take it as a good sign, but still I continued on with my decision. Because even though he was here right now, that didn't mean it would stay that way and having him behind bars meant that he couldn't run from me. But I was willing to risk that, for Draven to prove it all to me.

"Then prove it," I told him, walking closer to the door and

pulling out the key from my back pocket to show him. He stood quickly, now looking shocked at what I had in my hand.

"Keira, I..." he started to speak, but knowing it was the wrong type of tone, being one of doubt, I shook my head and said,

"Prove my greatest fear wrong, Draven." Then I raised the key and put it in the lock ready to turn. This was his one shot, to erase the past and prove to me once and for all that all my lies were said in vain. Because he would never leave me like he promised not to. I kept eye contact with him and he knew this was his one chance to show me, but the battle I saw there was easy to see and, in the end...

He proved my lies right.

His hand shot out and the second I started to turn it, he snapped the lock back and took the key from me, keeping himself locked inside. I let the devastation wave over me and I lowered my head so that he wouldn't see how much that action killed me.

"I thought so," I muttered and turned ready to go back to my seat when suddenly he grabbed me by the sweater and pulled me up against the bars, then he took my face in his hands and said fervently,

"Don't give up on me." Then he kissed me through the gap and gripped my sides, holding me there as if he was afraid if he let me go it wouldn't just be for a moment in time, no this time it would be for good.

"Just give me time, that's all I ask of you," he whispered, putting his forehead to the bars as he couldn't reach my own. His eyes were closed, and his voice was pleading.

"Time is something we don't have much of, Draven," I told him softly looking down at my belly that I had cradled in my hands for he knew then what I meant.

"I would never forgive myself if something were to

happen...can't you understand that?" he told me, and I tried to pull away, but he wouldn't let me go, not yet. So, to prove my point I reached through the bars and cupped his cheek, telling him.

"You wouldn't hurt me."

"I wouldn't *want* to ever hurt you, but that doesn't mean I can't," he told me in return, making me close my eyes against the painful truth.

"You won't hurt me," I repeated, closing my eyes this time and when I felt him let me go I knew I had lost him and with it our moment.

"I think you're forgetting, Keira, *I already did."* he said painfully before turning his back to me and I watched as his muscles tensed as the stolen memory came back to him, one taken from Takeshi.

"Draven I..."

"And once again it was Lucius who came to the rescue," he said bitterly, and I winced when he said it, knowing how much that must have hurt him.

"Please don't be angry, I just...I didn't want anyone to know and he was the..."

"The first person you thought of that could beat me...Yeah, I get it, Keira!" he snapped and again I hated the sound of his pain.

"That's not...okay, so yes, I got scared and panicked."

"Scared of me, which is my point!" he said and damn him, but he was making this harder to argue against.

"I wasn't scared of you Draven, I was scared *for you*. Scared for us both. I didn't know what was happening, but I knew one thing and that was Lucius was the only one I knew had the power to make your Demon stop," I told him, and I knew he hated every word of that sentence.

"Great, then maybe we should ask him to move in with us,

there we go, problem solved!" he said sarcastically and unusually for Draven showing me that bite of bitter humour I rarely ever saw.

"That's not funny," I told him.

"No, we are in agreement there, that's for damn sure!"

"Well, if it helps with your ego at all, then I think Lucius has a pretty clear idea of what he considers all the crazy shit I would do because I love you!" I snapped back at him.

"You think this is my ego talking?" I didn't answer him, but I just folded my arms across my chest hoping my look said it all.

"Fuck my ego and the Vampire who has been in love with you for nearly as long as I have, this is only about keeping you safe for me…not for him, or anyone else for that matter, for the fucking world could crumble for all I care! You are mine and you are not going to get hurt at my hands, I don't care what I have to do to achieve that!" he threw at me slashing an angry hand through the air.

"So, what about in the meantime, Draven, are you going to live down here in a prison behind a set of bars? And for how long are we talking for here, days, weeks, months or fucking years!? You want me to introduce our child into the world on my own and then bring the baby down here to meet its father for the first time down in this Hell!?" I snapped back, getting angry and making his chest rumble a barely contain growl at the thought.

"What do you want from me Keira, to just walk out of here with your hand in mine and take the chance?" he said after finally letting go of his anger and me now doing the same.

"That's exactly what I am saying, Draven. Look, I know it won't be easy, but it will be a damn sight easier if we do this together, not alone. All I am asking for is a chance to prove it to you. To prove that we can do this," I told him, and he sat back down on his bench giving me his answer right there.

"You know I can't give you that, Keira." he said without looking at me and sounding like those words should have been utterly foreign to him, as there was nothing that Draven wouldn't want to give me…but only if it was in his power to give and it looked like this was the first thing that wasn't.

"Then I think you will find me unable to give you the same when you ask me to leave your side," I told him, deciding to sit down and this time doing so on the floor with my back up against the bars facing away from him.

"Keira, please be reasonable here," he said after releasing an exasperated sigh.

"You have your choices, honey, and I have mine, this being one of them, for I am not ever leaving your side again…that's a promise I made Draven and one I intend to keep," I told him hearing his response being another sigh. Then I heard him moving and glanced over my shoulder to see that he too had come to sit on the floor with his back to me with only the bars in between us.

And this was how we remained for some time. Our heads back against the bars with our legs stretched out in front of us, just listening to the sound of hopeless silence and an endless space between us that these few bars held.

"I guess this means the honeymoon is over then," I commented after a while, making him chuckle and at least break some of the tension between us.

"Yeah, I guess it does," he agreed.

"Why does this keep happening to us, Draven?" I asked him softly turning my head sideways so that my cheek was against the cold stone and metal. I watched as he did the same and answered me,

"I don't know, sweetheart…*I just don't know,*" he whispered again, and this was the last thing I remembered him saying before I must have fallen asleep, for the next thing I knew I was dreaming. I knew I must have been, because I reached out my hands finding the floor cold beneath my fingertips. And then I felt a hand reaching through the bars I felt at my back. The next thing I knew my hair was being moved out of the way. Then I felt a single touch at my neck where I knew there shouldn't have been.

I woke up, my eyes wide as I screamed,

"NOO!" But I was too late as I felt the hand at my neck holding me close to the bars and just before I could struggle, I heard his demon say…

"Sittu, Wardum…You will rest, my little Slave…for now it is my turn," he told me and the second he said the first foreign command, it started to feel as though he had injected me with a drug, as my eyes started to close on their own and my mind's fog started to cloud my thoughts of anything but sleep. I couldn't understand how he had this power over me, whereas Draven had lost his long ago.

But as I heard the slide of a lock and felt myself being lifted up in a pair of strong arms, I knew I was helpless to stop it.

Helpless to stop him.

The last thing I heard as he walked away from the cell with me firmly in his grasp, was one thing I knew would stay with me,

For it was my own doing as I heard him say…

"Time to fight the war."

CHAPTER TWENTY-SIX

TABLES TURNED

I woke up that morning when the light in the room started to annoy me and I frowned as I stretched out and found the comforting feel of our bed beneath my body. It took me a while to ask myself why that would feel wrong, but the second it finally came to me, I bolted upright and instantly looked to Draven's side of the bed.

A side that was empty.

I looked down to see I was still in my clothes and wondered how the hell I got here? It seemed a bit odd that Draven would risk carrying me back up himself, especially with me in his arms, but how else…? The question lingered on as I started to try and remember pieces of last night. I knew that after a few bitter sweet moments with Draven at some point we both fell asleep leaning next to each other with only the bars between us. At one point his hand entwined with mine as I slept. I even felt a single tear fall as I heard him whisper how much he loved me.

But now? I just didn't know, which was why, as my heart

started to plummet in my chest, I jumped out of bed and started running as fast as I could.

"Keira wait, what happened?!" Sophia shouted as I slid around the corner, but I didn't stop. I couldn't stop. Not until I knew. Not until I could confirm that my biggest fear hadn't come true. So, I ran. I ran faster than it felt I ever had before, as I could feel the power in my blood giving me supernatural help to get there quicker. I could still hear people behind me, following to see what was wrong with me, but they wouldn't catch me.

Not now, not today.

I continued on, only stopping to gain access into the prison and cursing the tree for not doing so quicker. I ran through the light and out into the darkness, when I felt my blood start to run cold. I shook with fear as I rounded the corner I knew would hold my heart in the sight of a cell…

One, I found empty.

"NOOO!" I screamed collapsing onto my knees and screaming out at the world, whilst hammering my fists against the floor in anger, actually cracking it with my wrath.

"Keira what's wro…?" Sophia shouted as she came around the corner to discover for herself the root of my devastation.

"He's gone…he…he…*he left me…he lied to me,*" I said as I felt my heart break. I felt her take me into her arms and hold me on the ground as I buried my head in her shoulder and simply cried like I did that day I first lost him.

After this happened I didn't know how much time passed around me. I don't even remember walking back to the main part of the house, or even how I ended up on a couch with a cup of tea in my hands with someone telling me to drink it. I didn't remember how so many people ended up in the room or that someone put a blanket around my shoulders because someone saw me shivering.

I remembered nothing.

Nothing but Draven telling me that he wouldn't leave me again.

Nothing but the lies he told me.

The lies that slowly started to seep from my subconscious and take root in the form of anger.

Oh yeah, I remembered this and the second I did was when the room started to sink back into reality. Everyone around me was arguing, Jared was there with his men, asking those around him what was being done? Sigurd was downing a shot of something amber coloured, calling someone out saying it was,

"Fucking bullshit!"

Sophia was questioning Zagan and Adam, whilst Pip was looking worried pulling at a pigtail. Even Leivich was there asking where Vincent was and suggesting that he might know where Dom had gone. But then there was only one name that I heard out of the hum of noise.

"Well, we need to be asking the only one who isn't here, so where is that smug bastard Lucius at anyway?" Orthrus said snapping something within me and slamming a memory to the forefront of my mind. Lucius touching my birthmark. Him telling me that he saw Hell. But then there was more...what was it that he was going to tell me that day? The vision he had that I knew *he didn't want to tell me.*

I don't know why but I knew this was important, that what he had been shown had been a vision of the future not the past. I don't know how I knew that, but I just did.

So suddenly, to silence the room, before I knew what my anger was doing, I hammered my fist down on the coffee table in front of me. I did so dropping the tea and smashing most of the stuff on the table as the wood split, bouncing inconsequential things to the floor. The second this echoed through the room everything stopped, including the conversations. I calmly stood up and walked over to the large table most of our people were sat round, now recognising the dining room.

I then stood at the head, knowing that this was my place and it was about time I stepped up to it.

"The jet in Portland, how long before it's ready to fly?" I asked Zagan, knowing he would know being Draven's second in command.

"We could have it ready to fly within the hour it takes to get there," he answered me promptly.

"Good, get it ready."

"Where should I say the destination is?" he asked me, and I looked back before he left the room to do my bidding.

I gave him the only answer that mattered.

"To Munich."

It was amazing what you could get done when you applied anger to your daily routine. For example, I was showered, dressed and ready to go in record time thanks to angry body washing. I also had ordered men on a mission. Which included asking Jared to contact Bill and find out from his contacts in Hell, whether he had heard anything on the Hellvine about some pissed off demon King finally making it home? His answer had been a simple one,

"Gotya, Doll Face."

Next had been to ask Sigurd to find out which doors Draven might have used to go to Hell, that were in the Janus Temple. To which his reply had been,

"Sure thing, Lille øjesten, me and the old man are on it," he said taking his father with him. After this I left orders with the rest of them, one being for someone to let me know the second Takeshi was awake again, as after what Draven had done to him, he was predicted to be out of it for at least twenty-four hours, so should be waking up at some point when we were in Germany.

Something we were currently on our way to achieving as we were all five minutes away from the airport. Pip, Adam, Zagan, Sophia and I were all traveling together and so far, I think people had been too worried to approach me to ask what my plans were. I think people could tell that something in me had snapped and this was the last strand of hope I was holding onto. A hope that even if part of it started to unravel, then they didn't know what I would do. So, they watched as I remained silent, getting lost in my own private Hell and just praying that I could make it out alive with Draven in tow.

Of course, this silence would only be allowed for so long from my girls, as we were only thirty minutes in the air before they sat down opposite me. They found me staring out the window and watching as the sun got low, hating that I had nearly reached a whole day without him.

"So, come on, don't keep us in the dark any longer, what's the plan here?" Sophia asked me, making Pip add,

"Yeah, 'cause its rude you know." Hearing this made me give her a little smirk in return, my first hint of a smile since waking up before any of this began.

"It's simple, we go to Germany, I get the answers I need and then we go get him," I said really hoping it was as easy as it sounded, but deep down knowing that it really wouldn't be.

"And if that place is in Hell?" Sophia asked, and I looked towards the men on the plane and then back to the girls, knowing what I was going to ask of them.

"Then fancy another kick ass vacation somewhere hot?" I asked. They both looked at each other and I held my breath, really praying they wouldn't say no, because I wasn't sure I could do this on my own. But the second they started to smile, I knew their answer would be the one they gave me,

"Hell yeah."

"Fuckadoodle, yeah."

Okay, so I didn't know about the 'fuckadoodle' part but them agreeing to my crazy plan was definitely the outcome I had been hoping for.

"And what about Cronus?" Sophia asked, as I knew this was something Pythia had discussed with them before I had asked her to stay behind and help Takeshi out with his visions. She seemed more than a little relieved and seeing how she was terrified of Lucius, I couldn't say I blamed her.

"Yeah, what we going to do with that nob jockey?" Pip asked and once again, my answer was a simple one...

"We kill the bastard once and for all."

We got to Germany in good time, although any time it took me between now and getting Draven back was time I considered wasted. Which was why, when the car pulled up outside Transfusion, I was out of the car quicker than the rest.

"Back of the line." The door man said and I couldn't help my anger slipping, making my fangs spring free and I snarled at him, warning,

"Let. Me. Inside. Now!"

"Holy shit!" he shouted jumping back and I heard Pip giggle next to me before slapping him on the chest,

"Hey, well would you look at those cool fangs huh, this crazy chick really wants in my friend's club, so why not move that big bald ass of yours out the way and let us in, yea?" Pip said and the second he saw the rest of our gang show up behind us, he frowned, looking at us as if we were a bunch of misfits. He just folded his arms and shook his head repeating,

"Back of the line, freaks." I heard Adam sigh and Zagan chuckle before suggesting to his wife,

"Should we show him what freaks really look like, dear?" Then he removed his hood, startling the doorman and winking at him. Sophia smiled back at him and said,

"Behave, handsome."

"I take it he doesn't know who you are then?" I said, stating the obvious.

"Must be another newbie, damn it, I hate the newbies!" Pip said on a sigh, then she pulled out her shiny pink mobile phone that looked like someone had thrown up glitter on it and tapped the screen.

"Yo boss man, yeah be a doll and do us a fav, tell this big dickhead on the front door of your club to let us in…yeah, the Tootonator is in tow…okay cool, will do." Pip hung up and said,

"Hey Pinball, your boss just told me to tell you, that if you don't let us in right now then he's gonna come down here himself and rip off your cock before letting his guests use it as a straw."

"Winnie dear, play nice," Adam warned from behind, making her huff.

"Eww, he said that?" I asked as the man on the door went slightly pale at the vivid picture Pip just painted.

"I may have embellished a word or ten," she said making me chuckle. Seconds later another man appeared, who obviously wasn't a newbie, as the second he saw who was waiting to get in, he definitely paled for the right reasons.

"Dude, get the fuck out the way!" The new doorman said practically pushing this other guy out of the way.

"I am so sorry about that Miss Ambrogetti, Mr Ambrogetti, Sir, Miss, please go in."

"Thank you, George," Pip said sweetly as we passed, and I sniggered when I heard the new guy say,

"Your name's not fucking George!"

"Yeah, well when those two are here, then trust me, they want my name to be Cinderfuckinella, for the night, then that's what it is…you get me?"

"Wow, you really made a name for yourself, Pip," I said as I walked up the first lot of stairs to the VIP, briefly taking in the creepy picture of Andy Warhol's severed head in a soup can.

"Who me? Nah, I'm known as a freakin' saint around here…isn't that right honey bee bunches?" Pip shouted back to Adam who was smirking at his wife and currently mesmerised by her swaying pink ass, that had space cowboy kittens patterned all over her strange leggings.

"He loves these pants, he says that it looks like the kitten's winking at him as I dance," she told me after catching him staring at her ass. I couldn't help but look down at her legs and she gave me a little dancing wiggle as if to help me out with the visualization.

"Nice," I said grinning.

We made it upstairs and just as the next guard gave us a head nod before moving out the way, I couldn't help but remember the last time I did this all those years ago. In fact, it almost felt as though I had come full circle as this had been the start of where my fate had begun to unravel.

Everything was as I remembered it was back that day, from the polished dark wooden floors framed with a crimson carpet border to the wrought iron railings. I looked to the side as I took in the rest of the club, seeing them now as we were on the first level. And I did this knowing what I would find, seeing massive columns reaching all the way up to the top of the huge building.

In between were the wraparound balconies, wide enough to be filled with dancing bodies, so that everyone could see the band and dance floor below. I even shuddered, remembering the way I had vaulted from one level to the other in my stupid attempt at escape. And if I thought back then that I would be running from what would eventually be the Master of my own kind, then I would have ended in a mental hospital, talking to peanuts.

But now here I was, about to demand my once terrifying captor to help me...*again.* I shook my head to try and rid myself of the craziness my life had really become, and in doing so, taking note once more of the contradicting décor. A mixture of old world opulence meeting with the rough, hardness of the industrial revolution...something I now knew as Steampunk.

The next staircase however, and one I knew lead up to the man himself, was all gothic riches. High polished brass and thick lush black carpets, with a 'You pass, you die' vibe when being faced with brute strength in the guards positioned there. The type that would likely snap you in two and throw your broken ass in the dumpster before letting you pass.

But one look at me and my posse, and they couldn't move quick enough. I didn't know if this was down to their Master's warning of our arrival or seeing Adam, the scariest member of our little group for any supernatural.

We reached the top just as the chorus hit, blaring out heavy rock music that certainly fit well with the setting.

"Yey! We are home, Pooky!" Pip said jumping on the spot a few times and clapping before she went running off through the crowd like an excited child would at Disneyland. Hell, for all I knew this was her idea of the 'Happiest place of Earth' and one look at all the sex and naked bodies, then yeah, I had to say, that knowing Pip as I did, it so was.

Light boxes with naked ladies dancing behind were still as I remembered them, along with tables displaying naked men and women covered in food, mixed with what was clearly a face full of sexual fluids, as I really didn't think that was cream one of them was licking off the guy's penis.

I was surprised, because unlike last time, when I had been like a rabbit caught in headlights, that now nothing phased me. That and the fact that the crowd parted for us like we were celebrities come to spend the night. Then I took a deep breath as the man himself came into view and in pretty much the same as he had been that night.

Sat casually lounged back against that massive black velvet couch that could hold ten people at least. I even remembered the solid carved dragon's feet holding the couch forever in place thanks to its talons that were embedded into the floor beneath. As if at some point it had been brought to life and ready to charge, digging in its heels for extra strength behind the act.

"Lucius." I said his name, hoping it didn't sound as breathy as it should. Damn him, but his smirk told me all hope was lost in knowing how he still affected me. But Christ, who wouldn't be affected, for starters, you would have to be dead not to recognise how handsome and sexy this man was!

He was currently wearing tight fitting black trousers with dark grey pin stripes, that moulded to his strong thighs and down into his big biker boots that were only half tied. To this he had a tight fitted waistcoat that matched the trousers and a black shirt underneath that was rolled up his forearms. One long black leather glove hid its length as it disappeared up his shirt and also hid the damage I knew was beneath it. His shirt was also undone down to his waistcoat line showing a hint of his defined chest underneath.

Add to this an unforgiving, handsome face with stern features and lips that I regretfully remembered how they felt being kissed, and there we had the man himself.

"Ah, my little Keira girl, I would say it is a pleasure, but I think considering why you're no doubt here, then that would be a lie, for I did warn you."

"Great, Lucius, just great, 'cause that is what I came all this way for, a fucking I told you so!" I snapped making those around him gasp, as if they'd never heard anyone speak to their king this way. But then he just threw his head back and burst out laughing. Then he stood up and came over to me, placed a firm hand at my waist to pull me in for a kiss on the cheek, where he whispered,

"Oh, how I have missed you, pet."

"Yeah, because life would be boring without me, constantly getting myself into trouble and needing your help…right?" I replied hoping for sarcasm just to mask the way his hand was gripping my side and the nervousness that gesture was causing me.

"Oh, without a doubt…*very boring indeed,*" he hummed, and I cleared my voice making him grin as I stepped back putting space between us.

"Well, it's a lot different from our first time meeting here, that's for sure," I told him making him raise a honey coloured eyebrow in return.

"How so?" he asked.

"Well, for starters, no one has ended up impaled against a wall with your knife sticking out of them." He smirked and then said,

"Not yet no, but don't fear pet, there is still time." Then he winked at me before moving past me to shake Adam's hand, as if he had missed him. Of course, he just let it happen when Pip jumped into his arms and he caught her like he had done hundreds of times before, and like those times doing so with a warning,

"If you have that fucking coloured shit on your lips, don't even think about it, Squeak!" This then stopping her before she could cover his face in kisses. Of course, being Pip, she did indeed have 'coloured shit' on her lips, as today's choice was white with a black and red lipliner. So, she paused mid pucker and he let her slide down him with a smirk I could see he was trying to hide. It was obvious that he cared for Pip a great deal and more than he let on and Adam knew this, which was no doubt why he was so loyal. That and Lucius had also been his maker, helping him to remain with the love of his life for eternity. So yeah, lot to be thankful for with that one.

"Sophia," he said nodding down at her and then offering the same silent hello to her husband. Then he folded his arms over his chest and asked her,

"So, what has your brother gone and done this time?"

"He's fucked off again, so the usual," she remarked, folding her own arms and doing it with attitude as I wasn't the only one pissed off at her brother. It turned out that Sophia had been furious and managed to destroy a few things after she'd dealt with my meltdown. I think most of which were expensive bottles of spirts that, and I quote, she said 'Try fixing that shit when you get back, brother!'

"Figures," he responded as if he wasn't in the least bit surprised.

"And we are here because Tootie Angry Pants thinks you can help," Pip told him with a naughty smile, making him turn his attention back to me and say,

"Oh, I just bet she does." This made me frown at him, something he seemed to enjoy seeing because it made him grin at me.

"So, what is your grand plan here, or should I just guess?" he asked making me join the 'folding arms' club.

"I don't really have time for guesses, Lucius," I snapped, and he was back over to me in a second, like I hadn't even seen him move, that type of quick.

"Alright Pet, then seeing as I know you well, let me tell you what I know you are planning, without giving it a thought as usual…you think you can go running off down into Hell again and drag his ass out of wherever you think it is…am I right?" My growl said it all, as damn him, but I hated when he was right, smug ass.

"And you need my help why?" he asked making me frown up at him and tell him forcefully,

"Because you know where he is." At this he looked surprised and I watched as his eyes started to betray him ever so slightly. Yet he still kept up his facade.

"Do I now?" This was when I started losing my restraint and he clocked it straight away when my eyes started to change.

"Easy there, Pet, you don't want to go down this road with me," he warned in a stern tone, but this was the wrong thing to say right now as I felt my usual tingling in my fingertips as I slowly unfolded my arms. I was trying to hold it in for as long as I could, but it was like something had just snapped and now, I could barely contain it. So, I snarled up at him and felt my fangs drop, showing him just how serious I was.

"You saw it that day," I told him, feeling my voice becoming strained, but at least I now no longer had a lisp when I spoke, or that wouldn't have been very intimidating, despite the damage my demon side could do.

"Calm your shit, sweetheart, and we will talk but until then…" he started trying to get me under control, but I was too far gone for that. He knew this when I started walking him backwards,

"When I asked you that question, you didn't want to tell me, did you?" I accused for the first time making him look guilty.

"Keira I..." he started to say, backing up even more at the sight of the power now sparking from my hands. Because he knew what I was capable of, he saw it that day in the library. And with that one look realisation hit me about another day in the past, one not so long ago. And I looked down as if I could see it playing out in front of me.

It was back in the hallway after Draven had turned. He was just about to give me answers as to what he had seen when he touched my birthmark, when a strange look of concentration from him and Draven started to come back around. This was when I shot an accusing look back to Lucius and said in scary calm,

"You...you made it so it looked like Draven's mind control had worn off, so you could get out of telling me, didn't you?" Again, I pushed and this time when I took a step forward with it, he actually went back a step into the glass that just so happened to be the very same spot I had once been held up against.

When I felt the familiar tingling in my hand, I looked down and I suddenly knew why...I was far too close as the sparks now lashed out at the floor.

"Now easy Pet, let's just take a breath and..."

"TELL ME!" I screamed, demanding this from him and before I knew it my hand was around his neck and was pinning his big body back to the glass with a bang. I saw Lucius look behind me and shake his head telling whoever it was not to do something.

"Keira!"

"Toots!"

Both Sophia and Pip shouted in shock, but I was too far gone and past the point of caring that they saw me like this.

Then, as if I was reaching out with my over developed senses, I turned my head to the side and warned,

"Ruto, if you come any closer to me with that blade in your hand, you won't like where you will find yourself pulling it from."

"Drop it!" Lucius snapped before giving his attention back to me and saying,

"Looks like the tables have turned for me beautiful, question is, what do you plan on doing now?" he asked and again like Draven's voice had done to me down in the prison, it started to seep in and take hold. I shook my head trying to rid the rational side of me from taking control and I wondered if this was what it was like for Draven? But then just thinking that name was enough to get me to squeeze his neck a little harder.

"Tell me and you will find out," I told him, my voice now nearly completely transformed.

"Alright little Keira girl, have it your way," he said as if he had made an important decision, one he hated being forced to make in the first place. Then with a sigh he told me,

"I saw a palace in Hell." I frowned having a think about it before asking him,

"What palace?" Now this was what he really hadn't wanted to tell me and when he did I understood why, as my demon side erupted as I roared out my pain. And I did this all to the background sound of screaming and glass exploding.

And all because Lucius had said five little words,

Words that nearly destroyed Lucius' club,

And me with it...

"It's Draven's home in Hell."

CHAPTER TWENTY-SEVEN

WAITING IS HELL

I felt a pair of strong arms go around me, catching me when I fell as the power drained out of me like every single drop had been wasted on that one angry moment. But I had my answer and Lucius had saved me and everyone else from the Keira bomb going off and killing everyone. Because that scream I'd heard had been mine and that glass smashing had been caused by Lucius' actions, not mine.

It turned out I wasn't the only one with immense power and he proved this when he had taken my hand in his, bent it back and forced my hold on him to relax enough so that he could swap places with me. He had held me up against the glass, making it crack and shattered one of the panels further down the room from the impact.

Then he roared down at me like the Master of his domain and how dare I come there and treat him this way.

"Retract your fucking fangs and yield your demon to its Master, young one!" he snapped, snarling down at me, with his larger fangs and scarier face getting close to mine. I did as I was told instantly and the second he saw me submit to him, he too retracted his fangs and eased his hold on my neck. Then he stepped into my shaking frame and whispered down at me,

"Now this is like old times, Pet." His voice like this as a gentle hum was the last thing I needed to let go, and he knew it when my body started to relax and sag in his hold.

"Lucius?" I uttered his name in question as it was like coming down from a major high or adrenaline rush, it felt as though my body had been zapped and I tried to hold on to the only strength I had left right now…*Lucius.*

"It's alright love, I've got you." Then I felt my body being lifted and when he turned to face the others, I gasped as the whole room had been frozen. It was as if the whole world had stopped…that was other than those who held all the power in the room. So, Pip, Adam, Sophia, Zagan and Lucius' own council had been the only ones in the entire club to witness what had just happened. Then Lucius just snarled down at those we passed as he snapped out an order,

"I want an explanation and I want one fucking now!" Then he walked from the room with me in his arms, only allowing the club to have life back once he had walked us out of the room.

Which brought us to now and finding ourselves sat in a more private part of his club. I remembered being here once before when he had that asshole jailer Dimme killed. Lucius and I were alone for a moment, as I was situated in his lap whilst he was tucking my hair behind my ear. It seemed he was also giving me a moment to come back to earth, as it almost felt like being on drugs after having an operation. I looked around and he chuckled telling me,

"I had all the screens replaced if that's what you're wondering," he said referring to when my powers first started to emerge, and I freaked out smashing every TV screen without even thinking about it.

"Did that really just happen?" I asked in what sounded like a croaky voice.

"Yeah, that it did, Pet," he replied gently as if afraid of setting me off again.

"I am sorry, I don't know what is wrong with me, I have just been so angry, and I guess I just…"

"Took it out on your Vampire hero?" Lucius offered making me laugh.

"Yeah, well I won't be getting you a pair of tights and a cape anytime soon," I told him making me laugh when he replied,

"Thank fuck for that, those assholes look like sissies."

"Oh, I don't know, Thor is pretty hot…I mean if you like that big, muscular blonde, manly look," I said blushing when I realised who it sounded like I had just described.

"Don't say a word, not if you value these new TV screens," I warned, joking when I knew his smug ass wanted to comment.

"Mmm, it seems like you keep costing me money, sweetheart," he said making me suddenly think of all that money he had paid out for me back at the auction.

"Yeah, well lucky for you I am immortal now, so at least I have a chance at paying you back for buying me that day. Okay, so we might all look like spacemen living on the moon by the time that payment plan is finished, but still they say it's the thought that counts." This was when Lucius started laughing and I got the sense it wasn't just at my joke.

"What?"

"He never told you, did he?" Lucius asked making me frown.

"Tell me what?" I asked, wondering what had been kept from me.

"Dom gave me that money, Keira. Well, forced it upon me actually and I believe his exact words were, 'No one but I owns

Keira, now and forever'," he told me making my mouth drop in shock.

"No way," I whispered in disbelief.

"Wait, when was that?" I asked making him smirk.

"Shortly after you left Italy, he found out what happened to you during your kidnapping and yes, I believe you were still separated at the time," Lucius said, knowing this would mean something to me and I couldn't thank him enough for it. Which was why I threw my arms around him and hugged him, taking him off guard.

"Thank you, my friend." His reply had been a simple one,

"As always, you're welcome, *my little Keira girl.*"

After this sweet moment between us, Lucius had demanded to know what had happened to make my power come back the way it had and also what 'I had been getting up to this time'. The whole story came out with the colourful help of Pipisms that yes, this did also include the whole Nessie story.

"Seriously, only you could manage to sink a fucking boat on the Loch Ness," Lucius had said making me throw my hands up and say,

"Why do people keep saying that!? It wasn't even me, it was the bloody Loch Ness Mon…!"

"Don't say it!" Pip warned making me groan, one that quickly stopped the second I saw a familiar face walk through the door making me and Pip squeal,

"Percy!"

"So, I gotta ask, don't you think they are going to kind of notice us gone?" I asked after a night of chatting and catching up with old friends, the main one being Percy, who was looking happier and happier every time I saw him. When I think back to the shy, stuttering little man who I met that day who used to hide his face, to now seeing him standing proud, dressed like a punk rocker and caring little for the burns on his face, it made me want to cry with happiness for him. Me and Pip had both attacked him with kisses when we saw him, making his scarred puckered skin blush and look adorable.

He still had his stutter, but it wasn't as bad because now he had overcome most of his nervousness. The other surprising thing was not so much his connection to Lucius, who he seemed to adore as any loyal subject would. But more so Lucius' connection with him, as he seemed to have taken him under his wing and treated him with an extreme amount of respect. And because of this show of respect, others in his council reacted the same. Even scary, always pissed off Caspian, teased him affectionately by messing up his now styled hair when he sat down near both him and Liessa.

Throughout the evening Lucius would catch me watching Percy and smiling, which prompted him to lean into me and whisper,

"Don't be too happy for him, we have corrupted him to our level of debauchery, you can be sure of that." I giggled at his teasing and said,

"Oh, I have no doubt, with you as their leader after all...so I take it he knows all the big swear words then and can growl and snarl really loud when he's pissed at people?" Once finished with my teasing his eyes started to glow with amusement, but instead of laughing his lips twitched, along with a muscle in his jaw before he squeezed my shoulder and warned,

"Careful Pet, you are on the verge of being cute again."

The rest of the time with Lucius was spent first asking questions and answering them. Which took us into the evening, during which I had received three phone calls, one from Jared confirming from Bill that the news of Draven's return had lit

'Hellish hens' and they were clucking. Then he went on to explain that these were Bill's words not 'fucking his' as he said, but I could take it as a yes.

Then Sigurd had rung and told me that from what they could tell, no doorways had been used in the Janus gate, so this was a bust. Third and final call had been from Pythia, who told me Takeshi was now awake and he saw a vision of Draven leaving through a summoned portal. She also told us that during this time he also held back the other image he saw and that was the three of us in Hell looking for him. I thanked her and knew more firmly in my mind now what we had to do. And what we had to do, didn't include any overbearing protective men joining us.

Sophia knew this, Pip definitely knew this and taking one look at Lucius, I most certainly knew this. Because this would have been something that would never have worked had we had them with us.

For a start, Adam would have turned the second he made it through to the other side. Zagan's armies finding him would have drawn too much attention to our situation, something they were life bound to automatically do on his arrival. And Lucius, well one look at him from Demon Draven and the saying 'All Hell breaking loose', would have shifted quickly to 'All Hell being Broken'.

Not long after this we had all called it a night, after of course we had a bit of girl time in the toilets together so that we could finally have chance to make our plan in secret. And thus, talk about the fact that we had to do this alone. Which now prompted me to ask,

"What is going to happen to Adam when he finds you gone again, as it's not exactly like stepping back in time before he even finds out you're gone and therefore has no need to go King Demon Kong on them all."

"But he's here now, so it's all gravy," was her cryptic answer.

"What she means is that Lucius would control his mind, making him sleep before his anger could take hold...it's how certain circumstances have been avoided before."

"Yeah, like when I missed the bus that one time," Pip said shaking her head and making me nearly ask, but in the end we had more important things to do. Which was why we were currently on the rooftop of Transfusion looking for whatever Pip had promised us was up here.

Unfortunately, I also remembered the last time I was up here and that hadn't exactly ended well for me. I remembered waking up in a cell shortly before I found myself on a slab of marble about to be sacrificed by another unhinged megalomaniac that wanted to become a God. Jesus, but just how many of those guys were there in the world? I swear I could see the group catch line now, 'ever fancied becoming a God and taking over the world, hate kittens and furry cute things, have no friends and look kinda creepy, then join us and we will show you how!' I don't know why but I was seeing group sessions like in the movie 'Wreck it Ralph' with them all sat round sharing ideas and brainstorming.

"So, what are we looking for here?" I asked getting impatient and looking to Sophia who just shrugged her shoulders next to me and continued to check out her nails. We were both sat on a stone bench in Lucius' rooftop garden, with the amazing view of Munich city, lighting up the night sky all around us. Pip was, at this point in time, on all fours in front of us patting down the wooden decking. One that looked weathered and had turned a greyish shade that complimented the dark slate swirl in the middle of the round courtyard. I remembered thinking back then that it reminded me of a dark path to nowhere, because at the time that was how lost I had felt when seeing it.

"Mawhaa! Gotya!" Pip shouted pushing down on a hidden compartment and revealing what looked like a stone tablet underneath. It was filled with ancient text carved down in lines and it was framed in what looked like thick black tar, just floating there.

"Time for your blood, Missy," Pip said holding out a hand for me to take, making me frown.

"Christ, why is it always my blood we need for this shit, I swear I am going to get blood drawn at the doctors and start carrying it around with me in a water bottle labelled 'for the stupid time' if this carries on," I moaned as I dropped to my knees and scooted over to where she was leaning over the new discovery.

"Don't be a pussy…Miss Dramatic Much?" Pip said giving me a wink making me laugh before slapping a hand in hers with a lot more force than was needed, making her giggle, saying,

"Touché Toots, now show us some fang," I rolled my eyes knowing what was coming and concentrating on releasing my fangs like an obedient little Vampire puppy. Then she held my own palm out to me and said,

"Now chow down." I gave her a look and she gave me one back and said,

"Do you wanna go be a hero in Hell or not?" I didn't answer her with words but just released a sigh and bit down hard enough to say 'oww' around my hand with my mouth full, as like always, it bloody hurt.

"Good little Vampy baby," Pip said patting my head as she took my hand and held it over the tablet, letting my blood coat the symbols. Then I watched as it started to lower down into the thick black liquid before one large symbol started to appear, only this time it sizzled like it was being scorched to the stone.

It started to appear red as if it had transformed part of the black liquid to lava. Its shape was an upside-down triangle with the point extending out to create two hooks turning back in on themselves. Then a V shape cut through the bottom of the triangle, making a diamond pattern at the centre.

"Right, well that should do it," Pip said standing up and clapping her hands as if she had dirt on them and giving me a hand to help me up. So, I gave her my blood-free hand and looked back down at the symbol as it now started to fade.

"What was that?" I asked thinking it looked important to know and it turned out that it was.

"It's the Sigil of Lucifer, the mark of the Devil." Sophia stood up to join us and we all looked over to where the swirl of a path to nowhere had started to ooze and secrete the strange substance. This was before it bubbled up around the sides of the slabs and started to get overwhelmed by the black sticky liquid as if it was being pushed up beneath the stones.

"The sign of the Devil?" I asked following, as the two of them walked closer to the edge of the black substance, one that had now formed a circle covering the space with a black void.

"Yeah, Lucius is his son after all and now you, well technically speaking, are kind of like his daughter," Pip told me with a shrug of her shoulders, making me shoot her a look of disbelief.

"Uh, come again?!" I asked as Sophia took my still bleeding hand and held it over the black stuff making blood drip down onto it. The second it landed, it hissed as if it was acid eating away at metal.

"Ewww does that mean that you and Lucius are now like brother and sister?" Pip asked, teasing me and she laughed when I gave her an unimpressed look. Then I looked back to what I assumed would soon be a portal and swallowed hard as the stone path started to glow red beneath the black. Suddenly light exploded, shooting upwards, and nearly blinding me at first, it was so bright.

"Lucius gave you the blood straight from his heart...who did you think gave it to him? Now you have it, which is why Lucius is the only one who can open this portal... well Lucius and now you." Sophia was the one to answer me this time. And Pip joked,

"Yeah, so fancy a trip to meet your new daddy?" I groaned and said,

"Why the Hell not," I said holding my hands up and taking each of theirs in turn so that we could all step through together. And we did this all to the sound of Pip saying,

"Ha, why the Hell not...good one!"

Then we stepped into Hell and I only hoped that it would be for the very last time.

Stepping into Hell wasn't what I expected it to be as strangely, it started off in a room. I don't know why, but I was expecting all fire and brimstone. Although what in Hell brimstone really looked like was anyone's guess, as I always thought it was sulphur and if that was the case, then my reunion with Draven was certainly going to be a smelly one, that was for sure.

"Where are we?" I asked looking round and seeing what looked like a hotel lobby. Okay, so one that would have been run by the Adams family, owned by Tim Burton, and had a bell boy named Edward Scissorhands. Talk about having a Gothic unpleasant stay!

The floor was black and white swirls that looked like it went on forever, so that if you looked down it made you feel slightly sick, as if you were swaying. Sophia nudged me and shook her head telling me not to do that. The ceiling didn't help as it was a mirror and even looking up made you feel the same way, as if you would fall over backwards without even moving. Sophia saw me looking and I stopped, shrugged my shoulders at her and muttered,

"Can I look at the walls, is that safe?" I asked hoping to be sarcastic, but she didn't take it that way, as she wrinkled her nose and said,

"If you must, but I wouldn't recommend it." So of course, me being me, I did and at first, I couldn't understand what she meant. But then I looked closer and saw what she warned me of. All of the walls were completely covered in what looked like millions of white and red strands of thin wire against a black background, one that disappeared into a walled border painted crimson inside. But then I realised as I started to look closer that the red on the wire was moving slowly, dripping down the wire to the little river of blood that framed the large room.

Sophia saw my look of disgust and smirked, mouthing the words,

'Told you so.'

"So, is someone going to tell me where we are?" I asked wondering why we were just stood here waiting, which started to make sense when I was told,

"We are in a waiting room of sorts," Sophia whispered.

"Yes, but a waiting room for what?" I asked looking around, seeing that it was completely empty and other than there being a few mirrored benches, a mirror covered desk and a mirror elevator door, there was nothing.

"Who do you think?" Sophia asked, as though it should have been obvious.

"Well, I don't think it's Father Christmas, obviously?" I said on a snort.

"I think the only jolly fat man you will find down here

Toots, is King Henry VIII for killing so many of his wives, the horny bastard…damn, but you wouldn't have been the last one to marry him would you, not unless you wanted a quick way to die…like moving to Coronation street, you're just begging for something bad to happen to you there, hey speaking of which have you ever lived there…you know, on account of all your shitty luck and all?" Pip asked, leaving me with too much information to process and clinging on to the question, why Pip watched that show?

"I think that confused look means no, Pip…now can we please just wait for the Devil quietly, you know how he can get," Sophia said making me ignore what she asked and instead shout out,

"The Devil!?" This turned out to be a mistake, I knew that much as even Pip winced. But then so did I when suddenly a ding sound alerted us to the elevator doors that were about to open and when they did, well wouldn't you know, it was true what they said after all…

Speak of the Devil and he shall appear.

CHAPTER TWENTY-EIGHT

A MURDER OF CROWS

This time when I saw the Devil, I didn't expect to be seeing him looking dashing in an all-black suit, all but his tie of course which was blood red with a skull tie pin. Even his hair looked styled as if he were ready for a date or something. He looked, well he looked handsome as Hell.

But then he looked to each of us and whereas before he had a smirk playing around the edge of his mouth, now he looked dark and angry. It was almost as if he'd been expecting someone else to be here, not us.

"Uh-oh, he looks pissed," Pip said making Sophia swallow hard which I definitely took for a bad sign, as she wasn't ever scared of anything. I could see he was getting angrier by the second, so I decided to do something and hope for the best, as he hadn't exactly been horrible to me last time we met. Although that vision on the witness circle hadn't exactly been what I would call friendly, but then again, that hadn't been real...*right?*

So, I stepped forward making the girls gasp and Sophia try to hold me back. I looked down at her hand and told her,

"It's okay, trust me." She gave me a fearful look but let go anyway.

"Um, hello Sir," I said taking a step forward and I looked behind me to see Pip smacking her forehead and muttering,

"That's it, she's dead, it was great knowing her though." I ignored her and carried on with my insane plan, even though his impossibly tall frame was making me arch my neck back as he stared down at me expectantly.

"You may…um…well remember me a little differently, but you helped me…um, back when, well…" He raised a hand and said,

"I will stop you there before you give yourself a nose bleed. I remember you, although I must say you were certainly better dressed." This made blush as he looked down at me regarding my plain outfit of jeans, t-shirt and hoodie with distaste.

"You are here for the King I assume?" he asked making my heart soar with hope,

"Yes, we are, do you know where we can find him, only we…?" He held up his hand again and stopped me,

"A simple yes would suffice." I nodded making him grin in satisfaction.

"Then consider this a favour for if you are to succeed in fucking him, you will need to wear something better than that," he said making my mouth drop open in shock.

"I am not here to fu…" Suddenly, I found a hand around my mouth and Sophia coming up behind me correcting,

"She would be very grateful, wouldn't you Keira?" Sophia's voice told me that I would be most grateful, as he would let me live if I kept my big mouth shut and she proved this by nodding my head for me before letting me go.

"Yes, thank you." I said in a tense tone. Well, at least

Lucifer looked more amused than 'killer pissed off', a look that was likely to end with my head on a spike.

"Of course, I had been expecting more of you," he said making me frown and look back to the girls in question.

"More of us?" I asked knowing that I probably shouldn't.

"There was another girl among you, yes," he stated making me wonder how he knew that but not seeing any harm in it I said,

"Oh Pythia, yes she stayed behind." Hearing this he took a deep breath and with his reaction it suddenly struck me that she had been the one he had wanted to see here. I was so close to asking, but the second I saw his eyes turn hard in annoyance, I decided it wasn't wise.

"And why was that?" he asked, his voice now taking on that hard edge that told me to be very careful here. But then I thought what was best to hear if you had a thing for a girl, the fact that she was terrified and didn't want to be here or that someone else made her stay behind? So, I decided to take a chance and tell him what was a half-truth.

"It was my fault, I asked her to stay behind," I told him and the second his eyes turned into those that could only belong to the Devil, I nearly wet myself, unable this time to blame it on having a baby bladder. I heard the girls panic behind me as Sophia stepped up and was about to speak when Lucifer stopped her, and he did this by closing his fist and taking away her voice. It reminded me of when Draven had done the same thing to me that night by my truck when I was trying to scream for help and run from him.

"And why would you do that, I wonder?" he growled getting lower in my face, making Pip squeak in fear for me. So, I decided to keep going and hope that my reasons were good enough for him.

"Because I wanted her to be safe. She has never been down

here and from what I can tell, doesn't have the same means to protect herself as we do. I thought she would be vulnerable and didn't want her getting hurt…or worse." Now I watched as this realisation took root and instead of being annoyed at my reason, he now seemed pleased by it.

"You care for her?" he asked. I nodded trying not to show fear when I said,

"She is my friend and I helped her once when she had nowhere else to go." As soon as I had said this his eyes turned back to looking more human and I took a deep breath, along with Pip and Sophia who I hadn't realised until now, were not allowed to speak but weren't even allowed to breathe.

"Then it seems I am in your debt, as you will soon be in mine," he told me, having me quickly wondering why I would be in his debt, not exactly sure that would be the wisest of places to be. Then I looked down after feeling my legs go suddenly colder, and saw that my jeans had been replaced by a pair of black stockings.

This was also when I noticed what I was dressed in and I gasped as I now looked like a sexy virgin. I was in a tight corseted dress made out of shimmering white brocade that tied at the back with what felt like an endless amount of thick cord. It was low on my chest, showing an obscene amount of cleavage, making me instantly blush, one that also bloomed across the skin there.

But that wasn't the worst part, as the layers and layers of skirt were cut a lot shorter at the front, showing off the thick lace tops of the stockings and the hints of the four thick satin straps that went around each leg. These of course I could feel were attached to the suspender belt and lace thong I was wearing underneath, a set that was barely concealed if you asked me.

Even my hair had been styled half up with a cascade of

innocent curls flowing around my face and down my back. I could see all this through the elevator doors and that I even had on makeup. But that too had been done to make me look more like an angel than the demon I felt down here.

Pip wolf whistled, and this time Lucifer did grin at her antics.

"There now, that is better and more fitting for one of my Kings," he said, standing back and crossing his arms over his chest to admire his handy work.

"Now, if you can just make it there in one piece, you might have a chance at accomplishing your task, now go and try to tame your beast, for my own will have to wait," he said cryptically but I didn't ask, I was just grateful we had survived. The makeover however, I hadn't been expecting.

"So, does this mean you will grant us safe passage?" Sophia braved to ask, as Lucifer was about to turn his back to us. He paused and said,

"Now why would I do that, when the other option is far more entertaining." Then he clicked his fingers and the room around us disappeared and what now remained was the vision of Hell I had imagined. Everything but the demonic looking elevator doors which had turned into shattered pieces of a mirror. A broken glass that held desperate screaming souls in each damaged section. He walked to them and they opened, making me wonder where he was going to go now there was no building or floors for him to go up to.

"Enjoy my kingdom, won't you?" he said continuing into the elevator with his back to us. Once inside, he turned around and added,

"Be seeing you soon Keira, and next time..." The doors started to close just as he said,

"Without your white rabbit." Then they slammed shut and the elevator disappeared into the ground answering my earlier

question of where he would go. The doors let off a creepy echoing sound, as all the souls screamed out in horror until out of sight.

"Well, I would class that as a win any day of the week," Pip commented making Sophia scoff and say,

"Surviving the Devil when pissed off, uh yeah, I would say so." I tried to think about the reasons he had been pissed off, but in the end, all I could focus on was the last thing he had said to me about being without my white rabbit. How had he known that, if it had only been a vision and wasn't real?

"Come on, it shouldn't be that far from here, at the very least he transported us somewhere close," Sophia said, and it was the first bit of good news I had heard all day.

"That's good because now it looks like I have no choice but to walk it in heels," I reminded them as I looked down to see ivory satin shoes that were decorated with open lace along one side. They also had a strap in the same design that was as thick as my palm and covered my whole ankle and tied at the back with a satin ribbon.

"Oooh, pretty," Pip said with a clap.

"Yeah, but not for the pregnant lady who swore off heels for the next eight months," I commented dryly. After this we swapped shoe sizes and quickly realised it would be no good, as they both either had abnormally small feet or mine were abnormally big, which I had to say I was hoping for the first.

So, I soldiered on thinking that it could definitely be worse. Okay so yes, we were currently trying to find my husband in some palace he owned in Hell and having no idea what to expect to find when we got there. And I did so in heels. But we were all in one piece and had survived the Devil, so like Pip had said, win, win, on that front.

Then why was it I was nervous that I was about to walk into something I wasn't sure I could handle? Lucifer had mentioned something about 'taming the beast' and I was really hoping that was meant as a metaphor for something at this point.

I decided to shake these thoughts from my mind, before I sent myself insane and instead thought back to what Lucifer had wanted with Pythia. We were all just coming up to what looked like a mountain pathway that I had to say, wasn't going to do much for my nerves with heights. But thankfully, Sophia didn't take this way, but instead nodded to a cave entrance that was carved with an archway around the rough jagged rock. It looked like some demonic writing that was all harsh pointed lines that slashed through one another, making symbols of straight lined shapes.

"We are going in there?" I asked on a gulp.

"Well, I didn't think you would appreciate the mountainside route, as trust me, it only gets higher," Sophia said in a way that definitely made the cave seem a lot more appealing. So, inside we went and thankfully, Pip unhooked a torch from the fixture embedded in the wall and with a snap of her fingers lit it.

"Besides, this way we will draw less attention to ourselves." I thought this another good reason to add to what was starting to sound like one of many. So yes, it was creepy down here, but I thought what I needed was a distraction, so I found myself asking what I really wanted to know,

"Why did he want to know why Pythia was missing?" I asked, not understanding the chasm sized point I was obviously missing here.

"Don't worry about it, we'd better go before he releases the Gorgons just for kicks," Sophia said making Pip snort in agreement.

"Yeah, those mean bitches really like to…" I cut her off and said again,

"Sophia, tell me, why does he want to know about Pythia?"

"Uh, not like I was talking here or anything..." Pip muttered in the background.

"It's fine okay, just don't worry about it... now can we please...?" She started to say but it only managed to make me worry more, so I didn't let it go. I did the opposite.

"Sophia!" I shouted her name to get her to stop walking ahead and I knew I finally had her when her shoulders slumped in obvious defeat.

"Look, let's just say that even Devils have their obsessions and she is his," she finally admitted, making my mouth drop open in shock.

"What?!" I shouted on a screech, one that echoed down the large tunnel.

"Jeezy Peezy, should have just brought my demon fog horn, or sent out an invite for those bony suckers to come try some fast food," Pip said in response to me doing a crap job at keeping it down. I shot her a look and said,

"My bad." Then I carried on, pressing for more information, as again I felt like this was important.

"Right, now go back to the part where Lucifer, as in the King of Hell, is obsessed with the Oracle, because I take it you mean as in, wants her in a healthier, 'close to him so he could possibly use her to see the future type thing' but treat her right?"

"That would be a firm no."

"Or a Hell no...but firm, okay we can go with firm," Pip said, backtracking after receiving one of Sophia's scowls.

"Okay, so someone explain this to me," I said watching for the fallen rocks and boulders that had broken away from the rest of the cave's rock face. The cave had started opening up and I was starting to feel less claustrophobic. There were even walkways above us that made it look like an underground travel system, although granted, a pretty basic one.

"What's to explain, she is the ultimate forbidden fruit, never to have been touched by a man."

"At least not in a good way or the best way, or even better way…okay, shutting up now," Pip said adding to it and skipping over some rubble in her way.

"And Lucifer wants to bed her?!" I screeched in horror as no matter how hot he was to look at, it was giving new meaning to the whole 'beauty and the beast' scenario.

"To be honest no one really knows," Sophia said shrugging her shoulders before continuing,

"All we do know is that since the daughter of the God Janus was brought into the world, Lucifer has wanted her and the deal that was made for her, was that no one could touch her until after the Prophesy was completed. After that, well she was granted her one wish, which was to be released by the Fates to become human and to spend the rest of her days out in the world she first became a prisoner to," Sophia finished Pythia's tale of woe and from the look of Lucifer's anger at not seeing her, then I would say it wasn't over.

"Does she know?!"

"Oh yeah, she knows, which is why she changed her appearance so many times and all in hopes she wouldn't be appealing to the King of Hell," Sophia said with a hopeless expression as she too looked as though she felt sorry for the girl.

"Jesus, she was a bloody child when I met her!" I cried in horror, which again kept echoing making Pip wince.

"Sorry." I muttered, as I kept forgetting myself.

"Yes, and she has even been a man before now, but none of that matters to him, for he knows her true form and more importantly, what she is to him…or at least what he is convinced she is to him," she added as what looked like an afterthought.

"Which is?" I asked not preparing myself at all for the answer she gave.

"Well, as unbelievable as it sounds...*she's his Chosen One,*" Sophia told me with a tense smile.

"You're telling me she is destined to be with...*with the Devil!?*" This time when I went high pitched, I at least had the foresight to do it somewhat quietly. Pip mouthed the words 'Good Toots' at me but my mind was elsewhere. As in it started to race and suddenly my memories flashed back to that day in the library when she had seen Lucius. She had been beyond terrified.

"Is that why she is afraid of Lucius, because it has something to do with Lucifer?" I asked and Sophia and Pip both gave each other a look. I took it as my answer to be a resounding yes but still, I wasn't satisfied.

"What is it?" I asked, happy to at least have my mind focused on something other than what we were currently doing.

"Lucius is the son of Lucifer as you know, therefore he is charged with both the safety and capture of Pythia once the Fates no longer have need of her," Sophia said with a shrug of her shoulders and my mouth dropped open with this new bombshell.

"What! When they no longer have need of her!? Jesus, but it sounds like she just got kicked out of Heaven's VIP lounge and thrown to the bloody gutter and in the centre of a pack of circling Hellbeasts!" I said, now feeling about 400% more sorry for her.

"Technically, you don't get a pack of Hellbeasts, you just have Jared and everyone else...*that he owns*...but wolves, now wolves have a pack, and did you know what a group of monkeys are called...?" Pip asked, making me respond wryly,

"Pip, Sophia and Keira?" My sarcastic tone made Sophia

laugh and Pip, being Pip didn't get the joke but instead thought I was being serious because she replied,

"No, that's silly, they are called a troop or barrel…oh I get it, the game, a barrel of monkeys…you know I always wondered why a barrel…why not a crate or a box or better still a cage, although not better for the monkeys, as who likes living in a cage…well, other than our bed back at the lake house in Königssee, Adam loves it, oh and…"

"Pip, this stopped being helpful about five minutes ago, can we focus on the Hell part of this trip now?" Sophia said making Pip pout.

"Fine, but I was going to tell you that a group of crows is called a…"

"Murder, yes I know and if we don't all try and be a little quieter…" Sophia paused to shoot me a ray gun death look, one I was surprised didn't come with little 'pew, pew' sound effects, before she carried on,

"…That's precisely what we will be." I looked at Pip seeing her scrunch up her face in confusion, looking cute and at the same time a little crazy as she scratched at her plaited green and blue mohawk.

"But that's not right, I mean you can murder someone and be murdered but you can't *be a murder*…I think you fucked up there," Pip said to Sophia's back as she walked through the demonic rubble. However, Sophia's only response to this was a low growl as she continued to climb, turning back to me to help me across.

I don't know how long we had been walking for, but I nearly wept with joy when Sophia told me we weren't that far from reaching the other side of the mountain. To be honest I had been surprised that my appearance had held up to the task of trekking through Hell's underground.

"Okay, so listen to this one, did you know a collective of elk is called 'a gang'."

"Nope, didn't know that one Pip," I said moving to the side and dodging what looked like a shard of black ice the size of a car that had erupted from the ground at some point.

"Okay and a group of gorillas is called 'a band', right so if you then add a group of ferrets, which is called 'a business' and then you add them all together in the same room, you could say, 'oh look at that 'Gang, Band Business go' and you know what that sounds like right…?" Pip said waiting for our laugh and to be honest I would have, had we not heard another noise instead and this one sounded like a very distinct roaring of a beast.

"Well, it certainly doesn't sound like that!" Pip said looking behind her and then screaming,

"RUN FOR IT!" I looked behind us and saw what she had, now racing towards us. And my first and second thought after being scared shitless was to curse the day heels were invented and I also hoped my bladder held out until we were safe. But one look at the giant monster now charging at us and I didn't think it was up for the task. The only good thing about this was that all I could see was the red of his many eyes and the shadow of a body that was about the size of a bus.

"Come on, I can see the exit and it looks smaller than that thing so it can't follow us!" Sophia shouted back at us making our asses run like, well like a Hellbeast was on our tail and not the nice, handsome biker kind. I looked back and wished that I hadn't as it was gaining on us but thankfully so were we, on the glowing exit ahead. The second we could see where we were going, Pip threw the torch at it, giving us the extra time we needed to make it, as it landed straight on its head, making it stop for a few seconds.

Then we heard it bellow in rage behind us, and this time we heard it's many hooves stampeding its way towards us. Sophia managed to grab me at the last second before the creature launched itself through the gap, getting stuck the second it did.

"Holy shit, what is that thing, something from Hell or outer space?!" I shouted back, away from its snarling, hissing head that looked as if someone had taken the face of an alien and cut it down the centre to peel back the sides. Then someone stuffed a couple of eyes on there and a snake's tongue for good ugly measure.

"Come on, I don't think it's going anywhere," Sophia said but Pip being the first to turn her back on the thing said,

"Uhh, guys, sorry to tell you this, but I don't think we are either." Me and Sophia both turned around and were now faced with what Pip had seen…

A demonic army.

CHAPTER TWENTY-NINE

A DEMON'S WAY

"Uh okay, so what do we do now, 'cause I don't know about you guys, but I don't think we can take them," I said trying not to make any sudden moves as all three of us currently had our hands up in surrender.

"Oh, I don't know, you are wearing killer heels," Pip commented talking through one side of her mouth.

"Sophia, any ideas here?" I asked quietly without looking at her and trying not to take my eyes off the demon horde in front of us, all of which were holding out hellish long blades at us.

"Uh, nope, I have nothing here," she replied but this was when something happened as one of them stepped forward and snarled at Sophia in a different language, which impressively she started speaking back.

"Well, this looks promising," I said to Pip but then when I looked at her, she was frowning and told me,

"I wouldn't be too sure of that, Tootie." And when I glanced her way I saw Sophia stomping her foot and shouting back at the one that looked to be in charge. The only way I could really tell this was he had a bigger helmet, a bigger breastplate and a bigger sword...so all signs were pointing that way.

"What's going on?" I asked Sophia when she looked like she had no choice but to give up.

"They want to take you," she replied in a dire tone.

"Uh, come again?" I said hoping I had misheard her or at the very least, the 'me' part of that sentence.

"It is my brother's army and he has sent them out in search of us."

"Okay, so isn't that a good thing?" I asked looking first to Sophia and then to Pip, but neither of them looked as though that answer was a yes.

"No, as they refuse to take us with you," she told me making me want to cry out in frustration.

"But why?!"

"My brother's orders are simply to find the girl, *that being you,* ...and anyone else that is with her, have them removed," she told me.

"Removed?" This time I did screech my question and the one that had been arguing with Sophia snarled something at her.

"Yes alright, alright, hang on, dumb ass!" Sophia growled back and then turned to me once more.

"Their orders are to take us to the nearest gateway and grant us our passage home," she said as if hating this idea, which I had to say, I wasn't exactly loving it either.

"And me?" I had to ask.

"You're to stay here, so they can take you to their King...in other words, take you to Dom," she told me, and I turned my panicked eyes to Pip, who pretended to wave a little flag and say,

"It's as you wanted... Yay...so not yay?" she added after seeing my face drop.

"You mean to Draven's demon, right?" I corrected making them both sigh in return.

"I am afraid we have no other choice."

"Just so I know, what choices did they give us?" I asked in a hopeful tone that was quickly crushed when Sophia replied,

"You go with them freely and we get an escort home, or they take you against your will and we get put in chains and left to be eaten…either way, I think you can see where this is going to go." The shrug of her shoulders looked like it carried a lot more weight to it than the casual gesture it was usually done for.

"Can I just say at this point that I know that as the horny one of the group, you're all thinking I like chains, and many a time by Adam, to be eaten during these times. However, I do not like the idea of their version of events," Pip told us after putting her hand up as if addressing the class.

"It's okay Pip, no one is going to get eaten. I guess we have no other choice then," I said, unable to prevent my voice from sounding as dejected as it did.

"I don't think my brother will harm you or allow anyone else to do the same… the problem we do have is if he doesn't let you go and you can't get him to accept his Angel side back," Sophia told me looking worried.

"Then what you're saying is that I might not be able to get back…*right?*" I asked after swallowing down the fear in just saying it.

"We wouldn't…no just wait! Damn it, I said wait!" Sophia started shouting as I turned in time to see the main guy in charge storming this way, obviously hitting his limit on waiting. Either way, he now clamped a heavy gauntleted hand around the top of my arm and started yanking me away from Pip and Sophia.

"NO! Let me go! Oww your hurting me!" I shouted, trying to reach back to them.

"Let her go, you big bastard!" Pip shouted but the second she ran to me she was caught, as was Sophia.

"It will be okay Keira, listen to me, it will be okay, we will figure this out, we will find Cronus and put an end to this...!" Sophia kept shouting trying to reach me through the guards that had now surrounded them, as now I was being pulled in the opposite direction.

"Try bringing him back! Try bringing my brother back, I know you can!"

"I will, I promise!" I shouted back but this was the last thing I heard as I was yanked hard and then just as I was swung round, the idiot let me go, then looked at me, probably wondering why I couldn't keep my balance, as I fell to the side only to knock one of my cheeks against something hard, which strangely felt like the blunt end of a sword.

Then everything went black and to the echoing sound of my name being called in a desperate cry.

"You have trouble staying on your feet, don't you?" I heard his voice penetrate the darkness as if reaching out to me. It was a memory, I was sure of it. I knew this because I remembered him saying these same words to me once. So, I opened my eyes and found myself back in my bedroom at Libby's, wondering what had happened. Then I knew it was my turn to say something. I opened my eyes and found him there, my past Draven stood in my room where he shouldn't be. Because this had all come and gone.

"Umm...I mean...what are you doing here?" I asked him, playing my part, only this time, I was in my bed, not half stumbled over the window seat as I had been. I looked up at him as he stood at the end of my bed watching me, as if he too were asking himself if I were real of not. Then I watched as a smirk played around the edge of his lips before he told me,

"Yes, well apart from it being my right to see you, I also wanted to bring you something. You dropped this." He held out his hand to give me something, but like back then, I didn't reach for it. This time making him frown before leaning down to whisper,

"As I told you that day... there is no need to fear me... *I would never hurt you.*" And then just like that, he snapped his fingers, and everything was gone.

I jolted as if something was carrying me under my arms and had just dropped me to the floor. Then I heard something being said to me before I felt a nudge of someone's boot at my side, which I was glad to say didn't hurt. I decided this was my cue to move and I shook the fog from my mind before opening my eyes to find the most incredible sight.

Draven's palace in Hell.

It was as frightening as it was beautiful and seemingly half of it had been carved into a whole mountain, that's how big it was. The entrance was framed by two huge statues of demonic warriors, each on their knees. They held above them each side of a plinth with a figure held above it...

A figure of my husband's demon form.

The statue was of him stood with his legs slightly apart, his arms crossed to his front as if holding the two blades that came from his wrists, that reached down to the centre point between his feet. He was in full battle armour and the sight of him like this was glorious.

I shuddered at the sight, being that the whole entrance was at least the size of a twenty-story building. It was made up of staggered arches with turrets of jagged rock that had been carved in such a way that it looked half building, half fortress.

I looked up and up and then up some more and even when doing this I couldn't see it all, it was that high. I had never seen anything so big in all my life and wondered how many Scottish castles you could have fit inside it? I think more than what my fingers could have counted that was for sure. Hell, even Lucius' mountain home could have fit in here many times over.

Which had me wondering, if this was Draven's palace in Hell, then what the Hell did the Lucifer's look like? I wasn't given long to ponder this as a snarled voice spoke to me from behind in a language I didn't understand. I turned to face it knowing what I would find when I did and that was an army at my back. One with its general stood closest to me. They all looked the same except for this one. With black helmets that covered their entire faces, which was no doubt a good thing for me, as I can't imagine they were hiding anything pretty under there.

Each of them was heavy with armour that looked made out a combination of stone and metal, with spikes being the main theme of design. It looked as if no matter where they would have been hit, the damage would have been swiftly made to the other, as even their armour looked to be used more as weapon than as protection.

This time when that word was snarled at me again I could only guess that it meant it wanted me to move, so I stood up, having to work at steadying myself before I looked up at the endless steps leading to the entrance where it wanted me to go. So, with no other choice, I tugged off my shoes, throwing them to one side, knowing that if I were to make it up them, then there was no way I was doing so in heels. Thankfully, the steps were smooth beneath my feet, like highly polished black marble and one that continued throughout the palace.

I looked up at the mighty structure as I walked underneath it, wondering if this had been what it had been like for sailors, seeing the Colossus of Rhodes for the first time when sailing through its legs. Half of me wanted to turn around, claim I couldn't do this and run away taking my chances with an army chasing me. Seeing as I knew what was through the huge golden doors I could see up ahead.

But then, as if the whole purpose of my dream had been to ease my fear, I continued down the long imposing entrance hall we had now stepped into. Its arched ceilings were as high as those found in a church, but that's where the similarities ended quickly. What framed the way was massive granite pillars of tortured slaves, naked and twisted holding up the ceiling in what looked like pain and suffering.

Well, if this sight was meant to intimidate, then it was most certainly doing the job, as it felt more like a warning than a welcome. The closer I got to the doors, the more my heart dropped as it was as if they knew I was coming. The massive doors started to open, being themselves as big as a building. Their gold coating was highly polished, enough that I could see the reflection of the army at my back, like a black wave following me from behind. Then, as the doors opened fully they overtook me, splitting in the middle so that they could march either side of me and slightly ahead. Now this felt more like being delivered to the King.

A King I could now see.

But it wasn't the Draven I knew.

It was all his demon, the one he had shown me that night of the banquet, as if preparing me for the real thing…

It hadn't.

Because there he was, sat on a throne that looked to be made of shards of black glass and silver, as if it had been an experiment gone wrong and through its explosion a throne was created from the centre. A smooth section had been cut out for a large body to sit there looking the epitome of masterful, surrounded by deadly spiked tips and jagged edges. But nothing looked more dangerous than the man who occupied that seat, looking as he had that night.

With demonic armour that seemed to be a part of him, seeping from his pores and curling around his limbs. Casting itself into the form of a warrior and forging itself to wherever he wanted it to be. This, in contrast with his pale skin and harsh features, was enough to get me to think twice on my decision to come here.

I think I managed all of ten more steps before my nerves broke and he knew it as he was watching my every move. His gauntleted hand was tapping on the edge of his throne's armrest, with his talons hitting the metal, making for a haunting sound. The sound of impatience. A tapping that abruptly stopped the second I did. This action, although slight, was also a scary one as my heart started to pound in my chest even though I couldn't breathe. I knew my mistake the second he did as I had stopped walking towards him and found my steps going backwards.

He started to shake his head at me, telling me not to do what he knew I would do, but it wasn't enough of a warning. Because what sat ahead of me now was far scarier to face than what running from it could mean. So, I turned and started running down the centre of the army, most of which had become still like statues standing guard like a wall of black stone.

I heard the mighty roar of anger behind me and a whoosh of sound but as I looked back over my shoulder to see if he was making chase,

I found him gone.

I sucked in a needed breath at the sight of him missing, hoping that was going to last but unfortunately, this was far from the case. Because that giant whoosh sound I had heard, I now heard it again, only this time it was above me.

Then it stopped and the next sight I saw slammed another memory through me. It was on a rooftop and a storm raged around me, pelting my skin with heavy rain as a figure dropped from the sky.

"Draven." I let the name slip through my lips as I saw his demon do the same as he had done that night. And just like then, now he was showing me his true form in all its terrifying and mighty glory. He landed hard enough to crack the floor around one knee and he looked down for a few seconds as if letting me take in the sight of him. Huge wings spanned out behind him and unlike the ones I had seen before on him, they didn't hold a feather in sight. They reminded me a bit like Lucius' wings used to be, before he became half Angel. Only whereas Lucius' looked worn and torn in places, Draven's were all intact.

Massive sections of reddish skin stretched out between what looked more like extra limbs than the thick fingers that Lucius' wings had. And the ends were tipped with claws that looked as if they belonged on a dragon, they were that big...but then again, they were attached to wings that big. Black skin seemed to be closer to where they grew from his back and it looked like millions of tiny scales were rippling along them as they suddenly folded in on themselves, folding to the back of his body as he started to stand up, making me gulp.

"Arammu Shi, here at last," he said as if the words were ripped from him in a throaty growl. I started to walk backwards when he came towards me, but I was going nowhere fast and he was at me in seconds. Then he looked down at me from his great height as he had definitely grown and in all areas, from the looks of things.

A ring of flames seemed to burn brighter in his eyes as he

took in every inch of me, but then I knew something was wrong the second I saw those flames overtake the rest of his eyes in a second. I looked down at my arm to see what he was looking at and noticed a very distinct bruise in the shape of a large hand print from where the guy had grabbed me, yanking me from the girls.

"DALKHU!" he roared out making me flinch back in fear as I didn't know what it meant. I then saw all of his army suddenly stand to attention. Then he looked back at me and asked a dangerous question,

"Who touched you?" It came from a deadly voice and I bit my lip to stop it from trembling. He watched as I did this and something in him started to calm. The flames in his eyes started to simmer down back to a ring and he stepped closer to me, this time in a none threatening way. I tried to remain as still as I could when he bent lower towards me and said,

"Don't fear my wrath, for it is not aimed at you. Now tell me, which one touched you?" he asked, this time trying to make his words as soft as possible and like this I could almost see my Draven locked in there behind his demon skin. I took a few deep breaths before I nodded knowing that there was no way I couldn't do as he asked, so I swallowed down the lump of fear and said,

"The bigger one, I think he is in charge." Once I said this something strange happened as I watched him raise one brow at me and the gesture was so like Draven, I actually found myself relaxing next to him. He was in there, I knew it! And now, with this one slight expression, it gave me new hope that I could do this.

"There is only one in charge here, as you will soon learn, little one," he told me before he looked back up and he suddenly snapped back in his anger, now his attention was no longer directed at me. He called out what I thought was a name and motioned with his scary clawed hand for the one to step forward, who did so now looking fearful. I couldn't say I blamed him at that, as Draven towered above all of them in both size and authority.

I knew what was coming, but I didn't want to see it and as if Draven knew it too, he bent lower again and told me,

"If you do not wish to see death, my Shi, then I suggest you look elsewhere." The second he said this, adding to it a new unknown name for me, I quickly did as I was told and turned my head. Then I heard him swap his calm tone for one of death and wrath as he said,

"ANA SIMTIM ALAKU!" He roared this before I heard a sickening snapping sound and the fall of what I assumed was a body hitting the floor, but was then followed by a second thud, which left me to wonder about. Unfortunately, I wasn't left wondering for long as I cried out in fright when my legs were suddenly pulled from beneath me.

"Ssshh my Shi, I have you," he told me as he had picked me up and the height I now found myself at made me have no choice but to grip onto the horns at his shoulders. He had picked me up and flown upwards with me in his arms, and that second thud I had heard I could now see. Draven hadn't just snapped his neck, but he had snapped his whole head off, as now the body lay in two pieces on the floor.

"I...oh shit...I, um...really don't...DON'T like heights," I said screaming out one word as he went higher.

"You think I would drop you?" he asked me as he moved further towards the throne at the end.

"Well, I know you don't exactly like me but no, I don't think you would drop me," I replied making his lips twitch and again, it was such a Draven expression, that I almost wanted to reach out and touch his face to see for myself what it would feel like.

"Then you have nothing to fear in my arms, for my wings will not fail," he told me, before hovering over where he wanted to be and without warning, letting us suddenly drop, making me scream. I gripped on tight and closed my eyes as if readying myself for impact. But it never came.

"You can open your eyes now," he told me and I did so to see not only were his armoured boots back on the ground, but it also looked as though I had tried to climb up him. And I was clinging on to his neck like he would keep me safe from everything in this horrible world.

"Oh," I said letting him go with a little muttered,

"Sorry." He frowned as if he was silently wondering why I was sorry but, in the end, he never asked. No, instead he sat down and like the hundred times before, did so with me in his lap. It made me want to smile as it seemed that no matter which time we were in or which world, some things just never changed with Draven. Which was something I needed to realise before I could do what was necessary to bring him back. Because this was never about trying to drag him back from something I thought was wrong, without even giving it a chance. It was about understanding. About trying to understand what it was his demon wanted, and only then would I get the chance to reach him.

But it was also about getting him to understand me and why I was here. So, I decided to try a little humour and see where that got me.

"I thought you said your wings would never fail?" I said in a tone that was trying to be playful. He regarded me a moment as if trying to gauge this new tone, one that for once, didn't sound terrified of him.

"Ah, but not unless I wish them to," he told me, and I couldn't tell if he was teasing me or not but hoping that he was, as this would have been another big sign of Draven breaking through.

"And why would you do that, if you don't want to frighten me?" I asked now in more of a curious tone as I really wanted to know.

"Because sometimes fear is good," was his cryptic reply.

"Why do you say that?" I asked and when he grinned at me, I couldn't help but bite my lip as more of Draven came through. He seemed to study the habit, tilting his head slightly as if intrigued.

"It made you grip your body tighter to me, so why do you think?" he said shocking me, as that time there was no mistaking it, it was a definite tease. Then he seemed to notice something else on my face and before I could turn from him as my blush started to take hold, I felt a cold, smooth talon curl under my chin, forcing my face back to look up at him. Then he ran the back of his claw down my heated cheek before inquiring,

"And this, what is this?"

"Uh…knowing me, a bright red face from blushing," I said obviously amusing him as he smirked down at me before informing me,

"I know of your blushes my Shi, for I have seen them many a time before now, but I ask not of your blush but the bruise beneath it?" he said making my mouth drop on an unattractive,

"Oh." He raised a brow again, no doubt in question, the one I hadn't answered yet.

"I fell, but then if you know I blush a lot, then you will also know this too is a common occurrence." Hearing this he actually laughed, and it was a booming sound, one that made him hold me tighter in his lap so that I wouldn't fall. But then, looking at the spiked knee plates that rose high up above his knees, when sat like this I didn't think that was possible, as it was like a small wall preventing me from going anywhere.

"I do indeed, for I remembered the day you fell into our world," he said giving me my first insight to how this worked. He considered himself a separate being to Draven…that much was obvious.

Which would mean that it was almost as though Draven was three men in a sense. You had his Angel side and his Demon, whose lap I sat in now and then Draven who was ingrained in humanity. The man that held it all together and controlled these sides of him, commanding that they merge and live within his vessel as one. It had been confusing to think of before, but like this, after that one comment it all started to make sense.

"And when all your trouble began," I teased back making him scoff.

"He was weak!" he snapped making me flinch, but my action made him strangely want to comfort me in some way, as I felt his hand at my back rub circles there, being mindful of his claws.

"Why do you say that, because he fell in love with me?" I braved to ask. He snapped his intense gaze to me as if hearing the L word was one he was unfamiliar with.

"His weakness came from denying his desires and taking what is ours by right. And by denying them, he also denied me what is mine," he growled, and I knew now, this was the time to back off this conversation before I pushed him too far too soon.

But this was when I knew the saying, 'too little too late' came into play because that too far had just come and gone. I knew this when he declared,

"I have waited too long and now I need not wait any longer." I gulped when he suddenly stood with me in his arms. His army was still stationed where they were as they framed the huge throne room. It was only now I started to take in the room as I looked around in panic at what he could mean to do with me now. He dismounted the long stretch of large steps in front of him, one that put him at a higher level than the rest of the room as was Draven's way. A King that could watch over his kingdom, whether that be from an ancient far away Persian Palace, a Gothic nightclub in quiet little Evergreen Falls or a demonic fortress in Hell, it was all the same.

And like those times, I ended up asking the question...

"Why, where are you taking me?" The panic was clear in my tone. A panic that only increased when he answered me...

"To have my way with you."

CHAPTER THIRTY

THE POWER IN A NAME

When I had asked where he was taking me the last place I had expected it to be was to his bedchamber, as these actions weren't exactly coming from the Demon side of Draven that was supposed to dislike me and blame me for what he called Draven's weakness. But then again, what had his actions against me been so far? Yes, he had demanded his army to bring me to him and the girls thrown out of Hell but other than that, he hadn't purposely scared me. Or forced me to kneel at his feet, as I had been expecting. Which begged the question...

Why?

A question I found myself burning to ask more and more since he brought me to this space...*this very empty space*. It turned out that his home in Hell had been an endless amount of space filled with absolutely nothing. But then again, what was I expecting, hunted beasts as mounted trophies on the walls or portraits of him in his demon form? And as for furniture, I doubted that there was an antiques dealer with a shop down here in Hell somewhere. Although, I was sure there was at least an owner of a shop or two, as there must have been at least one evil man selling old furniture in the world.

No, it had just been bare stone walls with the occasional red banner here and there to break up the pale tones. That was until we approached a pair of black doors that looked to be the exact replica of the ones that led into Afterlife. I was so shocked I had nearly shouted this fact out, but one look at his tense gaze and I decided against it. No, instead I remained silent as the doors opened on their own and I watched in awe as I now stepped into this new space.

This new personal space.

"It's like Persia?" I said, unable to help myself as he walked further into the room that was like a gothic version of his bedchamber back in time. Everything was where it was, the bed (although very different), the sunken seating area, even the windows that now showed a very different view than what I remembered. It was all where it had been back then.

"Another foolish mistake that went unpunished," he commented putting me down and taking a step back making me gulp at the sound of that word coming from such a Being. One that looked as if he could have crushed me with little thought.

"What you call a foolish mistake was a choice made to save you," I corrected him, unable to help myself but making him snarl at me, one he only stopped when he saw me taking a fearful step back.

"You are the only choice we make!" he snapped and I frowned, not understanding what he meant by it. But I jumped when the doors slammed shut at the sight of his anger.

"And what of *my* choices, do you honestly believe I don't get to have any?" I asked making him frown at me and cross his arms before telling me,

"The last choice you made brought you to me and it is

foolish to believe I will allow you make another that will take you away again, not now I have you." I sucked in a deep breath and thought about what he was saying.

"But I don't understand, you...you hated me, all you wanted was to have him back, to control and to..."

"To have my control yes... to have that back is all I have fought for since you entered our life. For I have been forced to watch and wait for far too long as you endangered your life and for what, one foolish endeavour after another. Now that time is at an end, as is yours," he said walking towards me and now making me fearful once again that I had this all wrong. Had he wanted me down here to kill me once and for all? To get me out of the way so he could be free as a demon, forever.

"Please! Please don't...don't do this!" I shouted putting space between us and in doing so, nearly stumbling down the steps, forcing him to react by reaching out and grabbing me to him before I could fall.

"I will have you!" This was my only warning before he pulled me up to him, so that he could claim my lips in our first kiss as his demon. I would have thought it would have been different, but the second I opened up to him, it was my Draven I was kissing and no other.

I cried out in blissful knowledge of this and threw my arms around him, clinging to him to get closer. And he responded to it like a man starved of ever feeling this way. He picked me up and carried me towards the bed, doing so without breaking the connection. I broke away first to see what was happening around us when he growled at me, not liking that I turned away from him. I knew this the second his arm grew tighter around my waist. I swallowed hard when I saw that even though we may have been in a room I could call familiar, there was nothing familiar about that bed.

To begin with it looked more like something his father would own as the main theme to its structure was chains.

Lots and lots of chains.

He watched my panic rise and he seemed to feed from it as the hint of a grin reached the corner of one side of his dark grey lips. The whole bed was more like a cage as it was surrounded by thin pillars of black rock, with lengths of black chains in between. This meant that no one could escape if it hadn't been for the gap on one side. A gap big enough for him to step up to before he lowered me down, placing me inside.

Then he followed me down and I couldn't help my reaction as I scooted backwards across to the other side. This managed to put some distance between us as the bed was triple the normal size of ours back home. But my action caused him to grin as if this was a game and seeing my back was now against the stone bars was what he wanted to see. Then I watched as he raised up his hand and the gap that had once been there was now closing up as the same pillars grew like the others. This was now caging me in for good.

"I don't understand?" I said again.

"This was the last choice I allowed you to make, *the choice I knew you would make,*" he said, and I shook my head in confusion.

"I knew when he found out what you kept from him he would give in to his rage. It made me strong enough to take control and enough for him to allow me to be summoned," he confessed and as if being an outsider looking in, I could see it all start playing out for myself. Draven being taken over in that cell down in his prison. Fighting with himself as I slept on the floor just within his reach. I saw his eyes change into the demon I saw now. And with that one ounce of strength gained, he beat back Draven's control just long enough to reach out to touch the back of my neck. After that there had been no stopping him from becoming free of Draven's control and unlocking his cell, to then carry me from that place.

This was when it struck me. Draven hadn't lied to me. He hadn't just left me to keep me safe at all. He hadn't had a choice because his demon had taken it away from him.

Draven had kept his promise.

"It was you...you made him leave?" I said with both shock and anger lacing my words.

"I made him return," he corrected.

"And me?" I asked knowing he knew what I meant.

"You, I could not take with me," he told me making me clench my fists as I asked,

"Why?"

"Because the power of the portal summoned could only carry one of free will and I knew..."

"You knew I would be foolish enough to eventually come myself...that's what you meant about allowing me one choice left." He confirmed this with a nod before coming closer, now making me hold a shaky hand out to him.

"Wait, I thought it was him you wanted to control," I told him now getting up on unsteady legs and standing on the bed just to try and move quicker. I held on to the bars, surprised to find them warm to touch. He too rose up on the bed as he stalked towards me and just as I opened my mouth to speak again, he was on me!

"It was only ever one Being I wanted under my control... *You!*" he said as he raised my arms up above my head looking down at me and keeping my gaze captured with the intensity of his own. I barely even felt the chains he was wrapping around my wrists until suddenly he pulled on them and my body stretched out in front of him, like a prize ready for him to claim.

He looked down at me with a heated gaze, making the fire in his eyes burn brighter. Now my arms were captured, he took his time admiring my body, as he raised a hand to touch me. At first, I flinched from his touch making his features turn hard, but then he saw that my fear wasn't him touching me, it was with his razor claws cutting my skin.

This was when he must have realised that it was possible for him to hurt me and this was something he didn't want to do. I sucked in a surprised breath as I saw his gauntleted hand started to retract, seeping back into his pores like black liquid being absorbed into his skin. This left a strong male hand underneath with black fingernails and pale grey skin. I felt his other hand at my waist that still remained the same, so the threat of his talons was helping him in keeping me still. Something he was pleased about.

Then he went back to touching my skin, starting with holding the column of my neck.

"We like to feel your pulse beneath our touch, it brings us comfort to feel your life beating under our hold on you," he told me, as if now speaking for Draven and answering that long asked internal question as to why Draven in both the past and the present always held my neck.

After this his hand travelled further down and his eyes widened as I sucked in a breath at the feel of his hand skimming the nipple that was just peeking out of the top of my corset.

"You like my touch, little one?" He purred the question as it came out as rumbling in his chest. I found myself only able to nod and bite my lip from moaning aloud. Then I looked down to see the rest of his armour below has started to melt away, revealing beneath a very large and hard erection resting against the lower part of his abs.

"Then let's see how you like the touch of my cock!" he shouted on a growl suddenly lifting me up by taking hold of my behind in a firm grip. I cried out in shock as he wrapped my legs around his now bare ass. I tried to pull my arms down but they were locked there. Then he leant closer to my face and finished his sentence,

"My Wardum àm Kad nga Shi...*My slave who ties my life... you are mine now,*" he said before he kissed me and the second he did, I no longer fought my chains. It was as if I was lost the second his tongue fought mine, tasting me and devouring everything I had to give. I felt his hand reach down between my legs and he grasped his cock in his hand and used it to rub against my soaked clit.

I don't know how long he kissed me for, but I was nearly begging him to take me by the time he was finished with me. It was like sweet torture as he continued to rub his length against me at a maddening pace without making the contact I really wanted.

Lucifer had said about taming the beast, but it felt as if it was the other way around, for he was trying to tame me.

"Please...please." The only thing my pleas did was please him as a cruel smile appeared on his lips. I felt my underwear tear and with a hand holding my face secure, to make me look at him *and only him,* he watched my eyes as he surged up inside me. I cried out as the feel of him stretching me at his greater size making me realise now why he had spent the time in driving me to a frenzy...he wanted me ready to take him.

And take him I did.

He threw his head back and roared up at the rocky ceiling above making debris rain down with the power of it. He hammered into me, making me cling on to the chains just to hold on to something with the force of it all. But still, I wanted more. I didn't want to be chained to the bed, I wanted to be chained to him. So, I nipped at him with my fangs, to get his attention,

"Free me."

"Never!" he snarled back at me as he thrust in harder, done so as a warning.

"Then chain me to you, for I want to touch you," I told him surprising him still. I wondered what he thought of this but then I felt him reach up above my hands and yank the length of chain free. I felt it go slack as he gathered it up in his hand before turning us to face the bed. Then before he could lower me down I tightened my hips around him and raised myself up on his shoulders, using the horns there so that I was high enough to reach his ear.

"I want to claim you this time," I whispered making him growl the second he heard what I was asking of him. Then with a hand held to his face I started kissing him all over, making his resolve turn to dust. He didn't say anything more but this time when he lowered us to the bed he did so by falling to his knees before lying back on the bed, to let me sit on top of him. This new position made his size nearly too hard to take but I wanted it…wanted it all.

So, I took it.

I started to ride him, slowly at first and as I did, he grabbed my hands in front of me, wrapped the length of chain around them before wrapping the rest of its length around his fist. Just the sight of such ownership had me working myself harder and faster over him as I felt myself chasing my first orgasm. One that I knew when it hit, would be explosive.

"Yes, yes, yes!" I shouted as it started to rise and then, just as I was about to feel it erupt, I felt him yank hard on my chains so that my arms flew up above me. He held me immobile like this so that he could rip my corset down, freeing my breasts and baring my body to him. Then he took hold of one of my breasts with his mouth, bit down hard on my nipple and I screamed as my orgasm ripped through me,

"AAAHHHH YYEESSS!"

"Again!" he demanded of me, now taking over my movements as my body started to tire. He still had his hand above me, keeping my arms captured over my head by the chain he held in his fist. I was stretched out upright for him as he went back to feasting on my breast like a man obsessed. He hammered his hips up and, keeping a hand on my waist to steady me, I felt the slight pain of his hold that managed to morph into pleasure, and this was enough to have me hurtling once more up the next level of pleasure, only to find another screaming release.

"AAAHHH!"

"I want more," he demanded, but as my limbs relaxed around him he must have seen my weakness for he lowered my arms and gently, without removing himself, turned me around so that he was above me.

"I will give you more my Shi, but I do so taking care of what I own," he told me gently as he lowered my head back as if he was scared I would break. Then he unwrapped the chain from my hands and released them to wherever they would fall. The last orgasm had been so powerful, I felt as if I could barely move, but that was fine as the beast above me now wanted to take back control.

"Now I claim you!" he warned before claim me, *he did.* He lifted my legs up, so that my knees were to my chest and then he started to lose himself in the motion. This time building up his own release with every hard stroke of my core against his hard length. I knew he was near as he suddenly lifted me up so that I was in his lap with my legs locked at the base of his back.

His speed started to increase and his demonic voice made his next demand of me,

"We come as one, as I claim you, we come together chained together for eternity," he said this, and in the end, it wasn't meant metaphorically. As the second later I felt the length of chain wrap around my body as it tied me to his own. It was as though it had a life of its own as I even felt it wrap over my shoulders and around my breasts before tightening so that I was locked to him. I cried out at the sensation of being tied up all over my body and it sent my mind into sexual overload.

I could feel it once again build until soon his fangs lengthened and I knew what was about to happen. But he didn't want to take his hand from me, so instead, he commanded the chain to wrap dangerously around my neck. I gulped back the fear before I felt it slipping high enough under my chin to force my neck to one side and in doing so forcing me to submit to him. Then, not waiting another minute, he sank his teeth into me, and started drinking me down as if I was Heaven's forbidden nectar. I came screaming just as I felt the last of my energy being drained away, but yet he took more.

It was as though he couldn't stop.

I felt his body tense as he felt my release rippling along his cock sending him over so that he tore his bloody lips from my neck and he did so roaring out to his world, with enough force to crack the rocks around us.

We had come as one but the only difference being, that when he came, he did so screaming my name...

My real name,

"KEIRA!"

And he did this in panic as my body began to fall and my mind began to fade into the darkness. Feeling as though...well as though,

He had killed me.

I don't know what happened after that as I must have blacked out for a moment from the intensity of it all.

I opened my eyes to find myself staring into the eyes of the man I loved and at first, I couldn't understand how. I was lay down with his naked body now half over me. The body belonging to the man I fell in love with.

"Draven?" I called his name in confusion and I felt my hair being pushed back from my face before soft lips found my cheek. I don't know why but it all just felt like a dream, only when I opened my eyes I saw that we were still in the same bed.

"We're still in Hell!" I shouted bolting upright and making him grab my shoulders.

"Ssshh, calm down. Come on, lay back...you need your strength," he said in a soothing voice coaxing me to do as he asked.

"I don't understand...what...?"

"You're weak, my demon took too much from you and when he realised what he had done, he relinquished his control back to me," Draven told me in that gentle tone as if he was sorry any of it had happened. I could barely believe it, *I had done it*.

"I did it?" I questioned, needing to make sure. Draven looked at me asking me silently what I meant.

"I tamed your demon, I..."

"You made him realise his love for you was more powerful than his need to claim you. You made him realise what I had been trying to do since we met you," Draven explained as he gently stroked down my neck as if getting lost in the half naked sight of me.

"He was angry at you," I stated.

"Yes, and he had been for so long, but now thanks to you, for the first time in years, he is calm and acceptant...you might have just saved me centuries of headaches, love," he added making me chuckle.

"Well, you have plenty of time to thank me," I teased. But then he turned serious and said,

"He knew you would find a way." I frowned in question, so he said,

"He was counting on you coming to try and save me. He had it planned to make you suffer the wait he had to suffer. To see you kneeling by his feet and submitting to him for all to see but in the end, the second he saw you, he became lost to your power over us, lost to the love you made him feel... *As I knew he would,*" Draven told me, adding this last part spoken with his hand behind my head, pulling me closer to him. I smiled, kissing him after he said this, framing his face with my hands as I held him to me.

"You came back to me. You came back...you kept your promise and you never left me," I said as tears started to fall down my cheeks and he cupped my face,

Telling me the only words I needed to hear...

"I will always find a way back to you."

CHAPTER THIRTY-ONE

OUR HAPPY EVER AFTERLIFE

After this moment spent in each other's arms we soon left Hell behind, seeing it for what we both hoped was the last time.

And unbelievably life went on as planned. We had actually found the girls assembling a small army by the time we returned, as they readied themselves to storm the palace. The shock on their faces when we turned up at Afterlife after using one of the Janus doorways and strode casually into the dining room…aka, Supernatural army HQ, the only sound that followed was girly screams of joy. I had been declared the hero of the hour, which quickly turned to 'hero couple' of the hour as it had been both of us that had won.

We had no idea why, but the second that Draven's demon had said my true name, the birthmark on my neck changed back to how it always was. And we never battled his demon again.

In fact, the only battles Draven faced were those from his pregnant wife and learning the art of sensitivity by way of kissing me senseless when I did let the baby blues get in the way. But these were the moments that I would look at him and just know that my life really was perfect.

It wasn't the grand gestures or expensive gifts, like the new car he made me accept, finding it one day outside with the biggest purple bow wrapped around it. Or even the new necklace I now wore around my neck, not the one he had given me that day, but had unknowingly been tampered with. No, this one was a purple diamond in the shape of a heart, still one wrapped in his wings, but the difference was it was now inscribed with two simple words,

'My Shi'

It was forever to reminded me of the love I had conquered in not just having Draven by my side, but his demon as well. As I soon found out what this name meant. And I was shocked to find out that all this time his demon's name for me, was Shi, meaning...

'My life's soul.'

Of course, I had cried during this time.

But like I said, it wasn't the grand gestures that made it perfect, it was everything. The little things, the big things and everything in between. The time I got Draven a TV for our room for his birthday. It had been after our little Amelia Faith had been born. I remembered laughing when he looked slightly disappointed until I turned it on and images of me dressed sexy flashed on screen. It was the same outfit I had been wearing when I first dressed up for him. The night we made love on the bed of roses. Apparently, Sophia had pulled some strings with Victoria Secrets to get them to make me another, seeing as Draven had destroyed it the first time.

But as pictures of me posing sexy for him started to appear on screen one after the other he had first been transfixed. After this, I had laughed when his response to my bedroom boudoir photoshoot had been,

"Tell me quickly Keira, so that I may enjoy this without the rage that will soon follow, please tell me there were no male eyes behind the lenses of that camera?" I burst out laughing before then taking pity on both him and the remote control he was still holding.

"You will be happy to know dear, that the photographer was a woman and there were no other males in the building." I said this whilst patting him on the chest.

"And protection?" Again, his question made me smile.

"Zagan and Ragnar were both there, maintaining a perimeter so that no one came within seeing distance," I informed him making him now start to relax, but he wasn't yet finished.

"And the woman?"

"Oh my god Draven, seriously!?" I laughed.

"Yes, seriously," he replied making me shake my head at him and his caveman ways, part of which I now knew was down to his Demon, a part of him I very fell much in love with that day.

"Happily married, to a guy who was not in the building and knowing Zagan and Ragnar probably outside stopping traffic from getting too close...there now, are you satisfied?"

"With the beauty you gift me, *immensely,*" he said looking down at me before then looking back at the screen to take notice of what I was wearing.

"You look just as beautiful as you did that day." I grinned and reached up to kiss his cheek and say,

"Happy Birthday, Dominic." He put a hand to my cheek and told me,

"Thank you, my wife."

Then he kissed me.

After this, many wonderful things happened in my life, most of which included the new addition to our family. Seeing Draven as a father, well quite honestly there was nothing that gave me greater pleasure than being gifted to see it every day for the rest of my life. Watching him bath that tiny bundle in his large hands, being so gentle with her was the cutest thing. Watching him playing with her and making silly noises as she grew to be a toddler, would have me laughing alongside them.

Because it wasn't just about witnessing the first time your child did things, like trying food for the first time and spitting it out as if you had given them poison. Or giving them nicknames like 'Peedini' because they managed to leak from their nappy no matter what you did. Or it wasn't about seeing them walk for the first time, seeing them run, climb things they shouldn't like Ragnar for example. To take to the world like they owned it, and nothing could possibly stand in their way, which in this was my daughter very much reminding me of her strong willed Father.

But for me it was all about seeing it with Draven. Being able to not only witness it myself, but to watch as he did too. To watch as he discovered what human life was all about and to come to love it as he never thought he would.

To see Draven finally find his humanity and embrace it.

And as for us as a married couple, well after that time in Hell, we finally started to view things differently. We spent our time looking back on what had happened and learning a valuable lesson, as now we knew nothing was left standing between us.

Because in the end the only Beings strong enough to get in between our love was…well, *it was us*.

It was us and the stupid mistakes we had made. The lies we had told and the guilt we were then left with to weigh down our hearts. And my greatest fear in losing Draven by his own decision was now proved to never happen again. For he had never left me to go to Hell, his demon had, and all in order to lure me into it with him.

But in the end, it had been his demon's discovery of loving me, just as Draven did, that had made him submit willingly. Doing so all to keep me safe for where he felt he couldn't. He had taken too much blood from me in his moment of passion. And the realisation of this had terrified him enough to know that he didn't have the restraint around me not to do it again.

But one man did…

My Draven.

He knew the master of that demonic side of his soul was strong enough, because he had known the pain and suffering endured and all to see the woman he loved be safe and protected. And now, instead of his demon thinking him weak and resenting his choice, he had learned of this pain for himself. He had learned of this fear at the sight of almost losing me and therefore started to respect Draven for his decisions, instead of fighting against them.

And me, well I had managed to tame his demon enough to make us realise, that through all of this…

We had finally won the battle of love.

EPILOGUE

LUCIFER

A DEVIL'S BARGAIN

I watched as the two lovers fled my land hand in hand as if they had won a battle they had no idea I myself had inflicted upon them.

"I told you she would do it." The sound of Asmodeus' voice was one I expected to hear as long before I had sensed his arrival. I knew of his fondness for his daughter-in-law, a law that extended even down here for she had wed his son in our own traditions. A tradition the Prince of Lust no doubt missed out on and felt the annoyance of the fact daily as he had missed sight of their fucking, himself.

"So, you did old friend, and therefore you may have your night with your precious Sarah, as was our bet," I told him feeling him tense behind me. I was in tune with all of the creatures under my rule and that were forced to live in my world. But this extended further to one of my presidents and even more so to Asmodeus, being that he was part of the first hierarchy and one of 'Lust' no less. The fact that I also considered him a friend was another matter entirely.

"And for that I thank you… *eternally,"* he answered bowing his head to me as I knew he would.

"Yes, but no doubt she won't be," I replied making him laugh as he understood my meaning. After all, we both knew the bitter aftertaste forbidden fruit could leave in your soul, especially when they were taken from us and seemed forever from our grasp.

"And you, when will you claim your Chosen One, for now she grows more human by the day?" he asked me, making me clench my teeth at the thought of being foolish enough to think of it being this day. But then my plans hadn't exactly turned out the way I thought they would have, an unusual cup of knowledge for me to be forced to swallow. However, my brand and my Hex placed on her neck when she was in my grasp will mean that one day she will owe me her loyalty, for only then will I truly remove it.

And I knew just the task I had in mind for her future.

"Yes, and soon she will be fully so and my time in waiting will be at an end," I replied not because I owed him one, but more to voice it to myself as saying such things brought me comfort.

"And the sigil you placed on my daughter-in-law, your summoning mark, is it to remain?" he asked, this time making me grin as I watched that fiery soul disappearing with her tamed demon in hand. She certainly had spirit and a bravery rarely seen in one so young.

This made me think of my own Electus and wonder if she would be as she was when I haunted her dreams. An act that, although had near driven her to insanity, it had for much longer kept me sane. For it was my only connection to her, as even the Fates couldn't protect her mind as she slept.

But that has all come to an end as did the prophecy. And each day she grows less powerful and the lingering remains of who she was to Heaven's elite is dying as it should. The fucking Fates can say goodbye to their puppet for she will soon have a new master.

Me.

"It will remain hidden until I have need of it again," I told him, and silence descended as we both thought of times ahead. Mine consumed by the nights her mind was mine and soon to be the days her body would be too.

"Do they know it was you who cursed them?" Asmodeus asked me and for a moment I had been so lost in my thoughts of her, that I almost forgot he was still there.

"No, they believed for a time that it might have been Cronus."

"Ha, you had your fun with that bastard too quickly." Asmodeus sniggered.

"And you also as I do recall, what was that thing you had fucking his ass for days?" I asked making my friend throw his head back, this time a laugh as if the thought amused him as much as it had watching it.

"A cross breed, something I am working on, but the harpies bitches love it."

"I bet they do," I commented dryly making him chuckle once more. No wonder the bastard was always happy with the amount his cock saw action. I had little care to see my sexual thirst sated these days for the only body I wanted to take as my cock's slave was hers and she wasn't that far from reach now. I simply couldn't wait to play with her.

"What will you do with her when she is fully human?" Asmodeus asked of me, now that the sickening lovers were out of sight. I turned my back on the vast dead land I owned, and this time looked at him when I delivered my answer,

"Why, kill her of course, how else is she to get into Hell." Then I walked past him back to my own castle home,

"And then?" he asked being the curious bastard he was by nature. So, I looked back over my shoulder and told him what I had recently learned was possible…

"Time to see, if she too, can tame her master's beast."

The Happy Ever End

I hope you all enjoyed reading this saga, as writing it was my greatest accomplishment in life other than bringing my children into the world and I am honoured to have been able to share it with you all.

But this isn't the end and if you all enjoyed reading the story of Keira and Draven, then you may now enjoy reading Lucius story, in his own saga, starting with Transfusion.

Also, if you wish to discover the story of the Children of Afterlife then why not try the Glass Dagger, the first book in the Afterlife Chronicles.

Plus watch this space for more from our Kings in the saga, as they too find their own Chosen Ones and do what is needed to protect them against what the fates may throw in their way.

ABOUT THE AUTHOR

Stephanie Hudson has dreamed of being a writer ever since her obsession with reading books at an early age. What first became a quest to overcome the boundaries set against her in the form of dyslexia has turned into a life's dream. She first started writing in the form of poetry and soon found a taste for horror and romance. Afterlife is her first book in the series of twelve, with the story of Keira and Draven becoming ever more complicated in a world that sets them miles apart.

When not writing, Stephanie enjoys spending time with her loving family and friends, chatting for hours with her biggest fan, her sister Cathy who is utterly obsessed with one gorgeous Dominic Draven. And of course, spending as much time with her supportive partner and personal muse, Blake who is there for her no matter what.

Author's words.

My love and devotion is to all my wonderful fans that keep me going into the wee hours of the night but foremost to my wonderful daughter Ava...who yes, is named after a cool, kick-ass, Demonic bird and my sons, Jack, who is a little hero and Baby Halen, who yes, keeps me up at night but it's okay because he is named after a Guitar legend!

Keep updated with all new release news & more on my website
www.afterlifesaga.com
Never miss out, sign up to the
mailing list at the website.

Also, please feel free to join myself and other Dravenites on my Facebook group
Afterlife Saga Official Fan
Interact with me and other fans. Can't wait to see you there!

- facebook.com/AfterlifeSaga
- twitter.com/afterlifesaga
- instagram.com/theafterlifesaga

ACKNOWLEDGEMENTS

Well first and foremost my love goes out to all the people who deserve the most thanks and are the wonderful people that keep me going day to day. But most importantly they are the ones that allow me to continue living out my dreams and keep writing my stories for the world to hopefully enjoy... These people are of course YOU! Words will never be able to express the full amount of love I have for you guys. Your support is never ending. Your trust in me and the story is never failing. But more than that, your love for me and all who you consider your 'Afterlife family' is to be commended, treasured and admired. Thank you just doesn't seem enough, so one day I hope to meet you all and buy you all a drink! ;)

To my family... To my amazing mother, who has believed in me from the very beginning and doesn't believe that something great should be hidden from the world. I would like to thank you for all the hard work you put into my books and the endless hours spent caring about my words and making sure it is the best it can be for everyone to enjoy. You make Afterlife shine. To my wonderful crazy father who is and always has been my hero in life. Your strength astonishes me, even to this day and the love and care you hold for your family is a gift you give to the Hudson name. And last but not least, to the man that I consider my soul mate. The man who taught me about real love and makes me not only want to be a better person but makes me feel I am too. The amount of support you have given me since we met has been incredible and the greatest feeling was finding out you wanted to spend the rest of your life with me when you asked me to marry you.

All my love to my dear husband and my own personal Draven… Mr Blake Hudson.

Another personal thank you goes to my dear friend Caroline Fairbairn and her wonderful family that have embraced my brand of crazy into their lives and given it a hug when most needed.

For their friendship I will forever be eternally grateful.

I would also like to mention Claire Boyle my wonderful PA, who without a doubt, keeps me sane and constantly smiling through all the chaos which is my life ;) And a loving mention goes to Lisa Jane for always giving me a giggle and scaring me to death with all her count down pictures lol ;)

Thank you for all your hard work and devotion to the saga and myself. And always going that extra mile, pushing Afterlife into the spotlight you think it deserves. Basically helping me achieve my secret goal of world domination one day…evil laugh time… Mwahaha! Joking of course ;)

As before, a big shout has to go to all my wonderful fans who make it their mission to spread the Afterlife word and always go the extra mile. I love you all x

ALSO BY STEPHANIE HUDSON

Afterlife Saga

A Brooding King, A Girl running from her past. What happens when the two collide?

Book 1 - Afterlife

Book 2 - The Two Kings

Book 3 - The Triple Goddess

Book 4 - The Quarter Moon

Book 5 - The Pentagram Child /Part 1

Book 6 - The Pentagram Child /Part 2

Book 7 - The Cult of the Hexad

Book 8 - Sacrifice of the Septimus /Part 1

Book 9 - Sacrifice of the Septimus /Part 2

Book 10 -Blood of the Infinity War

Book 11 -Happy Ever Afterlife /Part 1

Book 12 -Happy Ever Afterlife / Part 2

Transfusion Saga

What happens when an ordinary human girl comes face to face with the cruel Vampire King who dismissed her seven years ago?

Transfusion - Book 1

Venom of God - Book 2

Blood of Kings - Book 3

Rise of Ashes - Book 4

Map of Sorrows - Book 5

Tree of Souls - Book 6

Kingdoms of Hell – Book 7

Eyes of Crimson - Book 8

Roots of Rage - Book 9

Afterlife Chronicles: (Young Adult Series)

The Glass Dagger – Book 1

The Hells Ring – Book 2

Stephanie Hudson and Blake Hudson

The Devil in Me

OTHER WORKS FROM HUDSON INDIE INK

Paranormal Romance/Urban Fantasy

Sloane Murphy

Xen Randell

C. L. Monaghan

Sci-fi/Fantasy

Brandon Ellis

Devin Hanson

Crime/Action

Blake Hudson

Mike Gomes

Contemporary Romance

Gemma Weir

Elodie Colt

Ann B. Harrison

Lightning Source UK Ltd.
Milton Keynes UK
UKHW011829170321
380525UK00002B/764